PRAISE FOR LEGEND

"*Legend* is an incredible odyssey that will leave you breathless. With its gorgeous art and sharp dialogue, this post-apocalyptic fable is compelling and mesmerizing. Imagine *Dark Knight Returns*, *Animal Farm*, and *Saga* all rolled into one." —Peter Tieryas, author of *United States of Japan*

"Gripping." —*Dogster*

"Thought-provoking." —*Catster*

"What happens when you combine the animalistic focus of *Homeword Bound* with the difficulty of forging a new world in the ashes of the old?" —*Comics Alliance*

"Chris Koehler is a drawing maniac. Readers are invited to see the world through a dog's perspective. We feel like one of the pack. We can smell the smoke, taste the grit in the air, and feel the sun at our backs." —Owen Smith

"Dog religion, armored cats, and more." —*io9*

"I could say that *Legend* is a post-apocalyptic *Watership Down* with dogs and cats and that might be enough. Instead I'll say that the story is fun, scary, and poignant, and the art absolutely gorgeous, melancholy, and menacing. I'm utterly and hopelessly hooked." —Paul Tremblay, author of *Disappearance at Devil's Rock*

"*Legend* easily maneuvers through multiple storytelling genres." —*Fanboy Comics*

"Proves that apocalyptic tales can comment on a variety of social issues without lecturing or talking down to readers." —*Freak Sugar*

"Koehler's artistic style sets a moody stage, with panels colored in unexpected hues, representing a world that's no longer seen through human eyes." —*CNET's Crave*

"Touching...profound...fascinating." —*Omnicomic*

"This is high-quality graphic storytelling, with writer and artist working in near-perfect tandem to produce an engrossing new fictional mythology using comics' unique tools... Thanks to remarkable world-building and a dynamic collaborative effort, Sattin and Koehler have crafted a fantastic adventure." —*Broken Frontier*

"Stunning." —*Black Gate*

"Samuel Sattin and Chris Koehler's *Legend* is a lot like what would happen if Harlan Ellison wrote *Call of the Wild*, while being possessed by Cthulhu. It's an epic tale of loyalty, courage, and defiance." —David Gallaher, author of *The Only Living Boy*

"Fascinating." —*The Nerd Machine*

"*Legend* is an endearing tale, filled with darkness and mystery, beautifully illustrated to capture every threat, every surreal horror, and every glimmer of hope." —Richard Thomas, author of *Breaker*

LEGEND

WORDS
SAMUEL SATTIN

PICTURES
CHRIS KOEHLER

FLASHBACKS BY
SARAH HAWKINSON

MAPS BY
KATIE LONGUA

CAT CREATION MYTH BY
ANA VALDEZ

DOG CREATION MYTH BY
SARAH HAWKINSON

PUMPKIN'S LAST STAND BY
JUSTIN HALL

CAT TRIBE COMMAND BY
DAWN CARLOS

DEFEND THE GROUNDS BY
SPETH SZABO

BORIS THE BLACKSMITH BY
ABBY ROCHA

ADDITIONAL ART BY
MICHAEL MANIKUS, MAKAYLAH FAZZARI, AND MEECHELLE McNEIL

REFERENCE CREDIT/SPECIAL THANKS
SYLVAN FAWN (LEGEND/KUMA)
BRYNN MOHAGEN (HERMAN/ODINN)
ANTHONY JAMES HARMER (MYRA/TESSA)
MOLLY LOCKLIN (LEX) & DOLLY (ELSA)
Inigo Montoya/Atticus/Leeloo/Bagheera

Follow @Legend_Comic
www.facebook.com/dogsoflegend

Publishers:
Josh Frankel and Sridhar Reddy

"Be cunning, and full of tricks,
and your people will never be destroyed."
-Richard Adams, *Watership Down*

LEG

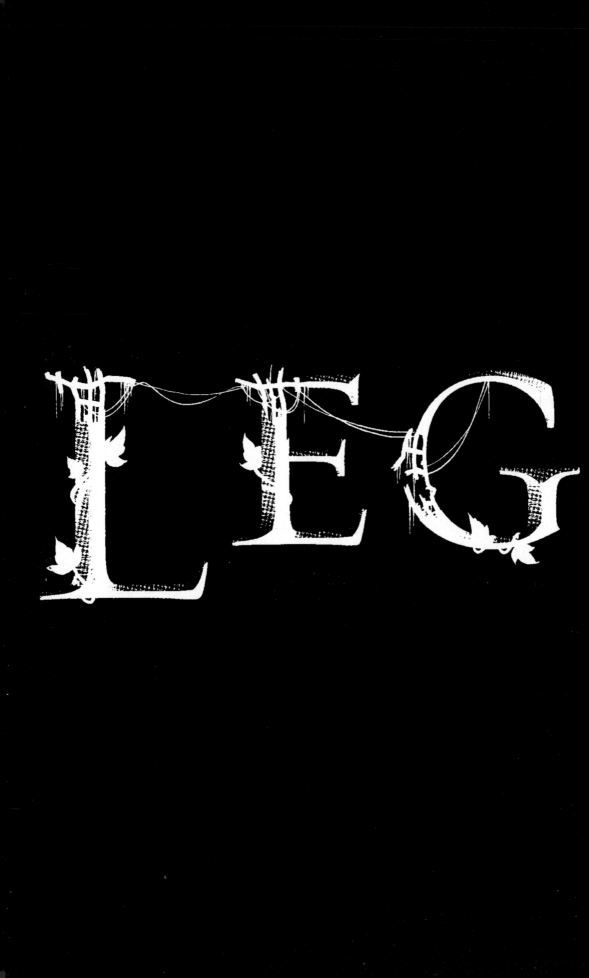

END

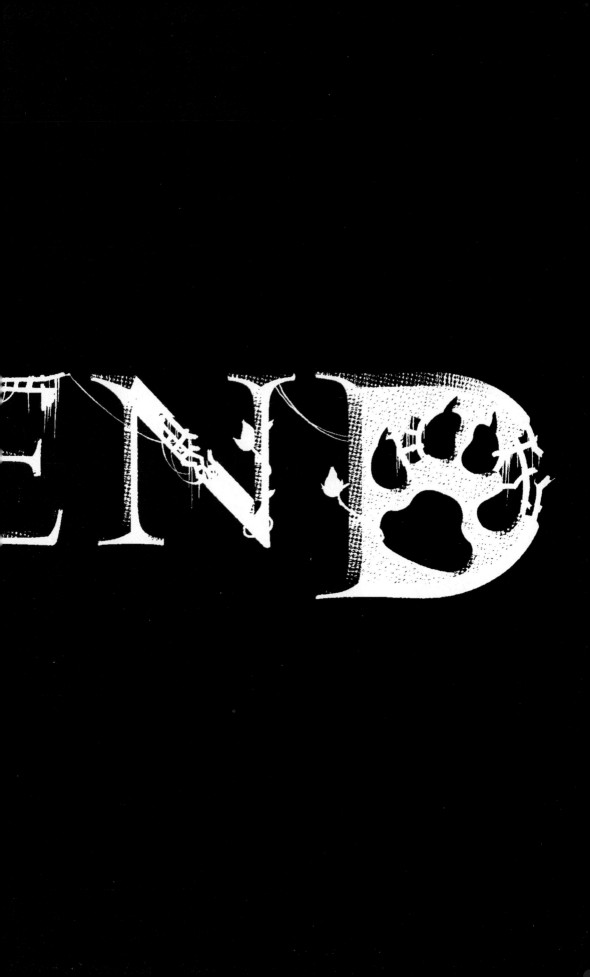

Let me tell you something, between you and me, okay? When Samuel first described *LEGEND* to me, I thought it sounded like good clean comics fun. A biological weapon wipes out humanity and leaves dogs and cats to fight and fend and rebuild. That's totally fun, right? I assumed I was in for a clever, jokey adventure, one that riffs on but wouldn't necessarily rise to the level of one of my favorite novels and movies, *Watership Down*.

From *LEGEND's* very first haunting pages and images of a ruined city and a pack of dogs mourning its fallen leader, I quickly realized that the story here is much bigger and weightier than a simple riff. *LEGEND*, living up to its title, is an epic in every sense of the word.

I read comics for that magical synthesis between images and word, the amplified power of two storytellers. What Samuel Sattin and Chris Koehler have managed to do in their shared yet singular vision is astounding. Within the first two pages, they built a world and a set of empathic characters, and a mood and a tone equal parts heroism and pathos. And then they expanded it throughout the five issues. The uneasy alliance between the two factions of survivors is always emotionally authentic, as is the palpable sense of mystery, menace, and danger they face.

I hesitate to say more for fear of spoiling anything. Only, I look forward to joining you on the blooded path.

-PAUL TREMBLAY, AUTHOR OF *A HEAD FULL OF GHOSTS*

"For Dolly the night thief, Gogo the one ear, and Miko the brave."
- SAMUEL SATTIN

"For Ayla, my harshest critic."
-CHRIS KOEHLER

CHAPTER ONE

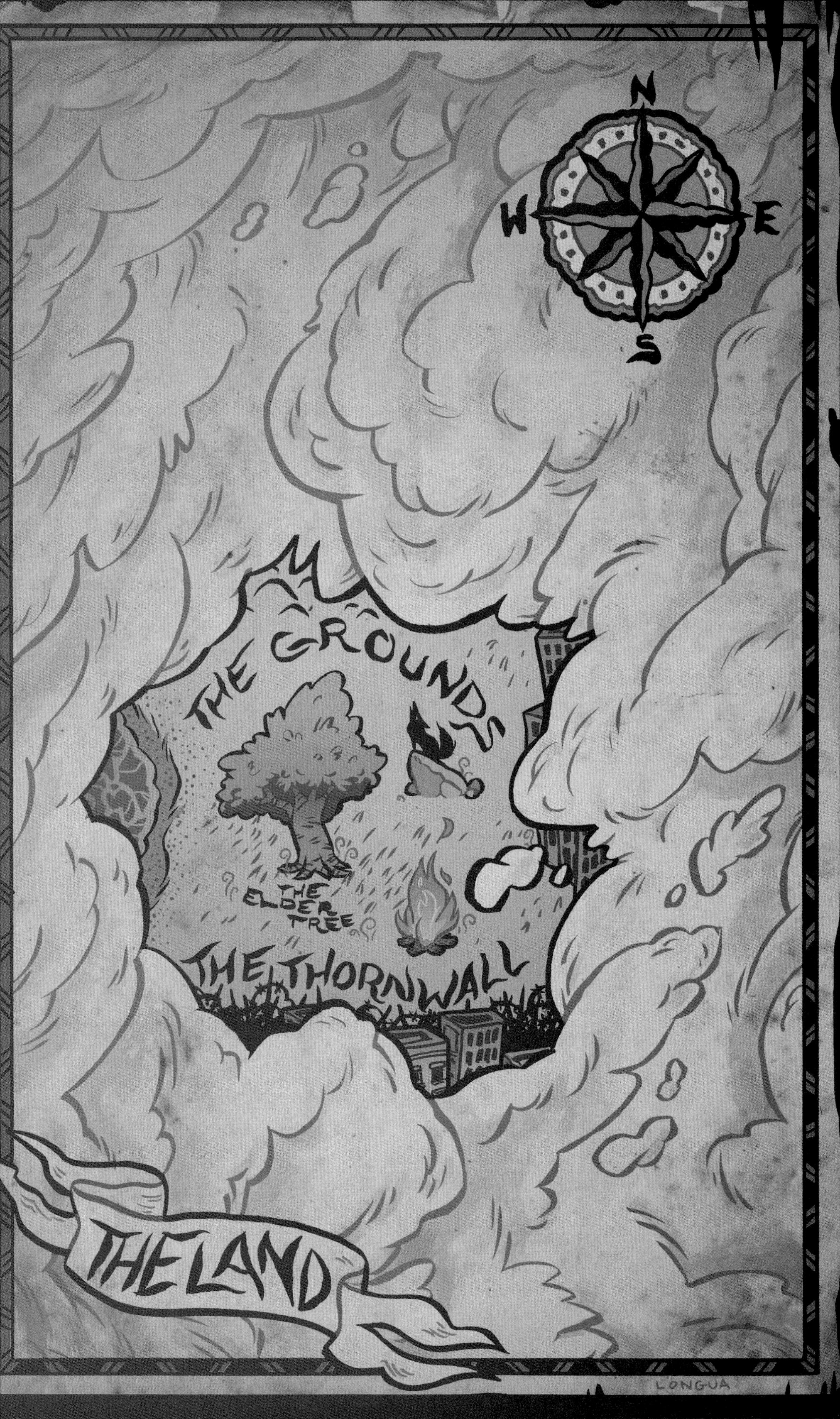
N
W
E
S
THE GROUNDS
THE ELDER TREE
THE THORNWALL
THE LAND
LONGUA

IN THE RUINS OF A DEVASTATED CITY.
IN A PLACE KNOWN AS THE GROUNDS.

"GATHER ROUND, SAD ONES.
FOR TODAY WE MOURN.

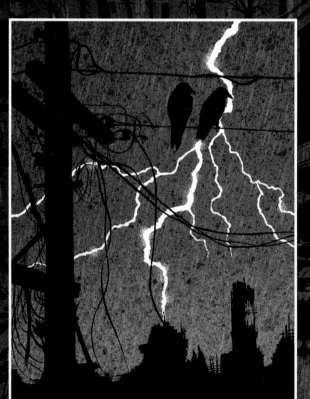

TRY NOT TO BE AFRAID."

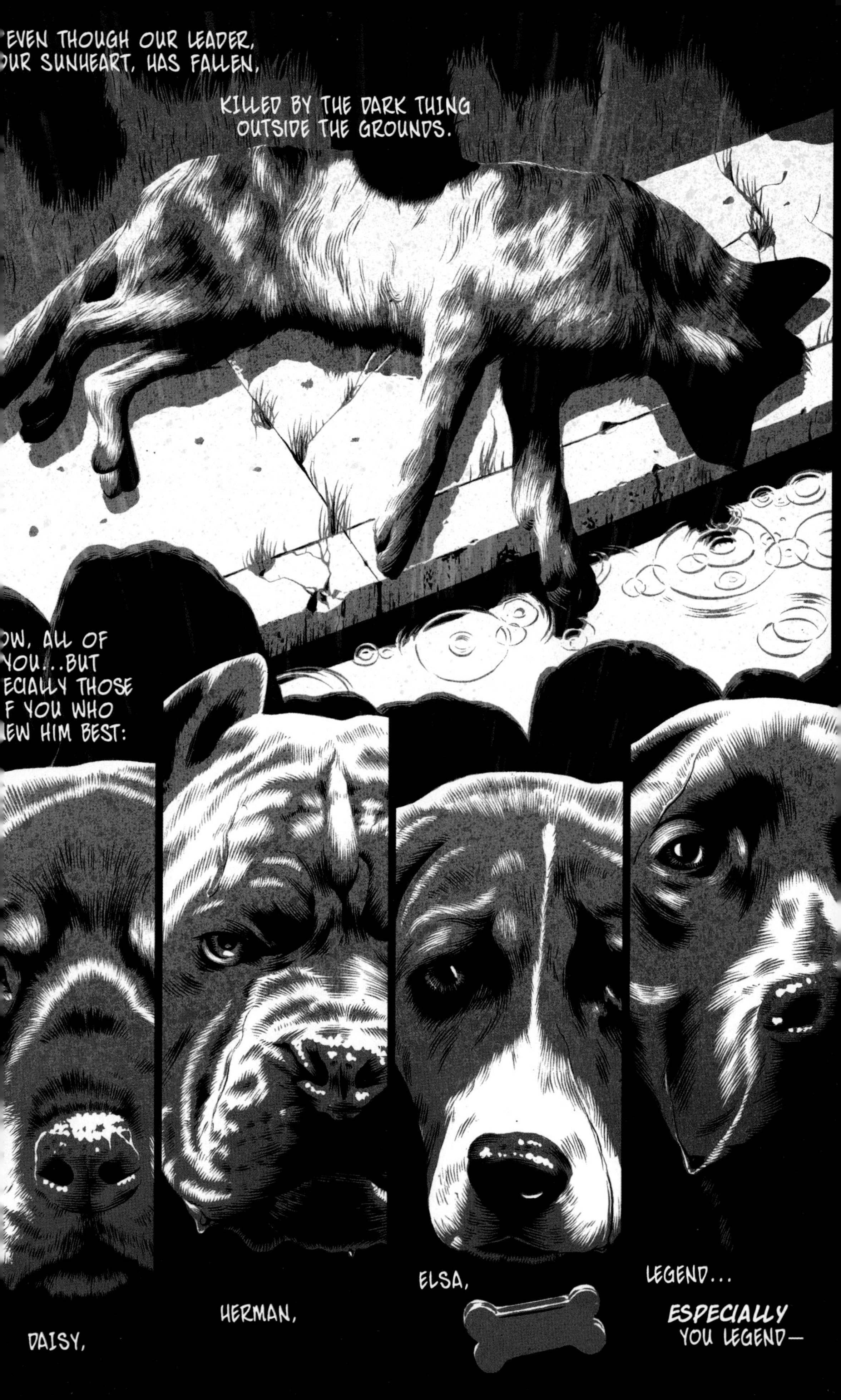

EVEN THOUGH OUR LEADER,
UR SUNHEART, HAS FALLEN,
KILLED BY THE DARK THING OUTSIDE THE GROUNDS.
W, ALL OF YOU...BUT ECIALLY THOSE F YOU WHO EW HIM BEST:
DAISY,
HERMAN,
ELSA,
LEGEND...
ESPECIALLY YOU LEGEND—

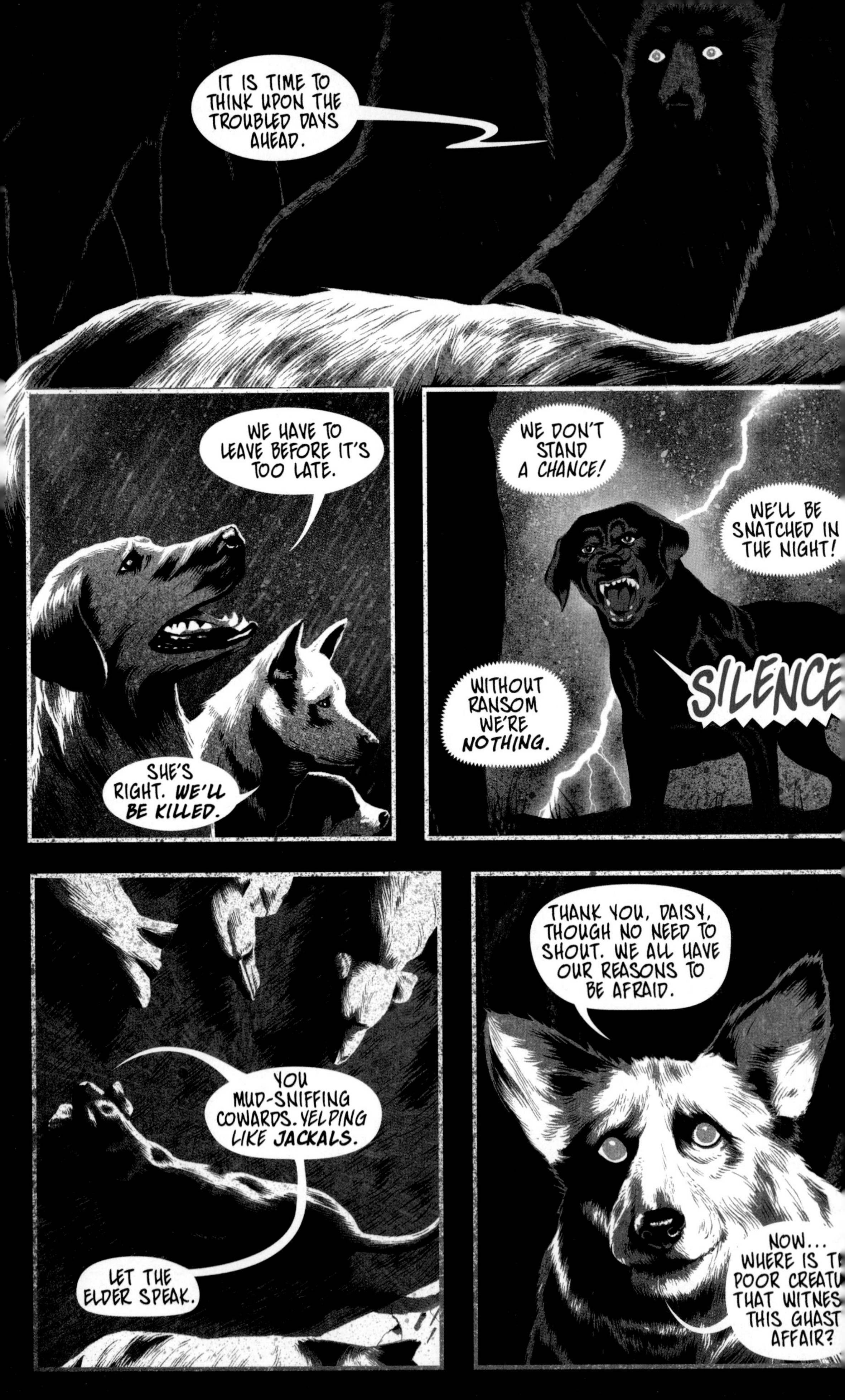
IT IS TIME TO THINK UPON THE TROUBLED DAYS AHEAD.
WE HAVE TO LEAVE BEFORE IT'S TOO LATE.
SHE'S RIGHT. WE'LL BE KILLED.
WE DON'T STAND A CHANCE!
WE'LL BE SNATCHED IN THE NIGHT!
WITHOUT RANSOM WE'RE NOTHING.
SILENCE
YOU MUD-SNIFFING COWARDS. YELPING LIKE JACKALS.
LET THE ELDER SPEAK.
THANK YOU, DAISY, THOUGH NO NEED TO SHOUT. WE ALL HAVE OUR REASONS TO BE AFRAID.
NOW... WHERE IS T POOR CREATU THAT WITNES THIS GHAST AFFAIR?

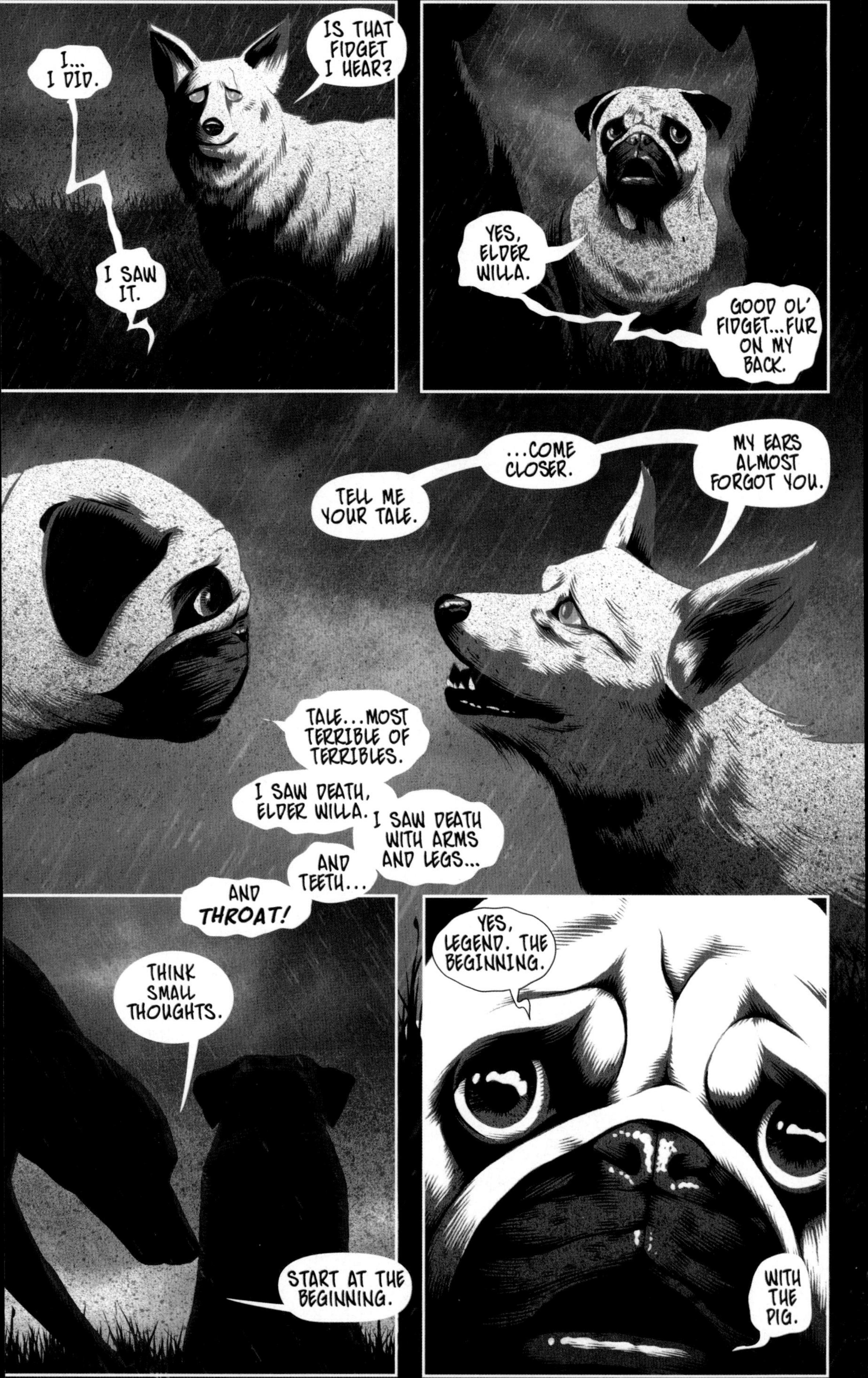
I... I DID.
IS THAT FIDGET I HEAR?
I SAW IT.
YES, ELDER WILLA.
GOOD OL' FIDGET...FUR ON MY BACK.
MY EARS ALMOST FORGOT YOU.
...COME CLOSER.
TELL ME YOUR TALE.
TALE...MOST TERRIBLE OF TERRIBLES.
I SAW DEATH, ELDER WILLA.
I SAW DEATH WITH ARMS AND LEGS...
AND TEETH...
AND *THROAT!*
THINK SMALL THOUGHTS.
START AT THE BEGINNING.
YES, LEGEND. THE BEGINNING.
WITH THE PIG.

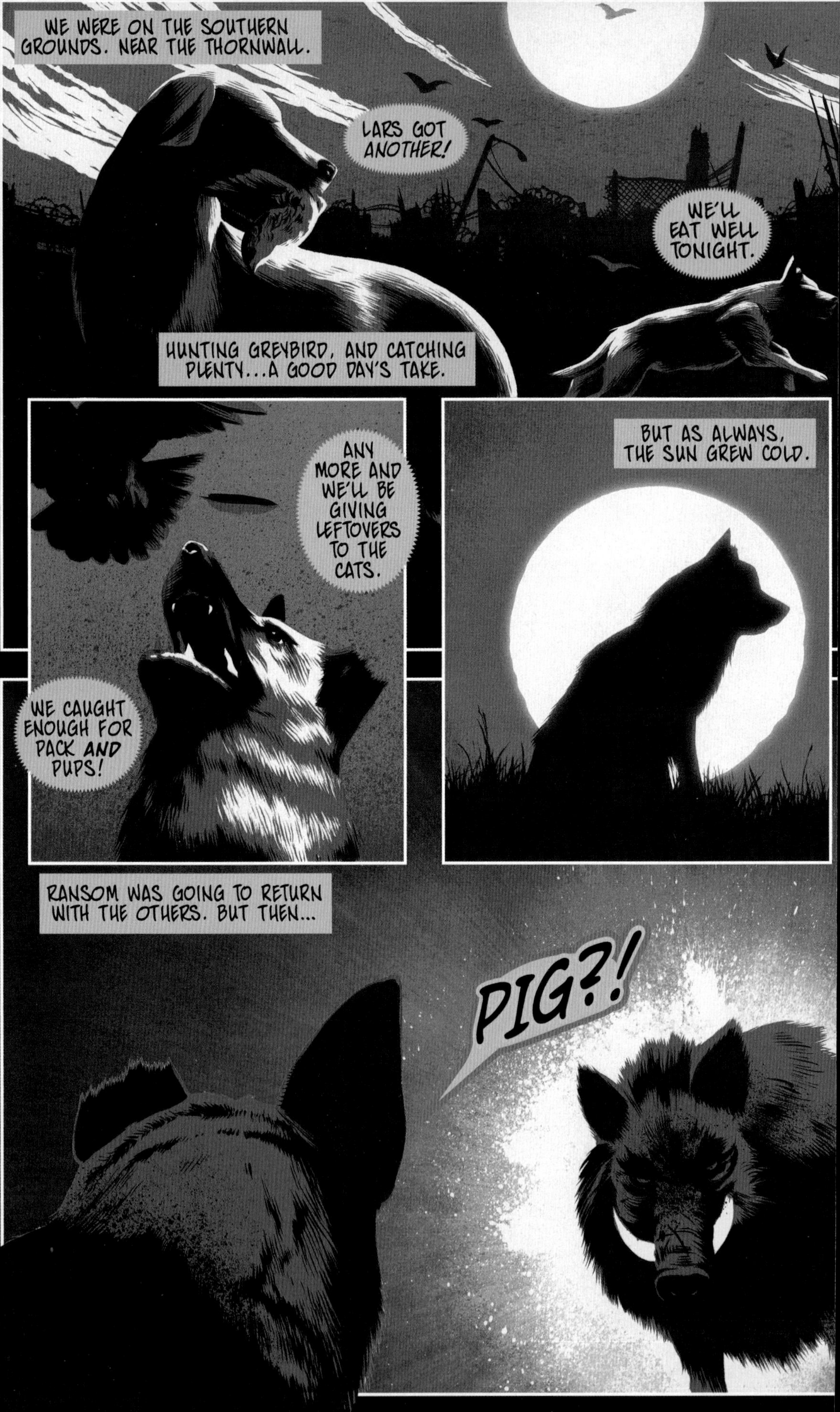
WE WERE ON THE SOUTHERN GROUNDS. NEAR THE THORNWALL.
LARS GOT ANOTHER!
WE'LL EAT WELL TONIGHT.
HUNTING GREYBIRD, AND CATCHING PLENTY...A GOOD DAY'S TAKE.
ANY MORE AND WE'LL BE GIVING LEFTOVERS TO THE CATS.
WE CAUGHT ENOUGH FOR PACK AND PUPS!
BUT AS ALWAYS, THE SUN GREW COLD.
RANSOM WAS GOING TO RETURN WITH THE OTHERS. BUT THEN...
PIG?!

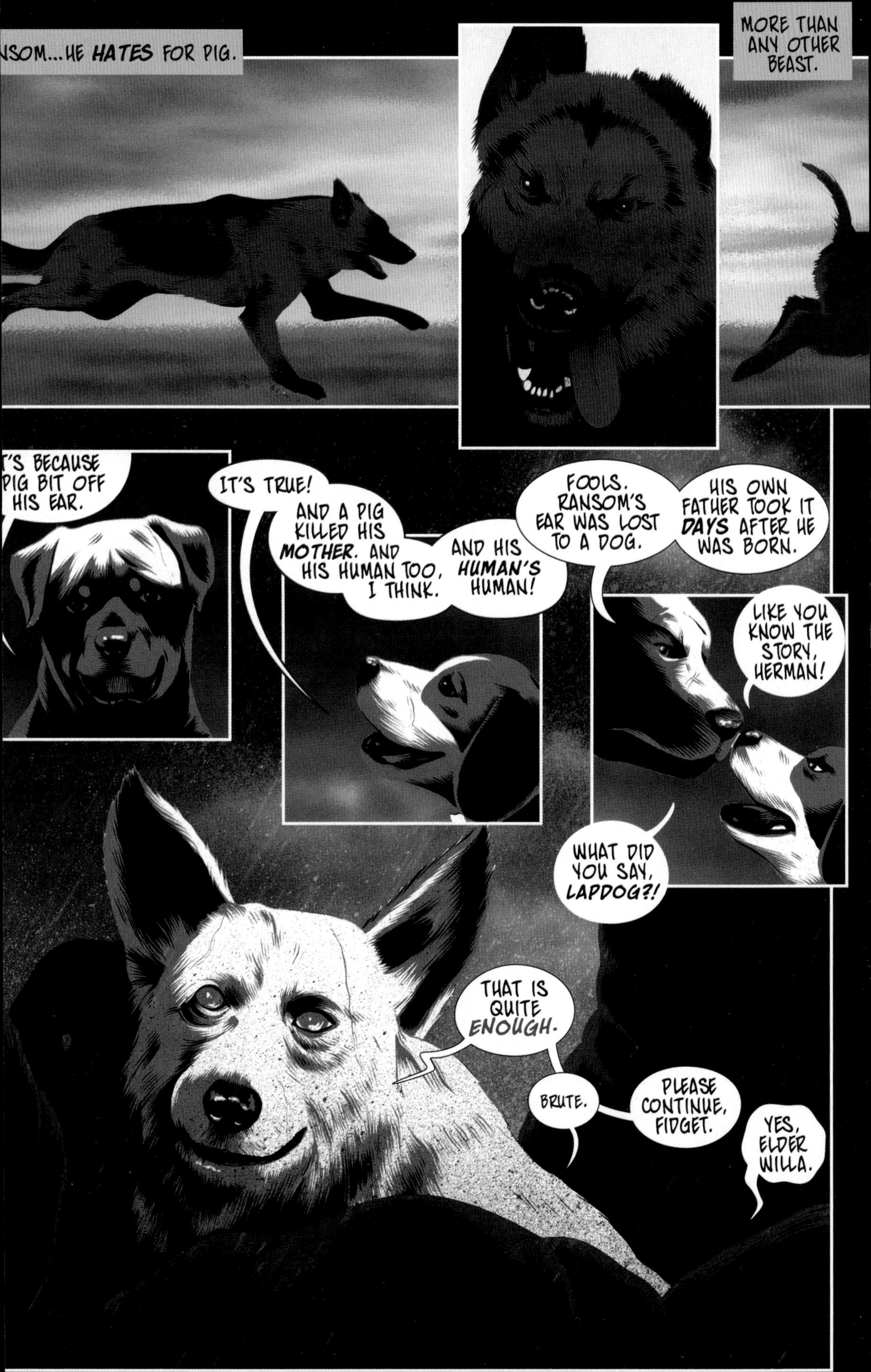
NSOM...HE *HATES* FOR PIG.
MORE THAN ANY OTHER BEAST.
'S BECAUSE PIG BIT OFF HIS EAR.
IT'S TRUE!
AND A PIG KILLED HIS *MOTHER*. AND HIS HUMAN TOO, I THINK.
AND HIS *HUMAN'S* HUMAN!
FOOLS. RANSOM'S EAR WAS LOST TO A DOG.
HIS OWN FATHER TOOK IT *DAYS* AFTER HE WAS BORN.
LIKE YOU KNOW THE STORY, HERMAN!
WHAT DID YOU SAY, *LAPDOG?!*
THAT IS QUITE *ENOUGH*.
BRUTE.
PLEASE CONTINUE, FIDGET.
YES, ELDER WILLA.

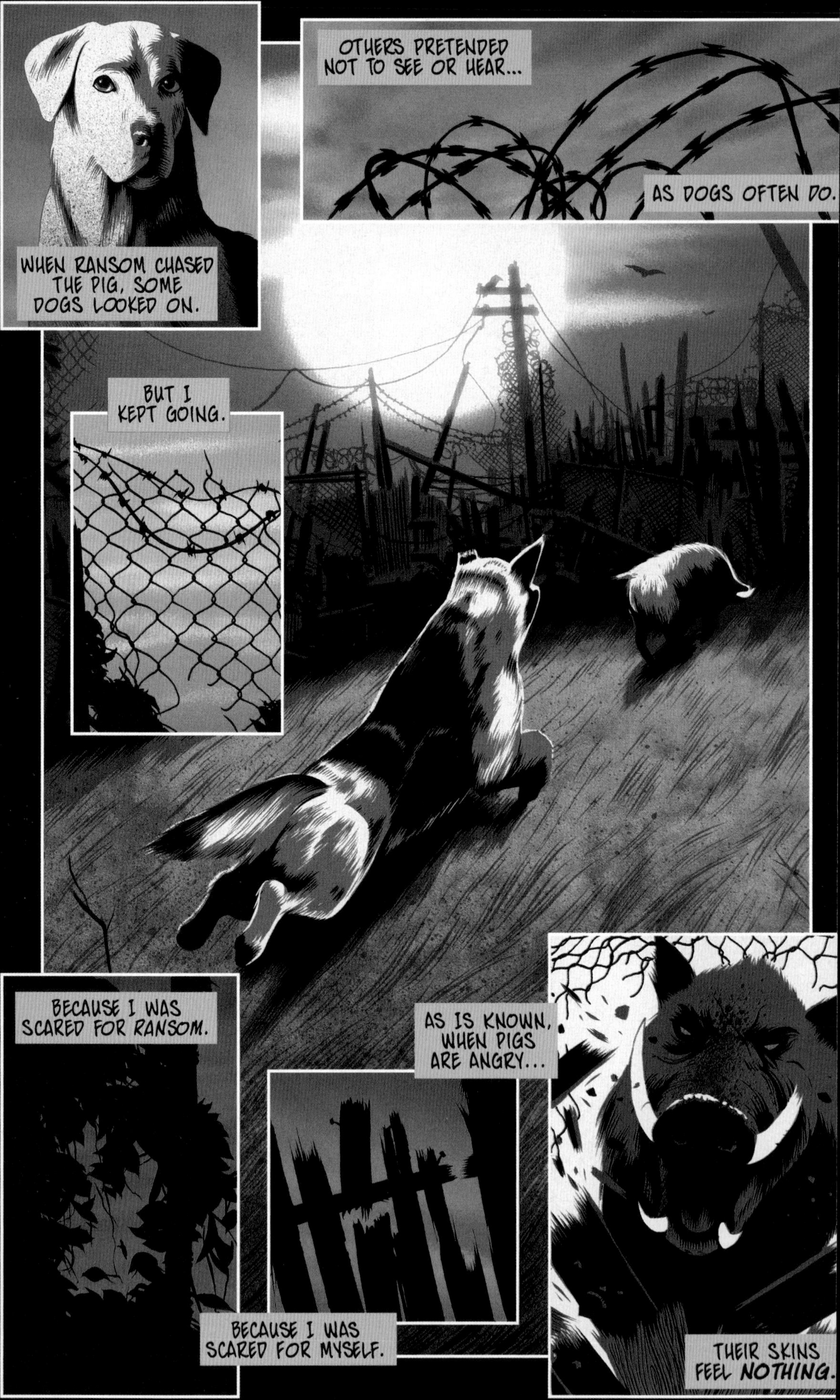
WHEN RANSOM CHASED THE PIG, SOME DOGS LOOKED ON.
OTHERS PRETENDED NOT TO SEE OR HEAR...
AS DOGS OFTEN DO.
BUT I KEPT GOING.
BECAUSE I WAS SCARED FOR RANSOM.
BECAUSE I WAS SCARED FOR MYSELF.
AS IS KNOWN, WHEN PIGS ARE ANGRY...
THEIR SKINS FEEL **NOTHING**.

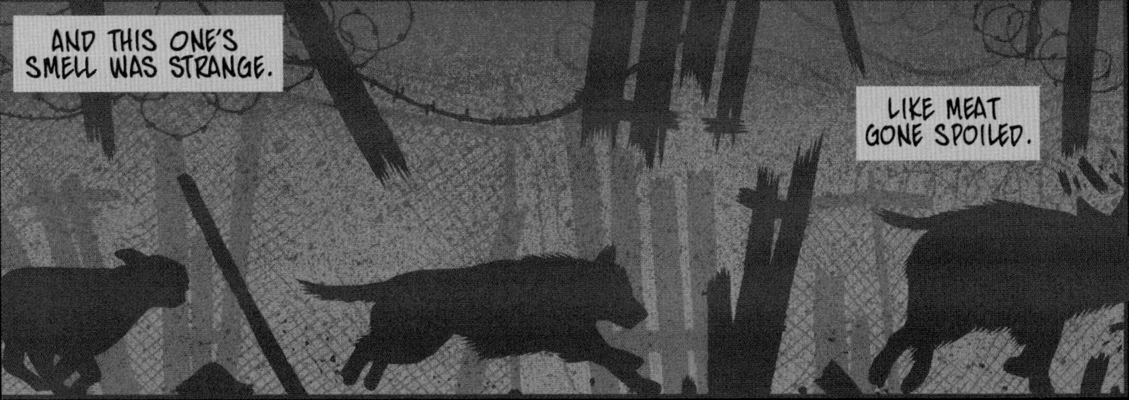
AND THIS ONE'S SMELL WAS STRANGE.
LIKE MEAT GONE SPOILED.

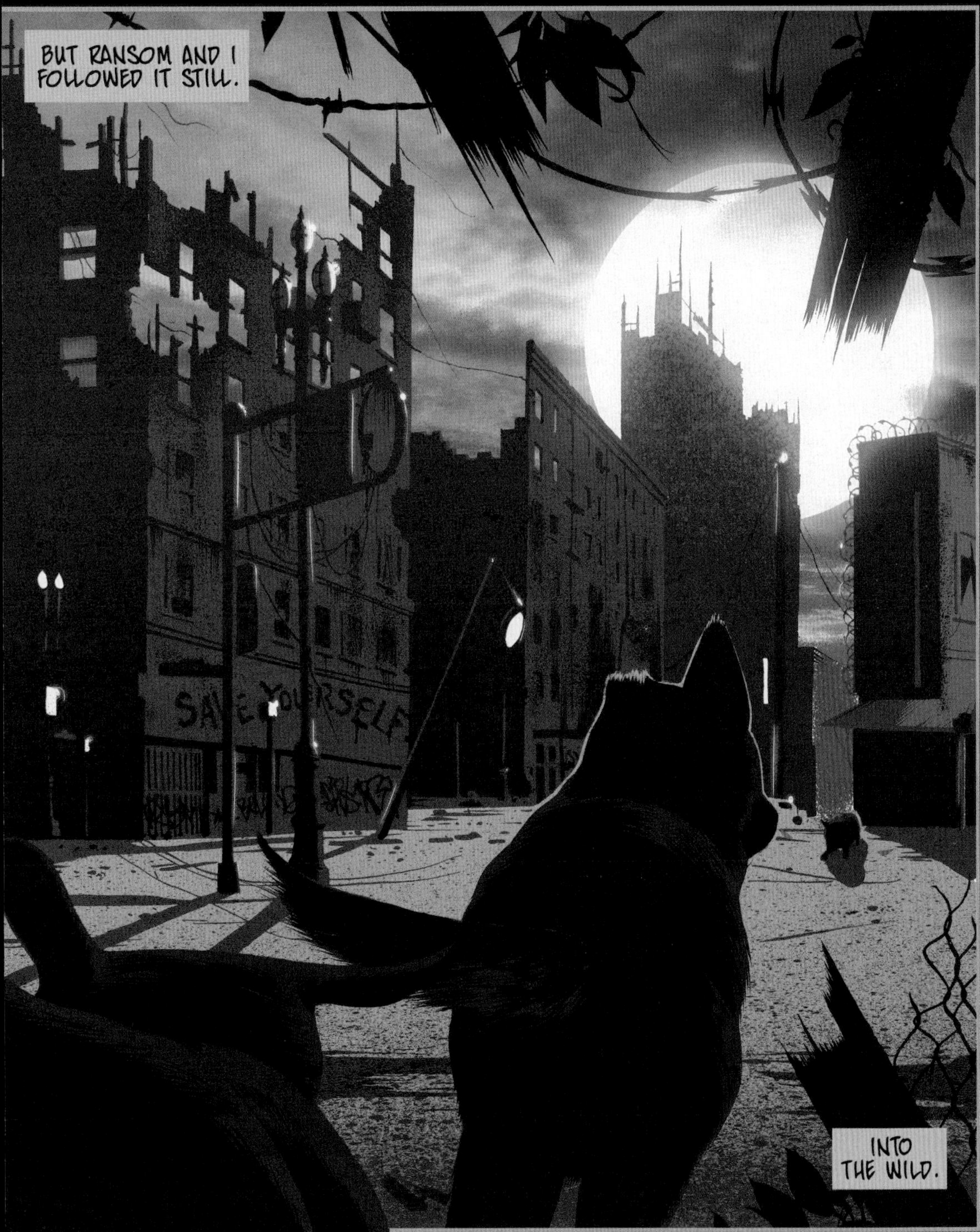
BUT RANSOM AND I FOLLOWED IT STILL.
SAVE YOURSELF
INTO THE WILD.

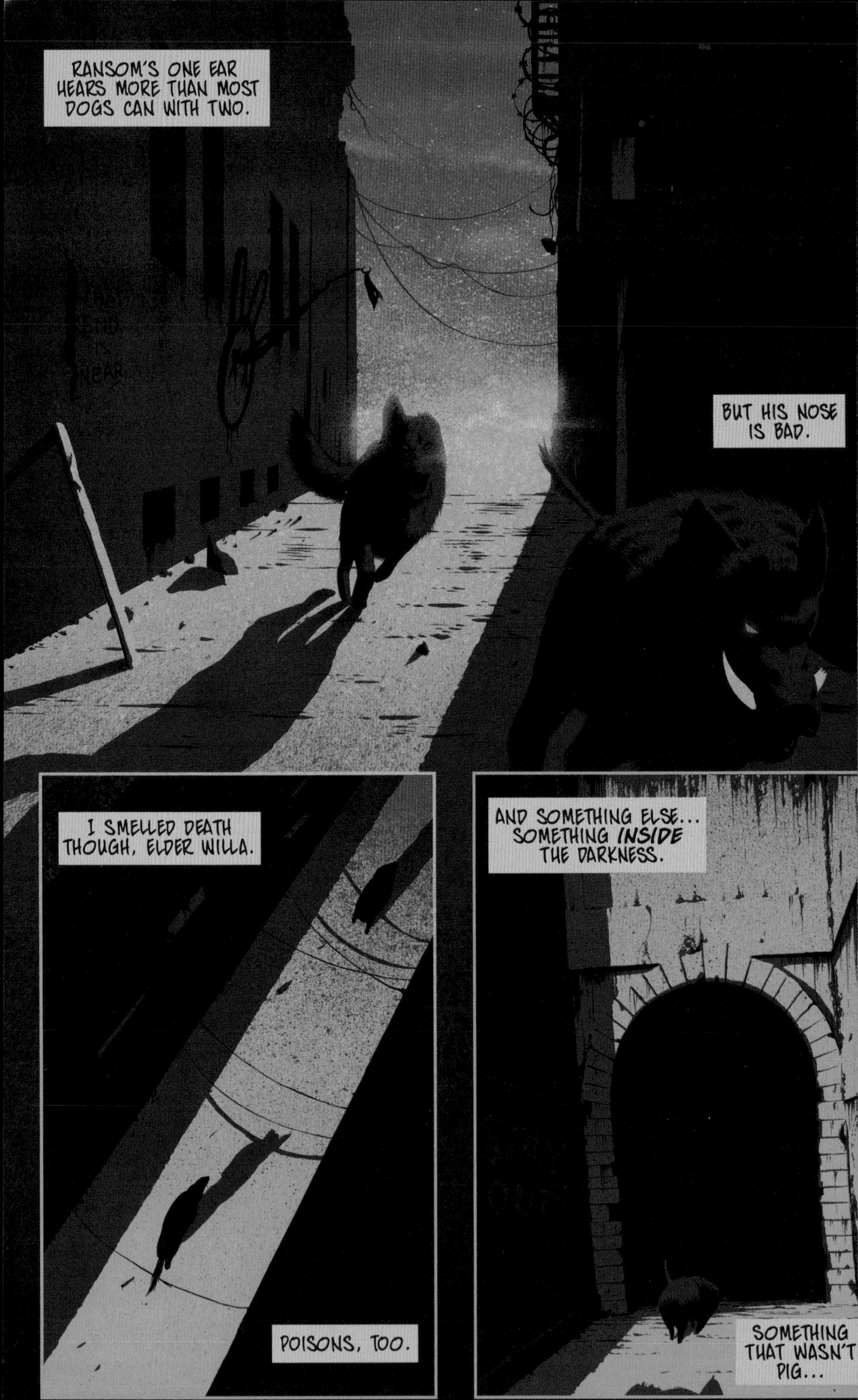
RANSOM'S ONE EAR HEARS MORE THAN MOST DOGS CAN WITH TWO.
BUT HIS NOSE IS BAD.
I SMELLED DEATH THOUGH, ELDER WILLA.
POISONS, TOO.
AND SOMETHING ELSE... SOMETHING INSIDE THE DARKNESS.
SOMETHING THAT WASN'T PIG...

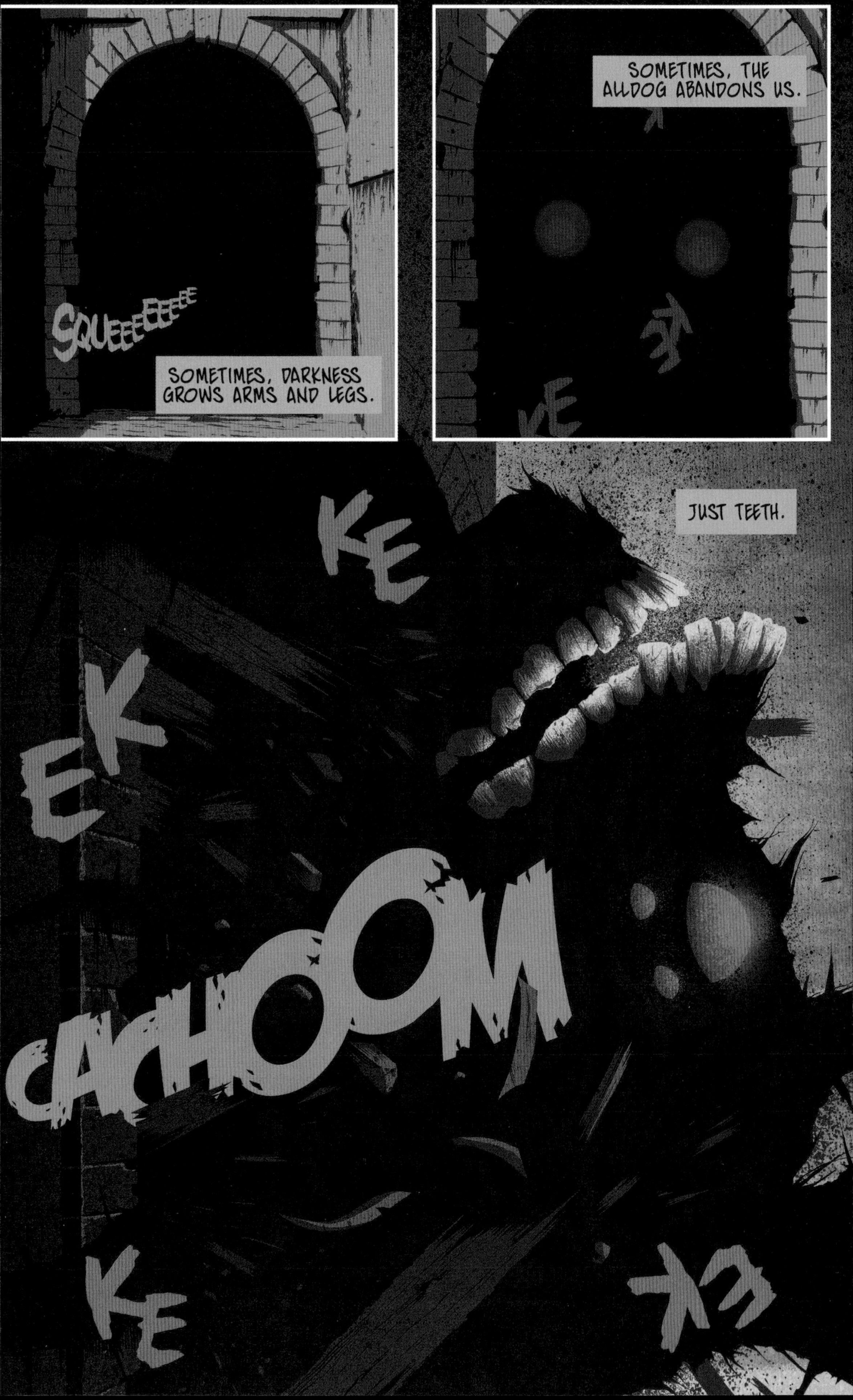
SQUEEEEEEEEEE
SOMETIMES, DARKNESS GROWS ARMS AND LEGS.
SOMETIMES, THE ALLDOG ABANDONS US.
KE
KE
JUST TEETH.
EK
CACHOOM
KE

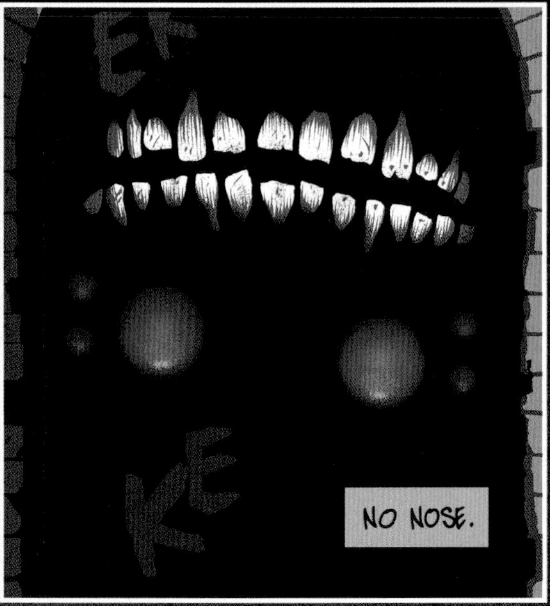
KE
NO NOSE.
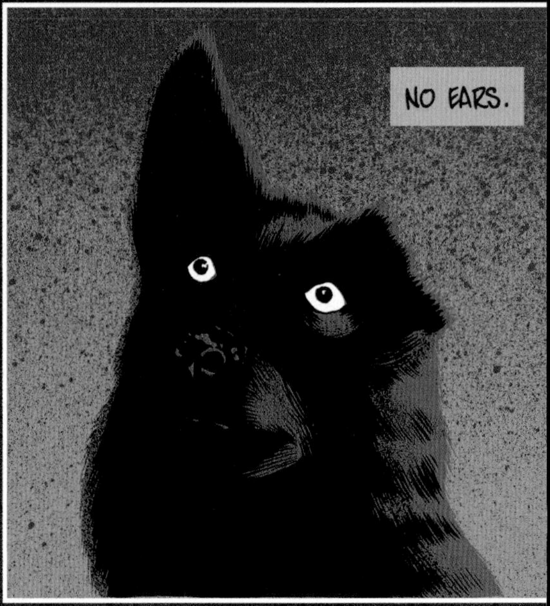
NO EARS.
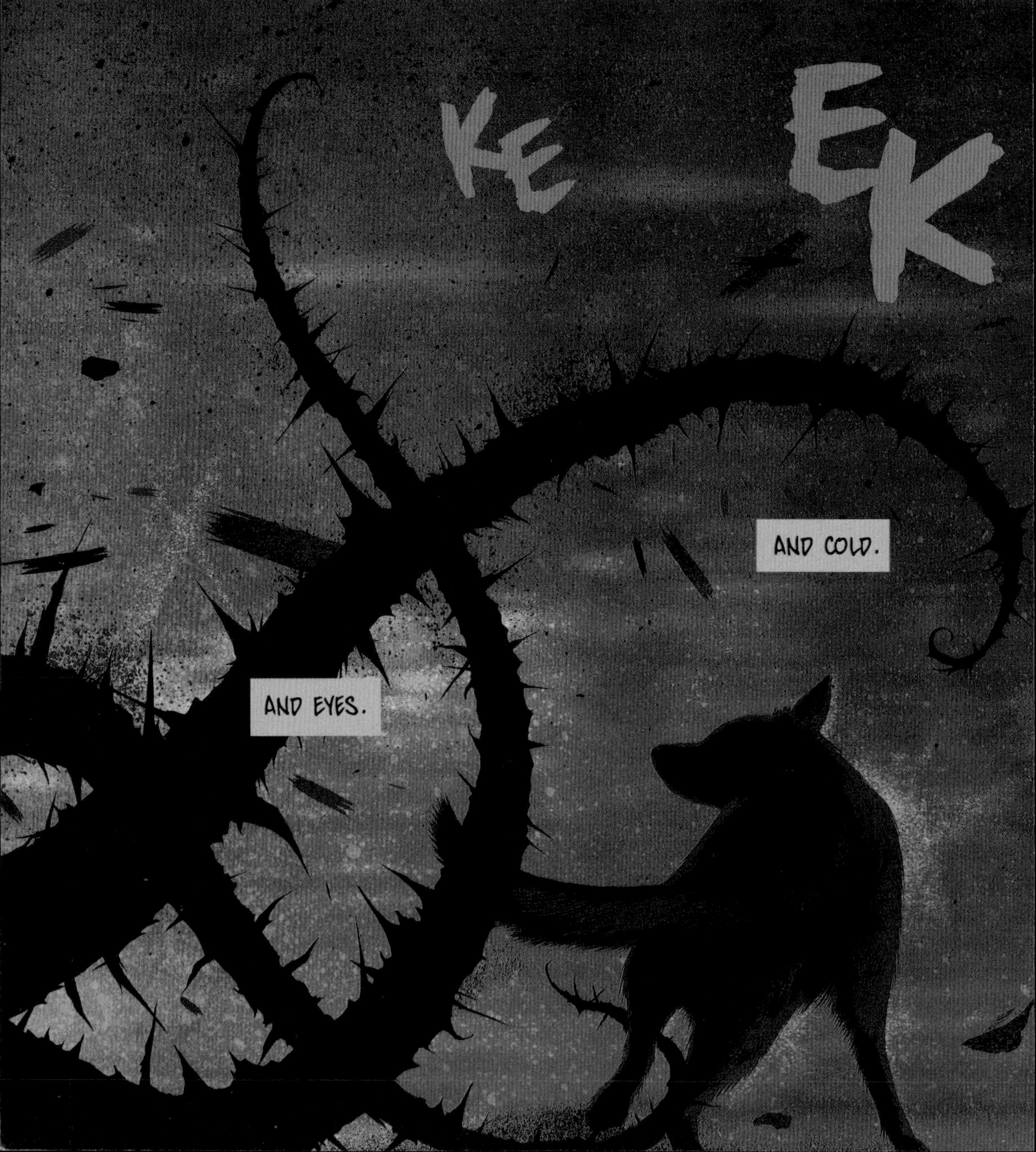
KE
EK
AND COLD.
AND EYES.

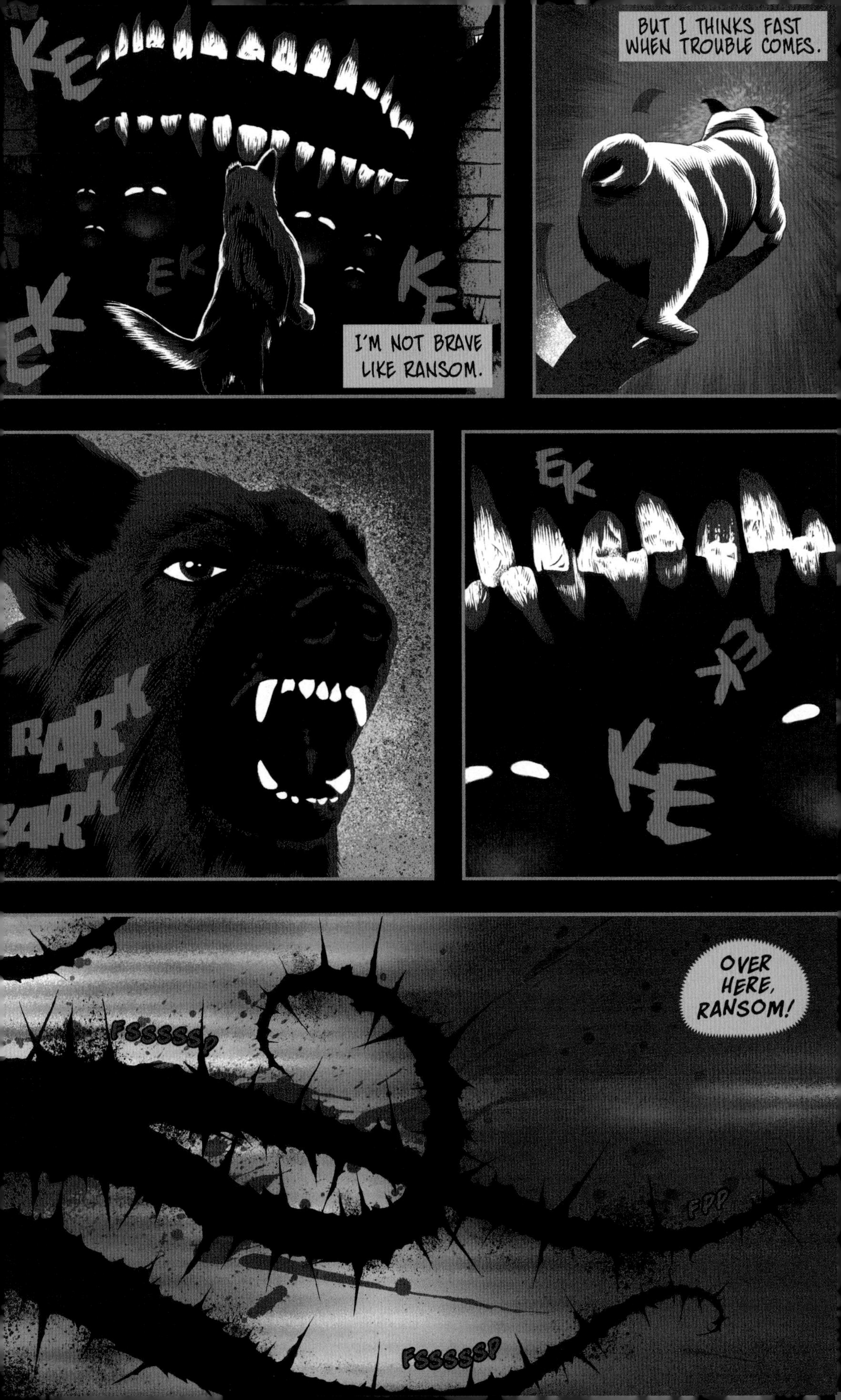
KE
EK
KE
EK
I'M NOT BRAVE LIKE RANSOM.
BUT I THINKS FAST WHEN TROUBLE COMES.
RARK
EK
EK
KE
FSSSSSP
OVER HERE, RANSOM!
FPP
FSSSSSP

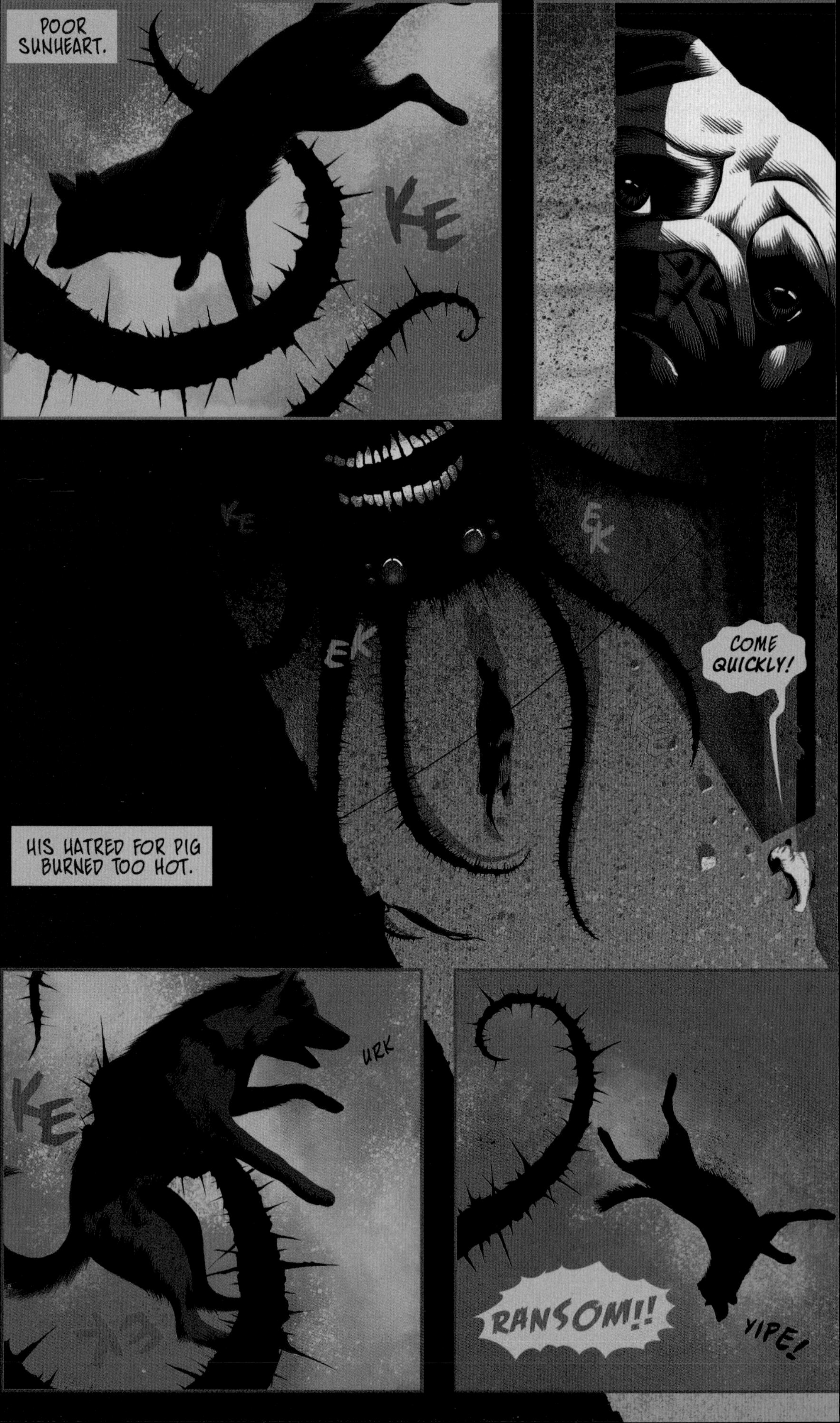

POOR SUNHEART.
KE
KE
EK
EK
KE
COME QUICKLY!
HIS HATRED FOR PIG BURNED TOO HOT.
KE
URK
RANSOM!!
YIPE!

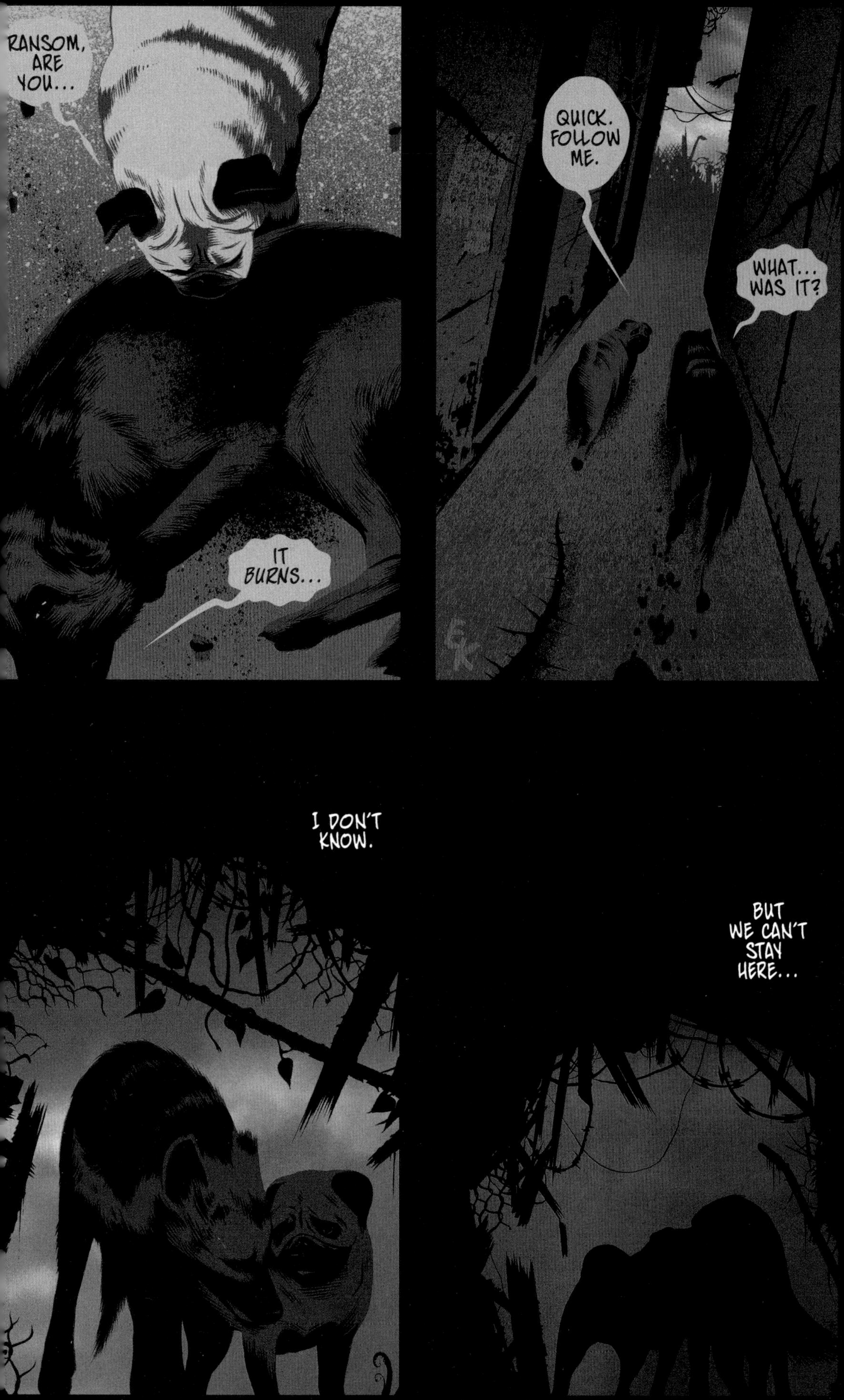
RANSOM, ARE YOU...
IT BURNS...
QUICK. FOLLOW ME.
WHAT... WAS IT?
I DON'T KNOW.
BUT WE CAN'T STAY HERE...

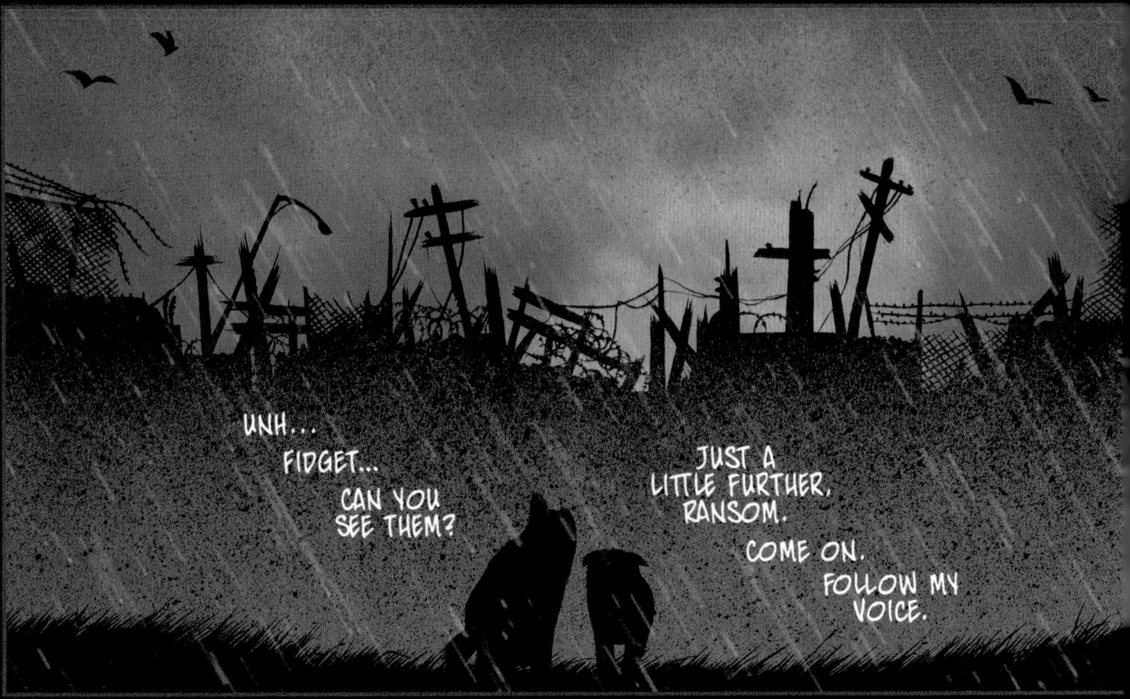
UNH...
FIDGET...
CAN YOU SEE THEM?
JUST A LITTLE FURTHER, RANSOM.
COME ON.
FOLLOW MY VOICE.
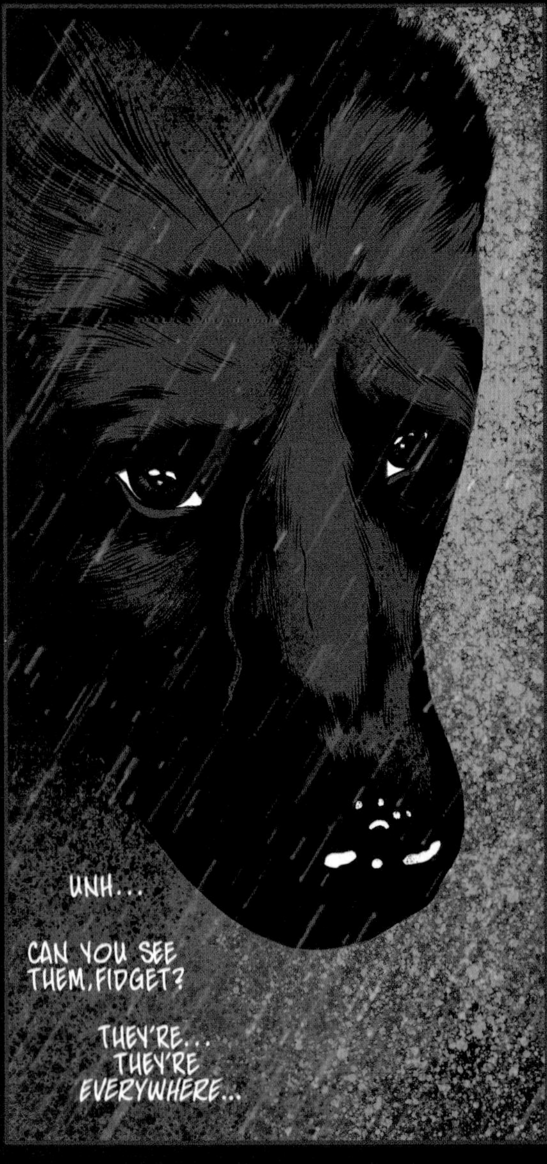
UNH...
CAN YOU SEE THEM, FIDGET?
THEY'RE... THEY'RE EVERYWHERE...
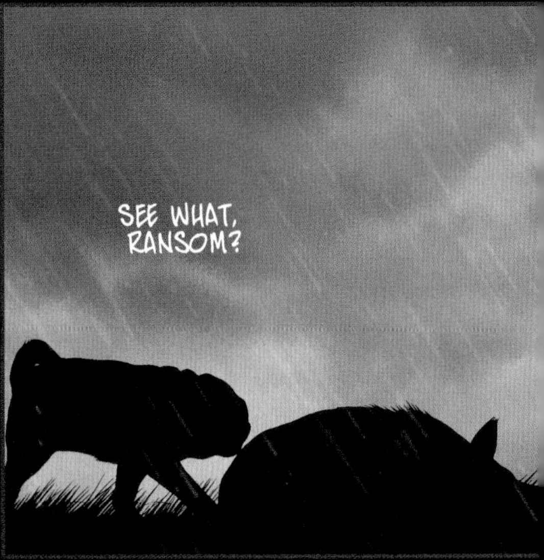
SEE WHAT, RANSOM?
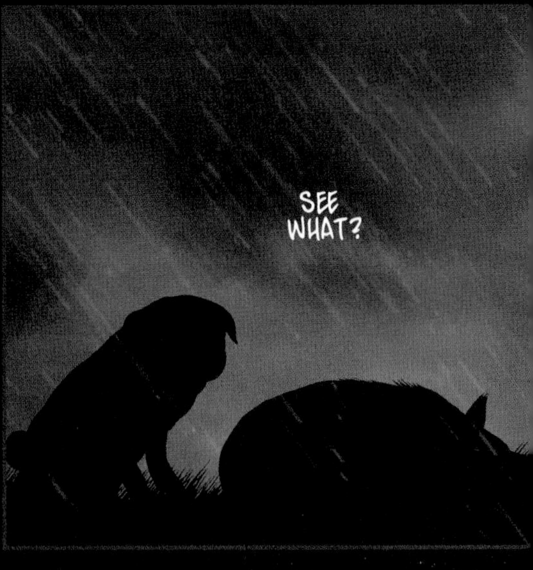
SEE WHAT?

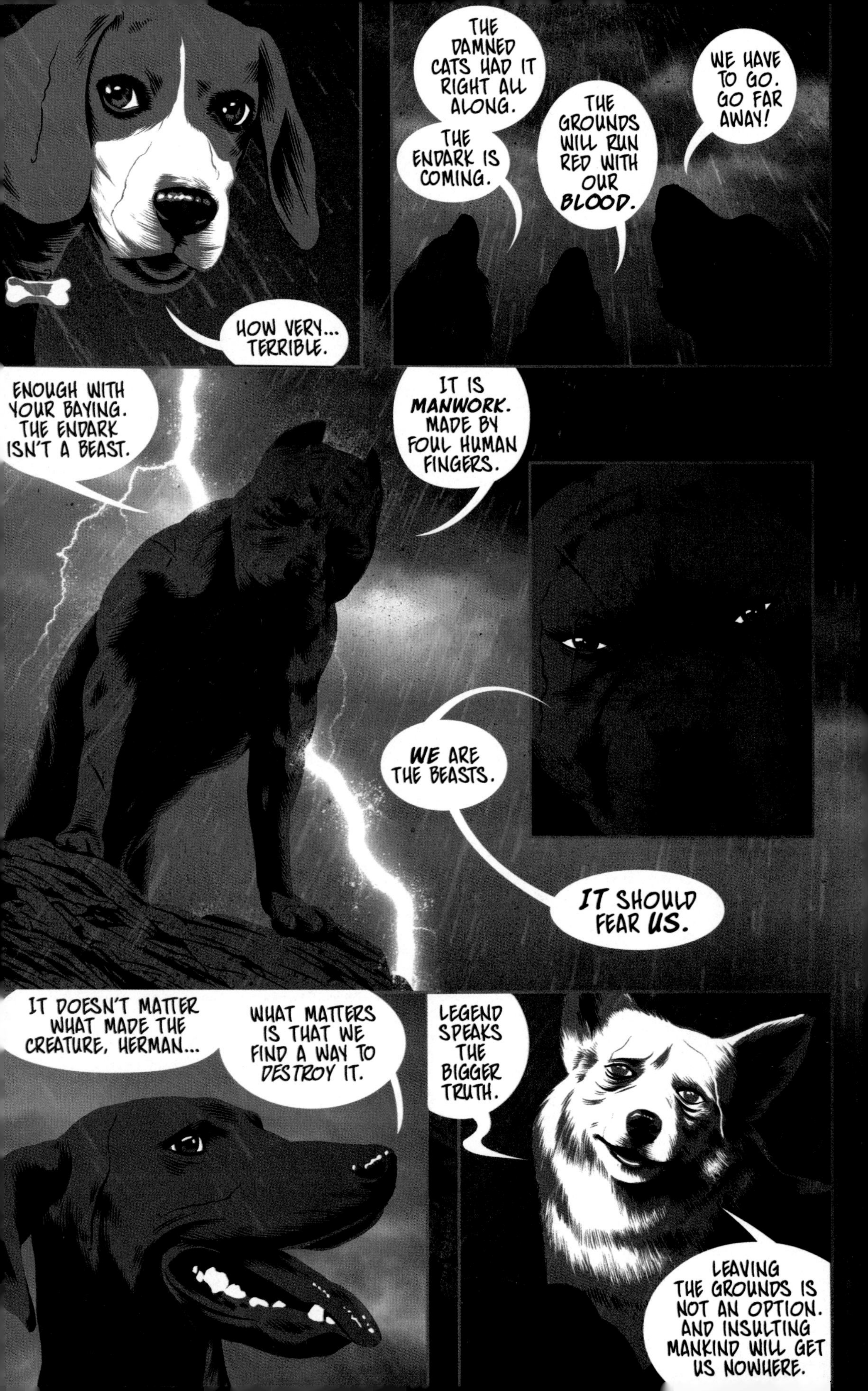
HOW VERY... TERRIBLE.
THE DAMNED CATS HAD IT RIGHT ALL ALONG.
THE ENDARK IS COMING.
THE GROUNDS WILL RUN RED WITH OUR BLOOD.
WE HAVE TO GO. GO FAR AWAY!
ENOUGH WITH YOUR BAYING. THE ENDARK ISN'T A BEAST.
IT IS MANWORK. MADE BY FOUL HUMAN FINGERS.
WE ARE THE BEASTS.
IT SHOULD FEAR US.
IT DOESN'T MATTER WHAT MADE THE CREATURE, HERMAN...
WHAT MATTERS IS THAT WE FIND A WAY TO DESTROY IT.
LEGEND SPEAKS THE BIGGER TRUTH.
LEAVING THE GROUNDS IS NOT AN OPTION. AND INSULTING MANKIND WILL GET US NOWHERE.

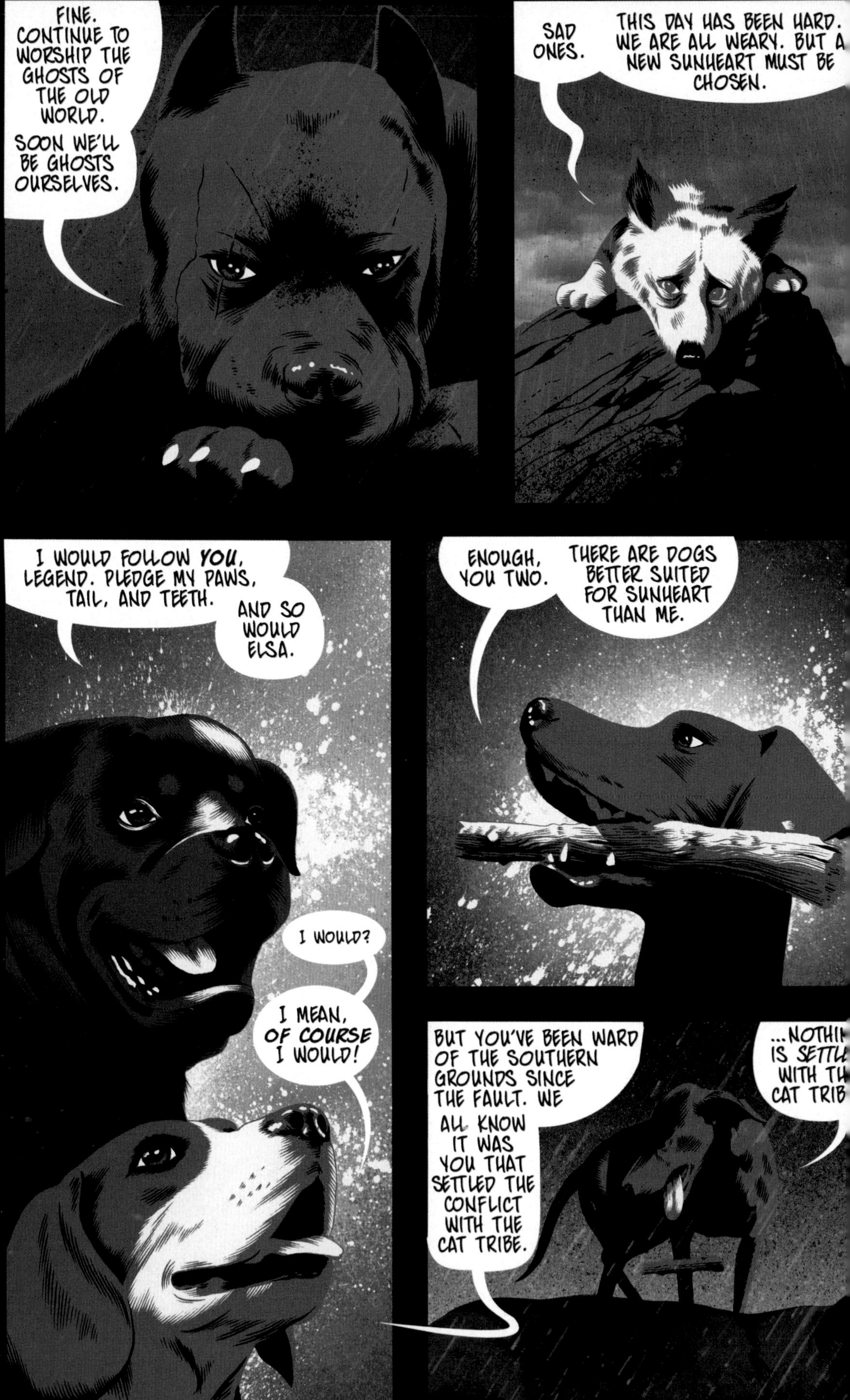
FINE. CONTINUE TO WORSHIP THE GHOSTS OF THE OLD WORLD.
SOON WE'LL BE GHOSTS OURSELVES.
SAD ONES.
THIS DAY HAS BEEN HARD. WE ARE ALL WEARY. BUT A NEW SUNHEART MUST BE CHOSEN.
I WOULD FOLLOW *YOU*, LEGEND. PLEDGE MY PAWS, TAIL, AND TEETH.
AND SO WOULD ELSA.
I WOULD?
I MEAN, *OF COURSE* I WOULD!
ENOUGH, YOU TWO.
THERE ARE DOGS BETTER SUITED FOR SUNHEART THAN ME.
BUT YOU'VE BEEN WARD OF THE SOUTHERN GROUNDS SINCE THE FAULT. WE
ALL KNOW IT WAS YOU THAT SETTLED THE CONFLICT WITH THE CAT TRIBE.
...NOTHI IS *SETTL* WITH TH CAT TRIB

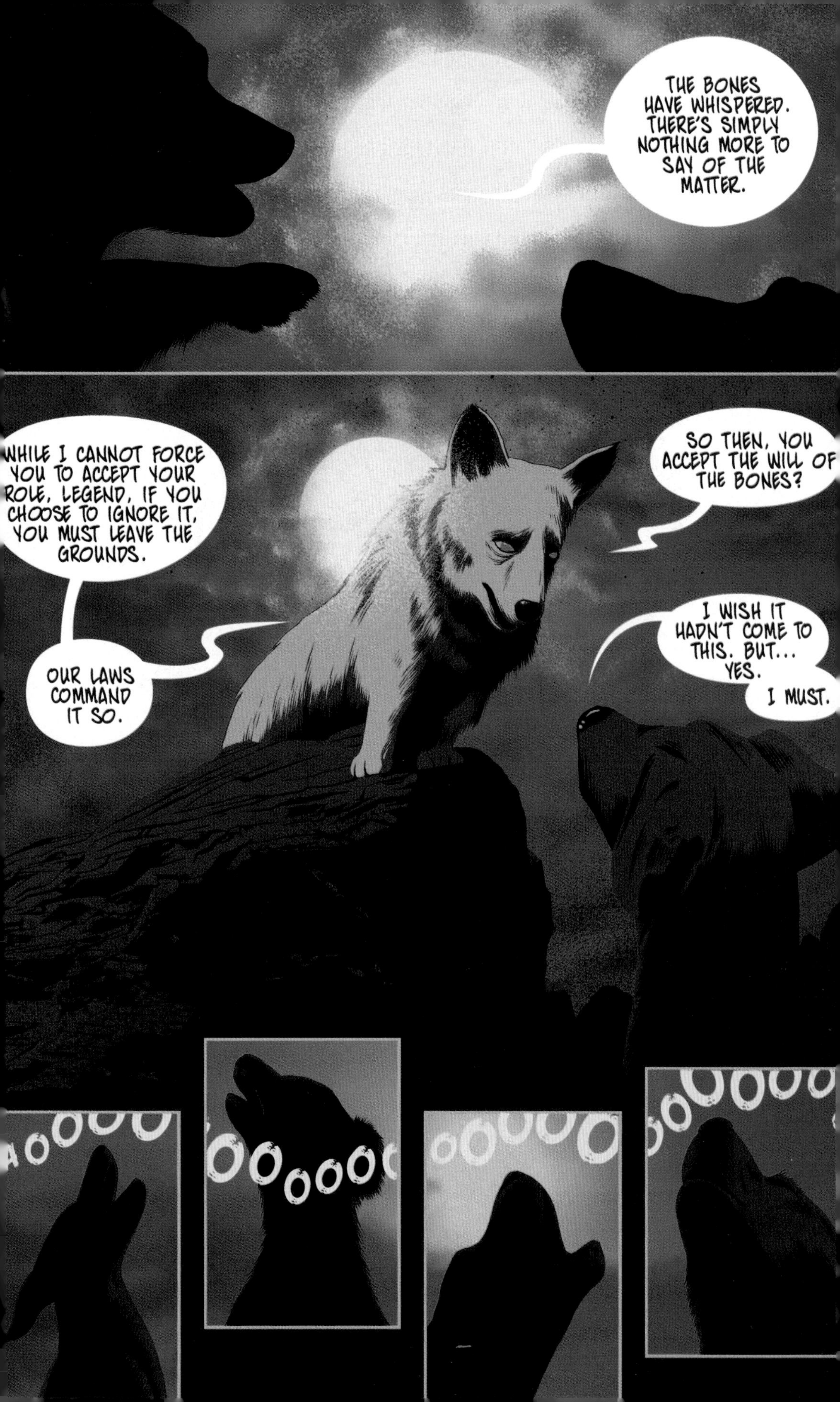
THE BONES HAVE WHISPERED. THERE'S SIMPLY NOTHING MORE TO SAY OF THE MATTER.
WHILE I CANNOT FORCE YOU TO ACCEPT YOUR ROLE, LEGEND, IF YOU CHOOSE TO IGNORE IT, YOU MUST LEAVE THE GROUNDS.
OUR LAWS COMMAND IT SO.
SO THEN, YOU ACCEPT THE WILL OF THE BONES?
I WISH IT HADN'T COME TO THIS. BUT... YES.
I MUST.
AOOOOO
OOOOOO
OOOOOOO
OOOOOOO

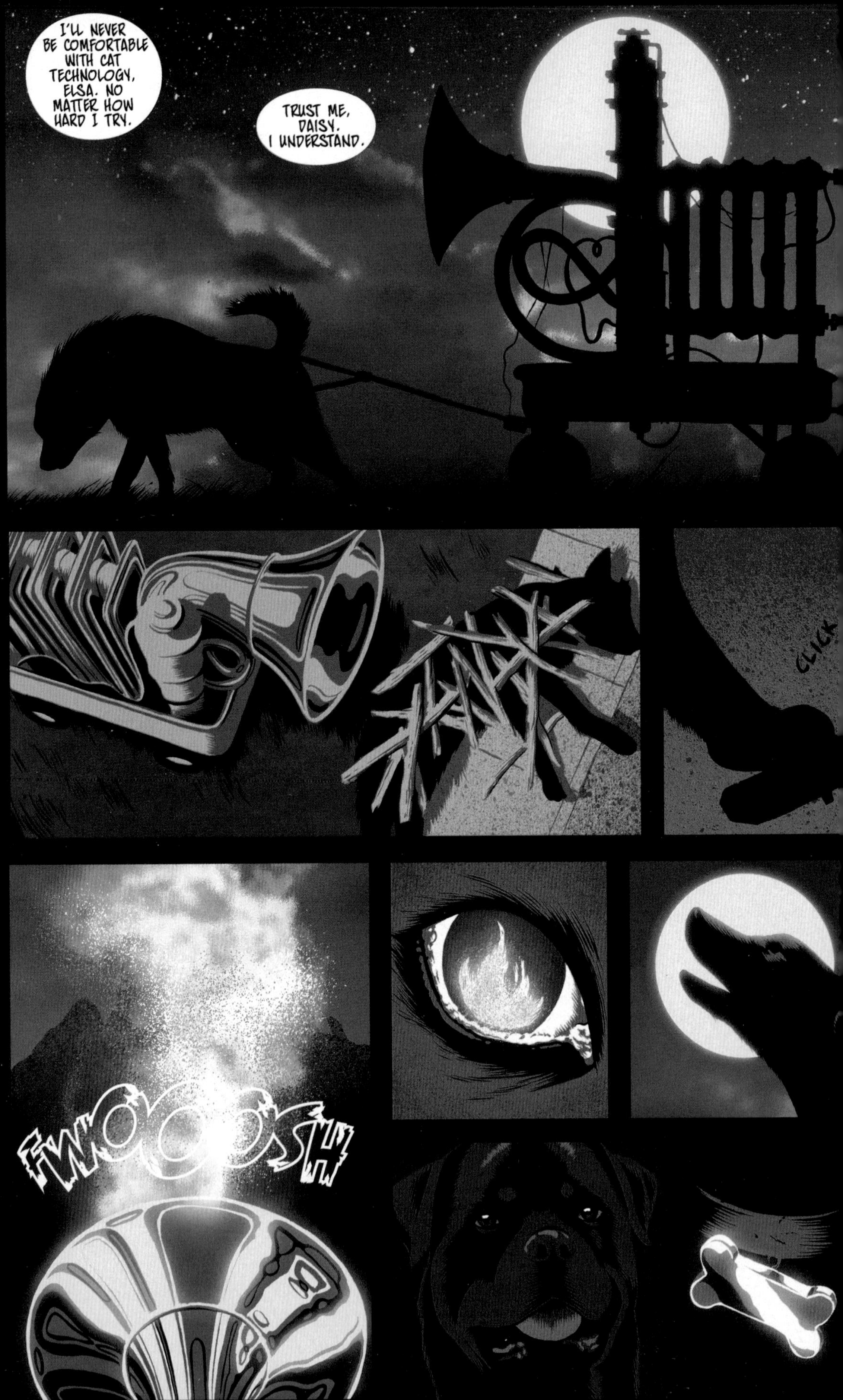
I'LL NEVER BE COMFORTABLE WITH CAT TECHNOLOGY, ELSA. NO MATTER HOW HARD I TRY.
TRUST ME, DAISY. I UNDERSTAND.
CLICK
FWOOOSH

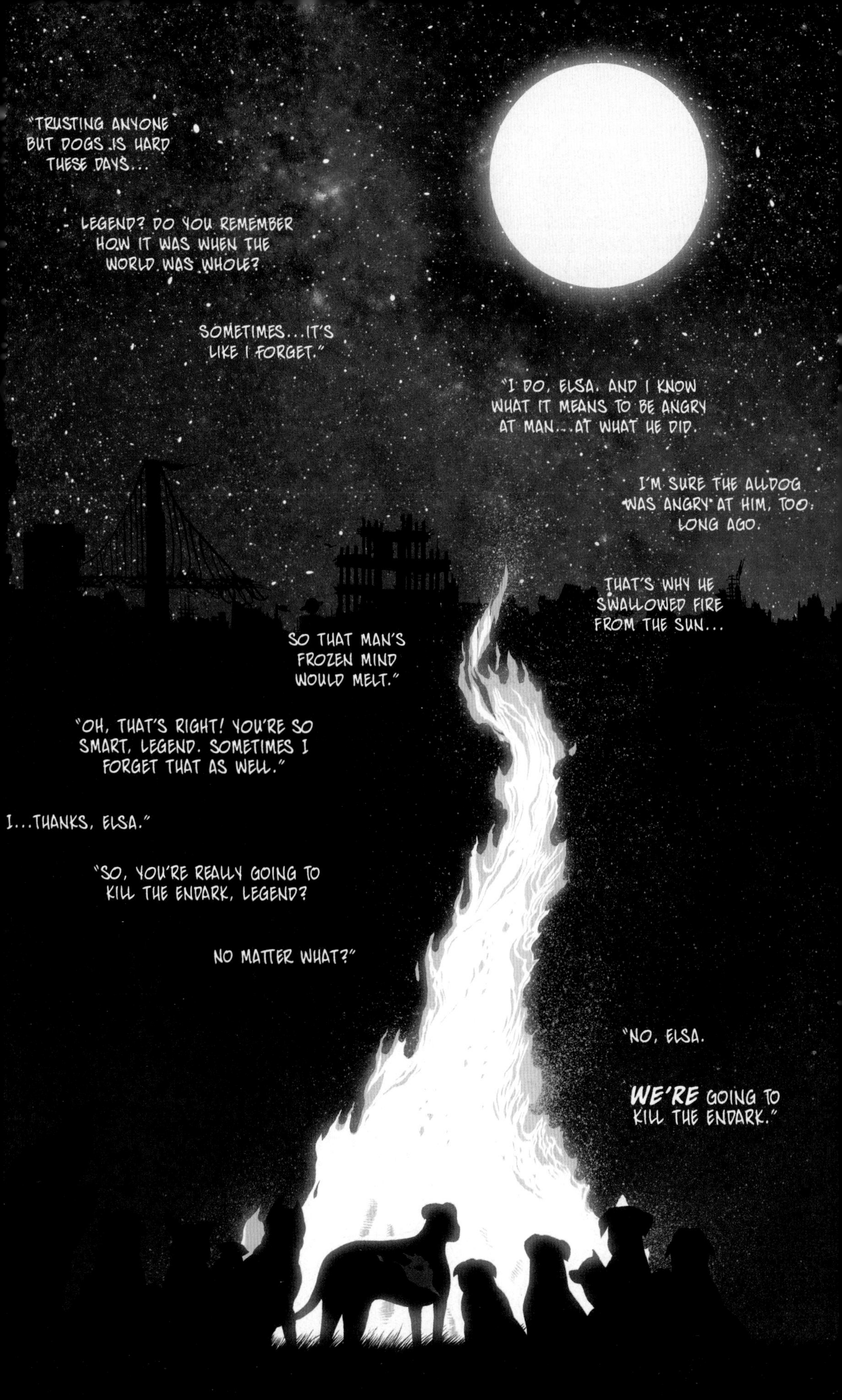
"TRUSTING ANYONE BUT DOGS IS HARD THESE DAYS...
LEGEND? DO YOU REMEMBER HOW IT WAS WHEN THE WORLD WAS WHOLE?
SOMETIMES...IT'S LIKE I FORGET."
"I DO, ELSA. AND I KNOW WHAT IT MEANS TO BE ANGRY AT MAN...AT WHAT HE DID.
I'M SURE THE ALLDOG WAS ANGRY AT HIM, TOO, LONG AGO.
THAT'S WHY HE SWALLOWED FIRE FROM THE SUN...
SO THAT MAN'S FROZEN MIND WOULD MELT."
"OH, THAT'S RIGHT! YOU'RE SO SMART, LEGEND. SOMETIMES I FORGET THAT AS WELL."
I...THANKS, ELSA."
"SO, YOU'RE REALLY GOING TO KILL THE ENDARK, LEGEND?
NO MATTER WHAT?"
"NO, ELSA.
WE'RE GOING TO KILL THE ENDARK."

CHAPTER TWO

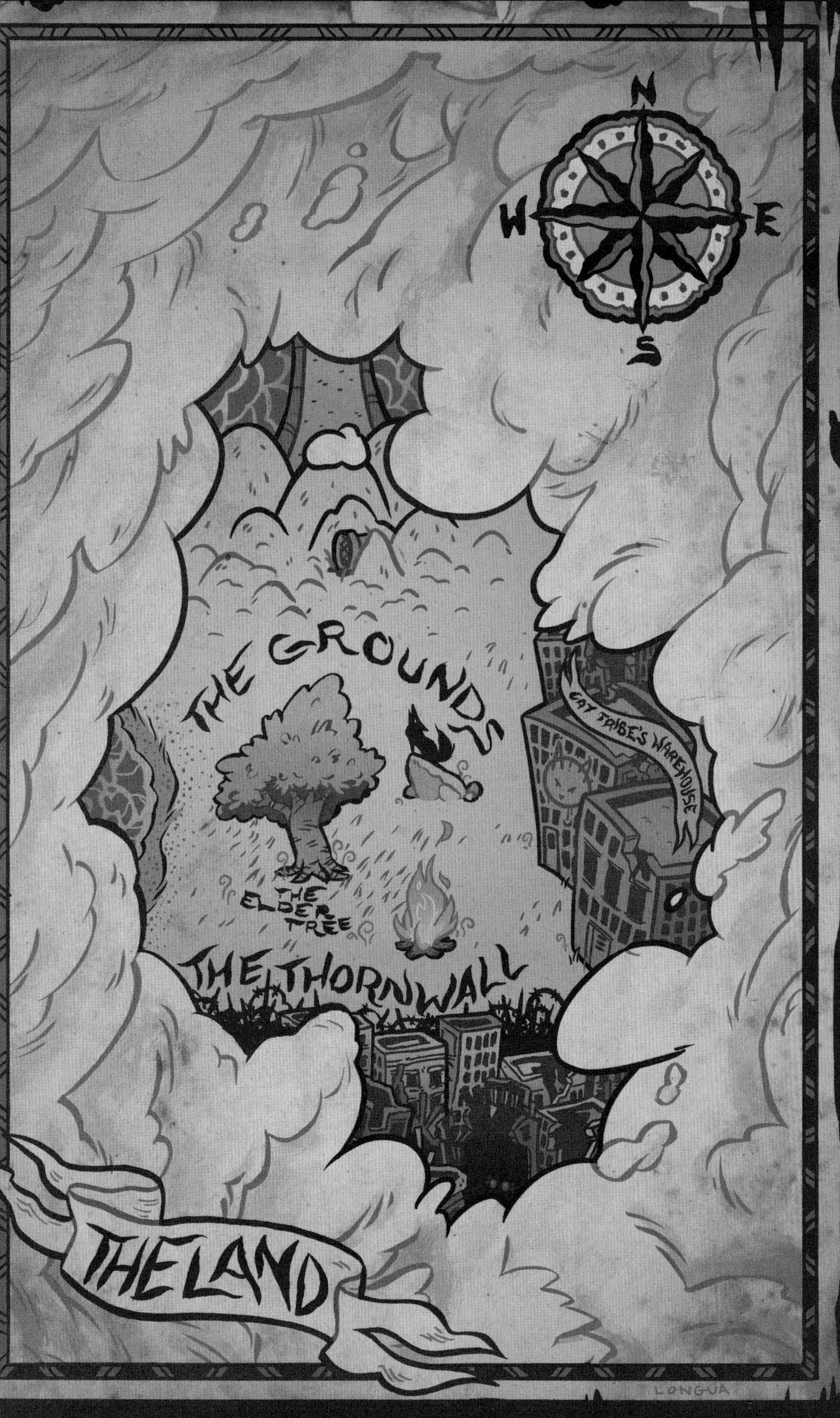
N
W
E
S
THE GROUNDS
CAT TRIBE'S WAREHOUSE
THE ELDER TREE
THE THORNWALL
THE LAND
LONGUA

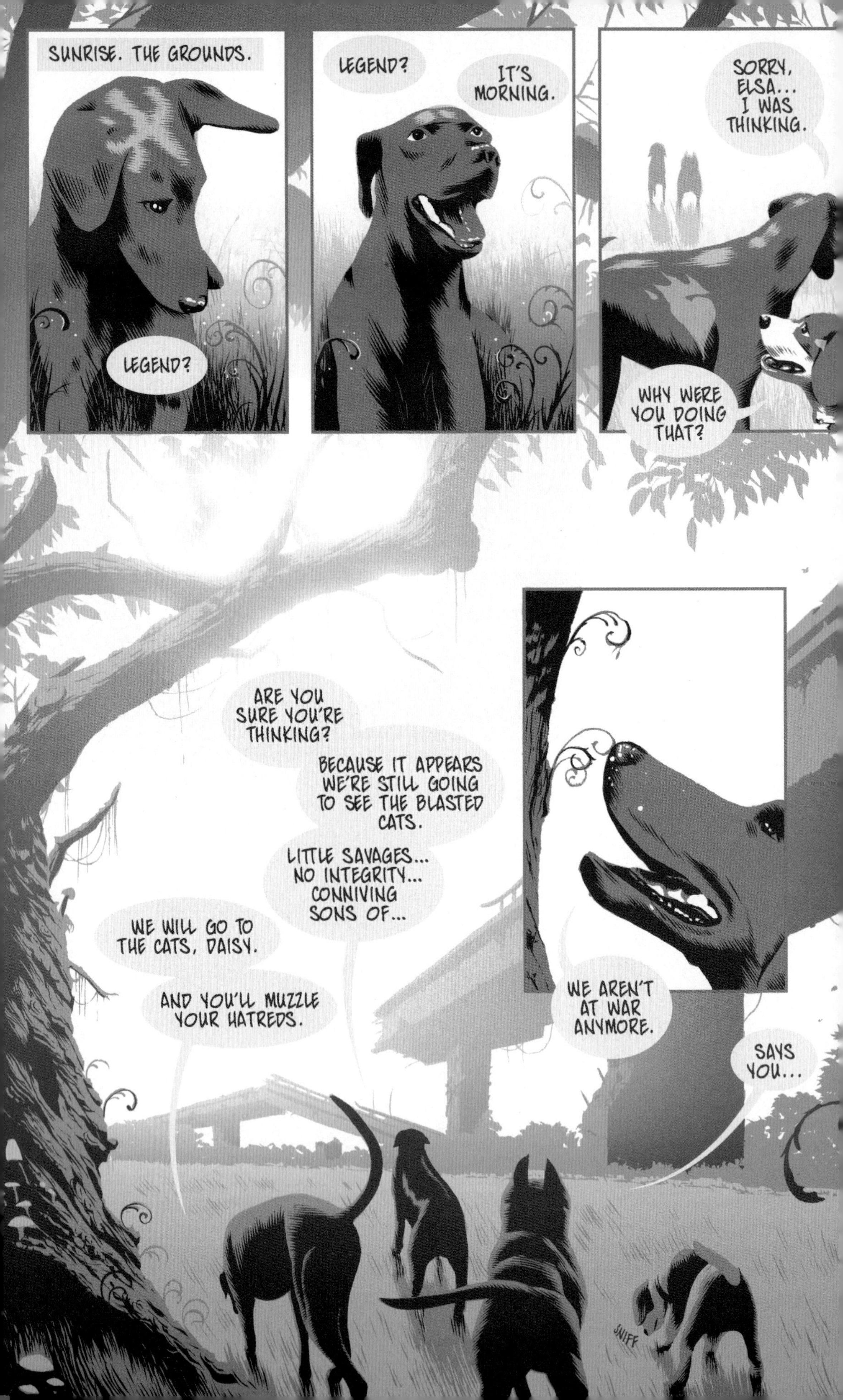
SUNRISE. THE GROUNDS.
LEGEND?
LEGEND?
IT'S MORNING.
SORRY, ELSA... I WAS THINKING.
WHY WERE YOU DOING THAT?
ARE YOU SURE YOU'RE THINKING?
BECAUSE IT APPEARS WE'RE STILL GOING TO SEE THE BLASTED CATS.
LITTLE SAVAGES... NO INTEGRITY... CONNIVING SONS OF...
WE WILL GO TO THE CATS, DAISY.
AND YOU'LL MUZZLE YOUR HATREDS.
WE AREN'T AT WAR ANYMORE.
SAYS YOU...
SNIFF

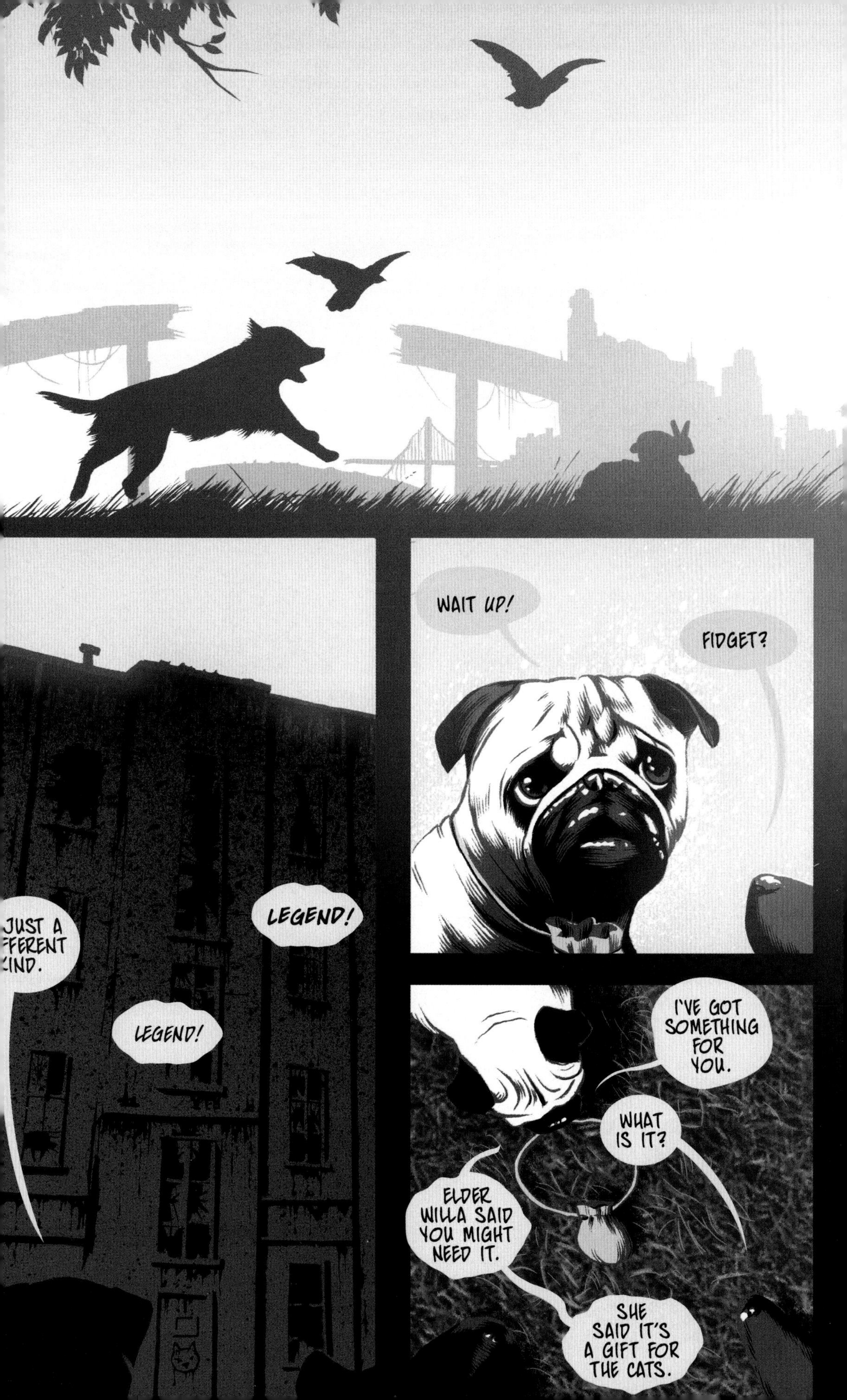
JUST A FFERENT IND.
LEGEND!
LEGEND!
WAIT UP!
FIDGET?
I'VE GOT SOMETHING FOR YOU.
WHAT IS IT?
ELDER WILLA SAID YOU MIGHT NEED IT.
SHE SAID IT'S A GIFT FOR THE CATS.

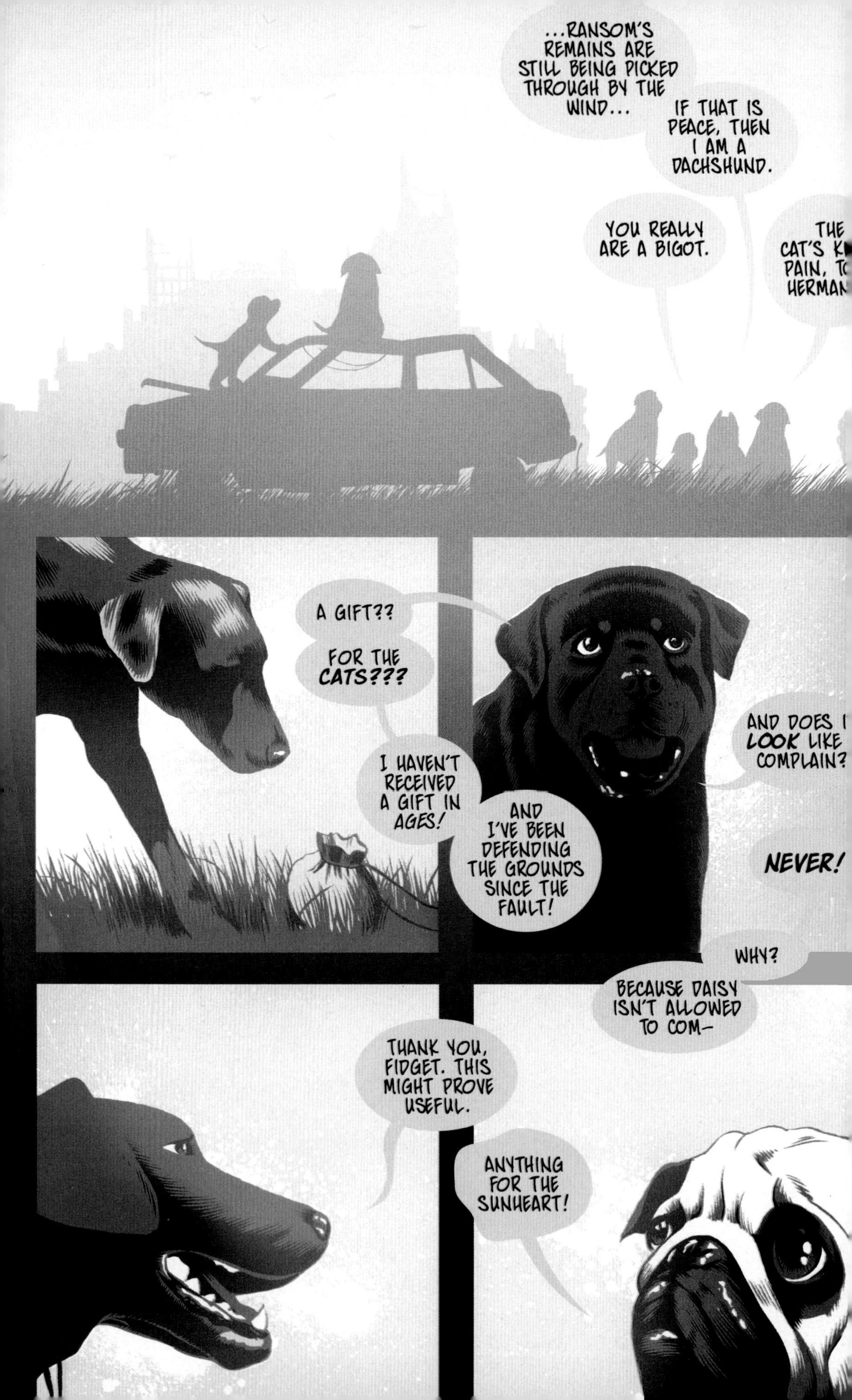
...RANSOM'S REMAINS ARE STILL BEING PICKED THROUGH BY THE WIND...
IF THAT IS PEACE, THEN I AM A DACHSHUND.
YOU REALLY ARE A BIGOT.
A GIFT??
FOR THE CATS???
I HAVEN'T RECEIVED A GIFT IN AGES!
AND I'VE BEEN DEFENDING THE GROUNDS SINCE THE FAULT!
NEVER!
WHY?
BECAUSE DAISY ISN'T ALLOWED TO COM–
THANK YOU, FIDGET. THIS MIGHT PROVE USEFUL.
ANYTHING FOR THE SUNHEART!

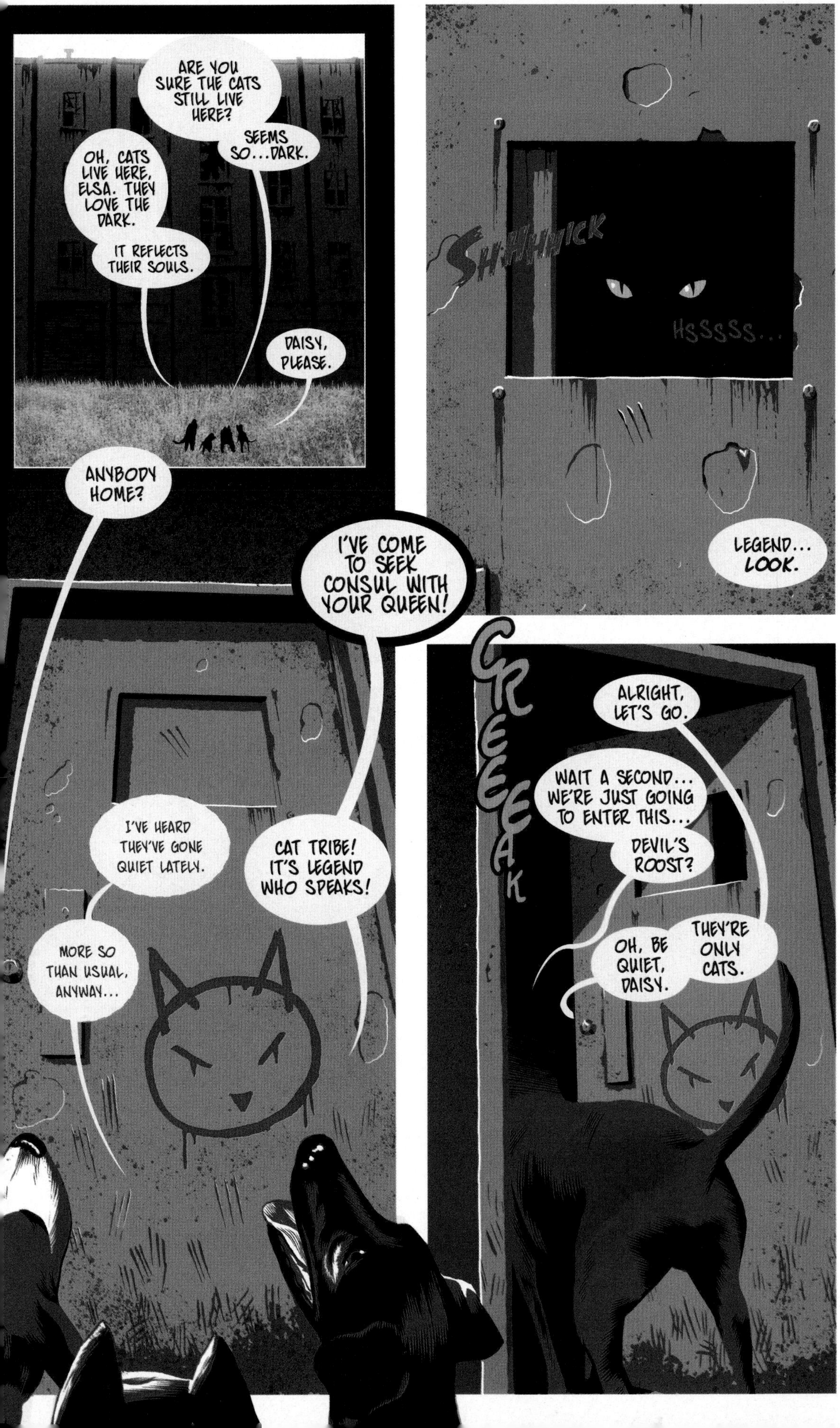
ARE YOU SURE THE CATS STILL LIVE HERE?
SEEMS SO...DARK.
OH, CATS LIVE HERE, ELSA. THEY LOVE THE DARK.
IT REFLECTS THEIR SOULS.
DAISY, PLEASE.
ANYBODY HOME?
I'VE COME TO SEEK CONSUL WITH YOUR QUEEN!
CAT TRIBE! IT'S LEGEND WHO SPEAKS!
I'VE HEARD THEY'VE GONE QUIET LATELY.
MORE SO THAN USUAL, ANYWAY...
SHHHWICK
HSSSSS...
LEGEND... LOOK.
CREEEAK
ALRIGHT, LET'S GO.
WAIT A SECOND... WE'RE JUST GOING TO ENTER THIS...
DEVIL'S ROOST?
THEY'RE ONLY CATS.
OH, BE QUIET, DAISY.

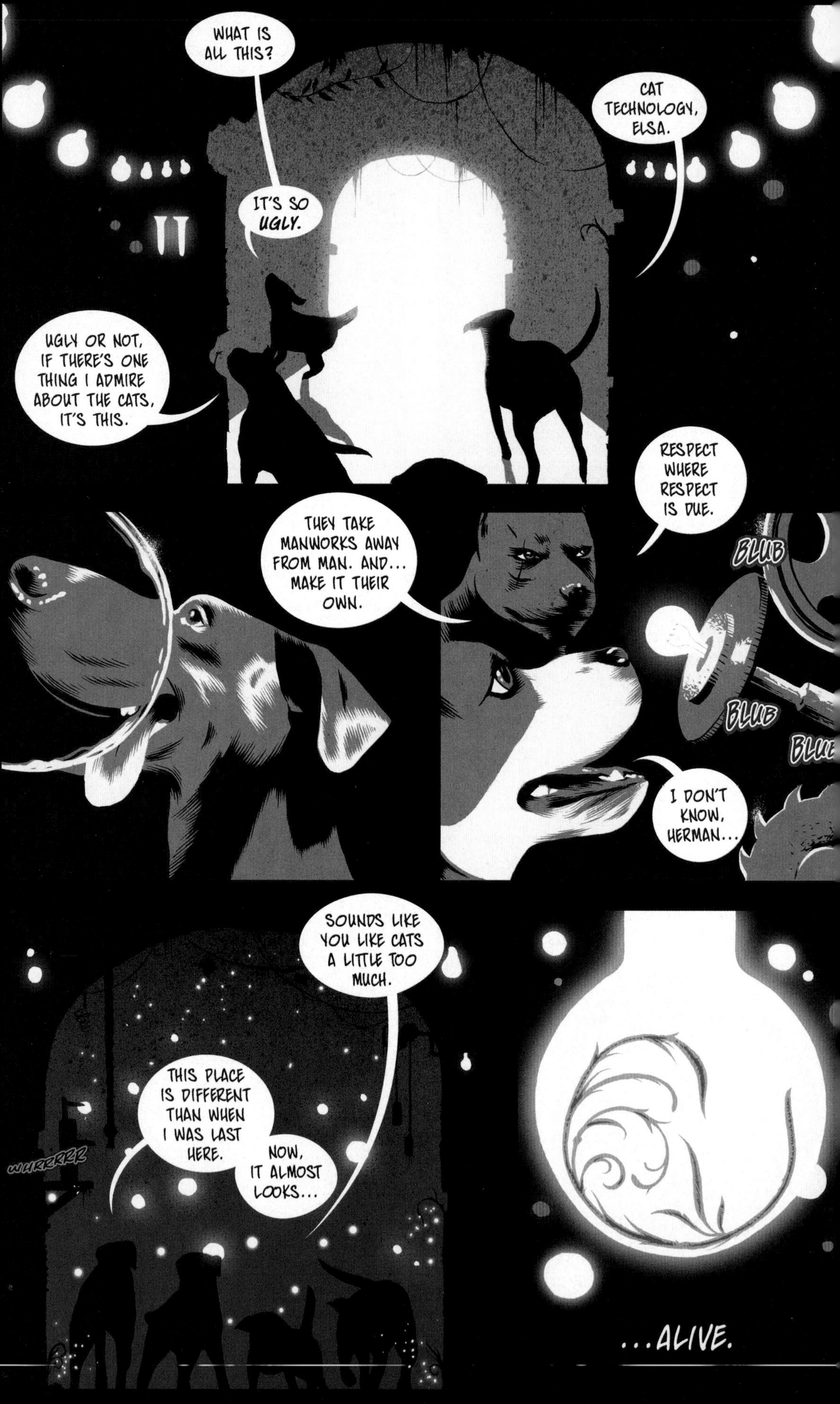
WHAT IS ALL THIS?
IT'S SO UGLY.
CAT TECHNOLOGY, ELSA.
UGLY OR NOT, IF THERE'S ONE THING I ADMIRE ABOUT THE CATS, IT'S THIS.
THEY TAKE MANWORKS AWAY FROM MAN. AND... MAKE IT THEIR OWN.
RESPECT WHERE RESPECT IS DUE.
BLUB
BLUB
I DON'T KNOW, HERMAN...
SOUNDS LIKE YOU LIKE CATS A LITTLE TOO MUCH.
WHRRRRR
THIS PLACE IS DIFFERENT THAN WHEN I WAS LAST HERE.
NOW, IT ALMOST LOOKS...
...ALIVE.

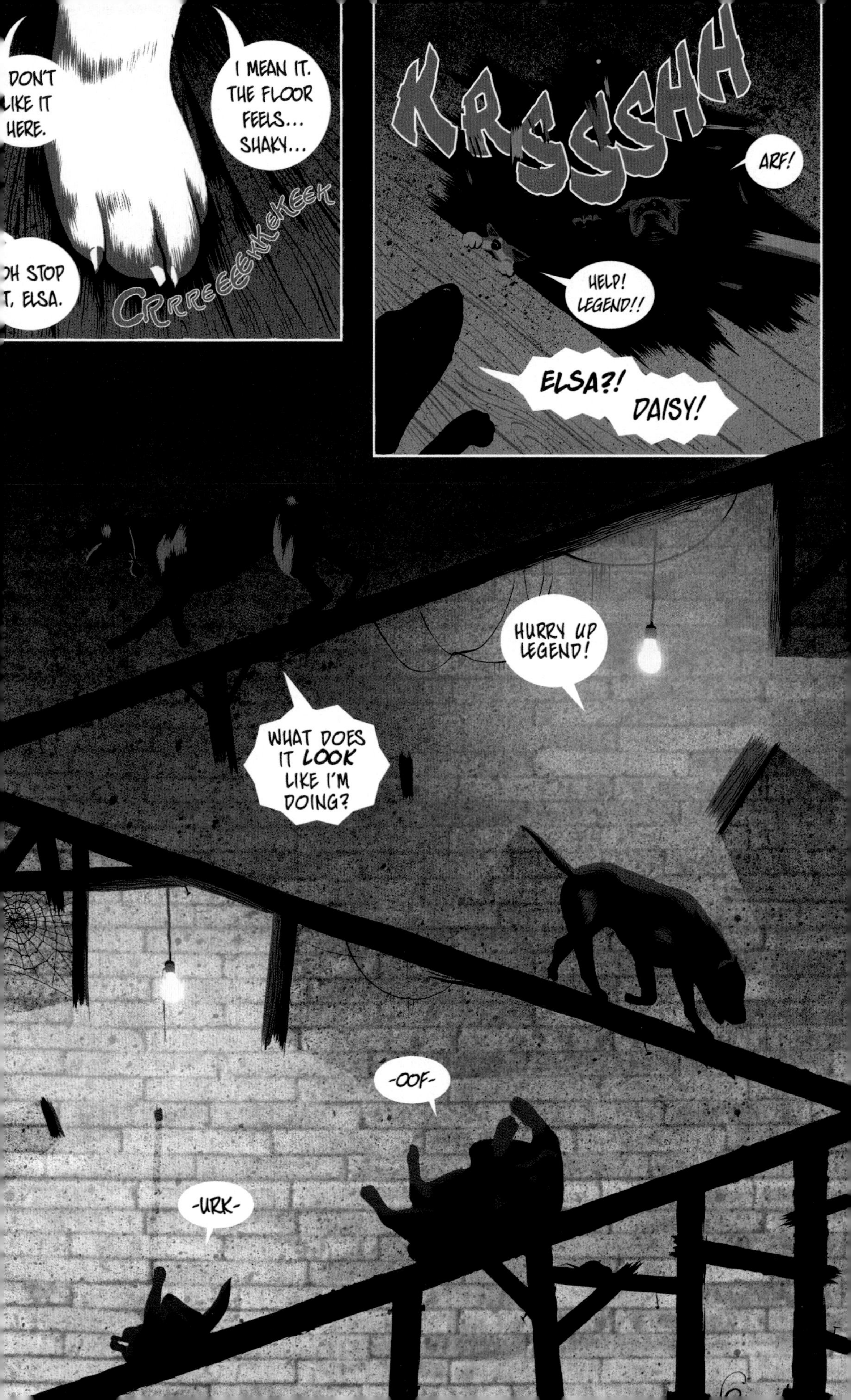
DON'T LIKE IT HERE.
I MEAN IT. THE FLOOR FEELS… SHAKY…
H STOP T, ELSA.
CRRREEEEKKEKEEK
KRSSSHH
ARF!
HELP! LEGEND!!
ELSA?!
DAISY!
HURRY UP LEGEND!
WHAT DOES IT LOOK LIKE I'M DOING?
-OOF-
-URK-

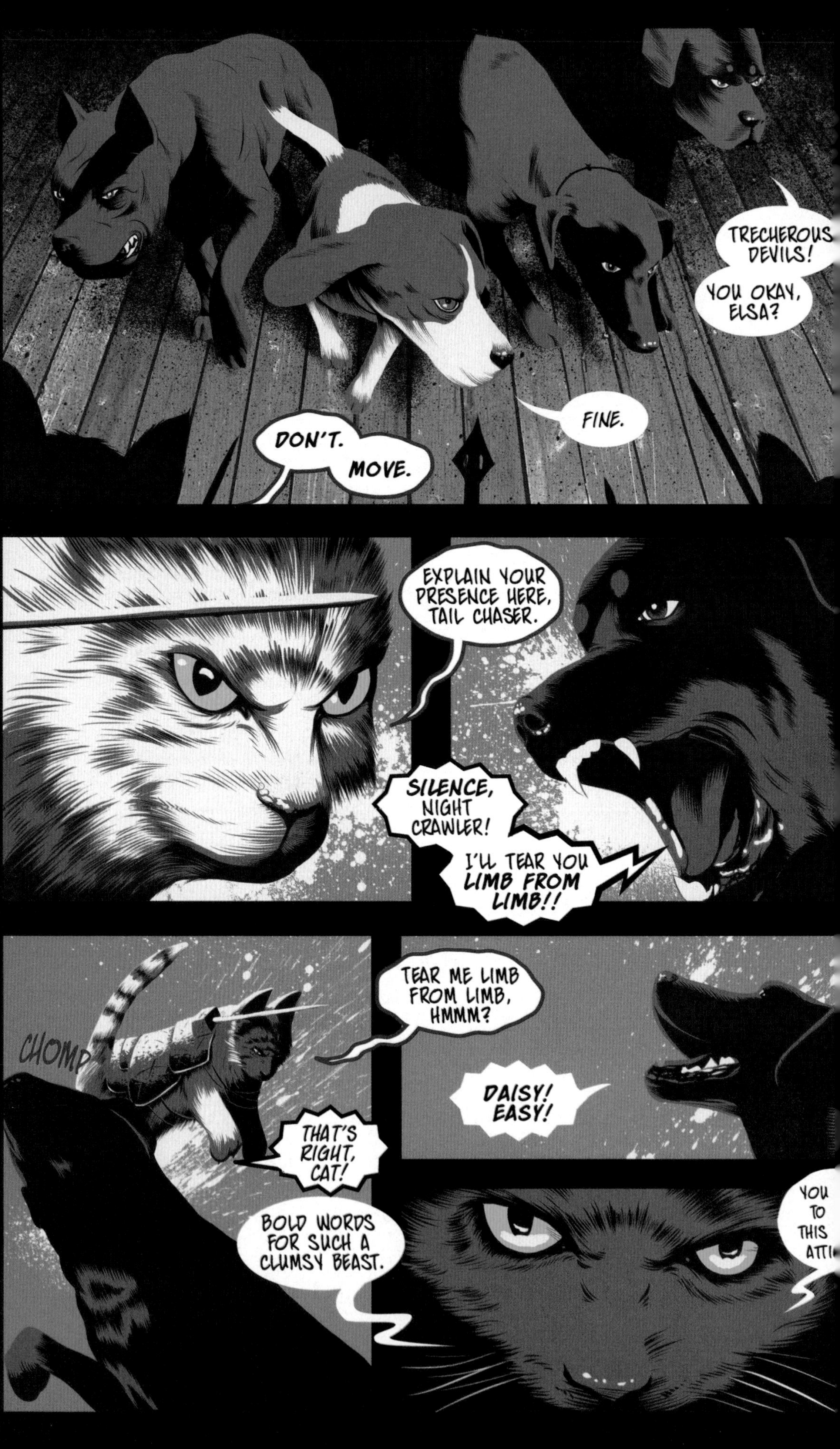
TRECHEROUS DEVILS!
YOU OKAY, ELSA?
FINE.
DON'T. MOVE.
EXPLAIN YOUR PRESENCE HERE, TAIL CHASER.
SILENCE, NIGHT CRAWLER!
I'LL TEAR YOU LIMB FROM LIMB!!
CHOMP
TEAR ME LIMB FROM LIMB, HMMM?
THAT'S RIGHT, CAT!
BOLD WORDS FOR SUCH A CLUMSY BEAST.
DAISY! EASY!
YOU TO THIS ATT

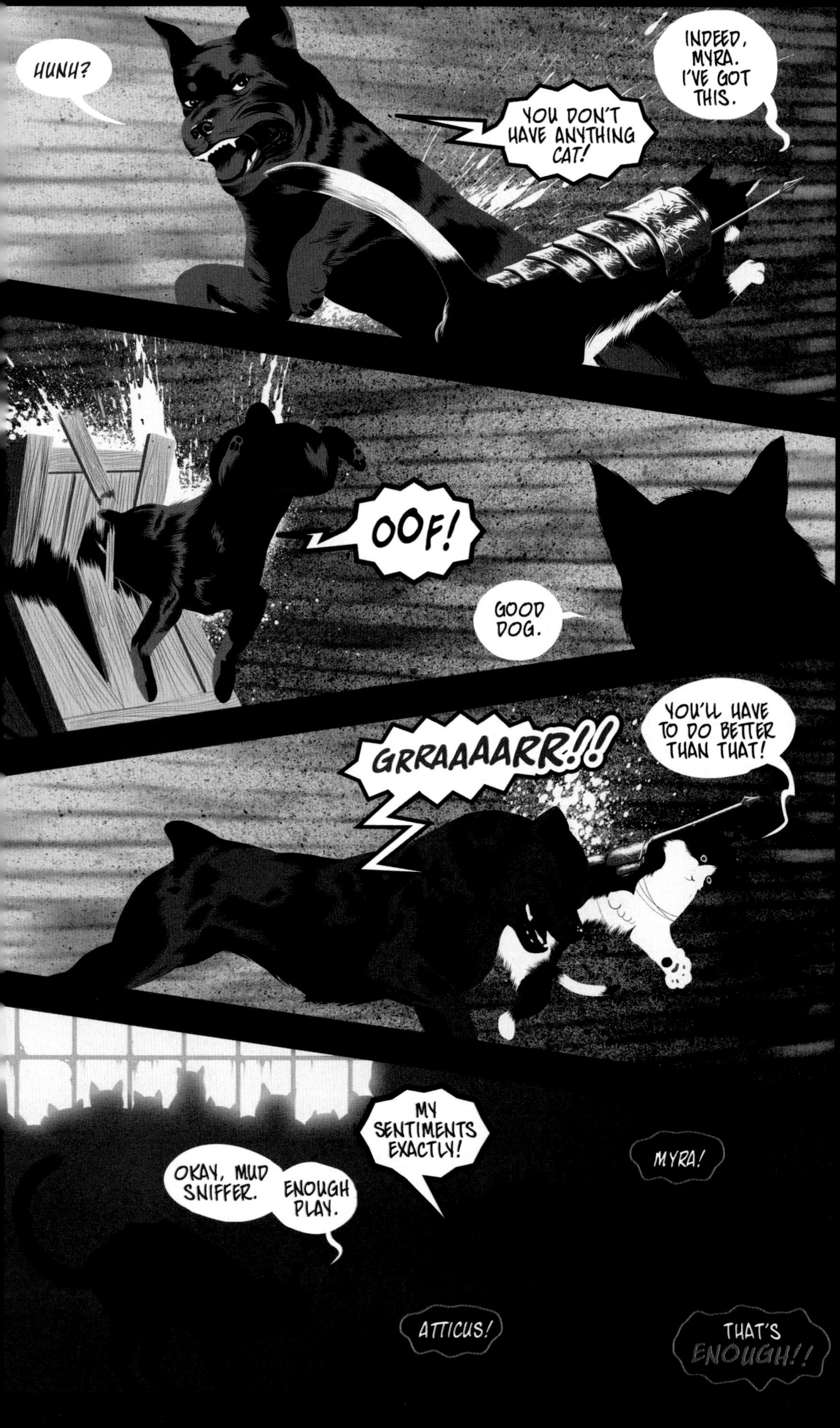
HUNH?
YOU DON'T HAVE ANYTHING CAT!
INDEED, MYRA. I'VE GOT THIS.
OOF!
GOOD DOG.
GRRAAAARR!!
YOU'LL HAVE TO DO BETTER THAN THAT!
OKAY, MUD SNIFFER.
ENOUGH PLAY.
MY SENTIMENTS EXACTLY!
MYRA!
ATTICUS!
THAT'S ENOUGH!!

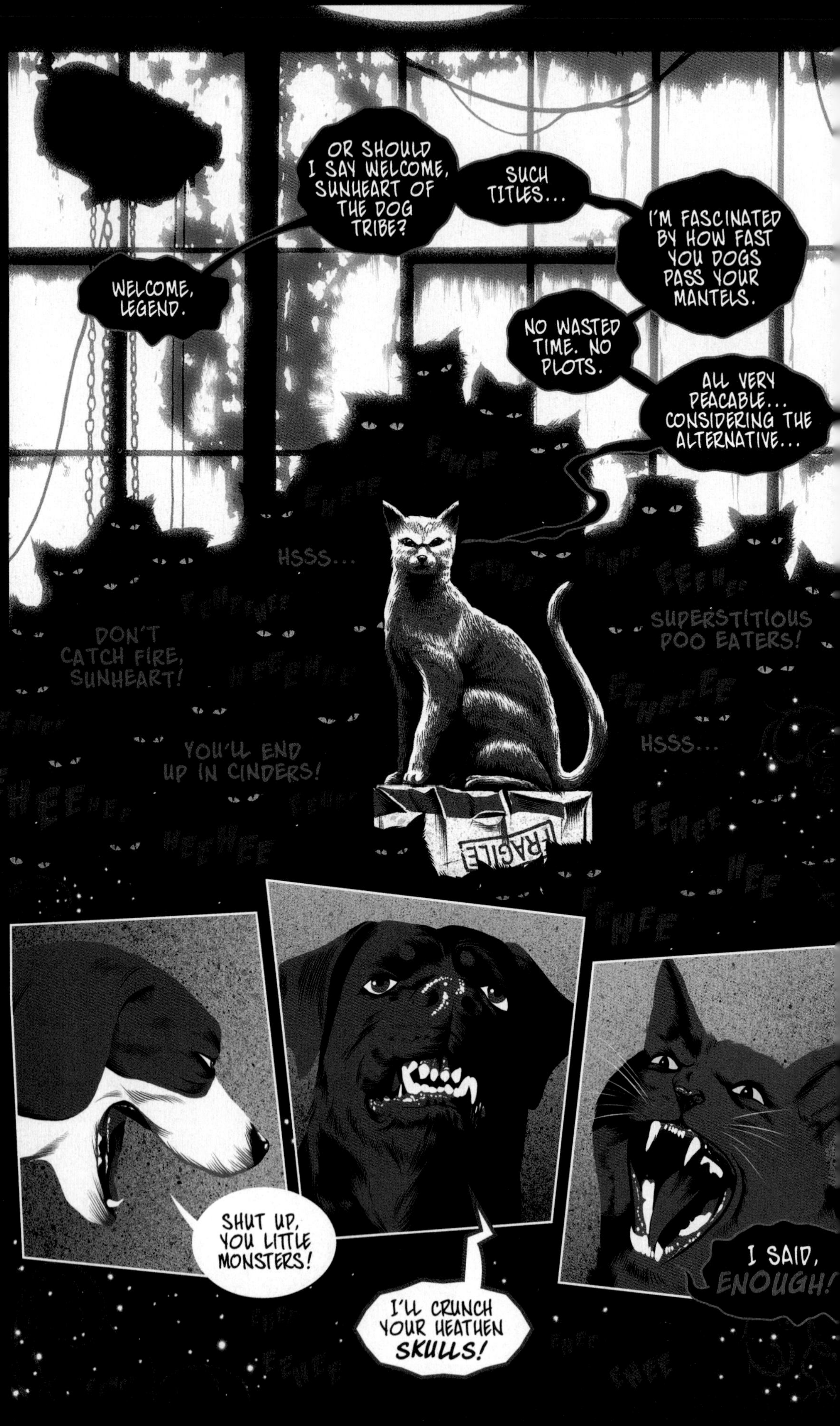

WELCOME, LEGEND.
OR SHOULD I SAY WELCOME, SUNHEART OF THE DOG TRIBE?
SUCH TITLES...
I'M FASCINATED BY HOW FAST YOU DOGS PASS YOUR MANTELS.
NO WASTED TIME. NO PLOTS.
ALL VERY PEACABLE... CONSIDERING THE ALTERNATIVE...
HSSS...
DON'T CATCH FIRE, SUNHEART!
SUPERSTITIOUS POO EATERS!
YOU'LL END UP IN CINDERS!
HSSS...
SHUT UP, YOU LITTLE MONSTERS!
I'LL CRUNCH YOUR HEATHEN *SKULLS!*
I SAID, *ENOUGH!*

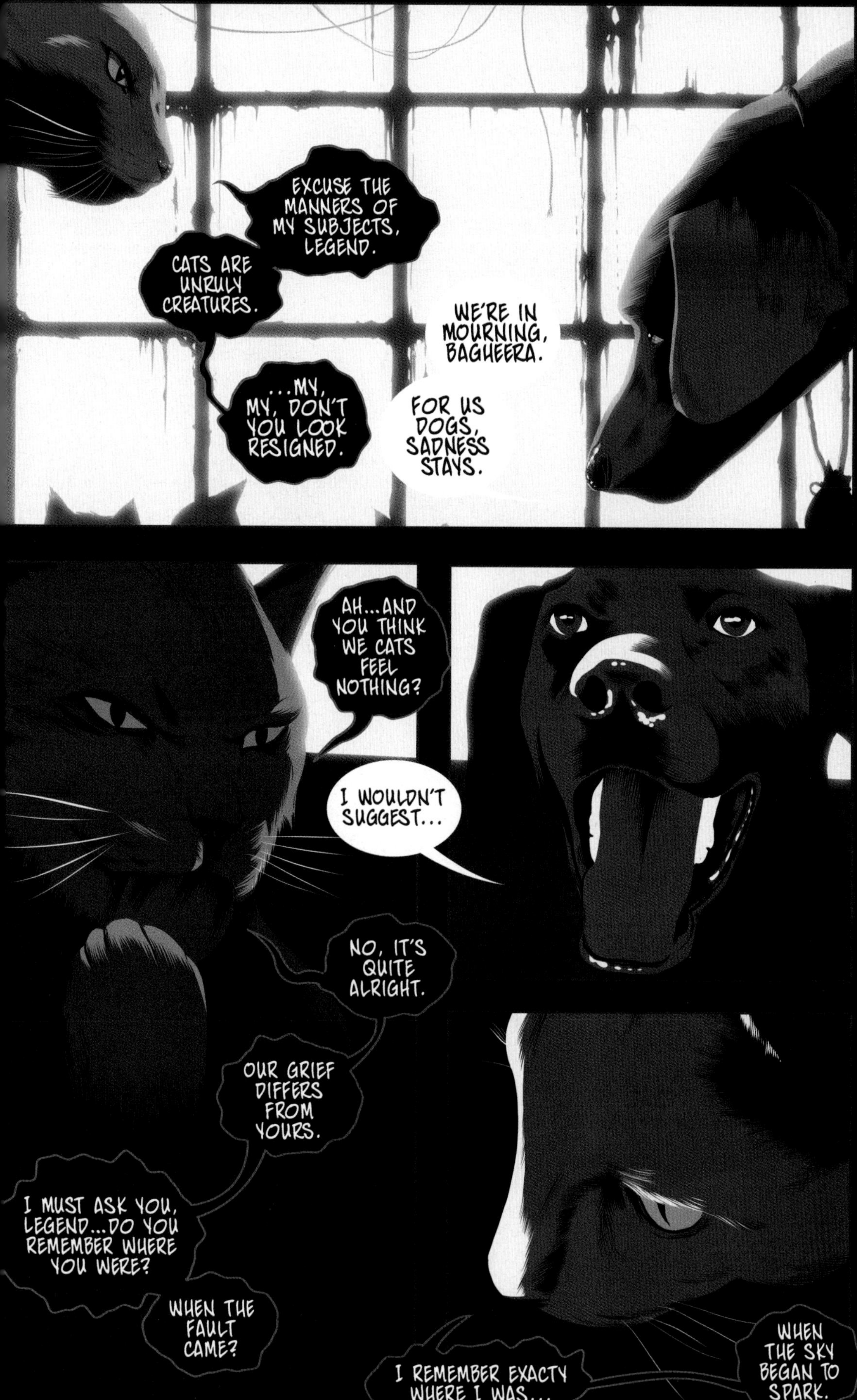
EXCUSE THE MANNERS OF MY SUBJECTS, LEGEND.
CATS ARE UNRULY CREATURES.
...MY, MY, DON'T YOU LOOK RESIGNED.
WE'RE IN MOURNING, BAGHEERA.
FOR US DOGS, SADNESS STAYS.
AH...AND YOU THINK WE CATS FEEL NOTHING?
I WOULDN'T SUGGEST...
NO, IT'S QUITE ALRIGHT.
OUR GRIEF DIFFERS FROM YOURS.
I MUST ASK YOU, LEGEND...DO YOU REMEMBER WHERE YOU WERE?
WHEN THE FAULT CAME?
I REMEMBER EXACTY WHERE I WAS...
WHEN THE SKY BEGAN TO SPARK.

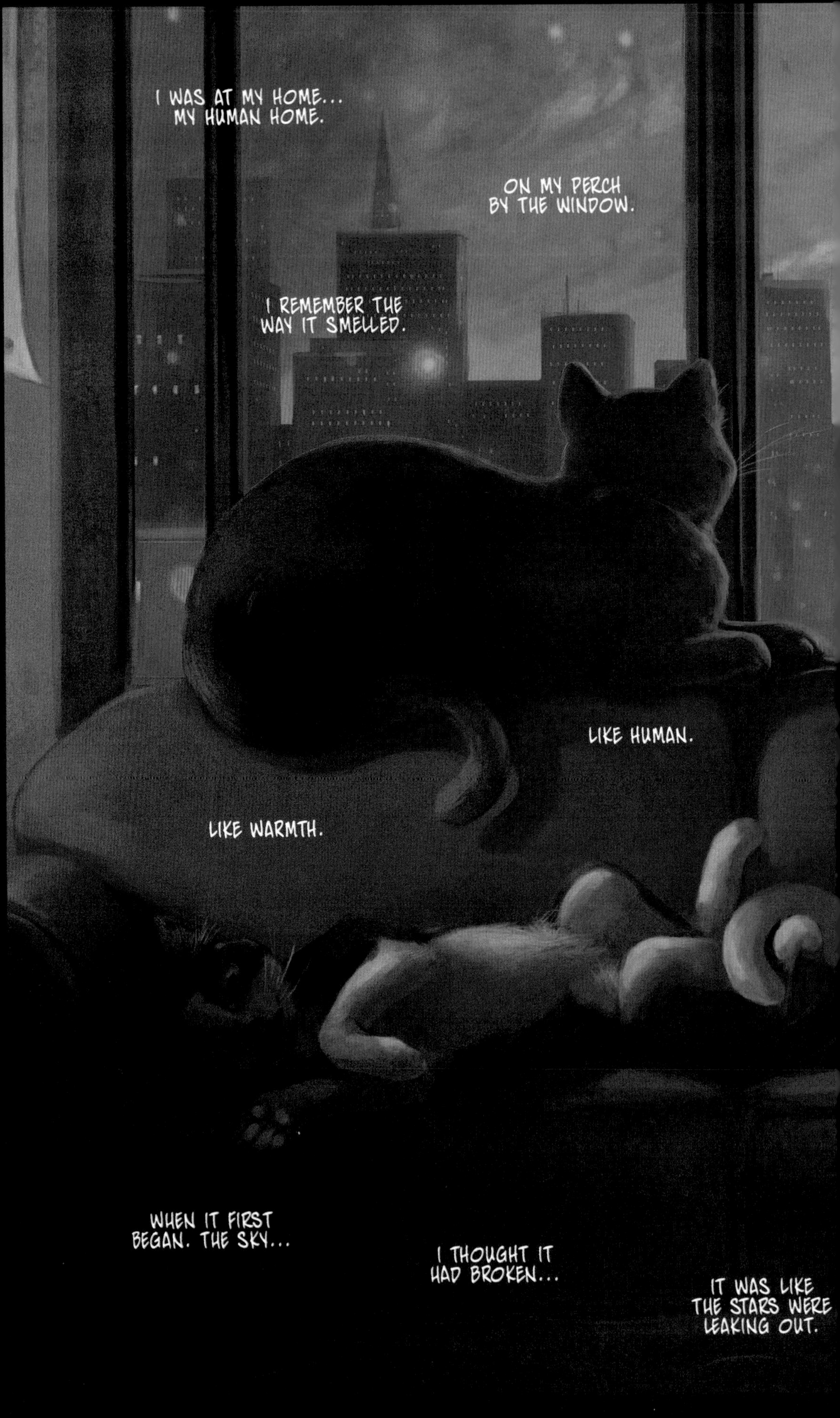
I WAS AT MY HOME...
MY HUMAN HOME.
ON MY PERCH
BY THE WINDOW.
I REMEMBER THE
WAY IT SMELLED.
LIKE HUMAN.
LIKE WARMTH.
WHEN IT FIRST
BEGAN. THE SKY...
I THOUGHT IT
HAD BROKEN...
IT WAS LIKE
THE STARS WERE
LEAKING OUT.

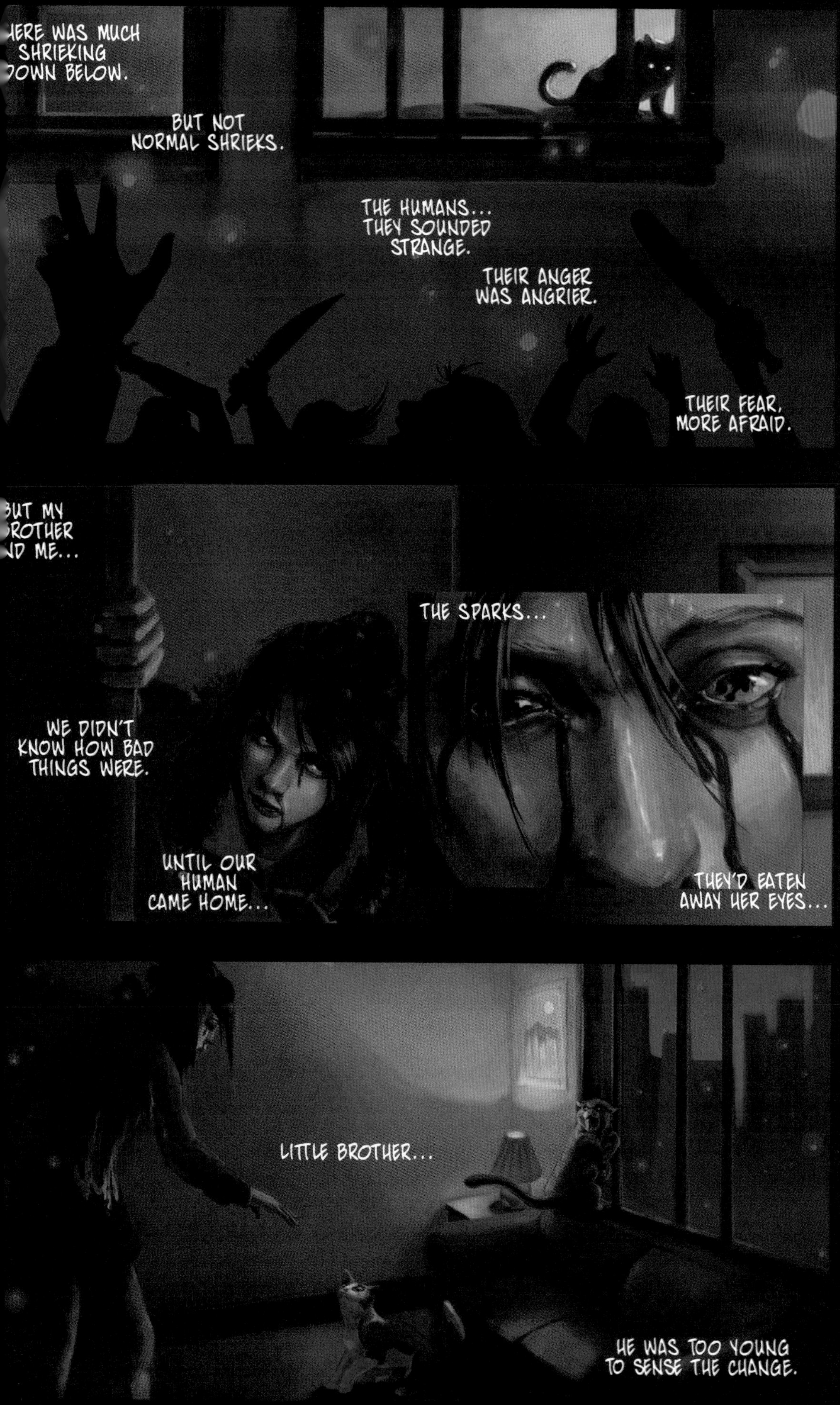
HERE WAS MUCH SHRIEKING OWN BELOW.
BUT NOT NORMAL SHRIEKS.
THE HUMANS... THEY SOUNDED STRANGE.
THEIR ANGER WAS ANGRIER.
THEIR FEAR, MORE AFRAID.
UT MY ROTHER ND ME...
WE DIDN'T KNOW HOW BAD THINGS WERE.
UNTIL OUR HUMAN CAME HOME...
THE SPARKS...
THEY'D EATEN AWAY HER EYES...
LITTLE BROTHER...
HE WAS TOO YOUNG TO SENSE THE CHANGE.

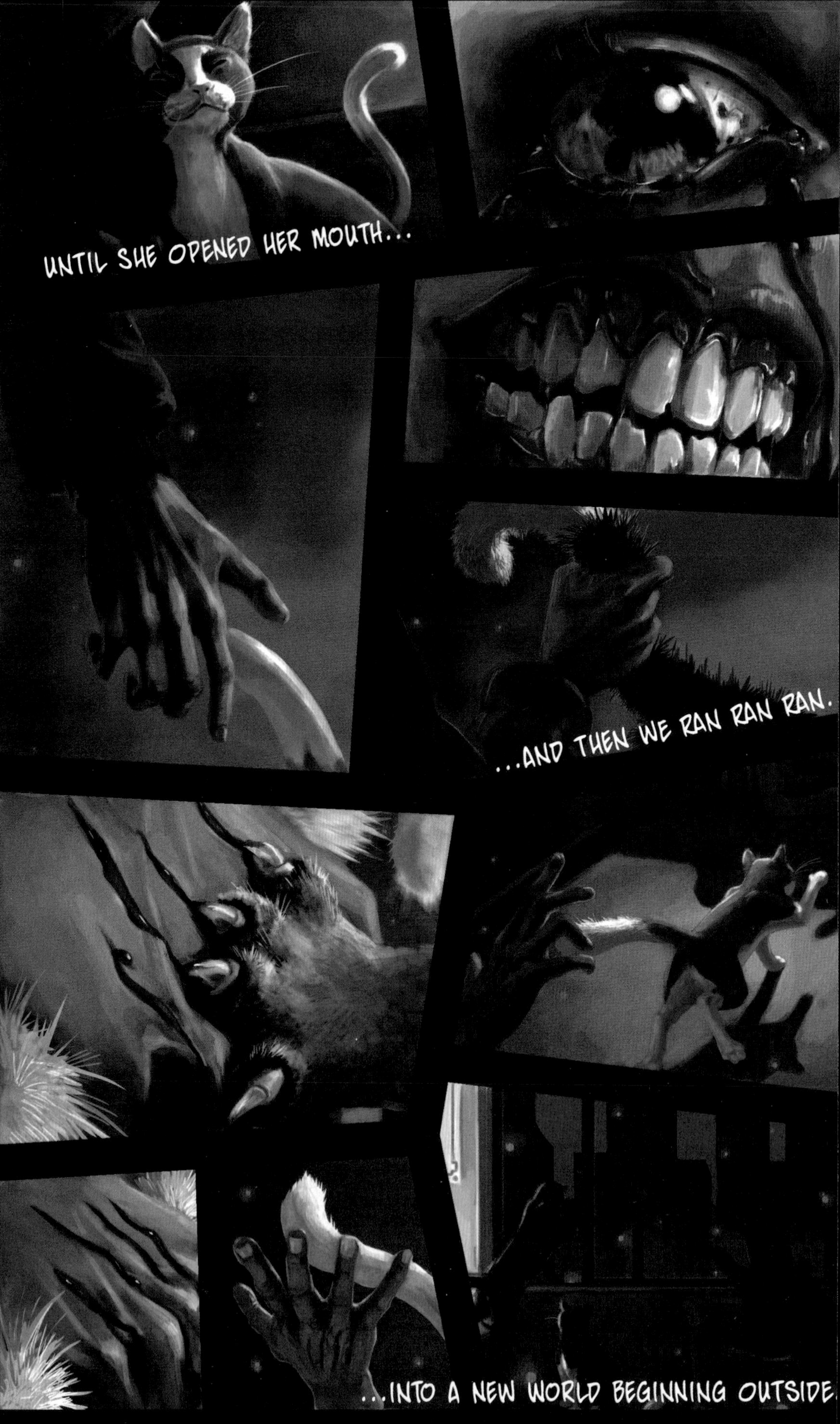
UNTIL SHE OPENED HER MOUTH...
...AND THEN WE RAN RAN RAN.
...INTO A NEW WORLD BEGINNING OUTSIDE.

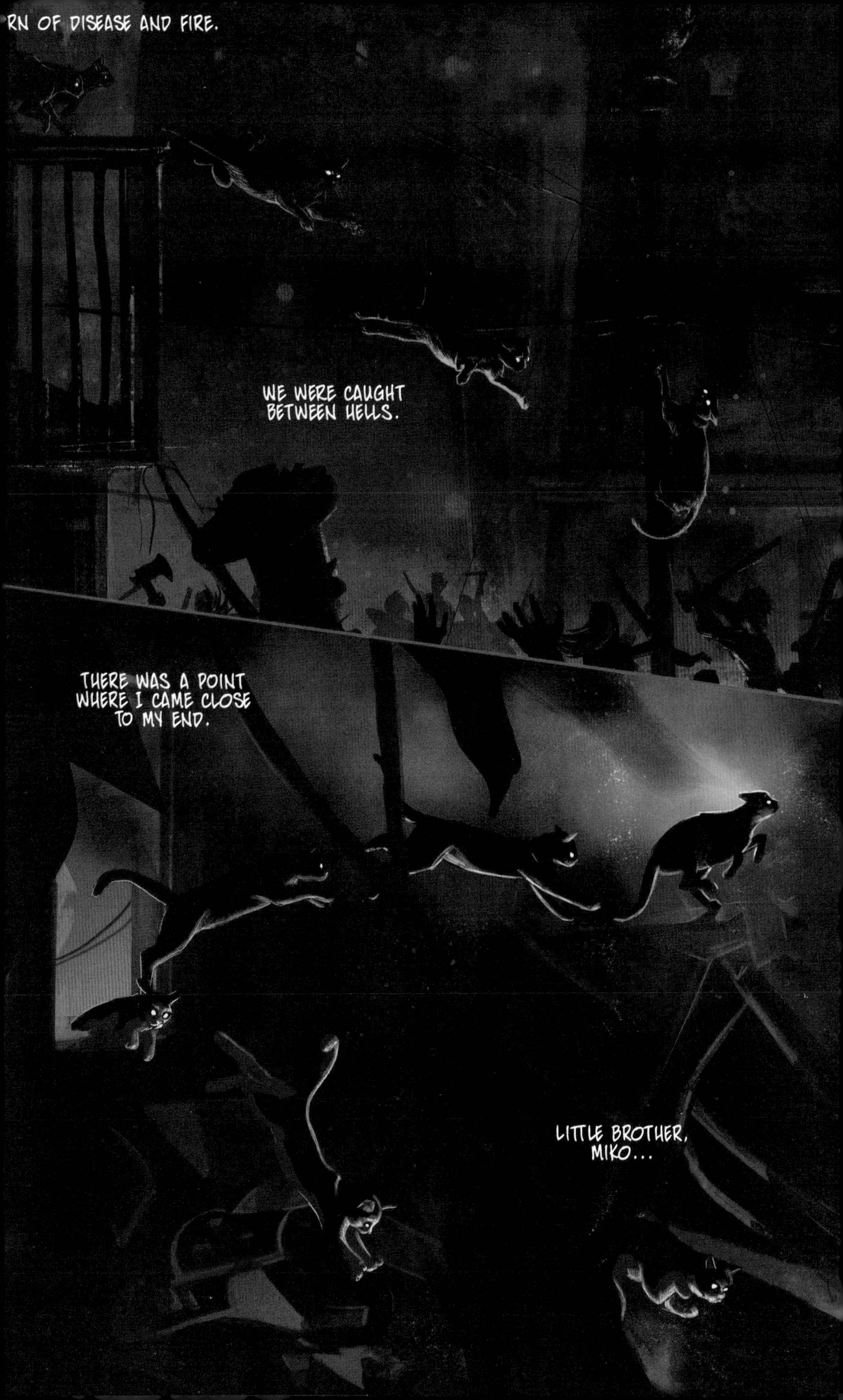
RN OF DISEASE AND FIRE.
WE WERE CAUGHT BETWEEN HELLS.
THERE WAS A POINT WHERE I CAME CLOSE TO MY END.
LITTLE BROTHER, MIKO...

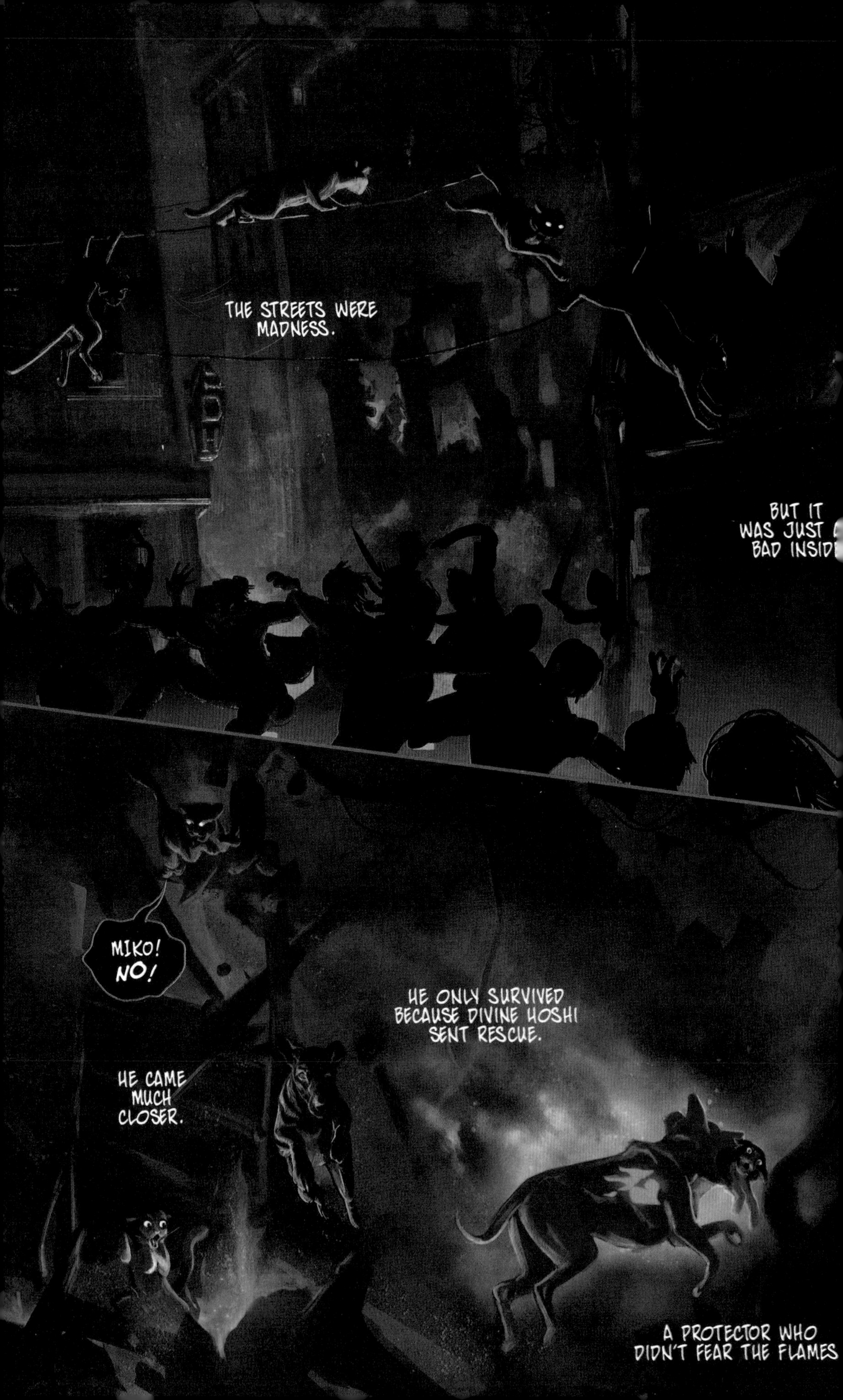
THE STREETS WERE MADNESS.
BUT IT WAS JUST BAD INSID
MIKO! NO!
HE ONLY SURVIVED BECAUSE DIVINE HOSHI SENT RESCUE.
HE CAME MUCH CLOSER.
A PROTECTOR WHO DIDN'T FEAR THE FLAMES

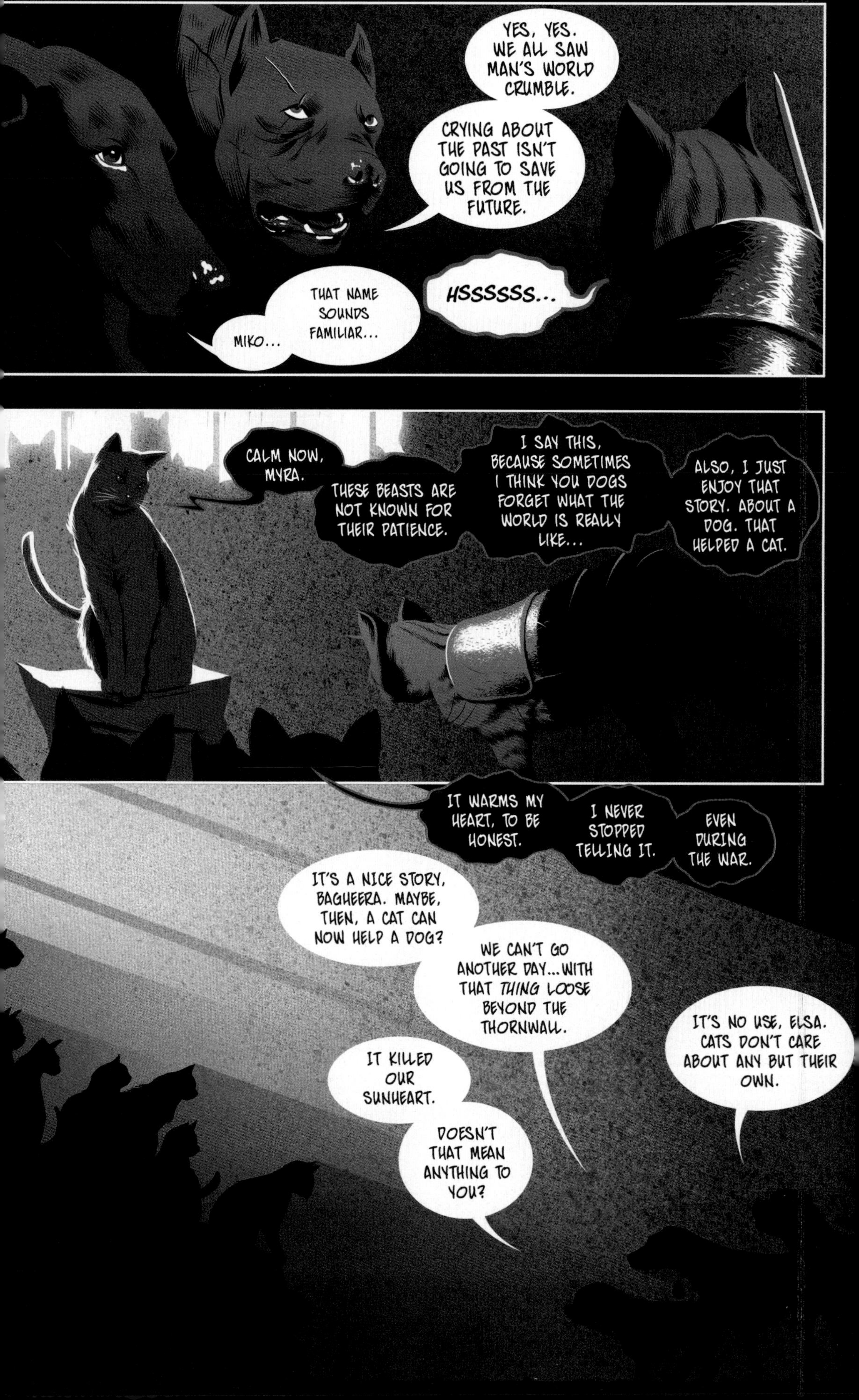

YES, YES. WE ALL SAW MAN'S WORLD CRUMBLE.
CRYING ABOUT THE PAST ISN'T GOING TO SAVE US FROM THE FUTURE.
MIKO...
THAT NAME SOUNDS FAMILIAR...
HSSSSSS...
CALM NOW, MYRA.
THESE BEASTS ARE NOT KNOWN FOR THEIR PATIENCE.
I SAY THIS, BECAUSE SOMETIMES I THINK YOU DOGS FORGET WHAT THE WORLD IS REALLY LIKE...
ALSO, I JUST ENJOY THAT STORY. ABOUT A DOG. THAT HELPED A CAT.
IT WARMS MY HEART, TO BE HONEST.
I NEVER STOPPED TELLING IT.
EVEN DURING THE WAR.
IT'S A NICE STORY, BAGHEERA. MAYBE, THEN, A CAT CAN NOW HELP A DOG?
WE CAN'T GO ANOTHER DAY...WITH THAT *THING* LOOSE BEYOND THE THORNWALL.
IT KILLED OUR SUNHEART.
DOESN'T THAT MEAN ANYTHING TO YOU?
IT'S NO USE, ELSA. CATS DON'T CARE ABOUT ANY BUT THEIR OWN.

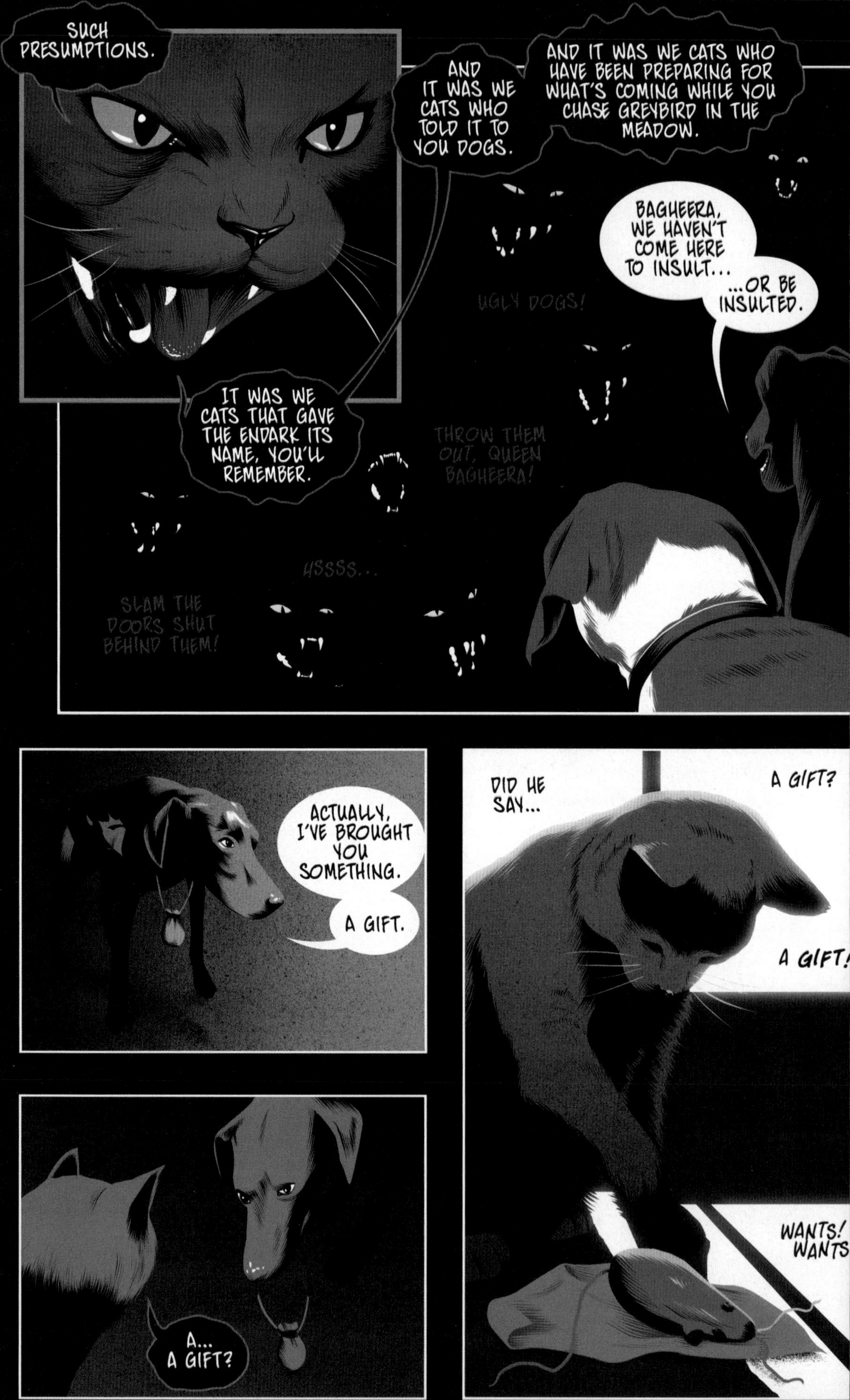

SUCH PRESUMPTIONS.
AND IT WAS WE CATS WHO TOLD IT TO YOU DOGS.
AND IT WAS WE CATS WHO HAVE BEEN PREPARING FOR WHAT'S COMING WHILE YOU CHASE GREYBIRD IN THE MEADOW.
BAGHEERA, WE HAVEN'T COME HERE TO INSULT...
...OR BE INSULTED.
UGLY DOGS!
IT WAS WE CATS THAT GAVE THE ENDARK ITS NAME, YOU'LL REMEMBER.
THROW THEM OUT, QUEEN BAGHEERA!
HSSSS...
SLAM THE DOORS SHUT BEHIND THEM!
ACTUALLY, I'VE BROUGHT YOU SOMETHING.
A GIFT.
A... A GIFT?
DID HE SAY...
A GIFT?
A GIFT!
WANTS! WANTS

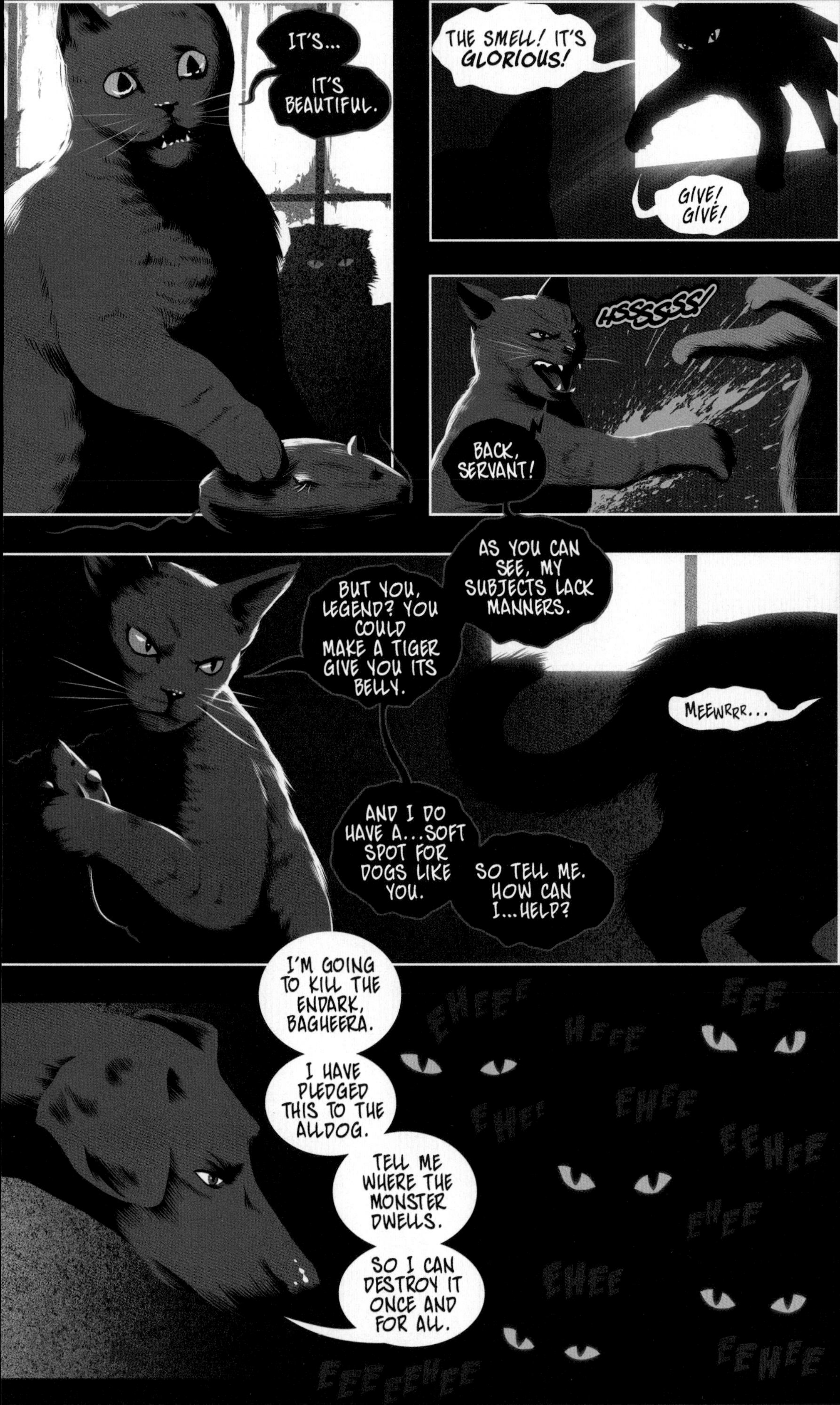
IT'S...
IT'S BEAUTIFUL.
THE SMELL! IT'S GLORIOUS!
GIVE! GIVE!
HSSSSSS!
BACK, SERVANT!
BUT YOU, LEGEND? YOU COULD MAKE A TIGER GIVE YOU ITS BELLY.
AS YOU CAN SEE, MY SUBJECTS LACK MANNERS.
MEEWRRR...
AND I DO HAVE A...SOFT SPOT FOR DOGS LIKE YOU.
SO TELL ME. HOW CAN I...HELP?
I'M GOING TO KILL THE ENDARK, BAGHEERA.
I HAVE PLEDGED THIS TO THE ALLDOG.
TELL ME WHERE THE MONSTER DWELLS.
SO I CAN DESTROY IT ONCE AND FOR ALL.

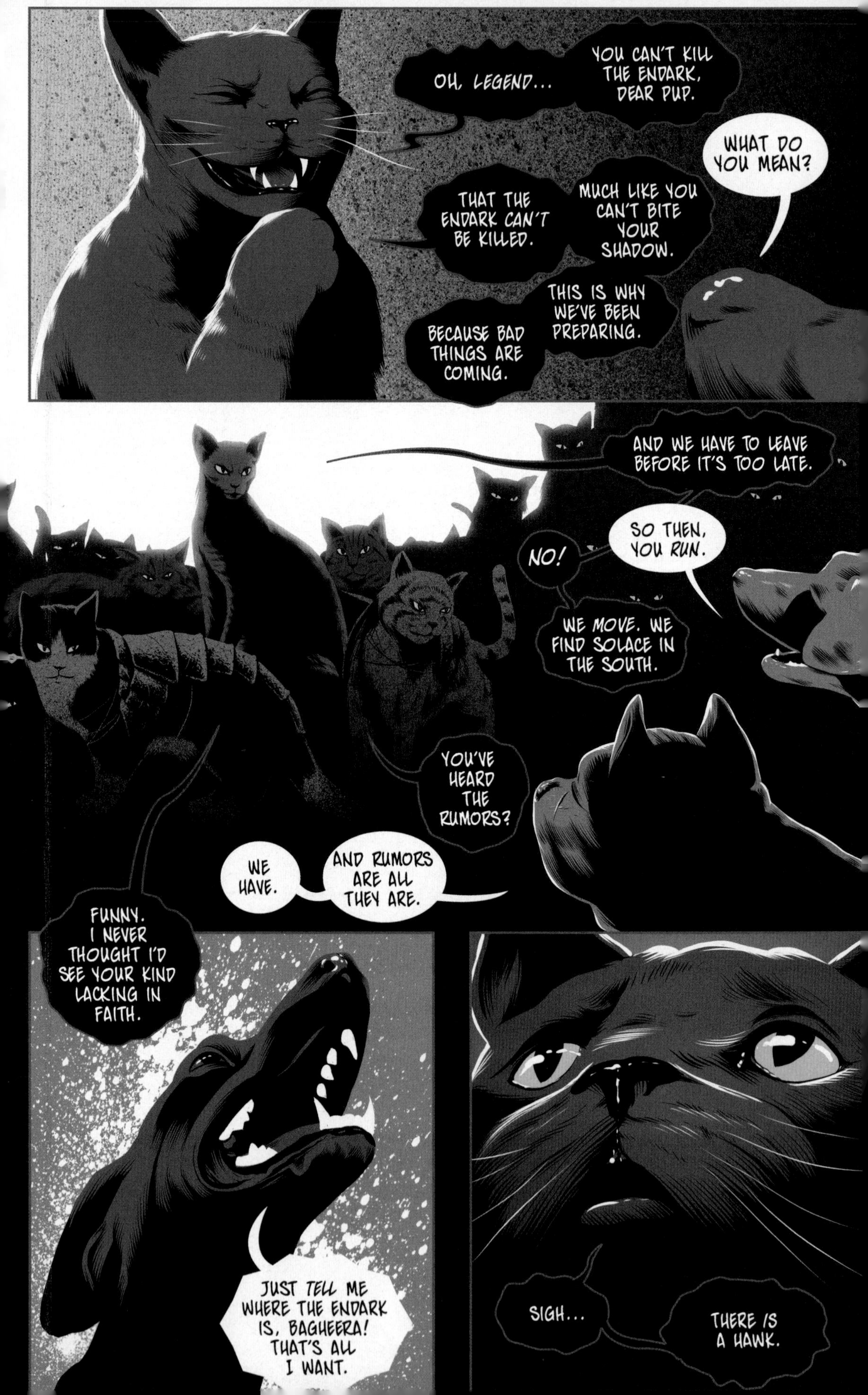
OH, LEGEND...
YOU CAN'T KILL THE ENDARK, DEAR PUP.
WHAT DO YOU MEAN?
THAT THE ENDARK CAN'T BE KILLED.
MUCH LIKE YOU CAN'T BITE YOUR SHADOW.
BECAUSE BAD THINGS ARE COMING.
THIS IS WHY WE'VE BEEN PREPARING.
AND WE HAVE TO LEAVE BEFORE IT'S TOO LATE.
SO THEN, YOU RUN.
NO!
WE MOVE. WE FIND SOLACE IN THE SOUTH.
YOU'VE HEARD THE RUMORS?
WE HAVE.
AND RUMORS ARE ALL THEY ARE.
FUNNY. I NEVER THOUGHT I'D SEE YOUR KIND LACKING IN FAITH.
JUST TELL ME WHERE THE ENDARK IS, BAGHEERA! THAT'S ALL I WANT.
SIGH...
THERE IS A HAWK.

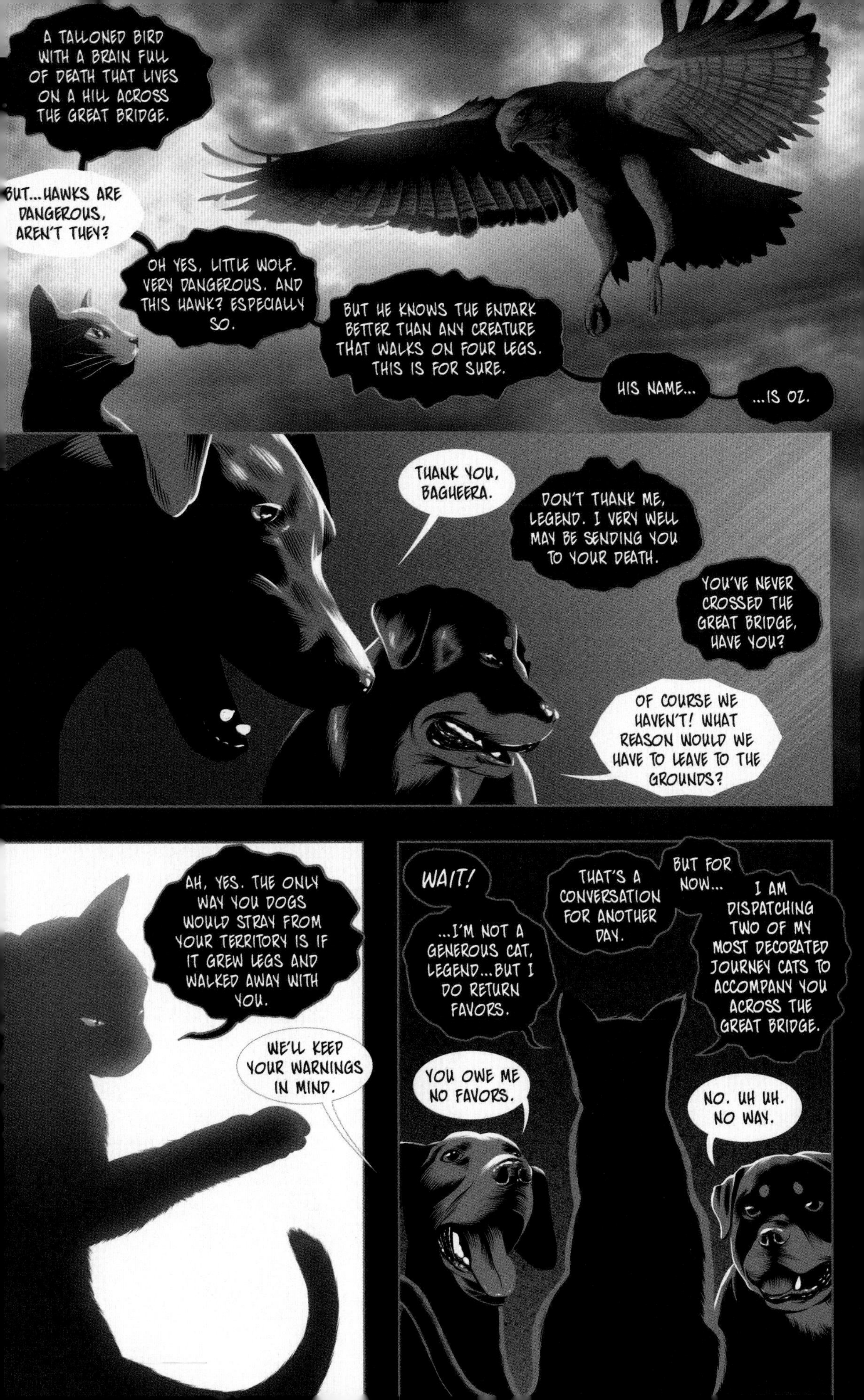
A TALLONED BIRD WITH A BRAIN FULL OF DEATH THAT LIVES ON A HILL ACROSS THE GREAT BRIDGE.
BUT...HAWKS ARE DANGEROUS, AREN'T THEY?
OH YES, LITTLE WOLF. VERY DANGEROUS. AND THIS HAWK? ESPECIALLY SO.
BUT HE KNOWS THE ENDARK BETTER THAN ANY CREATURE THAT WALKS ON FOUR LEGS. THIS IS FOR SURE.
HIS NAME...
...IS OZ.
THANK YOU, BAGHEERA.
DON'T THANK ME, LEGEND. I VERY WELL MAY BE SENDING YOU TO YOUR DEATH.
YOU'VE NEVER CROSSED THE GREAT BRIDGE, HAVE YOU?
OF COURSE WE HAVEN'T! WHAT REASON WOULD WE HAVE TO LEAVE TO THE GROUNDS?
AH, YES. THE ONLY WAY YOU DOGS WOULD STRAY FROM YOUR TERRITORY IS IF IT GREW LEGS AND WALKED AWAY WITH YOU.
WE'LL KEEP YOUR WARNINGS IN MIND.
WAIT!
...I'M NOT A GENEROUS CAT, LEGEND...BUT I DO RETURN FAVORS.
YOU OWE ME NO FAVORS.
THAT'S A CONVERSATION FOR ANOTHER DAY.
BUT FOR NOW...
I AM DISPATCHING TWO OF MY MOST DECORATED JOURNEY CATS TO ACCOMPANY YOU ACROSS THE GREAT BRIDGE.
NO. UH UH. NO WAY.

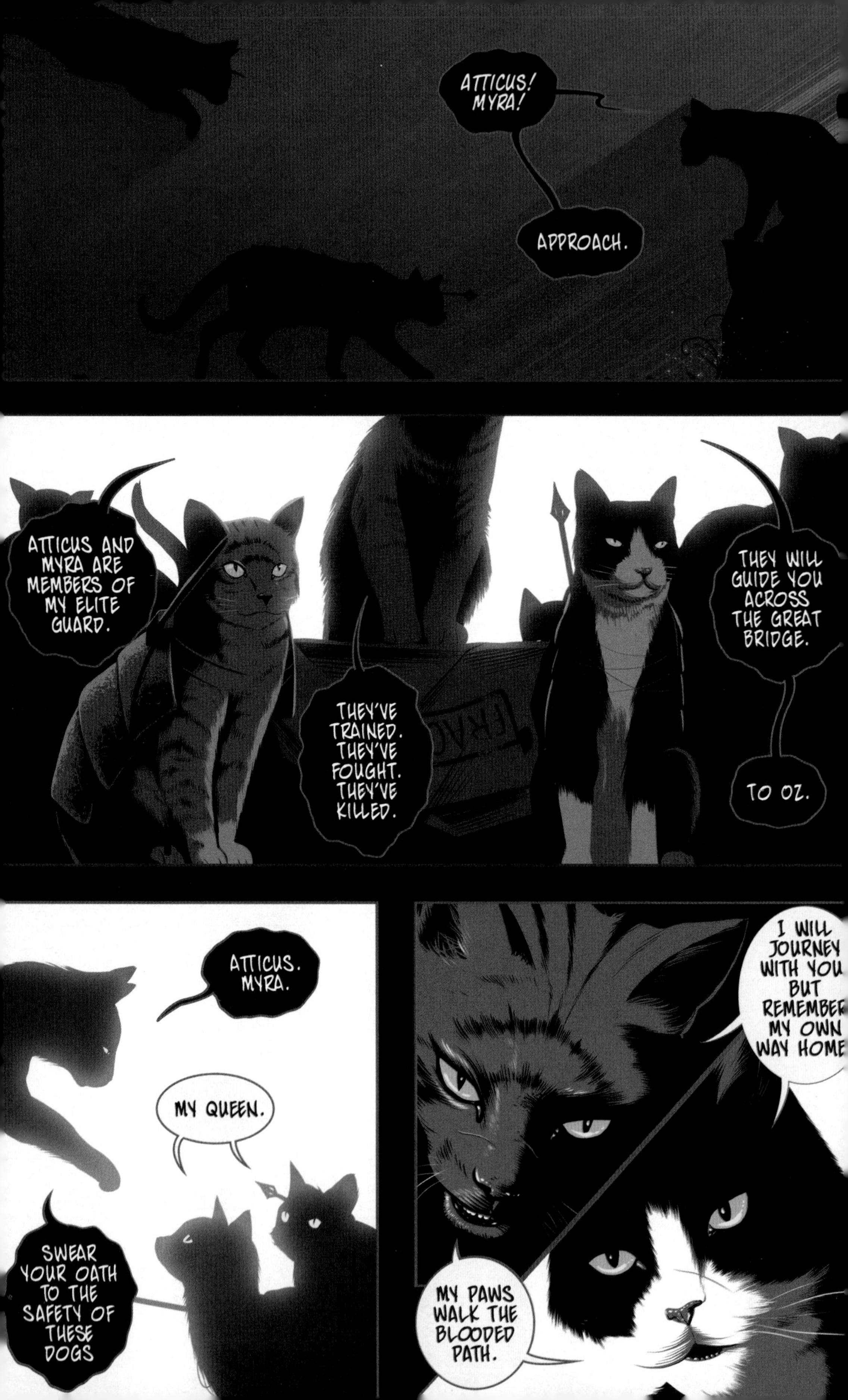
ATTICUS! MYRA!
APPROACH.
ATTICUS AND MYRA ARE MEMBERS OF MY ELITE GUARD.
THEY'VE TRAINED. THEY'VE FOUGHT. THEY'VE KILLED.
THEY WILL GUIDE YOU ACROSS THE GREAT BRIDGE.
TO OZ.
ATTICUS. MYRA.
MY QUEEN.
SWEAR YOUR OATH TO THE SAFETY OF THESE DOGS
I WILL JOURNEY WITH YOU BUT REMEMBER MY OWN WAY HOME
MY PAWS WALK THE BLOODED PATH.

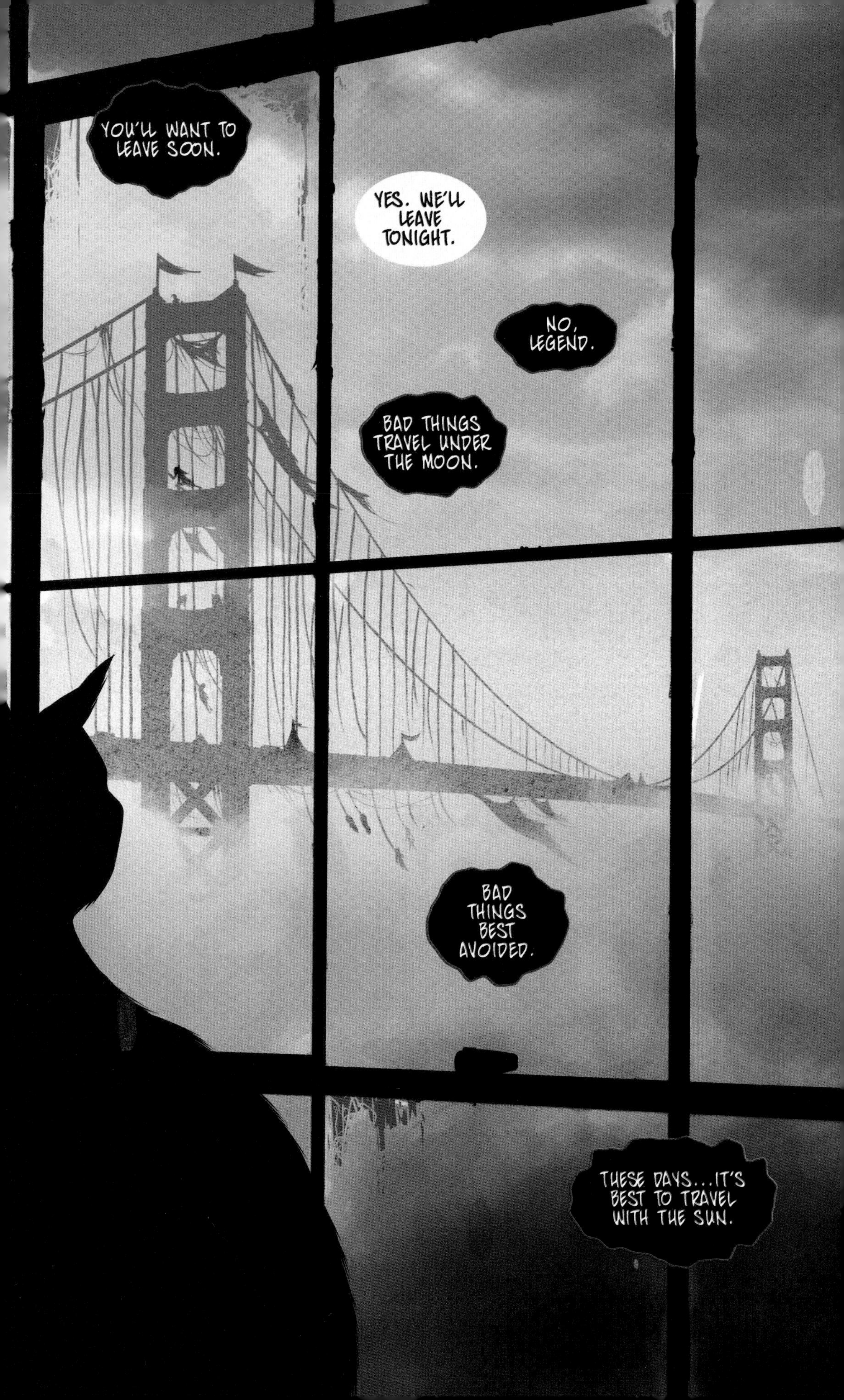
YOU'LL WANT TO LEAVE SOON.
YES. WE'LL LEAVE TONIGHT.
NO, LEGEND.
BAD THINGS TRAVEL UNDER THE MOON.
BAD THINGS BEST AVOIDED.
THESE DAYS...IT'S BEST TO TRAVEL WITH THE SUN.

CHAPTER THREE

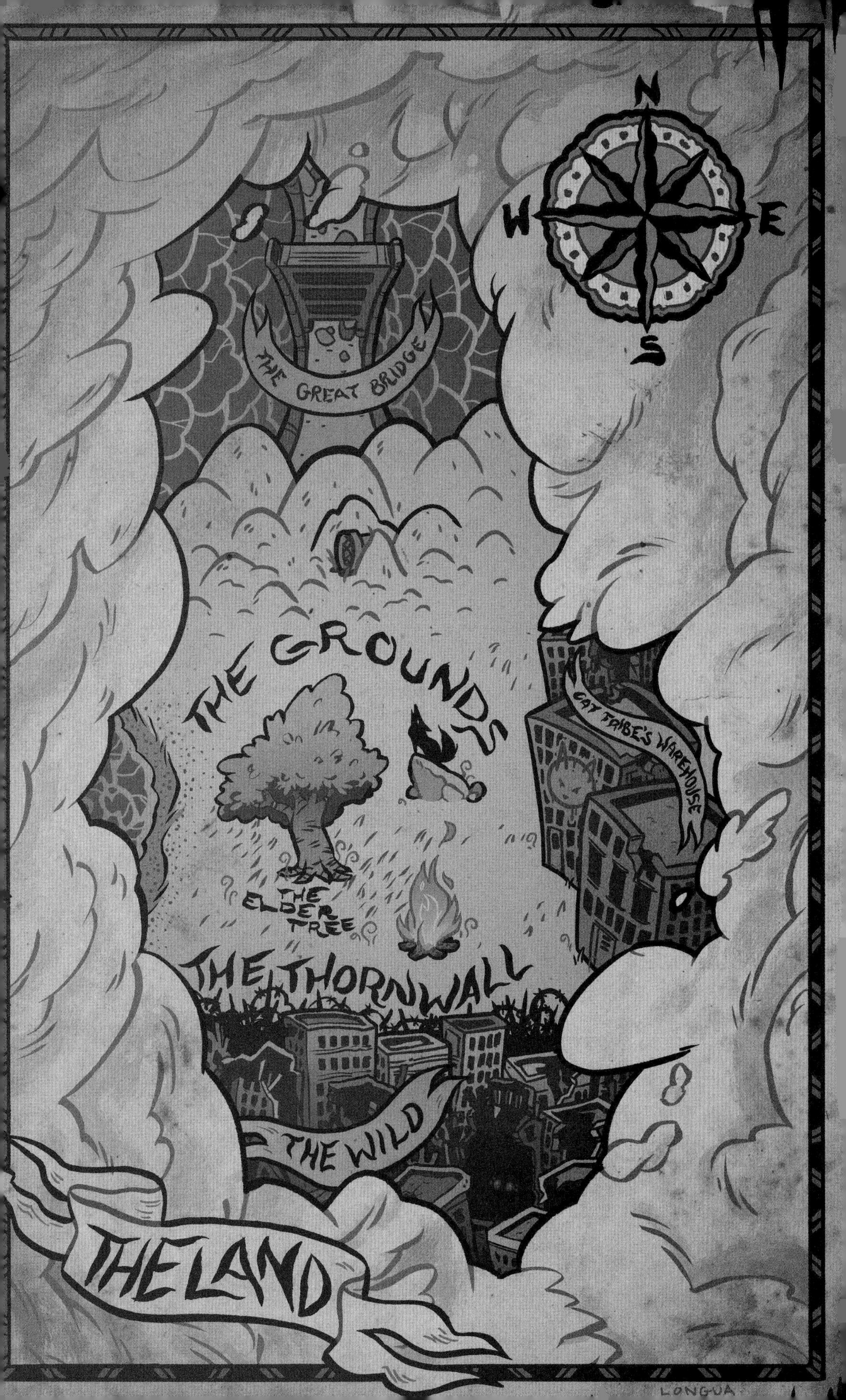

N
W
E
S
THE GREAT BRIDGE
THE GROUNDS
CAT TRIBE'S WAREHOUSE
THE ELDER TREE
THE THORNWALL
THE WILD
THE LAND
LONGUA

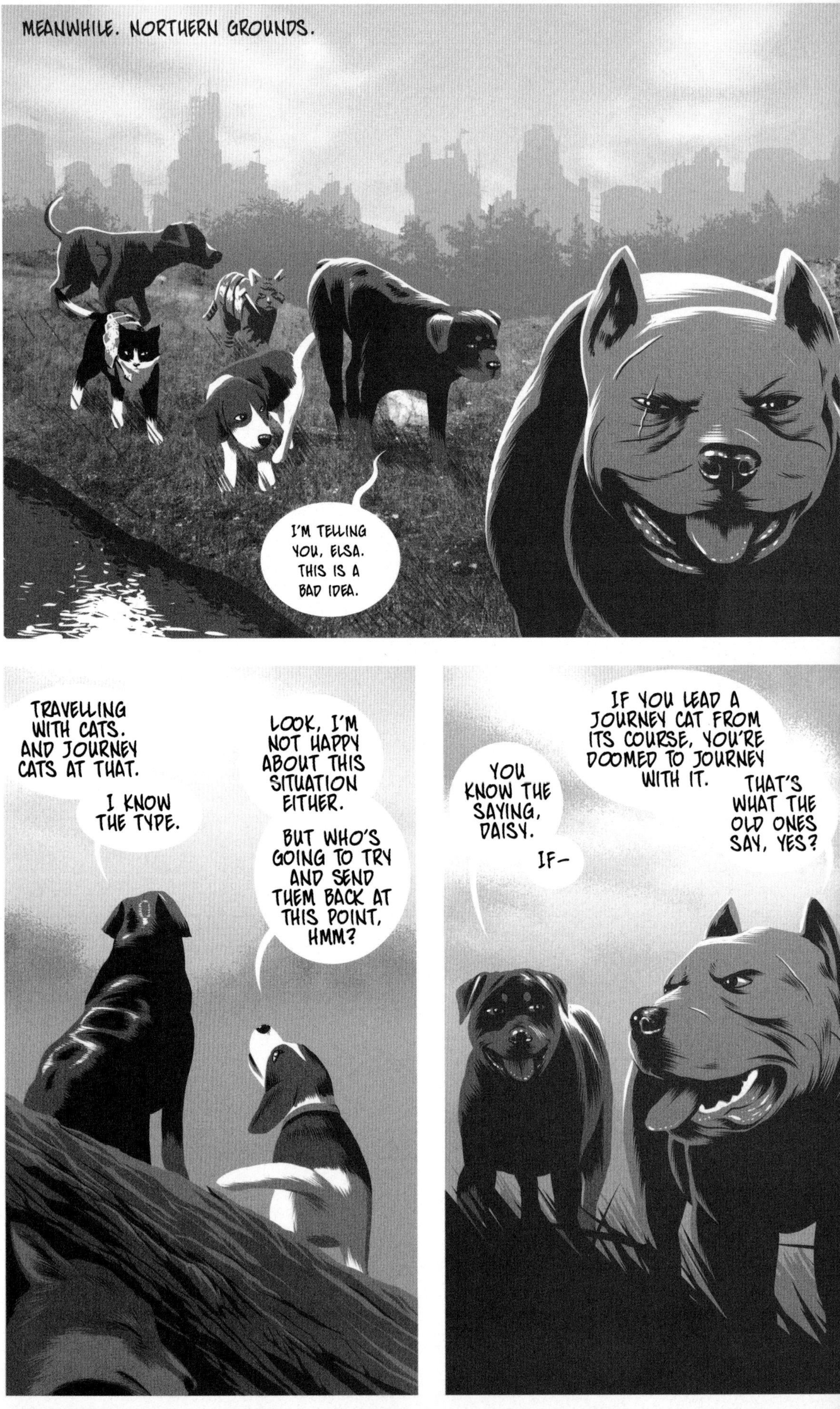
MEANWHILE. NORTHERN GROUNDS.
I'M TELLING YOU, ELSA. THIS IS A BAD IDEA.
TRAVELLING WITH CATS. AND JOURNEY CATS AT THAT.
I KNOW THE TYPE.
LOOK, I'M NOT HAPPY ABOUT THIS SITUATION EITHER.
BUT WHO'S GOING TO TRY AND SEND THEM BACK AT THIS POINT, HMM?
YOU KNOW THE SAYING, DAISY.
IF-
IF YOU LEAD A JOURNEY CAT FROM ITS COURSE, YOU'RE DOOMED TO JOURNEY WITH IT.
THAT'S WHAT THE OLD ONES SAY, YES?

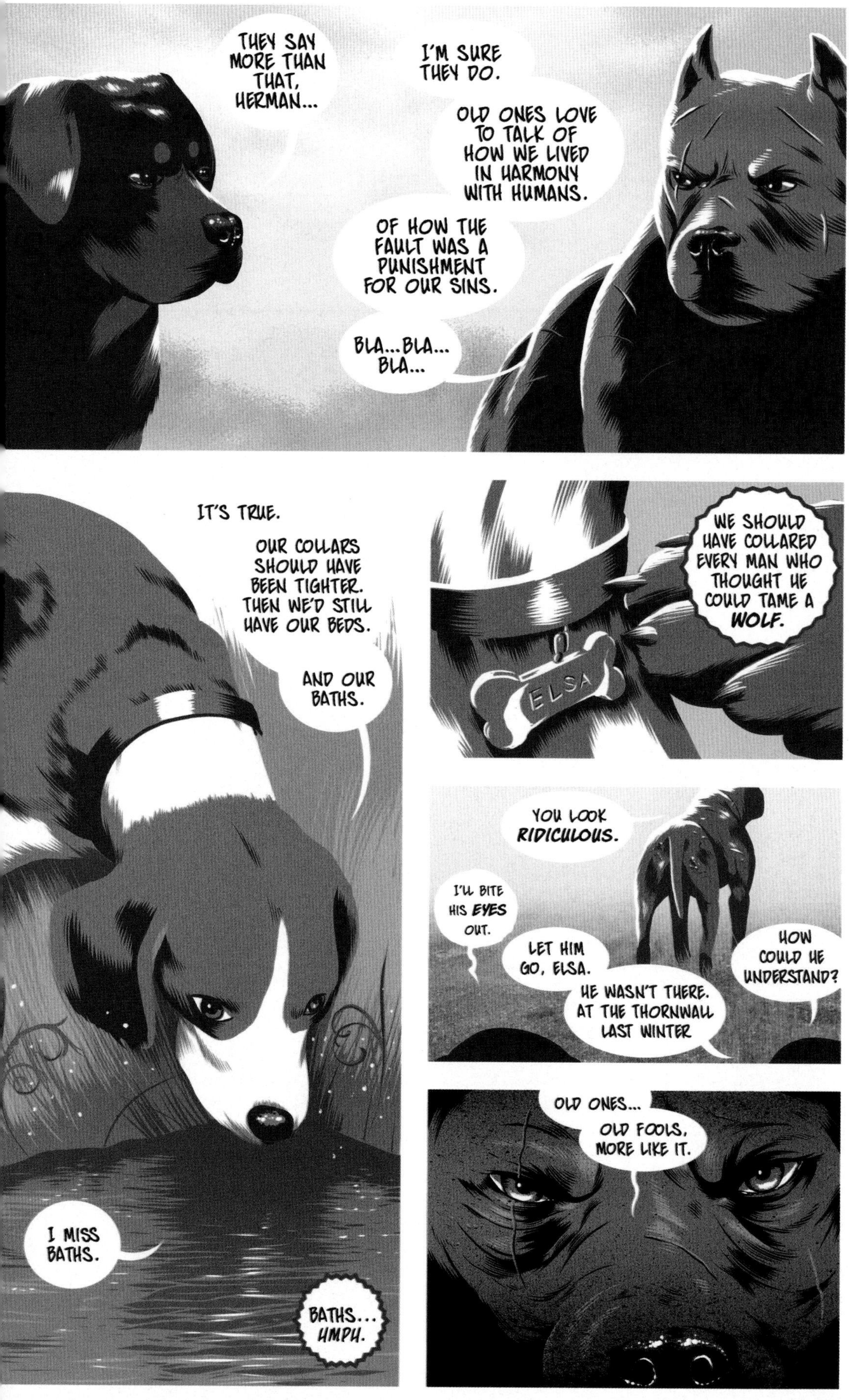
THEY SAY MORE THAN THAT, HERMAN...
I'M SURE THEY DO.
OLD ONES LOVE TO TALK OF HOW WE LIVED IN HARMONY WITH HUMANS.
OF HOW THE FAULT WAS A PUNISHMENT FOR OUR SINS.
BLA...BLA... BLA...
IT'S TRUE.
OUR COLLARS SHOULD HAVE BEEN TIGHTER. THEN WE'D STILL HAVE OUR BEDS.
AND OUR BATHS.
I MISS BATHS.
BATHS... UMPH.
WE SHOULD HAVE COLLARED EVERY MAN WHO THOUGHT HE COULD TAME A WOLF.
ELSA
YOU LOOK RIDICULOUS.
I'LL BITE HIS EYES OUT.
LET HIM GO, ELSA.
HE WASN'T THERE. AT THE THORNWALL LAST WINTER
HOW COULD HE UNDERSTAND?
OLD ONES...
OLD FOOLS, MORE LIKE IT.

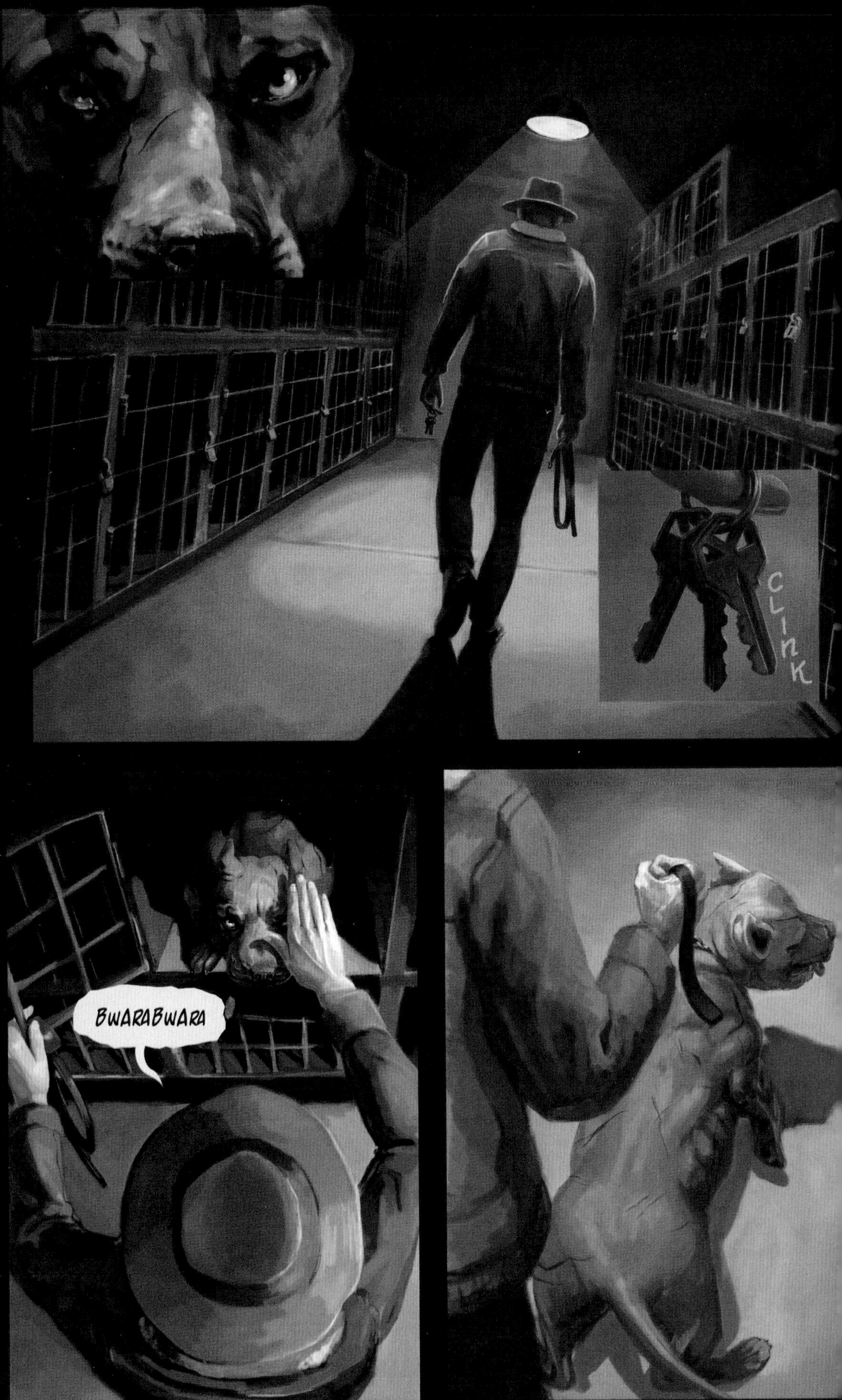
CLINK
BWARABWARA

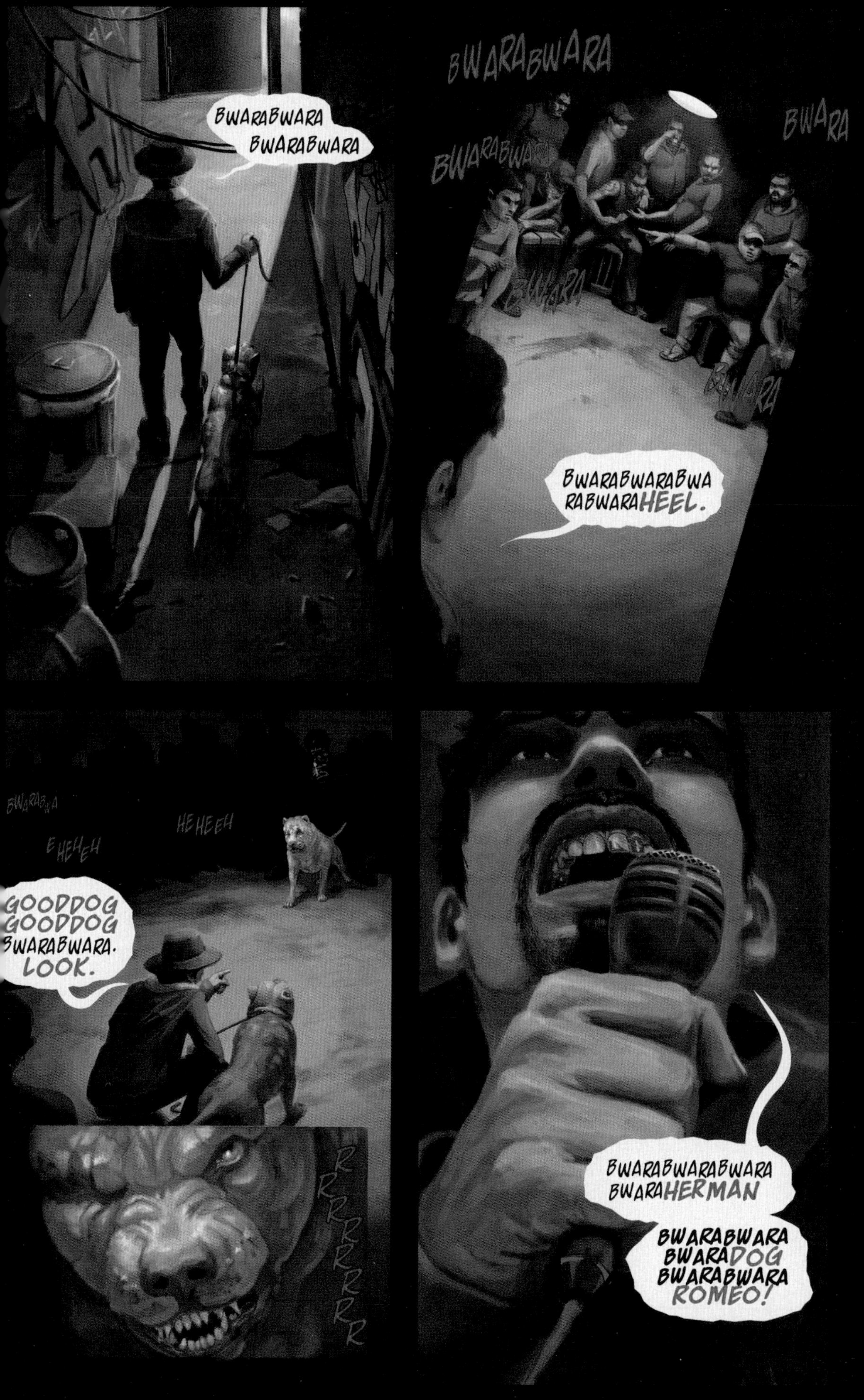
BWARABWARA BWARABWARA
BWARABWARA
BWARA
BWARABWARA
BWARA
BWARA
BWARABWARABWA RABWARAHEEL.
HEHEEH
EHEHEH
GOODDOG GOODDOG BWARABWARA. LOOK.
RRRRRRR
BWARABWARABWARA BWARAHERMAN
BWARABWARA BWARADOG BWARABWARA ROMEO!

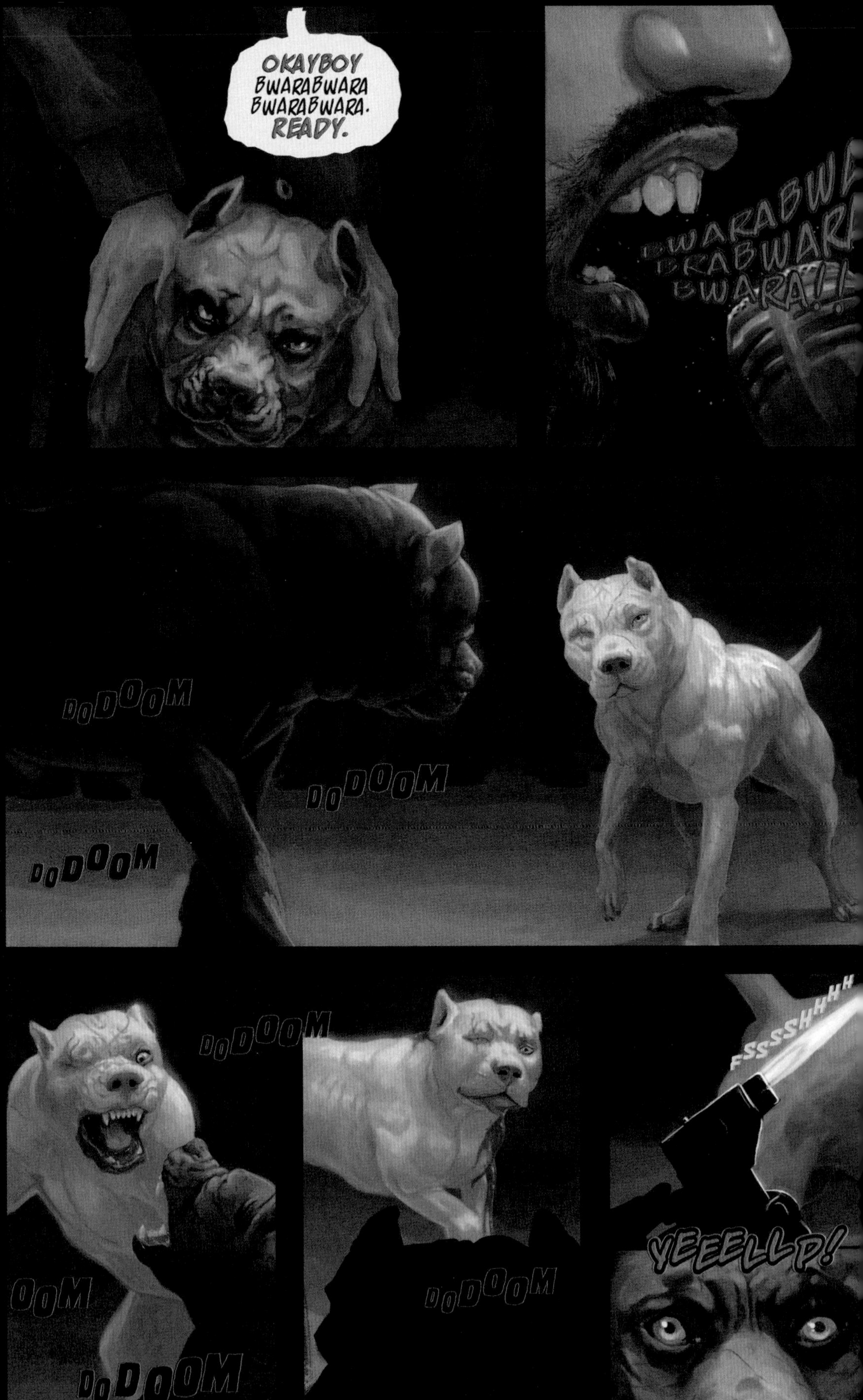
OKAYBOY BWARABWARA BWARABWARA. READY.
BWARABWA BRABWARA BWARA!!
DODOOM
DODOOM
DODOOM
DODOOM
OOM
DODOOM
DODOOM
FSSSSHHHHH
YEEELLP!

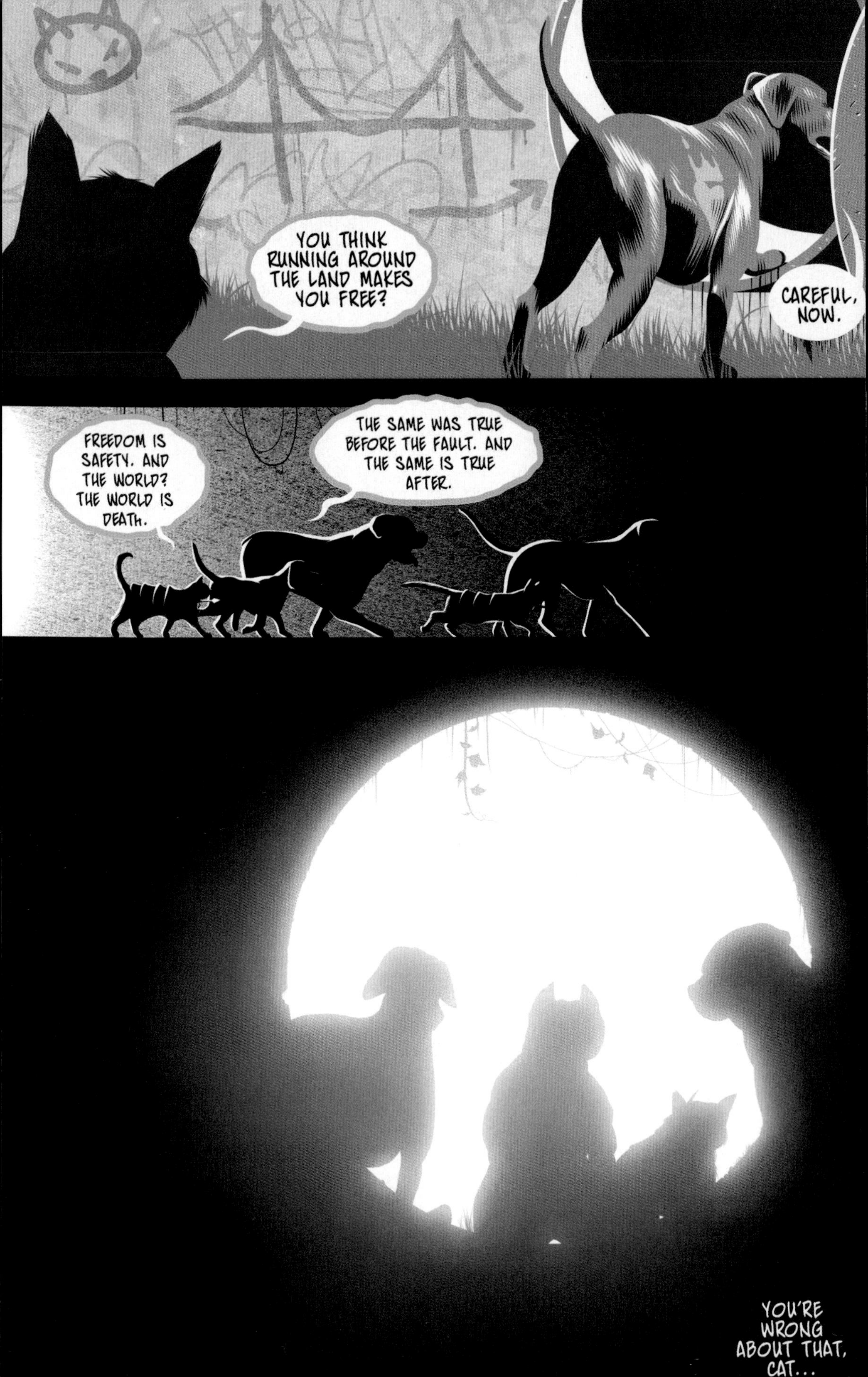
YOU THINK RUNNING AROUND THE LAND MAKES YOU FREE?
CAREFUL, NOW.
FREEDOM IS SAFETY. AND THE WORLD? THE WORLD IS DEATH.
THE SAME WAS TRUE BEFORE THE FAULT. AND THE SAME IS TRUE AFTER.
YOU'RE WRONG ABOUT THAT, CAT...

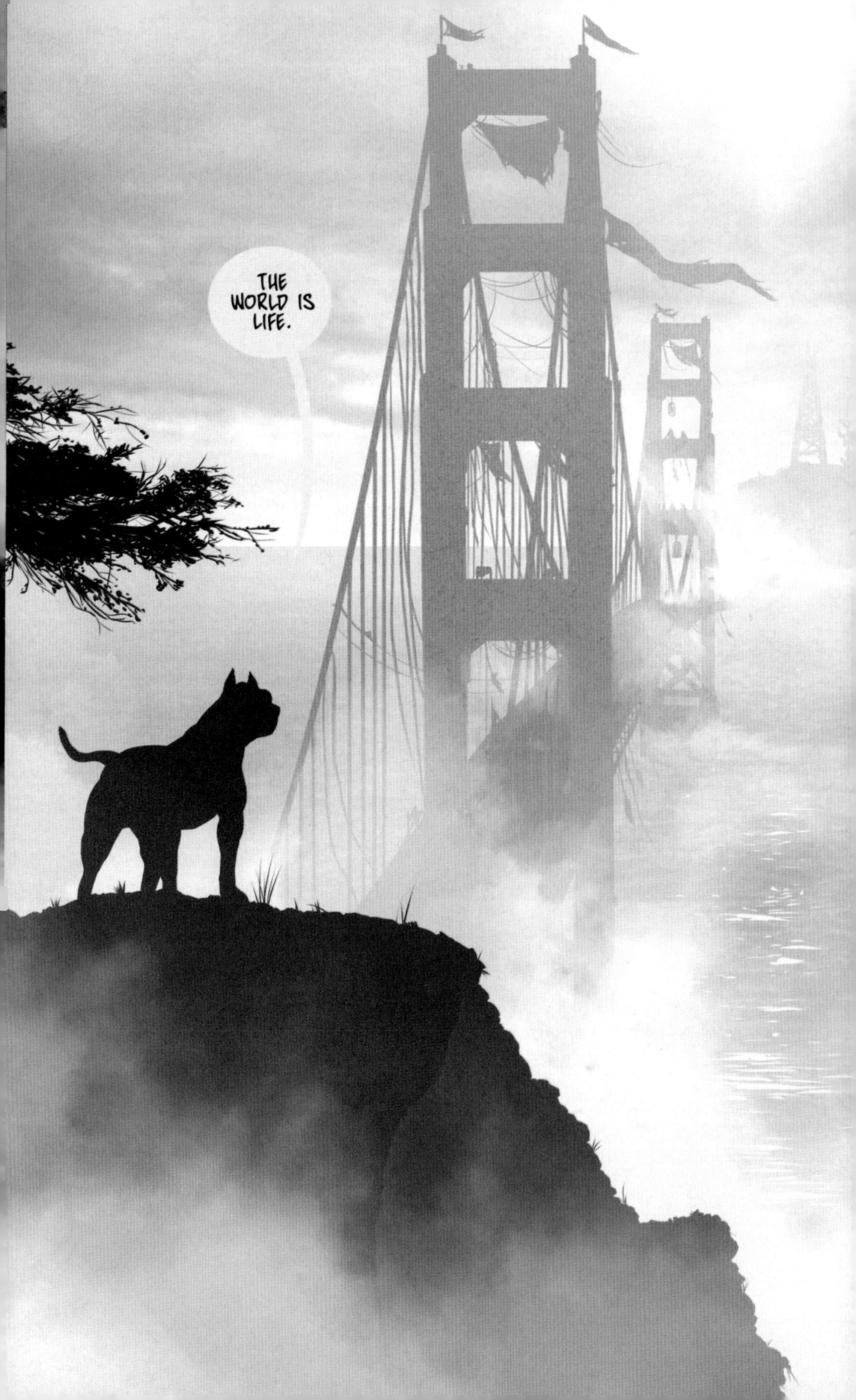
THE WORLD IS LIFE.

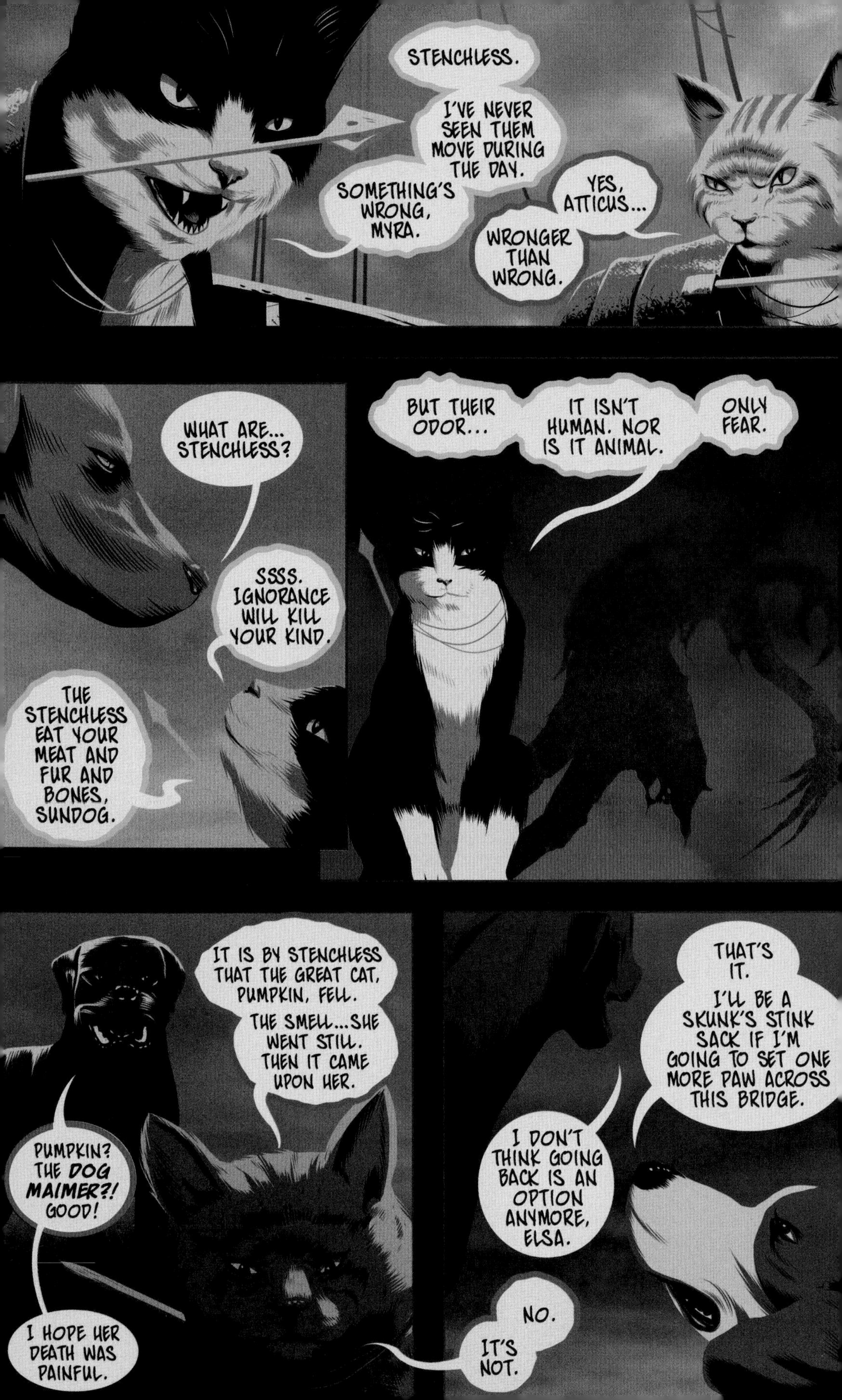
STENCHLESS.
I'VE NEVER SEEN THEM MOVE DURING THE DAY.
SOMETHING'S WRONG, MYRA.
YES, ATTICUS...
WRONGER THAN WRONG.
WHAT ARE... STENCHLESS?
SSSS. IGNORANCE WILL KILL YOUR KIND.
THE STENCHLESS EAT YOUR MEAT AND FUR AND BONES, SUNDOG.
BUT THEIR ODOR...
IT ISN'T HUMAN. NOR IS IT ANIMAL.
ONLY FEAR.
IT IS BY STENCHLESS THAT THE GREAT CAT, PUMPKIN, FELL.
THE SMELL...SHE WENT STILL. THEN IT CAME UPON HER.
PUMPKIN? THE *DOG MAIMER?!* GOOD!
I HOPE HER DEATH WAS PAINFUL.
THAT'S IT.
I'LL BE A SKUNK'S STINK SACK IF I'M GOING TO SET ONE MORE PAW ACROSS THIS BRIDGE.
I DON'T THINK GOING BACK IS AN OPTION ANYMORE, ELSA.
NO.
IT'S NOT.

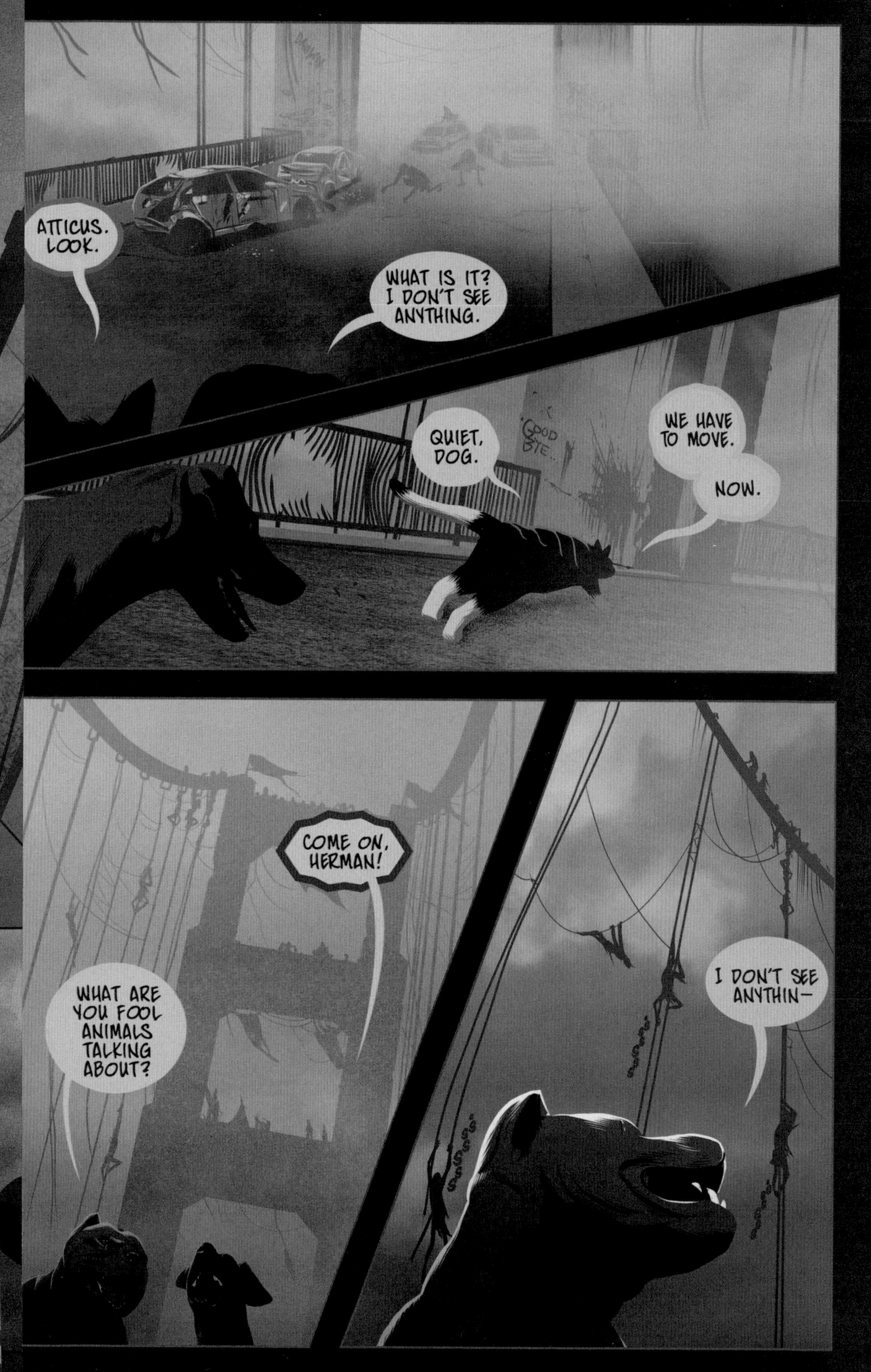
ATTICUS. LOOK.
WHAT IS IT? I DON'T SEE ANYTHING.
QUIET, DOG.
GOOD BYE...
WE HAVE TO MOVE.
NOW.
COME ON, HERMAN!
WHAT ARE YOU FOOL ANIMALS TALKING ABOUT?
I DON'T SEE ANYTHIN—

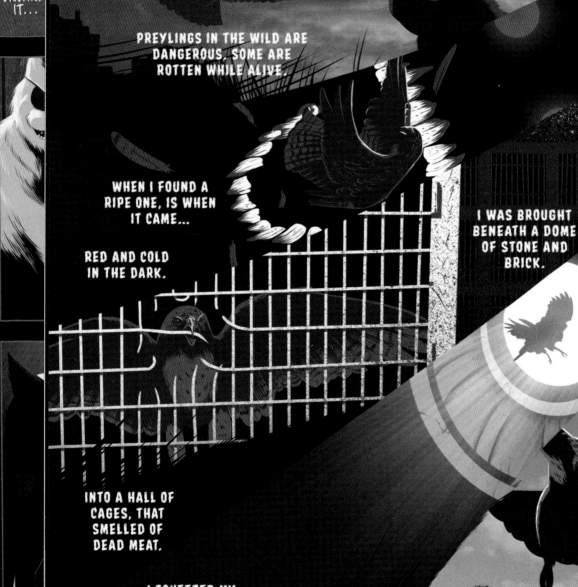

IT WAS A SCARCE WINTER. THE HILLS WERE BARREN.

I SEARCHED FOR FOOD UNTIL MY APPETITE SCREAMED AND I WAS FORCED INTO THE WILD TO SCAVENGE.

PREYLINGS IN THE WILD ARE DANGEROUS, SOME ARE ROTTEN WHILE ALIVE.

WHEN I FOUND A RIPE ONE, IS WHEN IT CAME...

RED AND COLD IN THE DARK.

I WAS BROUGHT BENEATH A DOME OF STONE AND BRICK.

INTO A HALL OF CAGES, THAT SMELLED OF DEAD MEAT.

I SQUEEZED MY WAY OUT.

TOWARDS THE AIR, CLIMBING...CLIMBING...

...WITH THE STENCH OF DEATH ON MY WINGS.

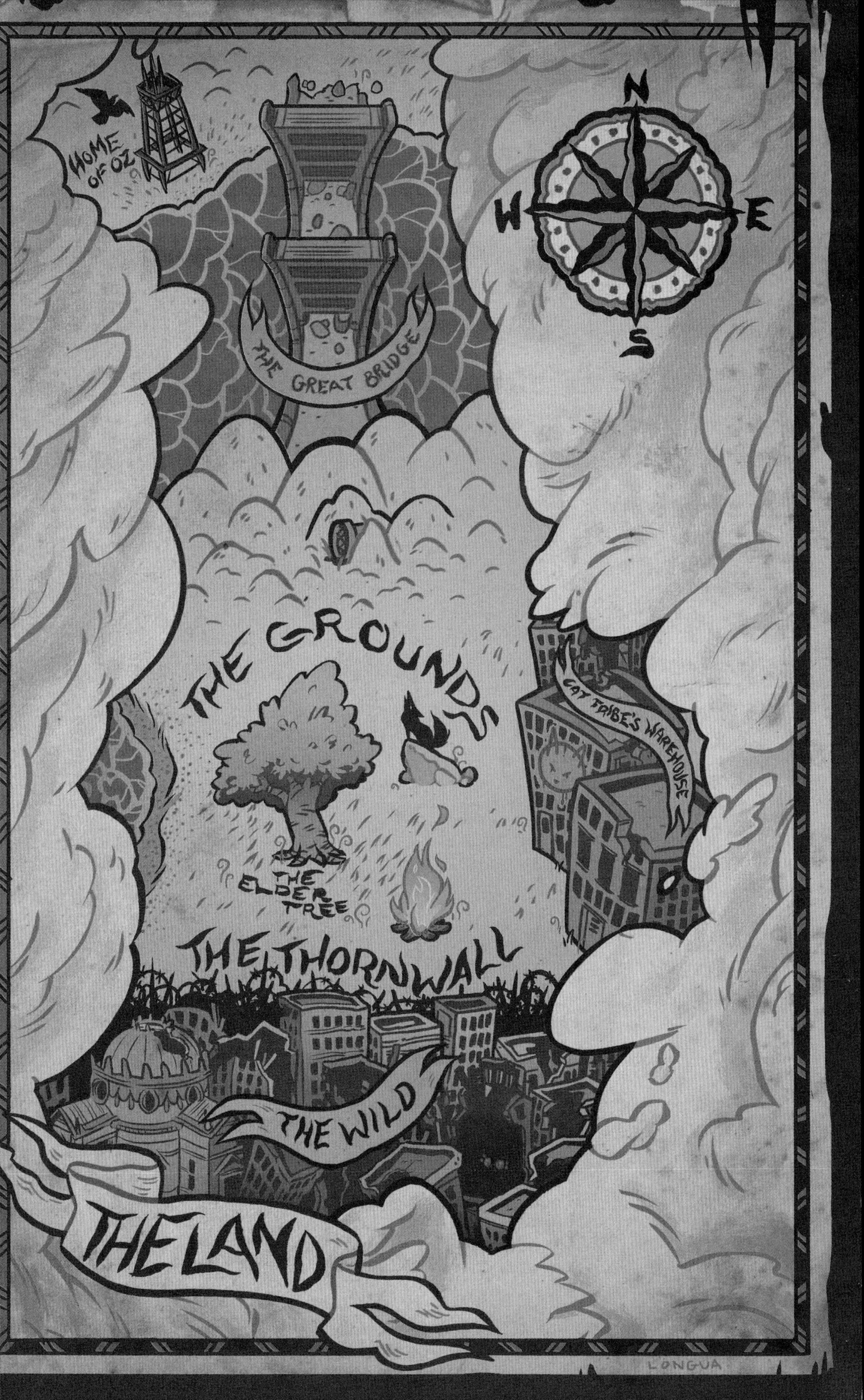
HOME OF OZ
THE GREAT BRIDGE
N
W
E
S
THE GROUNDS
CAT TRIBE'S WAREHOUSE
THE ELDER TREE
THE THORNWALL
THE WILD
THE LAND
LONGUA

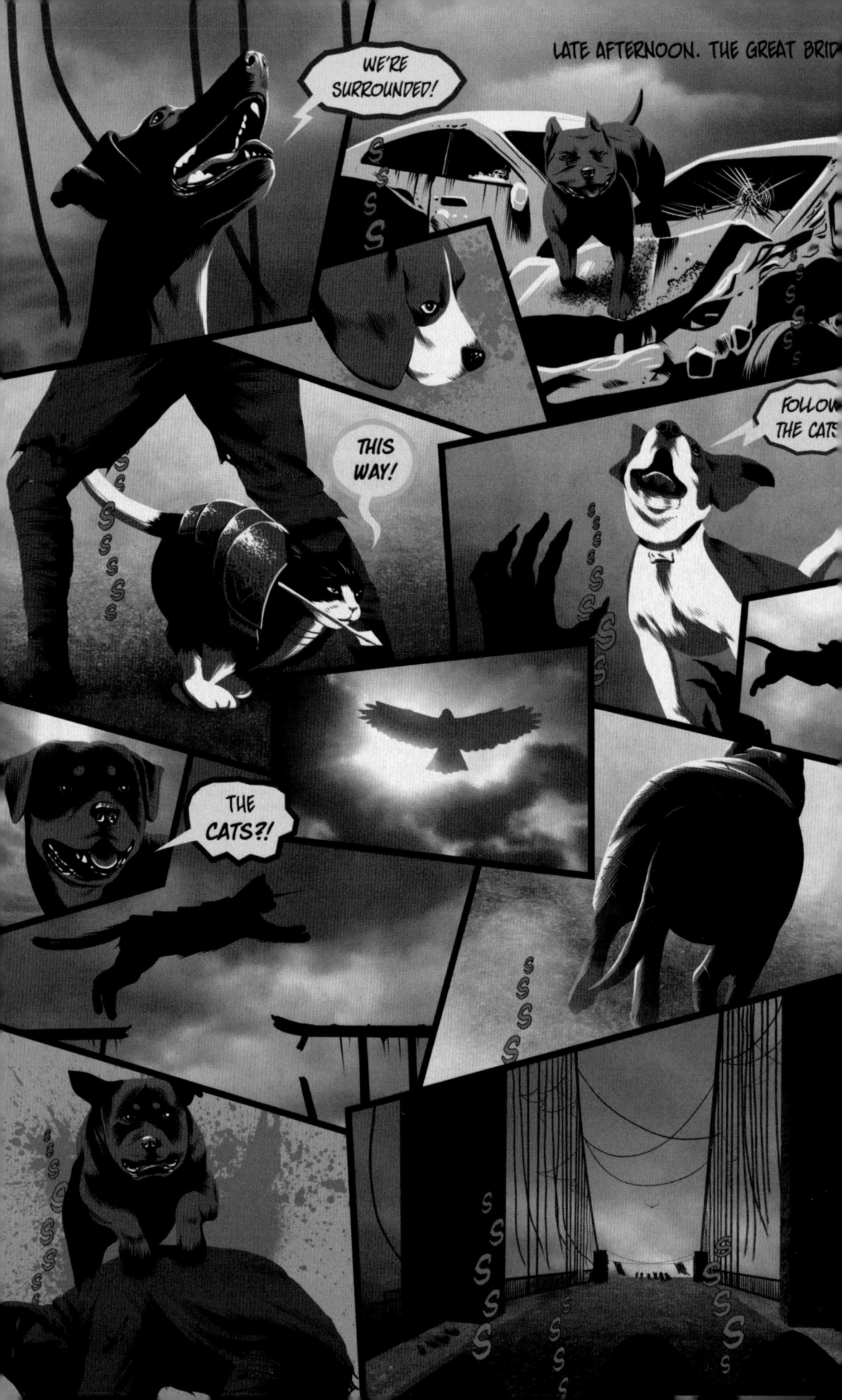
LATE AFTERNOON. THE GREAT BRID
WE'RE SURROUNDED!
THIS WAY!
FOLLOW THE CAT
THE CATS?!

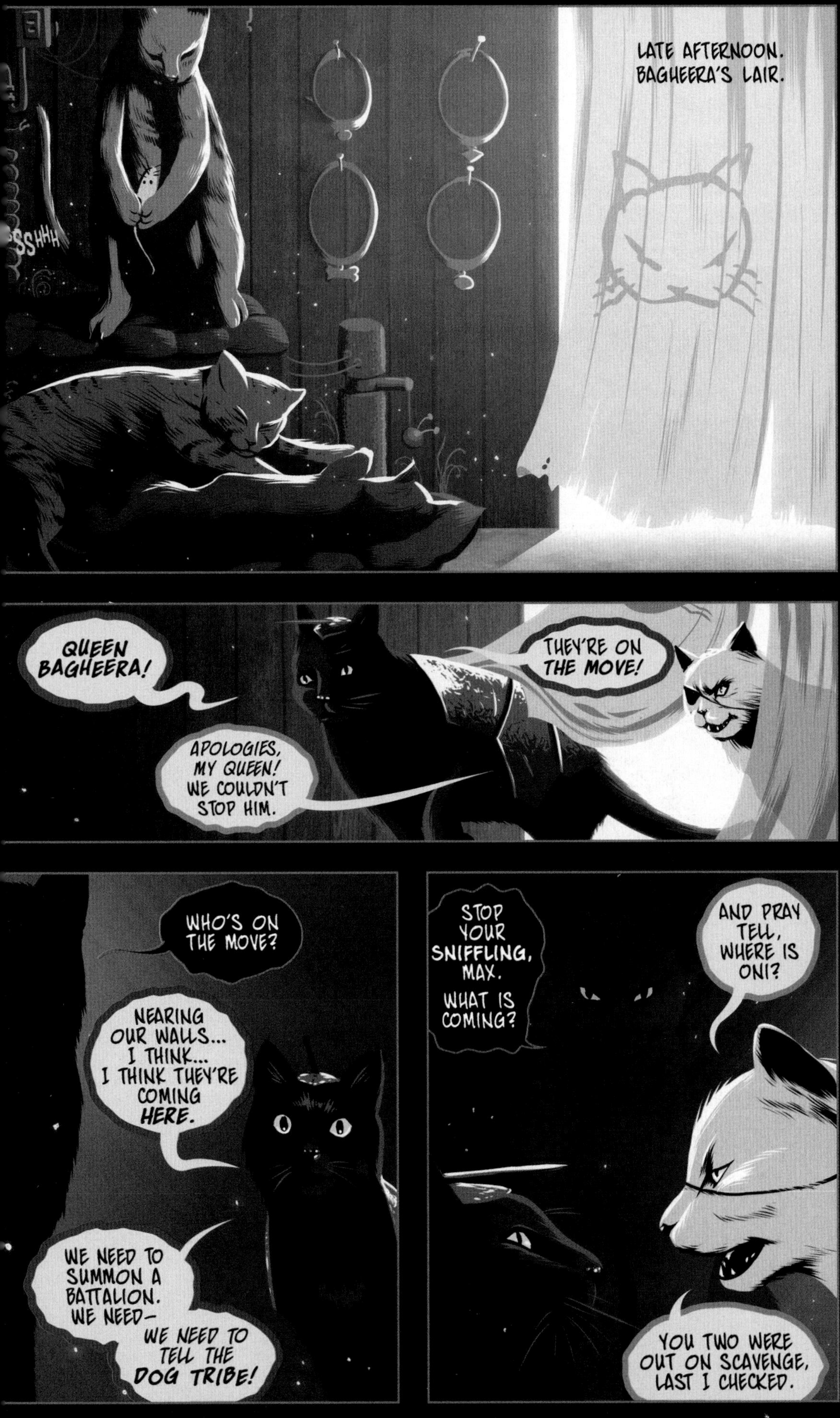
LATE AFTERNOON. BAGHEERA'S LAIR.
SSHHH
QUEEN BAGHEERA!
THEY'RE ON THE MOVE!
APOLOGIES, MY QUEEN! WE COULDN'T STOP HIM.
WHO'S ON THE MOVE?
NEARING OUR WALLS... I THINK... I THINK THEY'RE COMING HERE.
WE NEED TO SUMMON A BATTALION. WE NEED—
WE NEED TO TELL THE DOG TRIBE!
STOP YOUR SNIFFLING, MAX.
WHAT IS COMING?
AND PRAY TELL, WHERE IS ONI?
YOU TWO WERE OUT ON SCAVENGE, LAST I CHECKED.

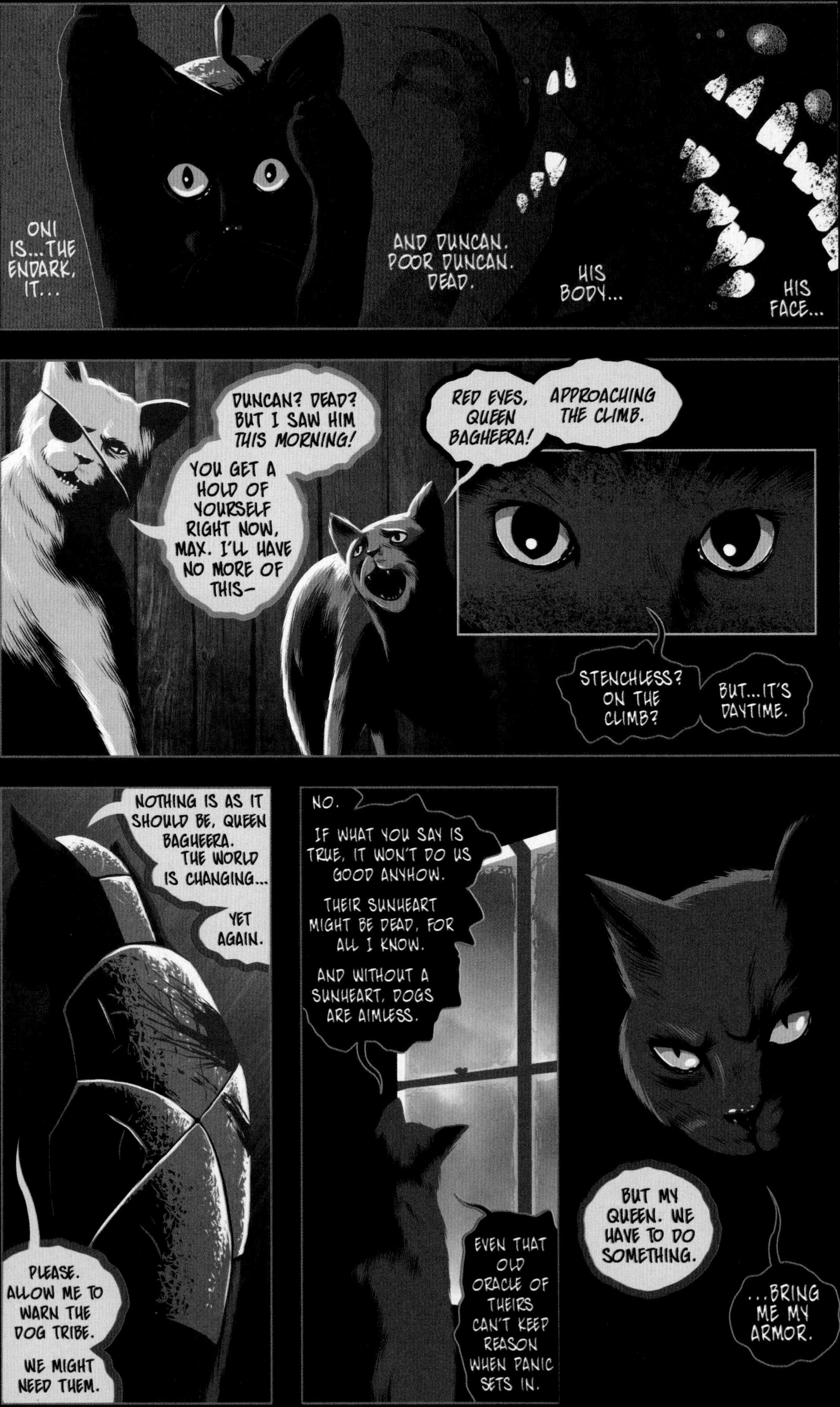
ONI IS...THE ENDARK, IT...
AND DUNCAN. POOR DUNCAN. DEAD.
HIS BODY...
HIS FACE...
DUNCAN? DEAD? BUT I SAW HIM THIS MORNING!
YOU GET A HOLD OF YOURSELF RIGHT NOW, MAX. I'LL HAVE NO MORE OF THIS–
RED EYES, QUEEN BAGHEERA!
APPROACHING THE CLIMB.
STENCHLESS? ON THE CLIMB?
BUT...IT'S DAYTIME.
NOTHING IS AS IT SHOULD BE, QUEEN BAGHEERA. THE WORLD IS CHANGING...
YET AGAIN.
PLEASE. ALLOW ME TO WARN THE DOG TRIBE.
WE MIGHT NEED THEM.
NO.
IF WHAT YOU SAY IS TRUE, IT WON'T DO US GOOD ANYHOW.
THEIR SUNHEART MIGHT BE DEAD, FOR ALL I KNOW.
AND WITHOUT A SUNHEART, DOGS ARE AIMLESS.
EVEN THAT OLD ORACLE OF THEIRS CAN'T KEEP REASON WHEN PANIC SETS IN.
BUT MY QUEEN. WE HAVE TO DO SOMETHING.
...BRING ME MY ARMOR.

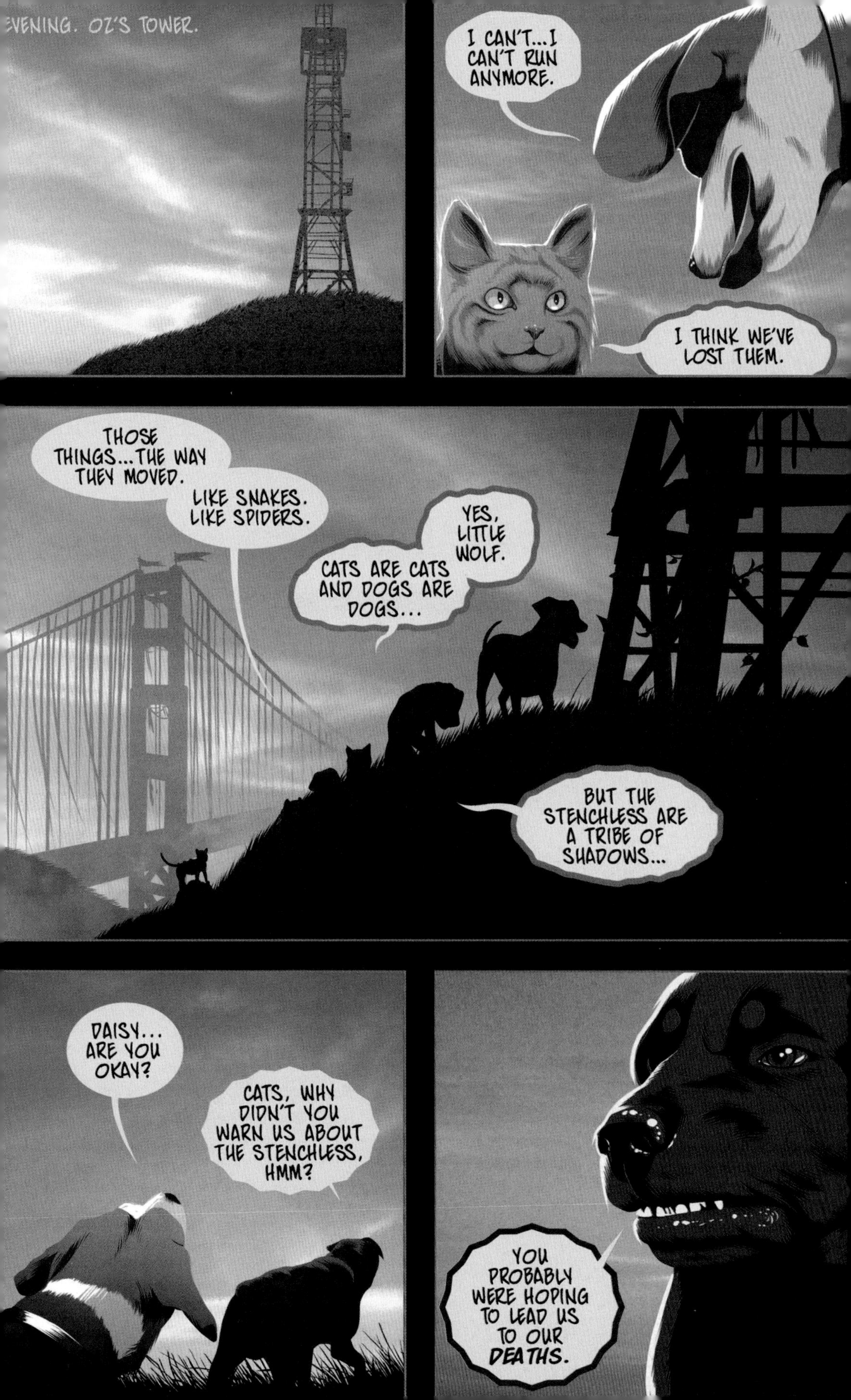
EVENING. OZ'S TOWER.
I CAN'T...I CAN'T RUN ANYMORE.
I THINK WE'VE LOST THEM.
THOSE THINGS...THE WAY THEY MOVED.
LIKE SNAKES. LIKE SPIDERS.
YES, LITTLE WOLF.
CATS ARE CATS AND DOGS ARE DOGS...
BUT THE STENCHLESS ARE A TRIBE OF SHADOWS...
DAISY... ARE YOU OKAY?
CATS, WHY DIDN'T YOU WARN US ABOUT THE STENCHLESS, HMM?
YOU PROBABLY WERE HOPING TO LEAD US TO OUR DEATHS.

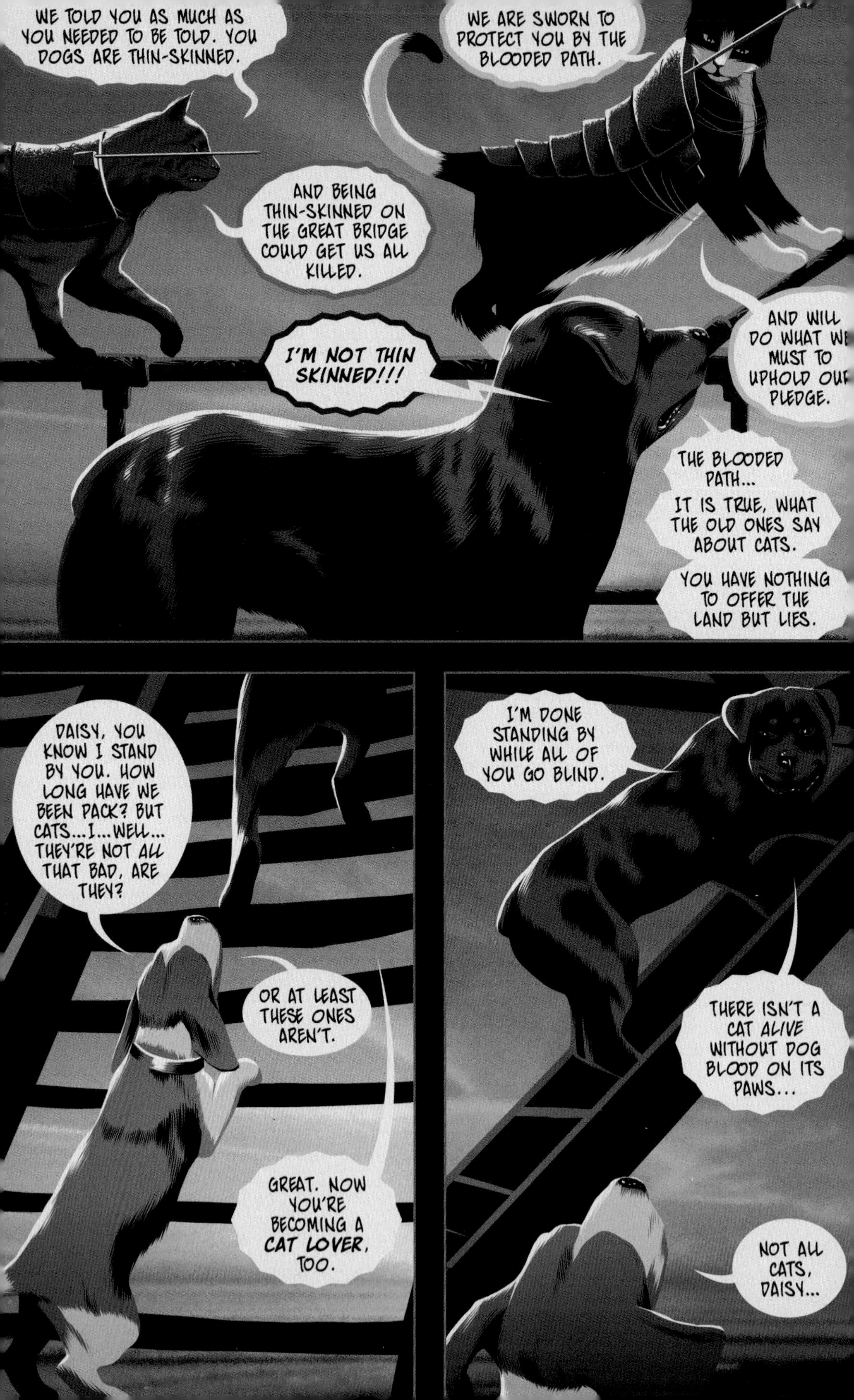
WE TOLD YOU AS MUCH AS YOU NEEDED TO BE TOLD. YOU DOGS ARE THIN-SKINNED.
WE ARE SWORN TO PROTECT YOU BY THE BLOODED PATH.
AND BEING THIN-SKINNED ON THE GREAT BRIDGE COULD GET US ALL KILLED.
I'M NOT THIN SKINNED!!!
AND WILL DO WHAT WE MUST TO UPHOLD OUR PLEDGE.
THE BLOODED PATH...
IT IS TRUE, WHAT THE OLD ONES SAY ABOUT CATS.
YOU HAVE NOTHING TO OFFER THE LAND BUT LIES.
DAISY, YOU KNOW I STAND BY YOU. HOW LONG HAVE WE BEEN PACK? BUT CATS...I...WELL... THEY'RE NOT ALL THAT BAD, ARE THEY?
OR AT LEAST THESE ONES AREN'T.
GREAT. NOW YOU'RE BECOMING A CAT LOVER, TOO.
I'M DONE STANDING BY WHILE ALL OF YOU GO BLIND.
THERE ISN'T A CAT ALIVE WITHOUT DOG BLOOD ON ITS PAWS...
NOT ALL CATS, DAISY...

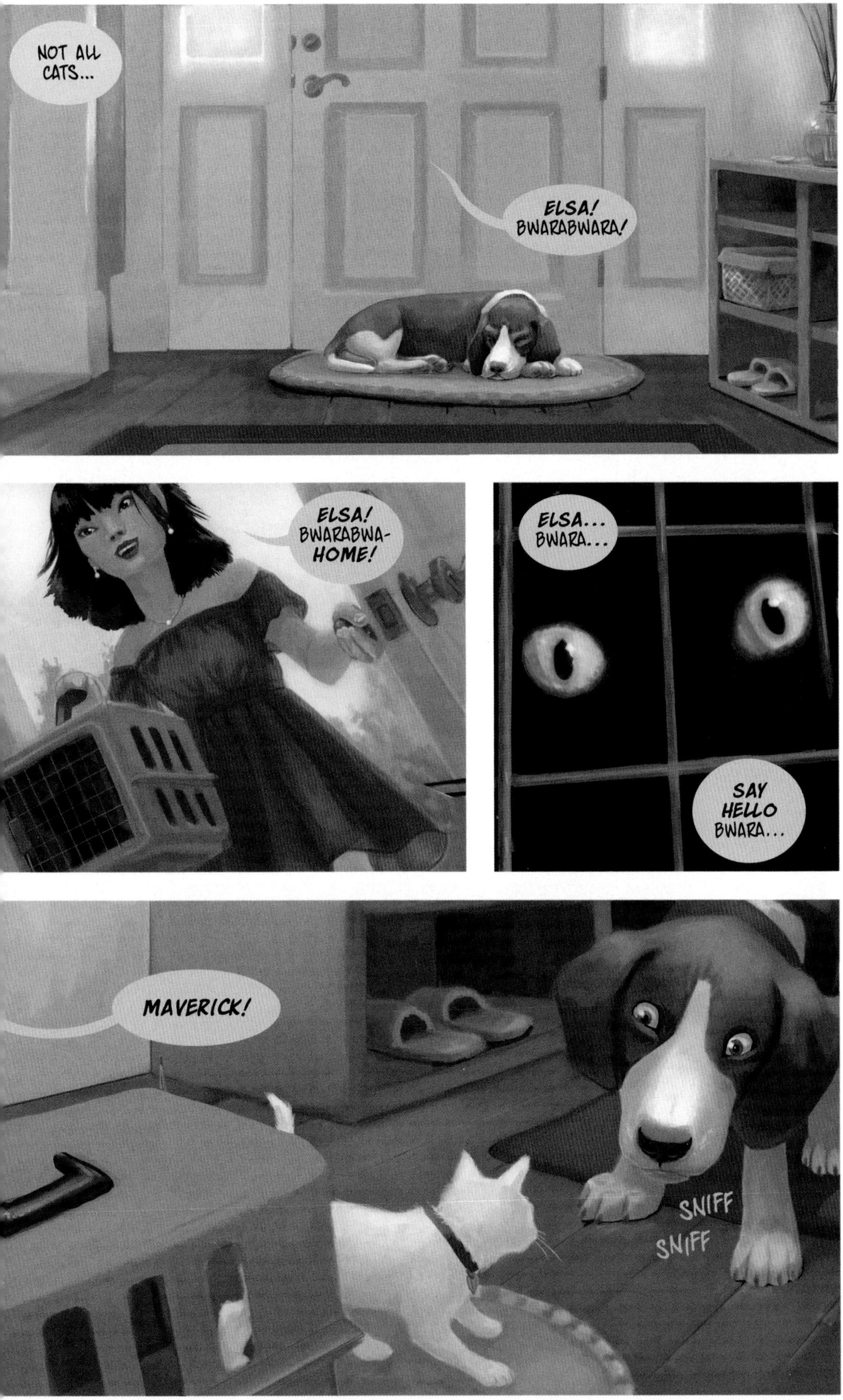
NOT ALL CATS...
ELSA! BWARABWARA!
ELSA! BWARABWA-HOME!
ELSA... BWARA...
SAY HELLO BWARA...
MAVERICK!
SNIFF
SNIFF

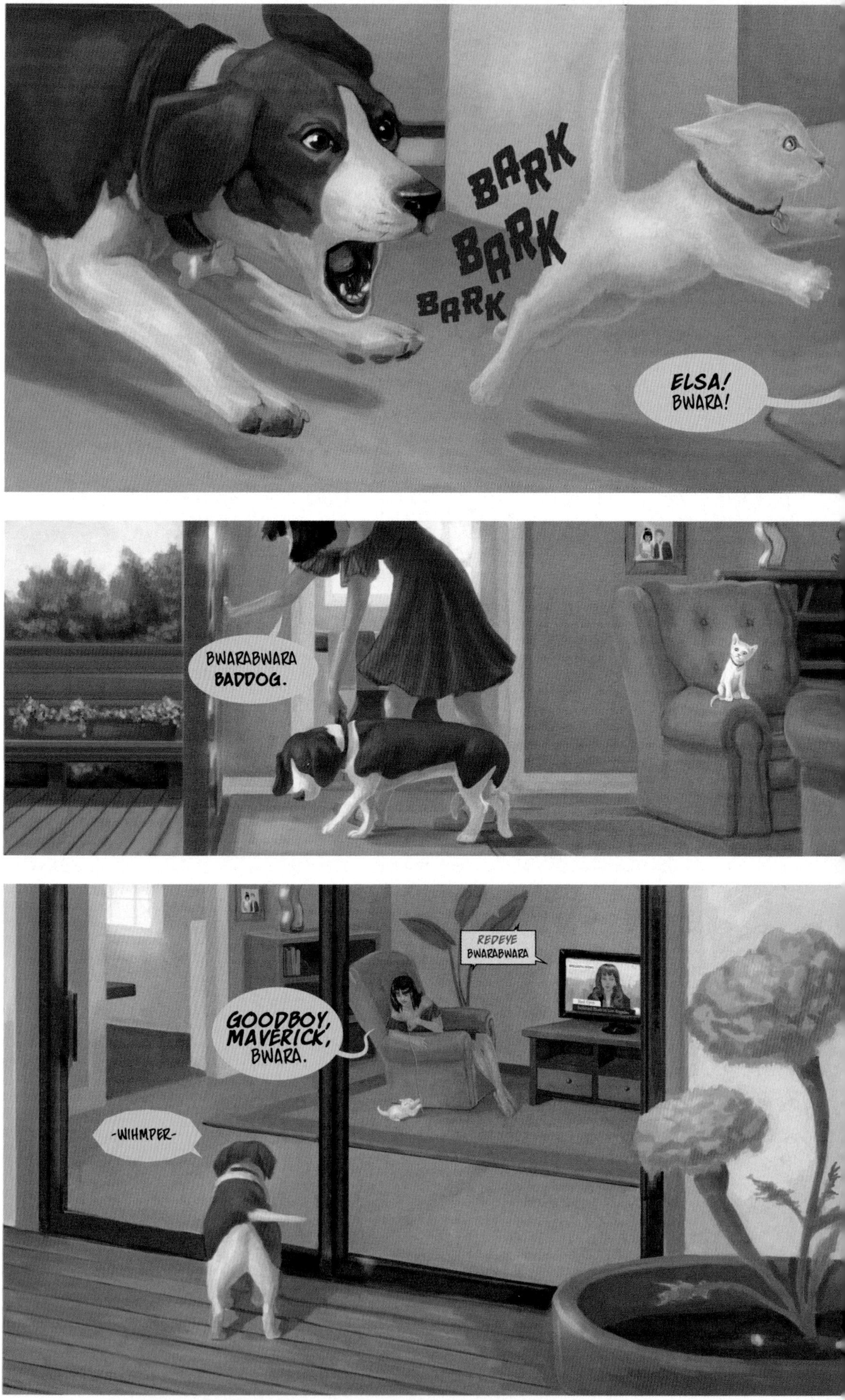
BARK
BARK
BARK
ELSA! BWARA!
BWARABWARA BADDOG.
REDEYE BWARABWARA
GOODBOY, MAVERICK, BWARA.
-WIHMPER-

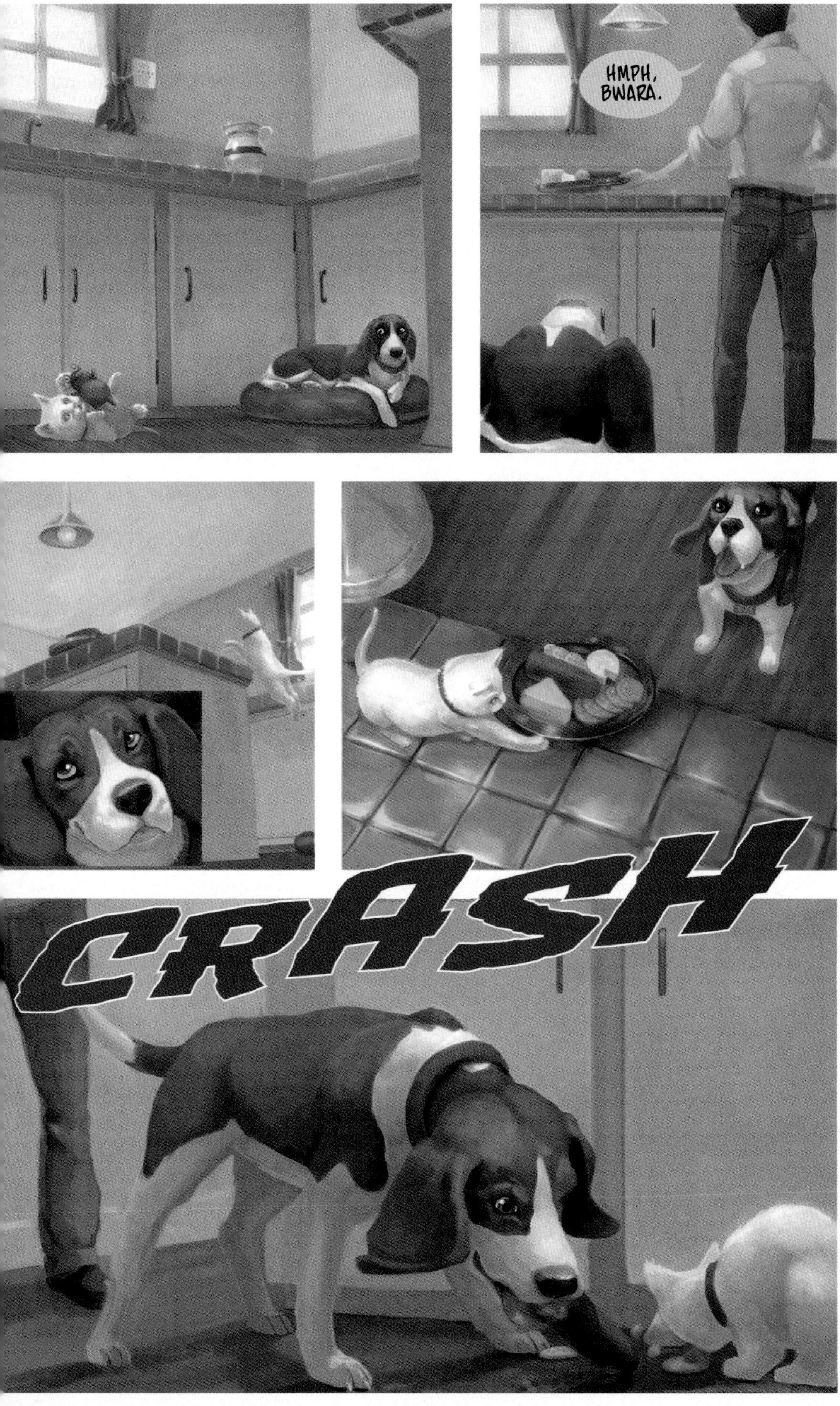
HMPH, BWARA.
CRASH

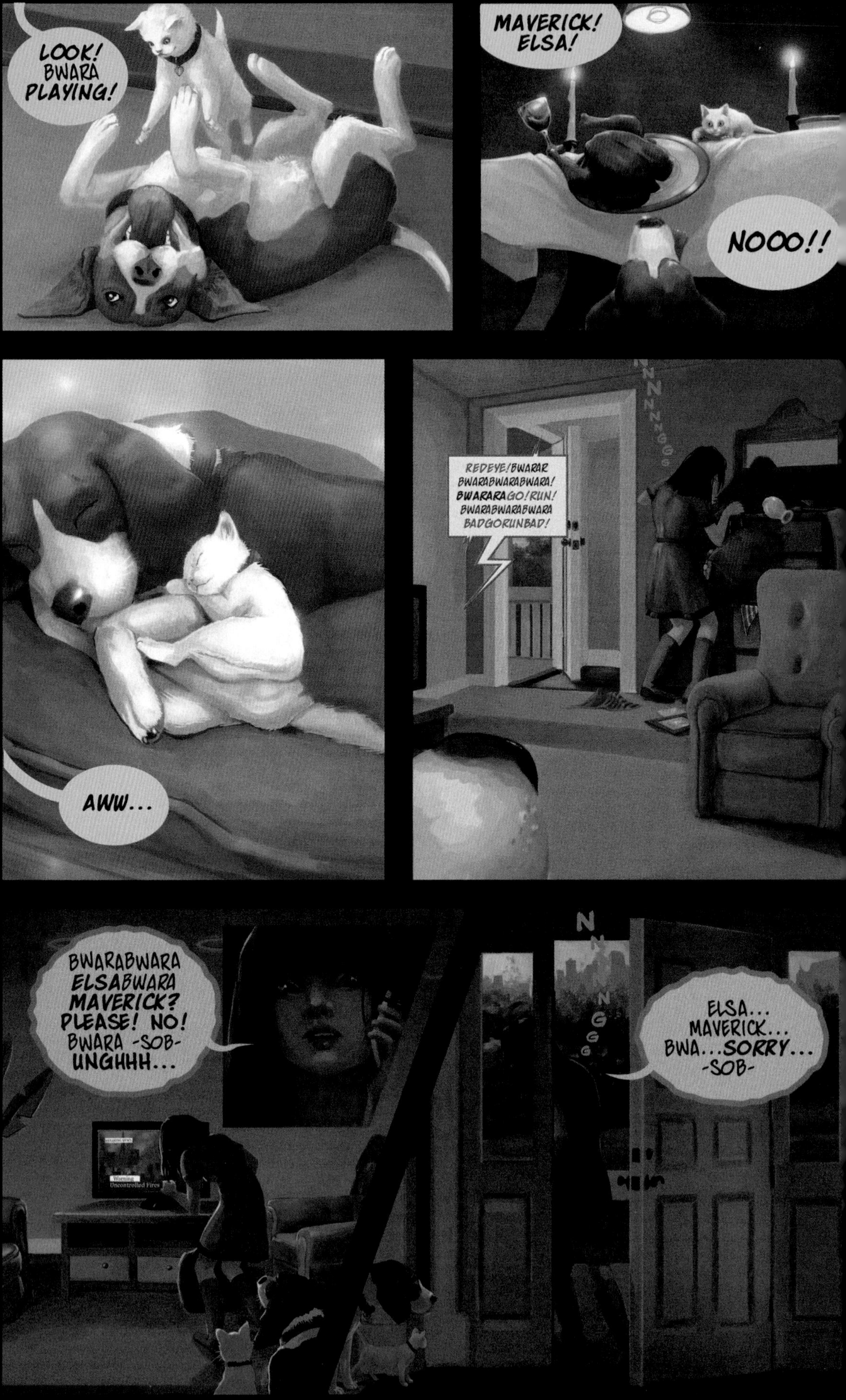
LOOK! BWARA PLAYING!
MAVERICK! ELSA!
NOOO!!
AWW...
REDEYE! BWARAR BWARABWARABWARA! BWARARAGO! RUN! BWARABWARABWARA BADGORUNBAD!
BWARABWARA ELSABWARA MAVERICK? PLEASE! NO! BWARA -SOB- UNGHHH...
Warning
Uncontrolled Fires
ELSA... MAVERICK... BWA...SORRY... -SOB-

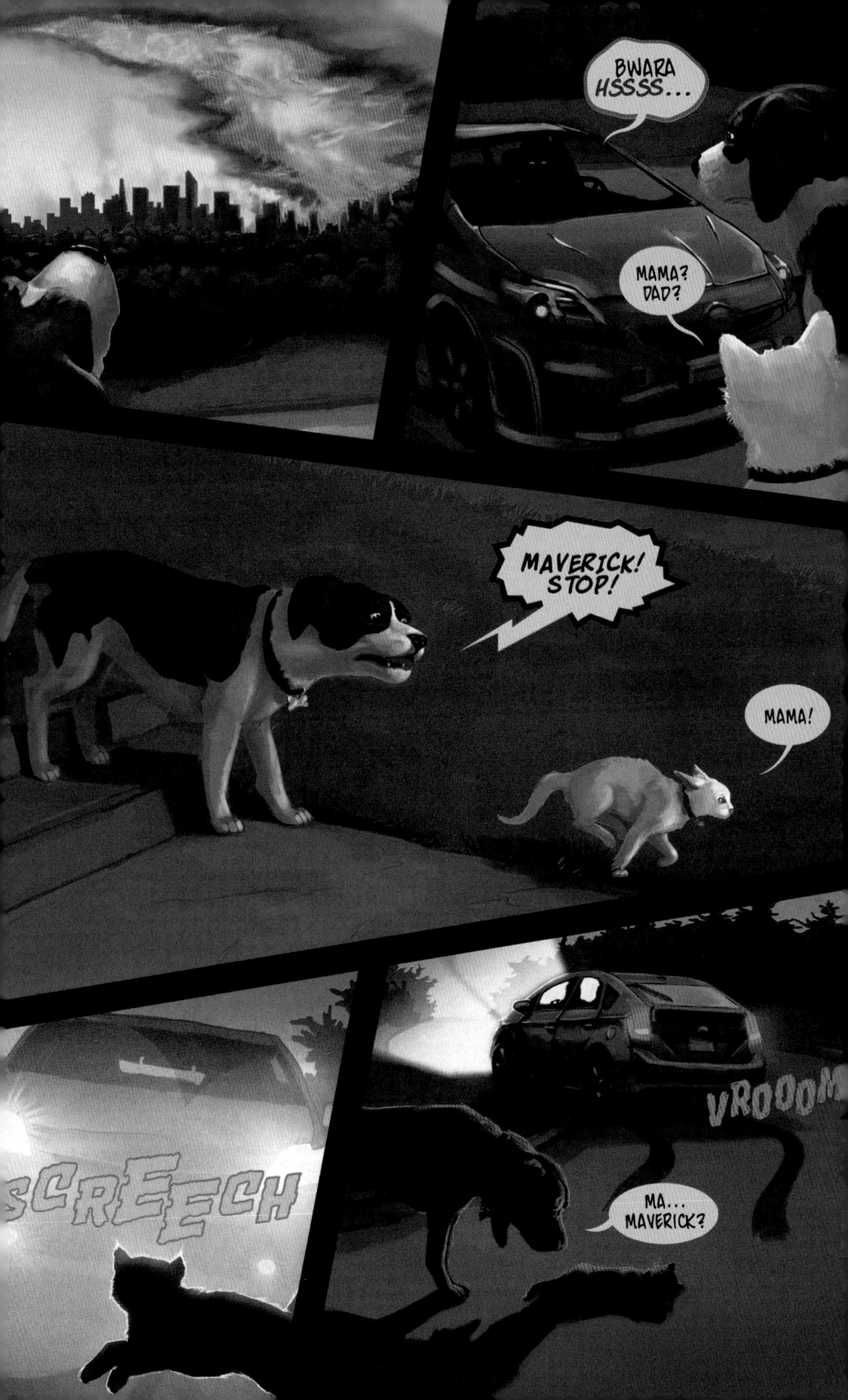
BWARA HSSSS...
MAMA? DAD?
MAVERICK! STOP!
MAMA!
SCREECH
VROOOM
MA... MAVERICK?

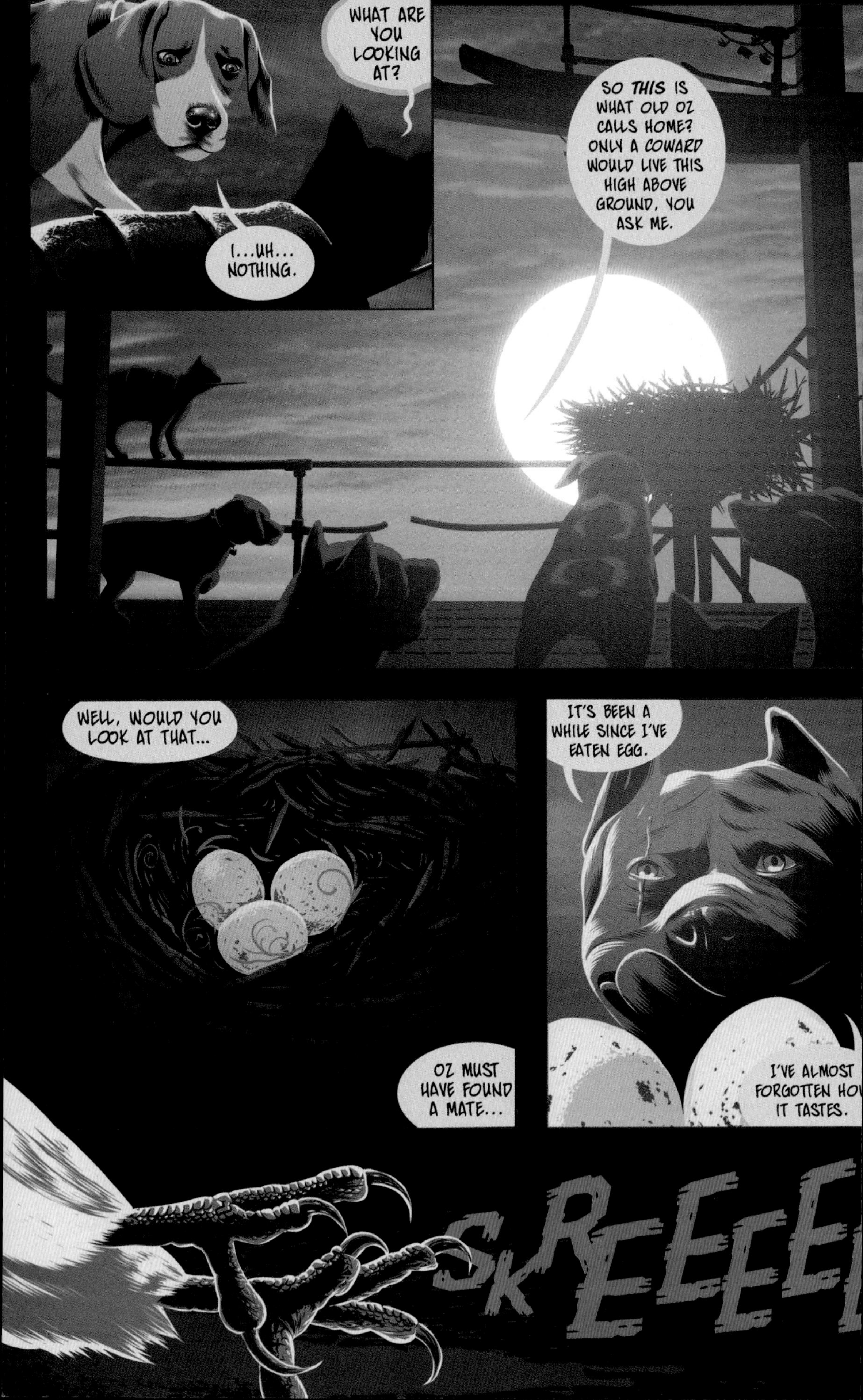
WHAT ARE YOU LOOKING AT?
I...UH... NOTHING.
SO THIS IS WHAT OLD OZ CALLS HOME? ONLY A COWARD WOULD LIVE THIS HIGH ABOVE GROUND, YOU ASK ME.
WELL, WOULD YOU LOOK AT THAT...
OZ MUST HAVE FOUND A MATE...
IT'S BEEN A WHILE SINCE I'VE EATEN EGG.
I'VE ALMOST FORGOTTEN HOW IT TASTES.
SKREEEE

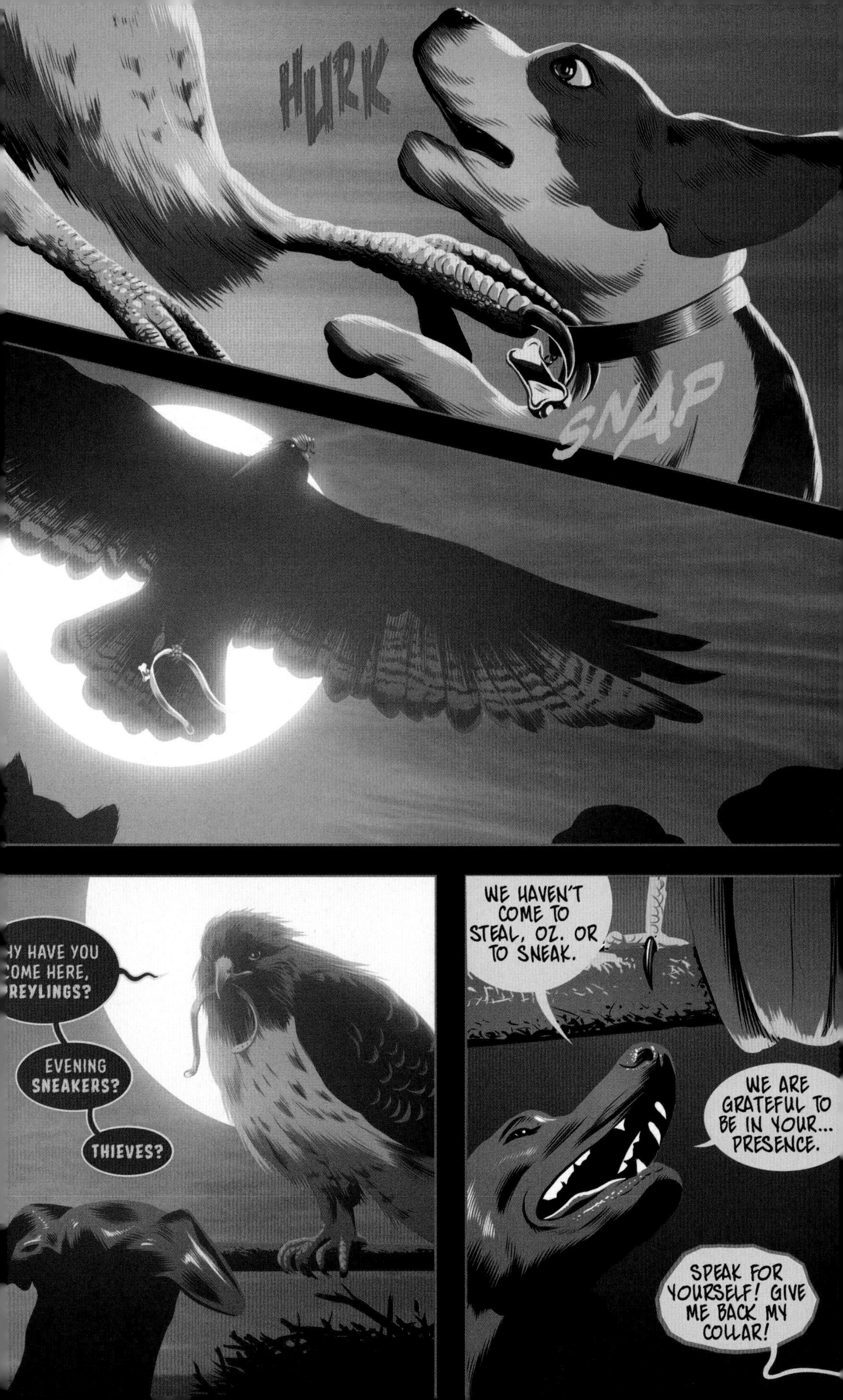
HURK
SNAP
HY HAVE YOU OME HERE, REYLINGS?
EVENING SNEAKERS?
THIEVES?
WE HAVEN'T COME TO STEAL, OZ. OR TO SNEAK.
WE ARE GRATEFUL TO BE IN YOUR... PRESENCE.
SPEAK FOR YOURSELF! GIVE ME BACK MY COLLAR!

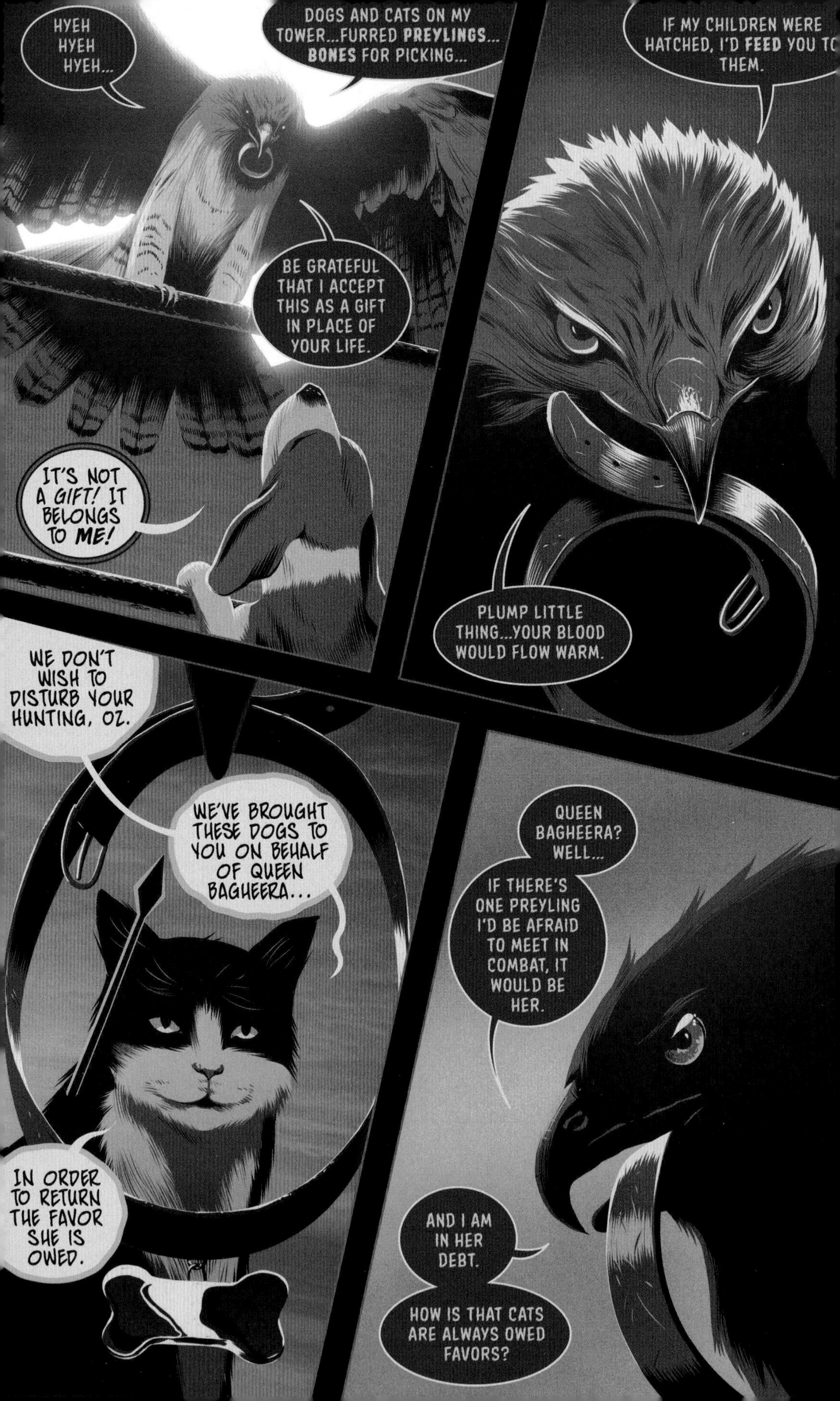
HYEH HYEH HYEH...
DOGS AND CATS ON MY TOWER...FURRED **PREYLINGS**... **BONES** FOR PICKING...
BE GRATEFUL THAT I ACCEPT THIS AS A GIFT IN PLACE OF YOUR LIFE.
IT'S NOT A GIFT! IT BELONGS TO **ME!**
IF MY CHILDREN WERE HATCHED, I'D **FEED** YOU TO THEM.
PLUMP LITTLE THING...YOUR BLOOD WOULD FLOW WARM.
WE DON'T WISH TO DISTURB YOUR HUNTING, OZ.
WE'VE BROUGHT THESE DOGS TO YOU ON BEHALF OF QUEEN BAGHEERA...
IN ORDER TO RETURN THE FAVOR SHE IS OWED.
QUEEN BAGHEERA? WELL...
IF THERE'S ONE PREYLING I'D BE AFRAID TO MEET IN COMBAT, IT WOULD BE HER.
AND I AM IN HER DEBT.
HOW IS THAT CATS ARE ALWAYS OWED FAVORS?

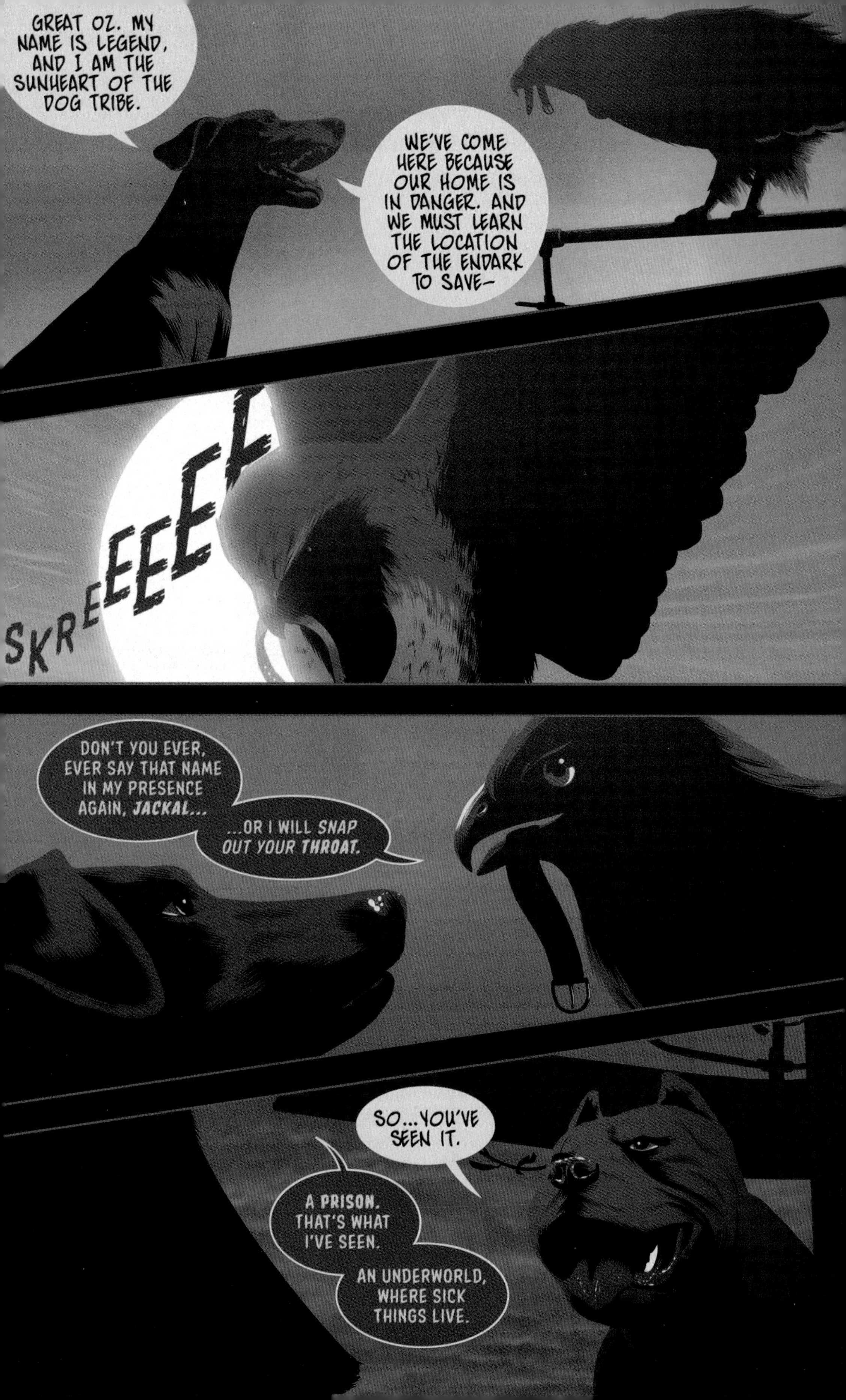
GREAT OZ. MY NAME IS LEGEND, AND I AM THE SUNHEART OF THE DOG TRIBE.
WE'VE COME HERE BECAUSE OUR HOME IS IN DANGER. AND WE MUST LEARN THE LOCATION OF THE ENDARK TO SAVE–
SKREEEEE
DON'T YOU EVER, EVER SAY THAT NAME IN MY PRESENCE AGAIN, JACKAL...
...OR I WILL SNAP OUT YOUR THROAT.
SO...YOU'VE SEEN IT.
A PRISON. THAT'S WHAT I'VE SEEN.
AN UNDERWORLD, WHERE SICK THINGS LIVE.

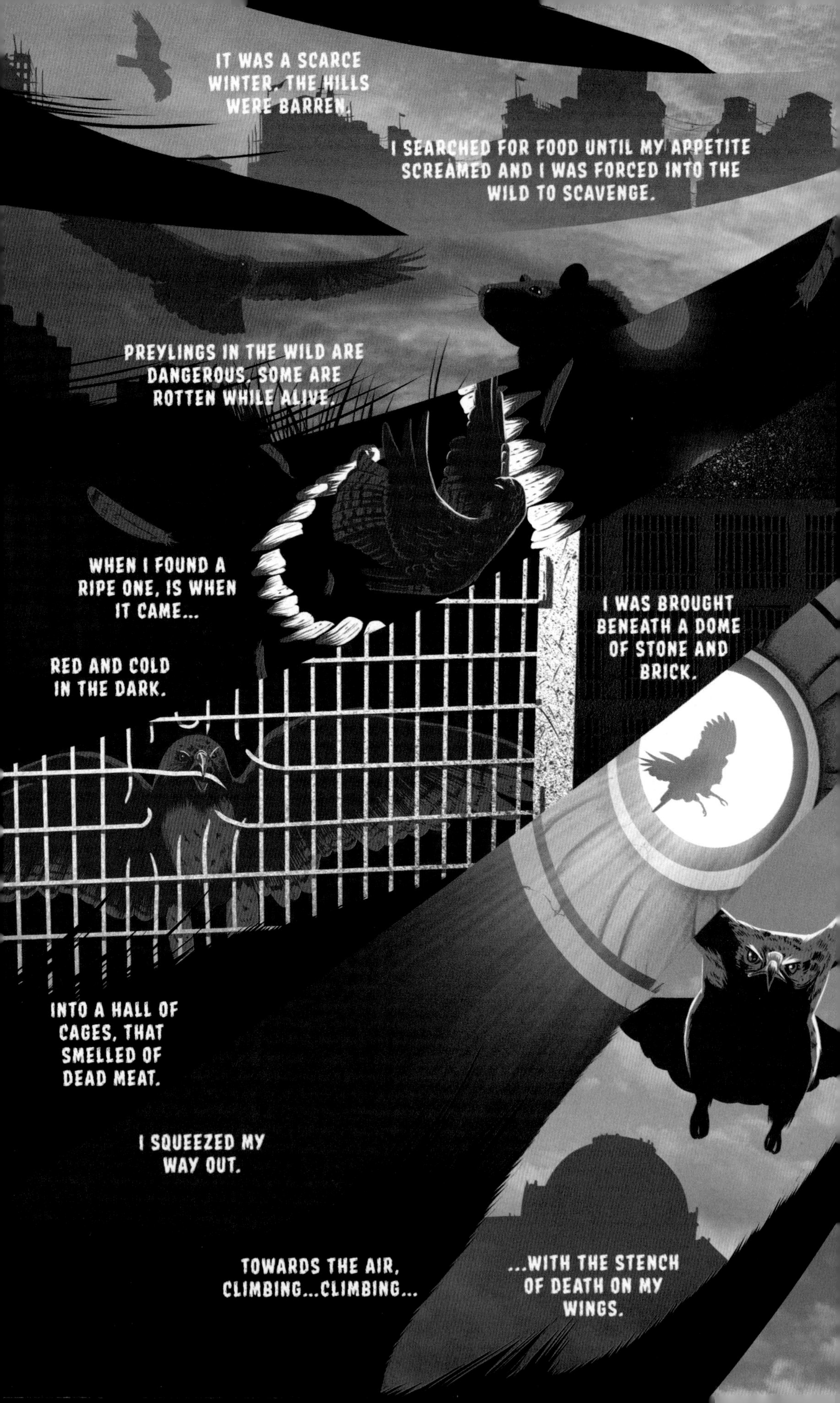
IT WAS A SCARCE WINTER. THE HILLS WERE BARREN.
I SEARCHED FOR FOOD UNTIL MY APPETITE SCREAMED AND I WAS FORCED INTO THE WILD TO SCAVENGE.
PREYLINGS IN THE WILD ARE DANGEROUS. SOME ARE ROTTEN WHILE ALIVE.
WHEN I FOUND A RIPE ONE, IS WHEN IT CAME...
RED AND COLD IN THE DARK.
I WAS BROUGHT BENEATH A DOME OF STONE AND BRICK.
INTO A HALL OF CAGES, THAT SMELLED OF DEAD MEAT.
I SQUEEZED MY WAY OUT.
TOWARDS THE AIR, CLIMBING...CLIMBING...
...WITH THE STENCH OF DEATH ON MY WINGS.

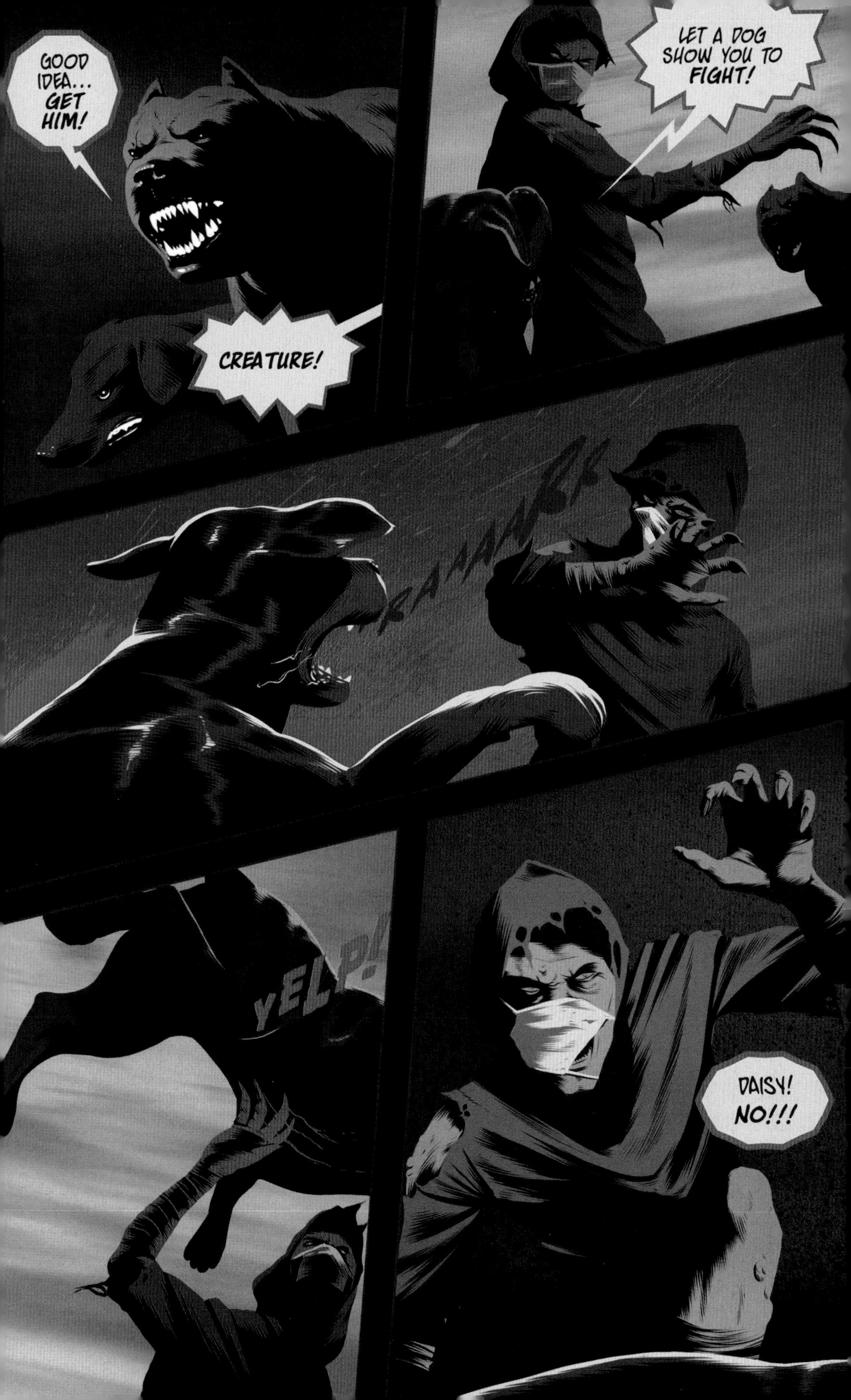
GOOD IDEA... GET HIM!
CREATURE!
LET A DOG SHOW YOU TO FIGHT!
YELP!!
DAISY! NO!!!

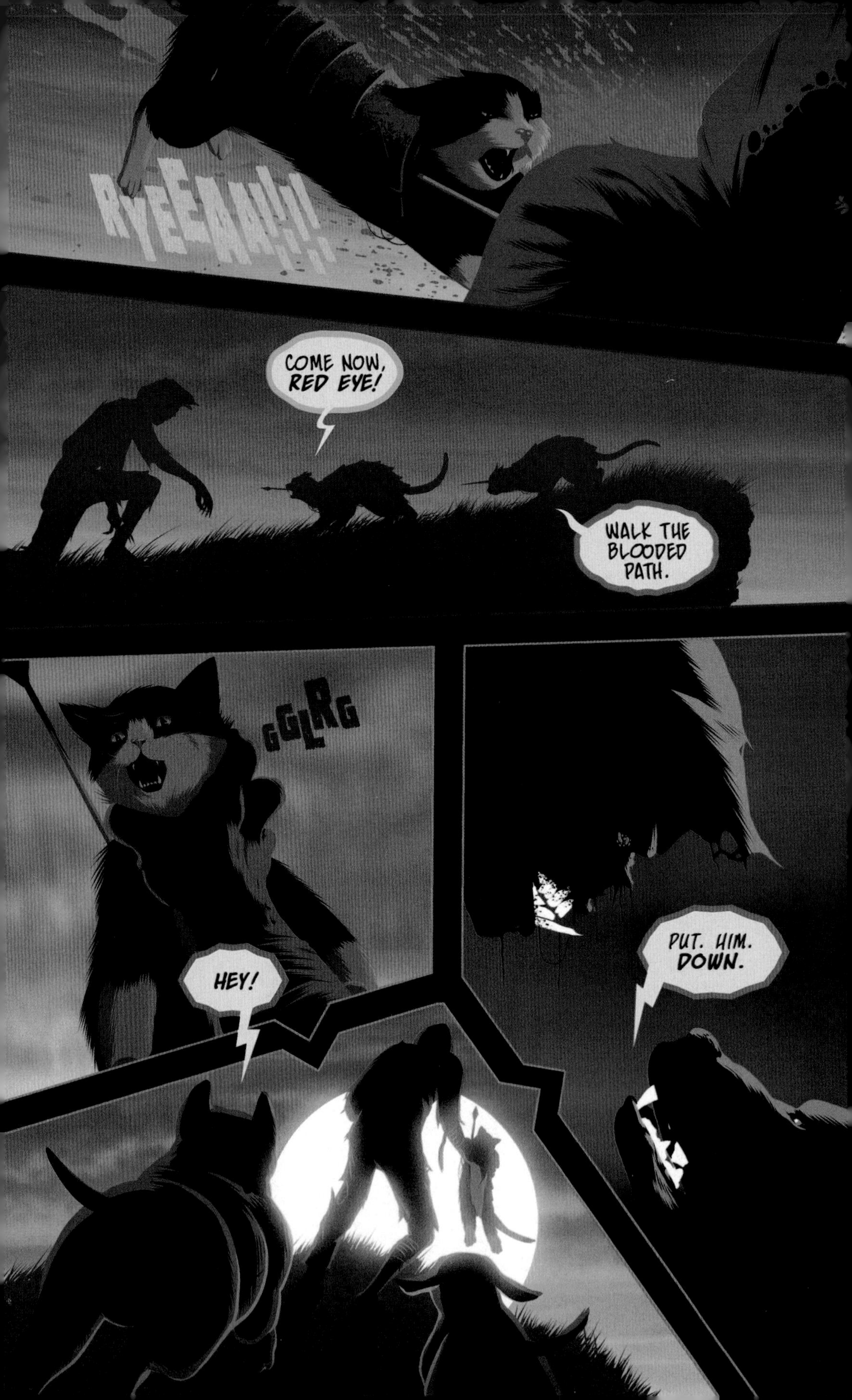
RYEEAAH!!!
COME NOW, RED EYE!
WALK THE BLOODED PATH.
GGLRG
HEY!
PUT. HIM. DOWN.

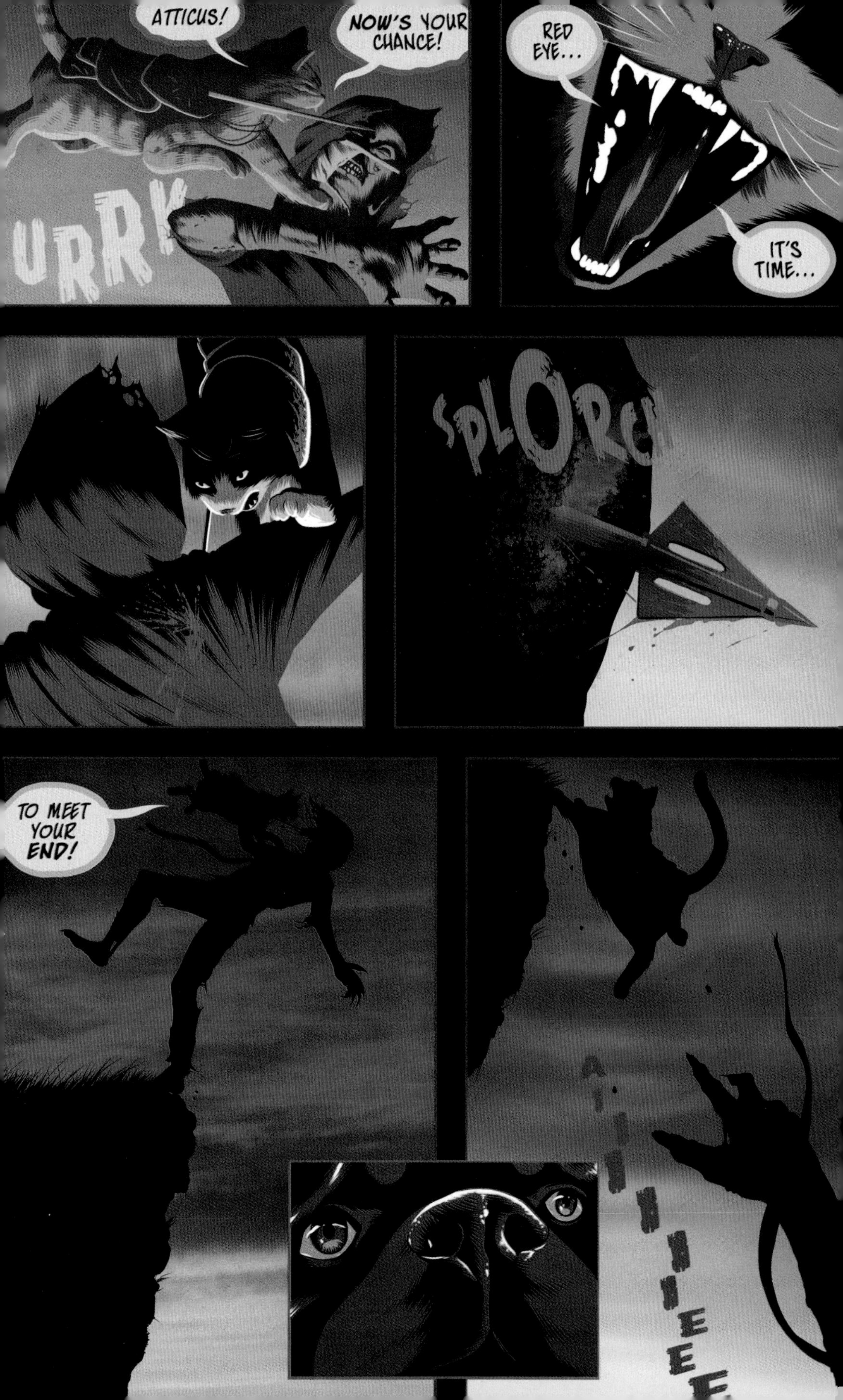
ATTICUS!
NOW'S YOUR CHANCE!
URRK
RED EYE...
IT'S TIME...
SPLORC
TO MEET YOUR END!
AIIIIIIEEE

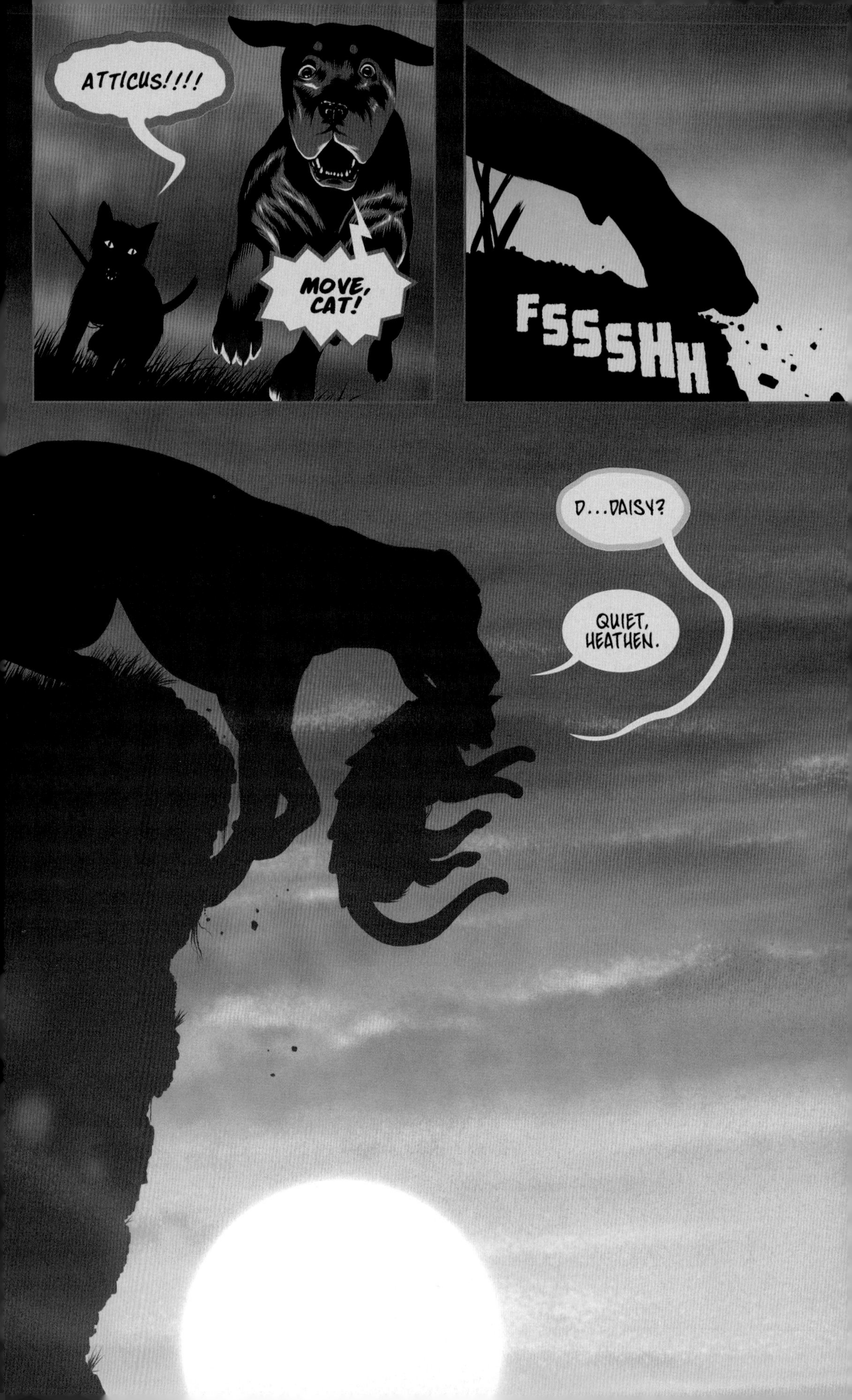
ATTICUS!!!!
MOVE, CAT!
FSSSHH
D...DAISY?
QUIET, HEATHEN.

CHAPTER FIVE

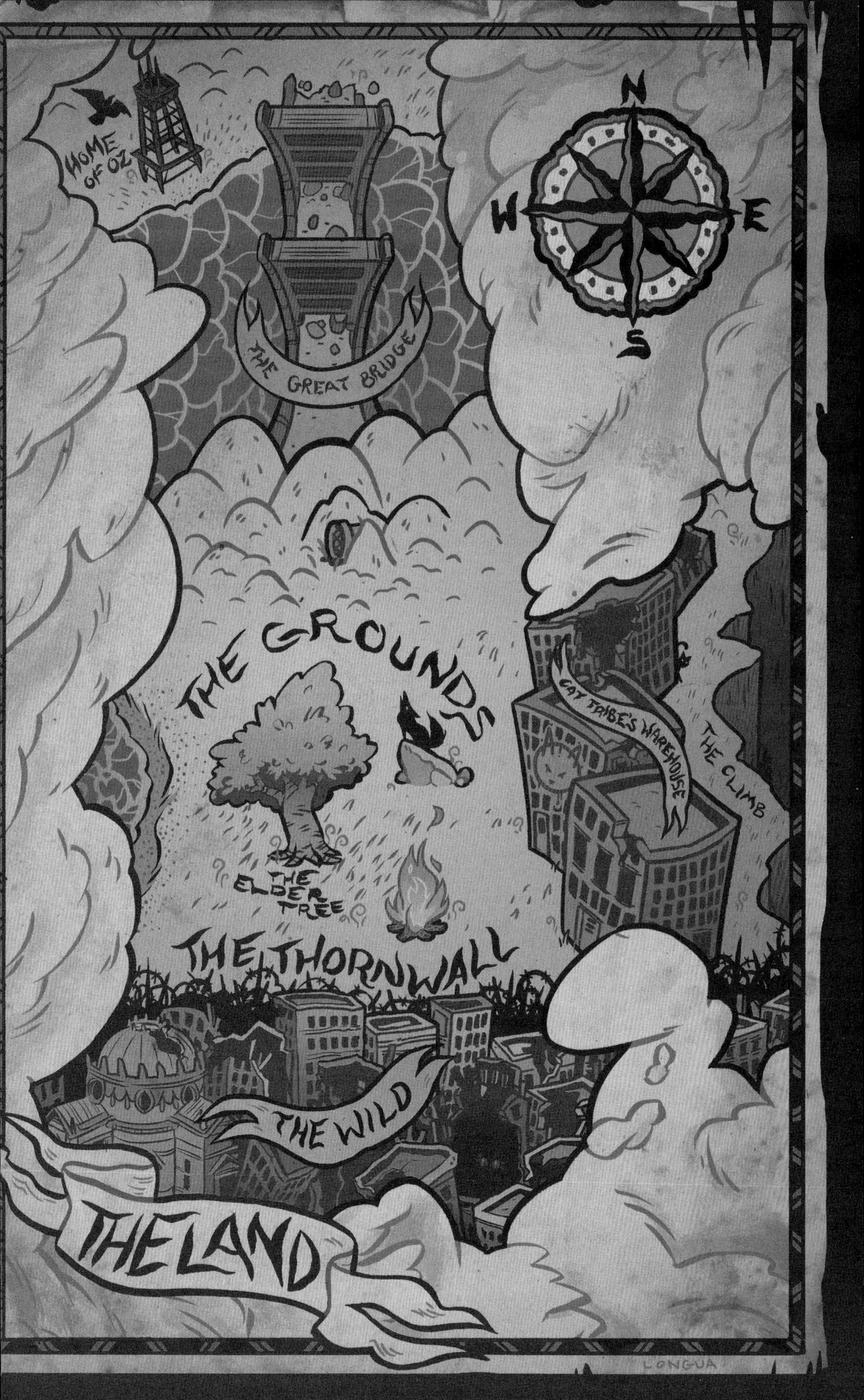
HOME OF OZ
THE GREAT BRIDGE
N
W
E
S
THE GROUNDS
CAT TRIBE'S WAREHOUSE
THE CLIMB
THE ELDER TREE
THE THORNWALL
THE WILD
THELAND
LONGUA

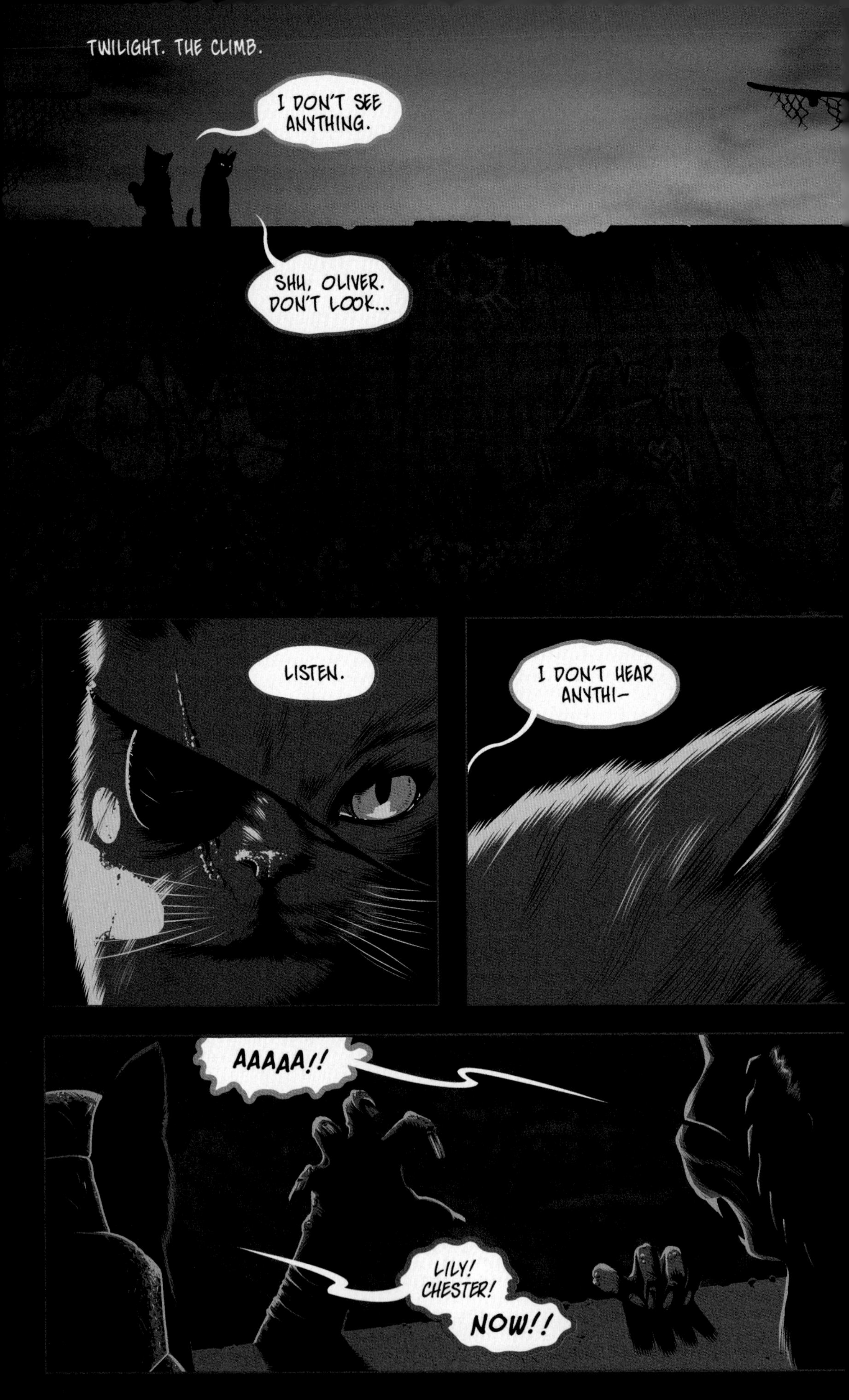
TWILIGHT. THE CLIMB.
I DON'T SEE ANYTHING.
SHH, OLIVER. DON'T LOOK...
LISTEN.
I DON'T HEAR ANYTHI–
AAAAA!!
LILY! CHESTER! NOW!!

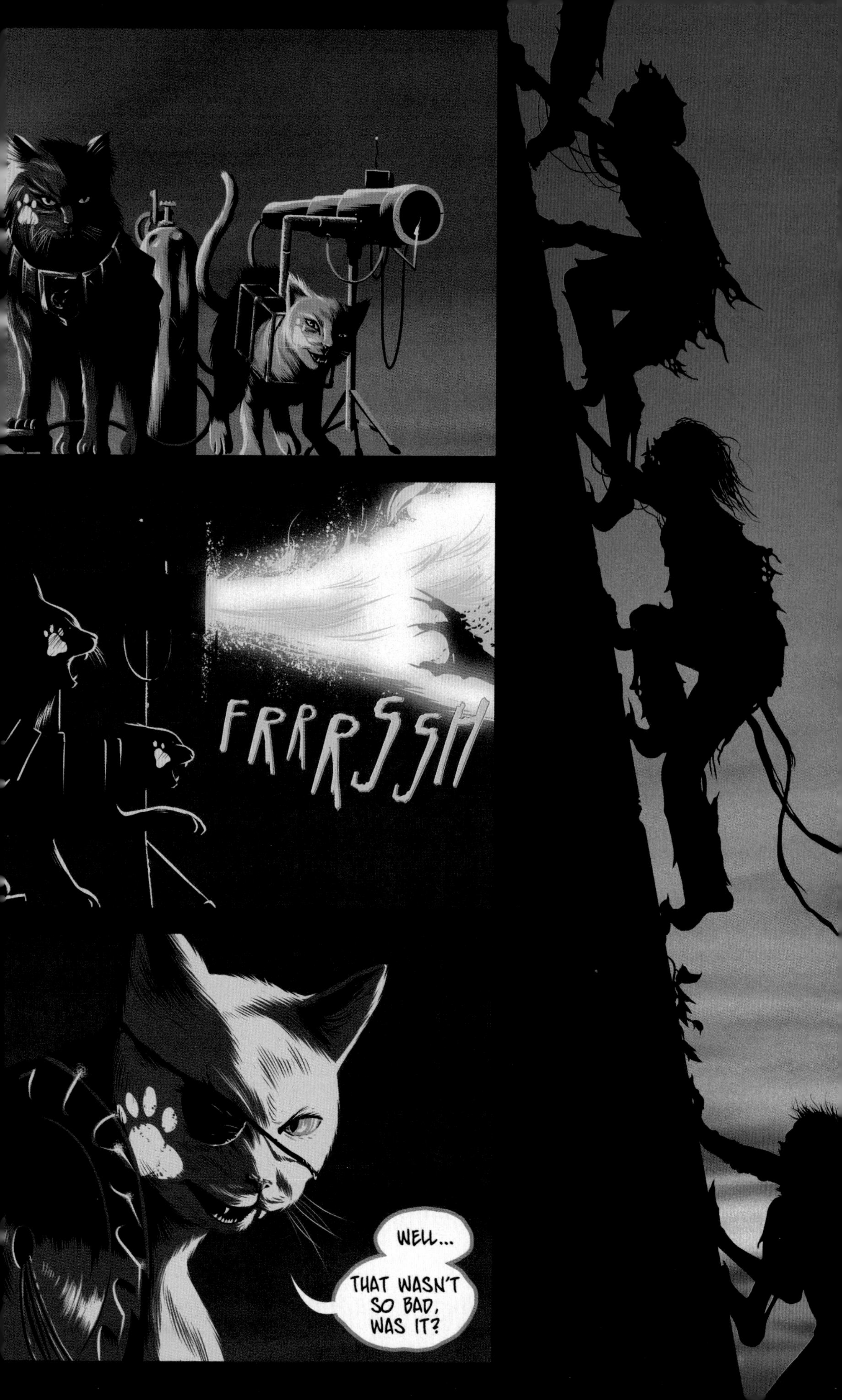
FRRRSSH
WELL...
THAT WASN'T SO BAD, WAS IT?

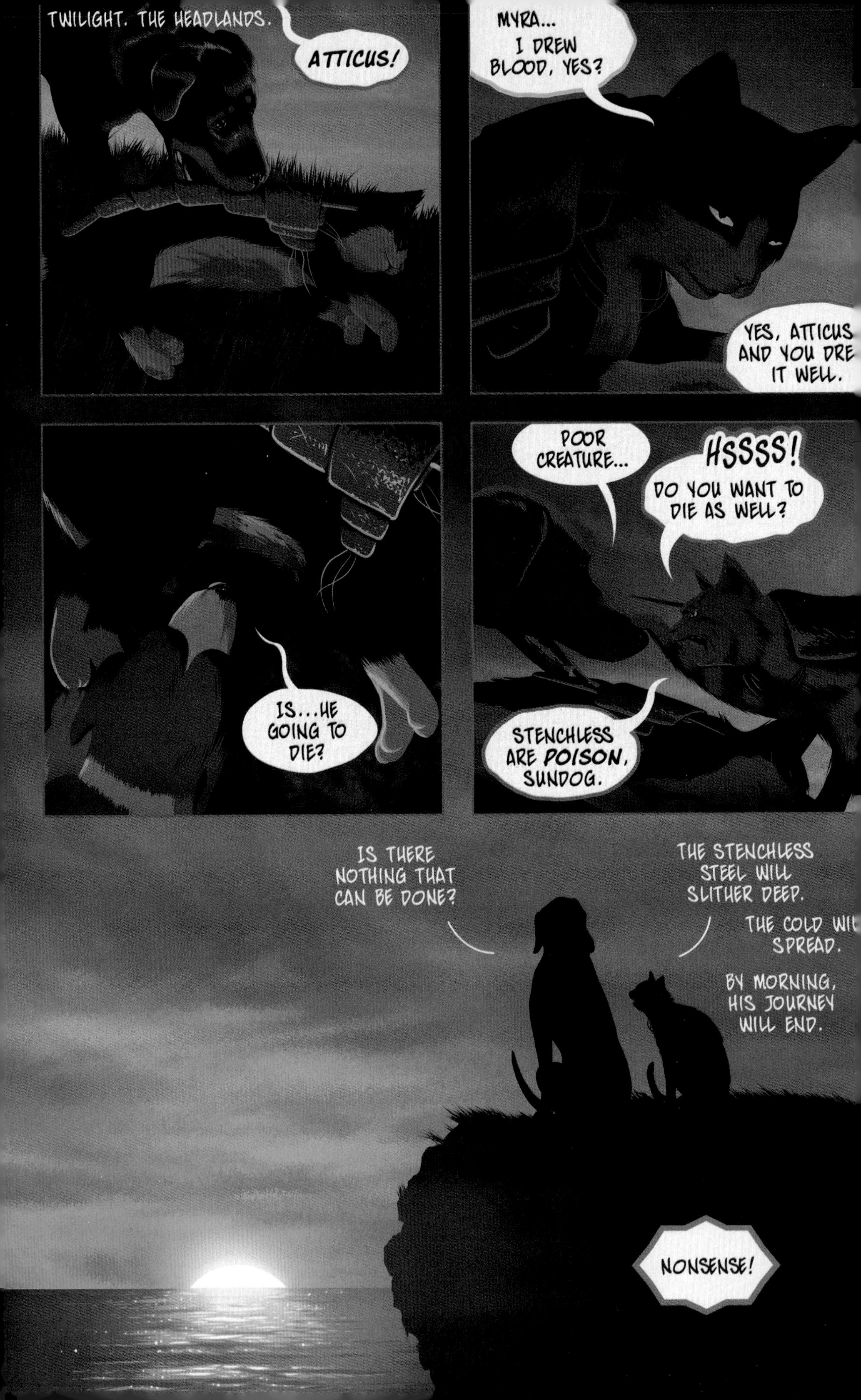
TWILIGHT. THE HEADLANDS.
ATTICUS!
MYRA... I DREW BLOOD, YES?
YES, ATTICUS AND YOU DRE IT WELL.
IS...HE GOING TO DIE?
POOR CREATURE...
HSSSS! DO YOU WANT TO DIE AS WELL?
STENCHLESS ARE POISON, SUNDOG.
IS THERE NOTHING THAT CAN BE DONE?
THE STENCHLESS STEEL WILL SLITHER DEEP.
THE COLD WI SPREAD.
BY MORNING, HIS JOURNEY WILL END.
NONSENSE!

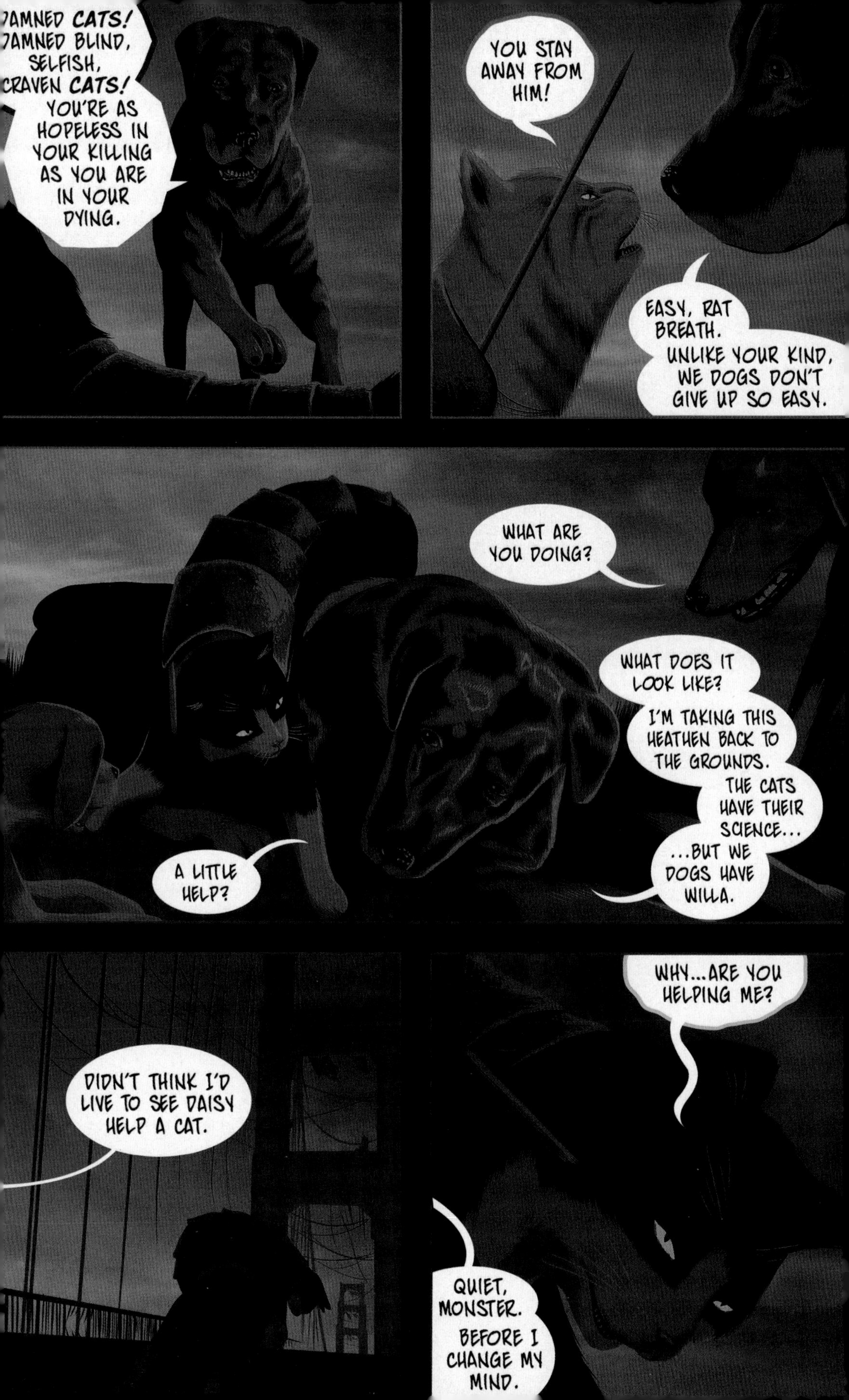
DAMNED CATS! DAMNED BLIND, SELFISH, CRAVEN CATS!
YOU'RE AS HOPELESS IN YOUR KILLING AS YOU ARE IN YOUR DYING.
YOU STAY AWAY FROM HIM!
EASY, RAT BREATH.
UNLIKE YOUR KIND, WE DOGS DON'T GIVE UP SO EASY.
WHAT ARE YOU DOING?
WHAT DOES IT LOOK LIKE?
I'M TAKING THIS HEATHEN BACK TO THE GROUNDS.
THE CATS HAVE THEIR SCIENCE...
...BUT WE DOGS HAVE WILLA.
A LITTLE HELP?
DIDN'T THINK I'D LIVE TO SEE DAISY HELP A CAT.
WHY...ARE YOU HELPING ME?
QUIET, MONSTER.
BEFORE I CHANGE MY MIND.

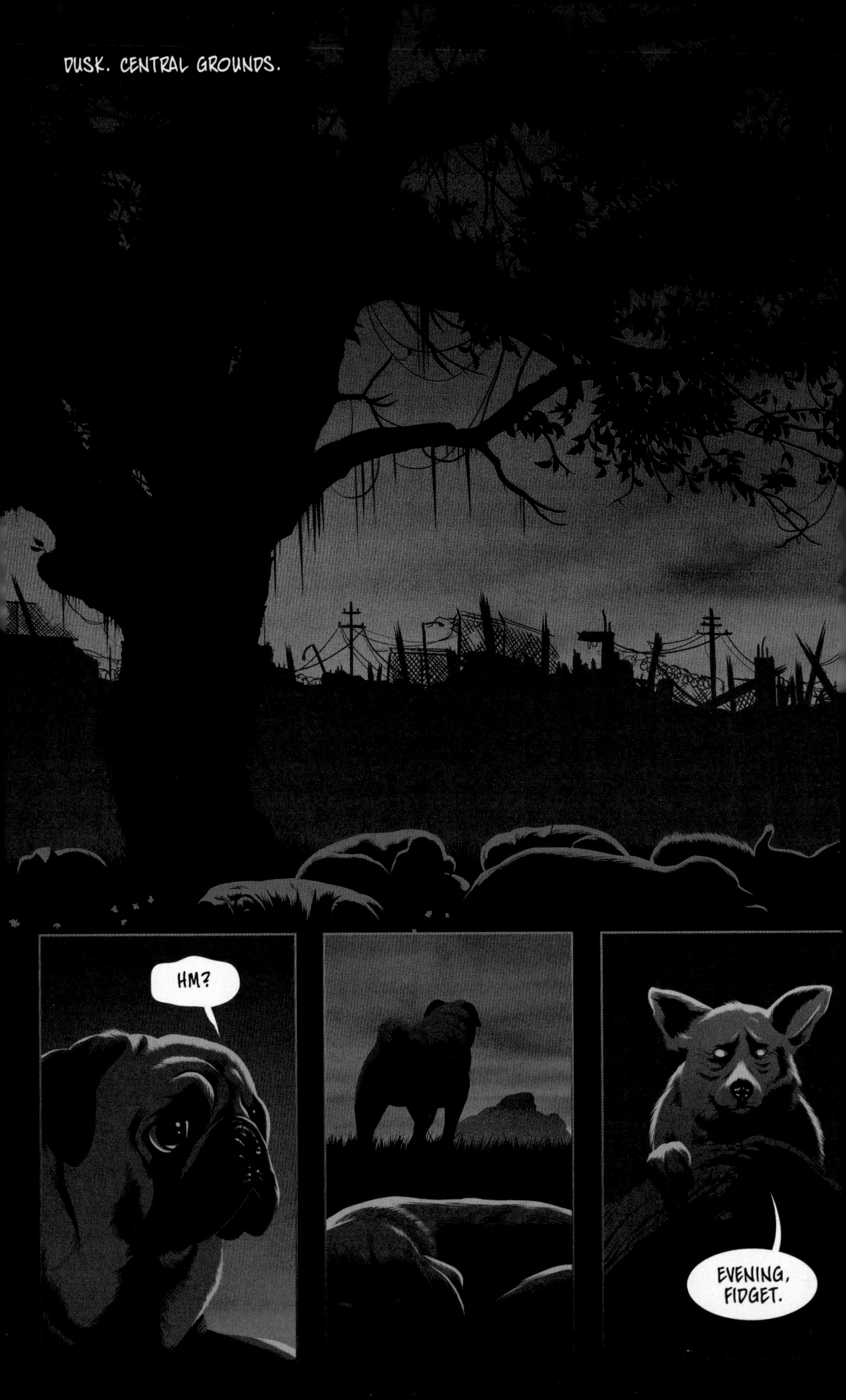
DUSK. CENTRAL GROUNDS.
HM?
EVENING, FIDGET.

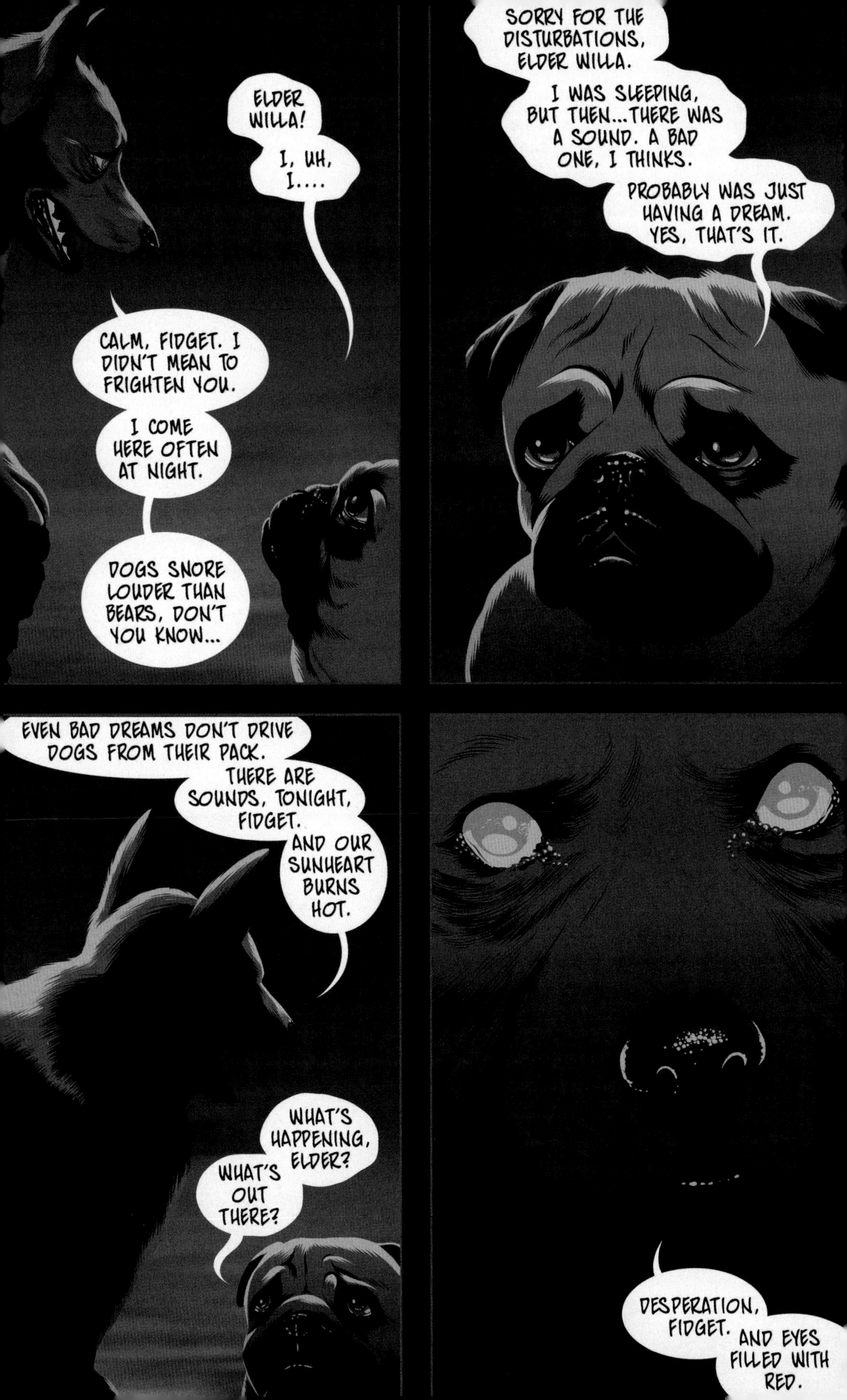
ELDER WILLA!
I, UH, I....
CALM, FIDGET. I DIDN'T MEAN TO FRIGHTEN YOU.
I COME HERE OFTEN AT NIGHT.
DOGS SNORE LOUDER THAN BEARS, DON'T YOU KNOW...
SORRY FOR THE DISTURBATIONS, ELDER WILLA.
I WAS SLEEPING, BUT THEN...THERE WAS A SOUND. A BAD ONE, I THINKS.
PROBABLY WAS JUST HAVING A DREAM. YES, THAT'S IT.
EVEN BAD DREAMS DON'T DRIVE DOGS FROM THEIR PACK.
THERE ARE SOUNDS, TONIGHT, FIDGET.
AND OUR SUNHEART BURNS HOT.
WHAT'S HAPPENING, ELDER?
WHAT'S OUT THERE?
DESPERATION, FIDGET.
AND EYES FILLED WITH RED.

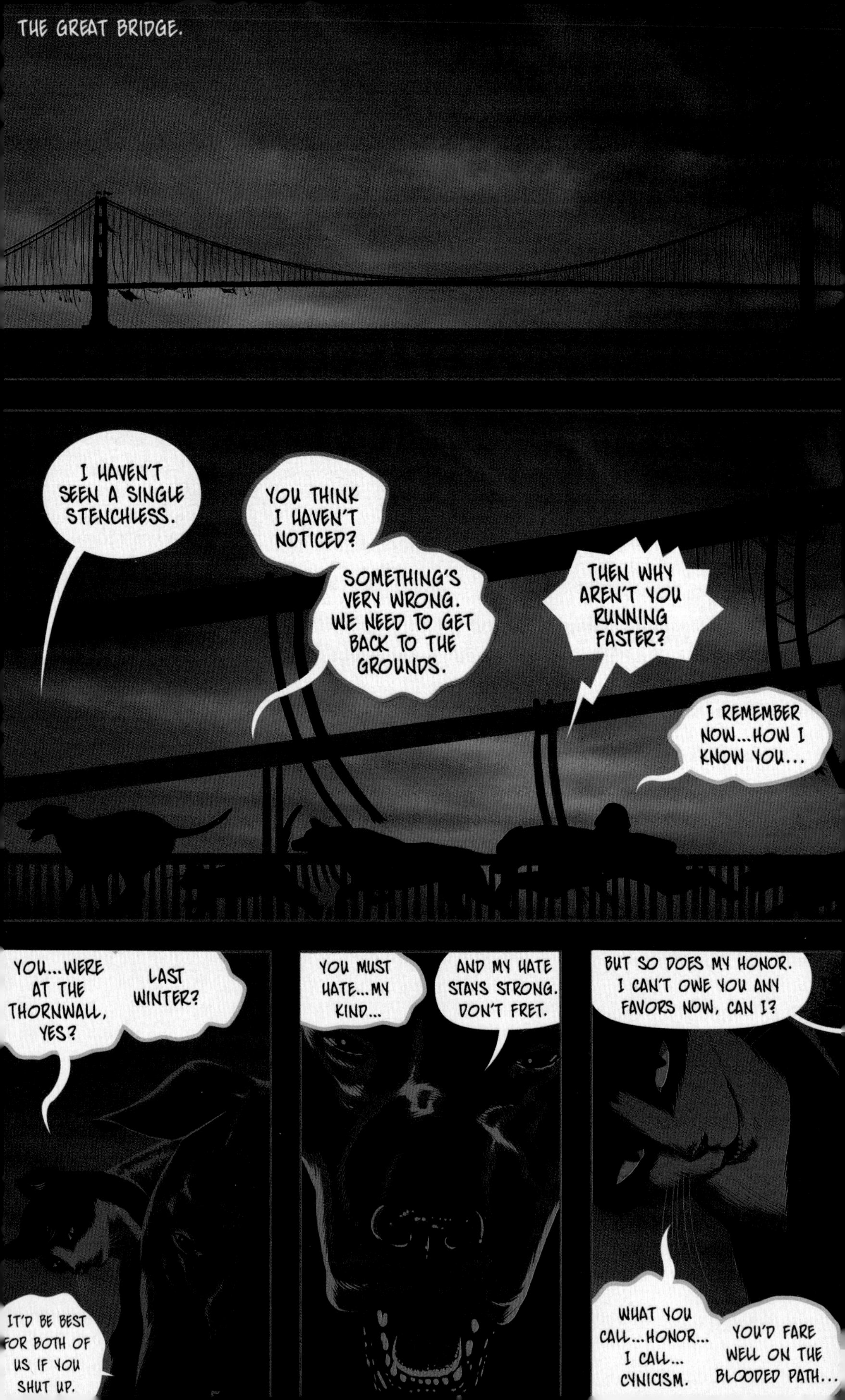
THE GREAT BRIDGE.
I HAVEN'T SEEN A SINGLE STENCHLESS.
YOU THINK I HAVEN'T NOTICED?
SOMETHING'S VERY WRONG. WE NEED TO GET BACK TO THE GROUNDS.
THEN WHY AREN'T YOU RUNNING FASTER?
I REMEMBER NOW...HOW I KNOW YOU...
YOU...WERE AT THE THORNWALL, YES?
LAST WINTER?
IT'D BE BEST FOR BOTH OF US IF YOU SHUT UP.
YOU MUST HATE...MY KIND...
AND MY HATE STAYS STRONG. DON'T FRET.
BUT SO DOES MY HONOR. I CAN'T OWE YOU ANY FAVORS NOW, CAN I?
WHAT YOU CALL...HONOR... I CALL... CYNICISM.
YOU'D FARE WELL ON THE BLOODED PATH...

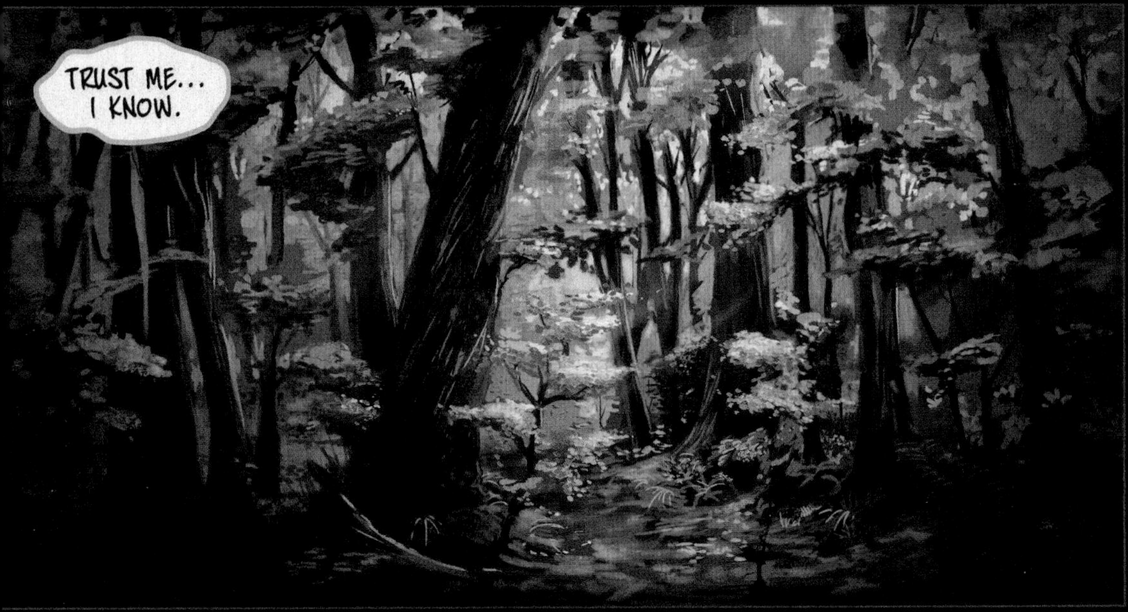
TRUST ME... I KNOW.
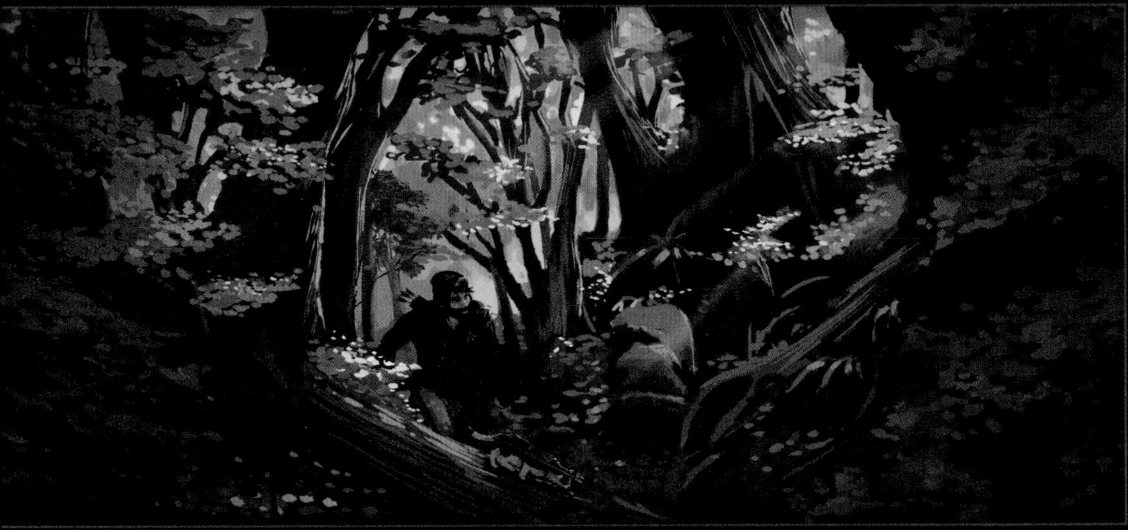
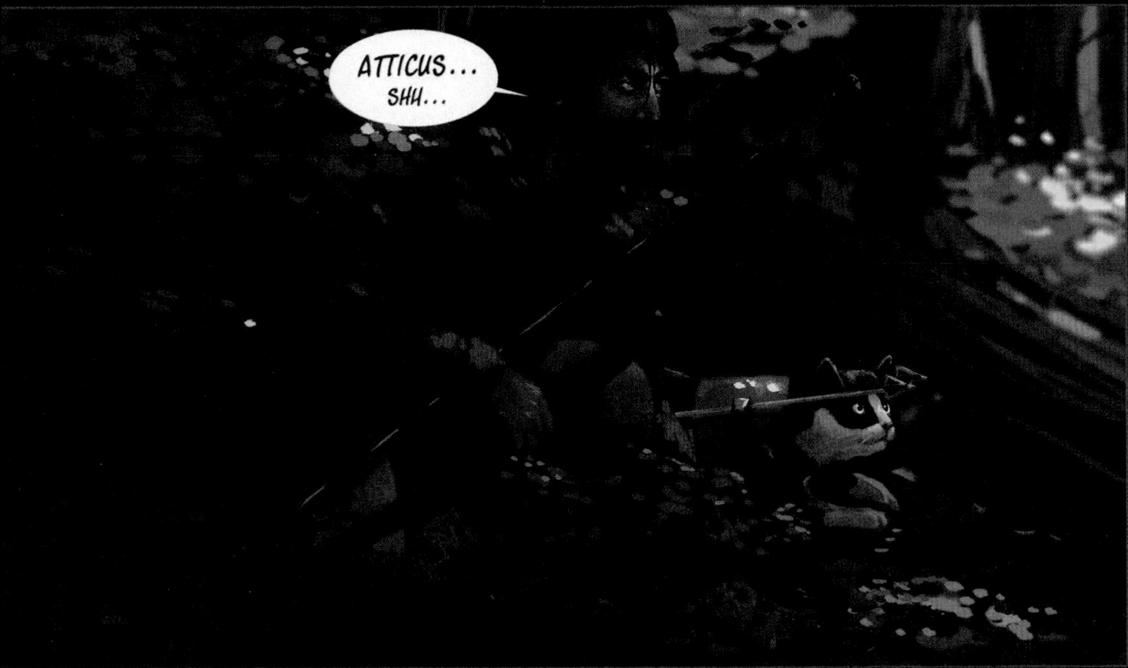
ATTICUS... SHH...

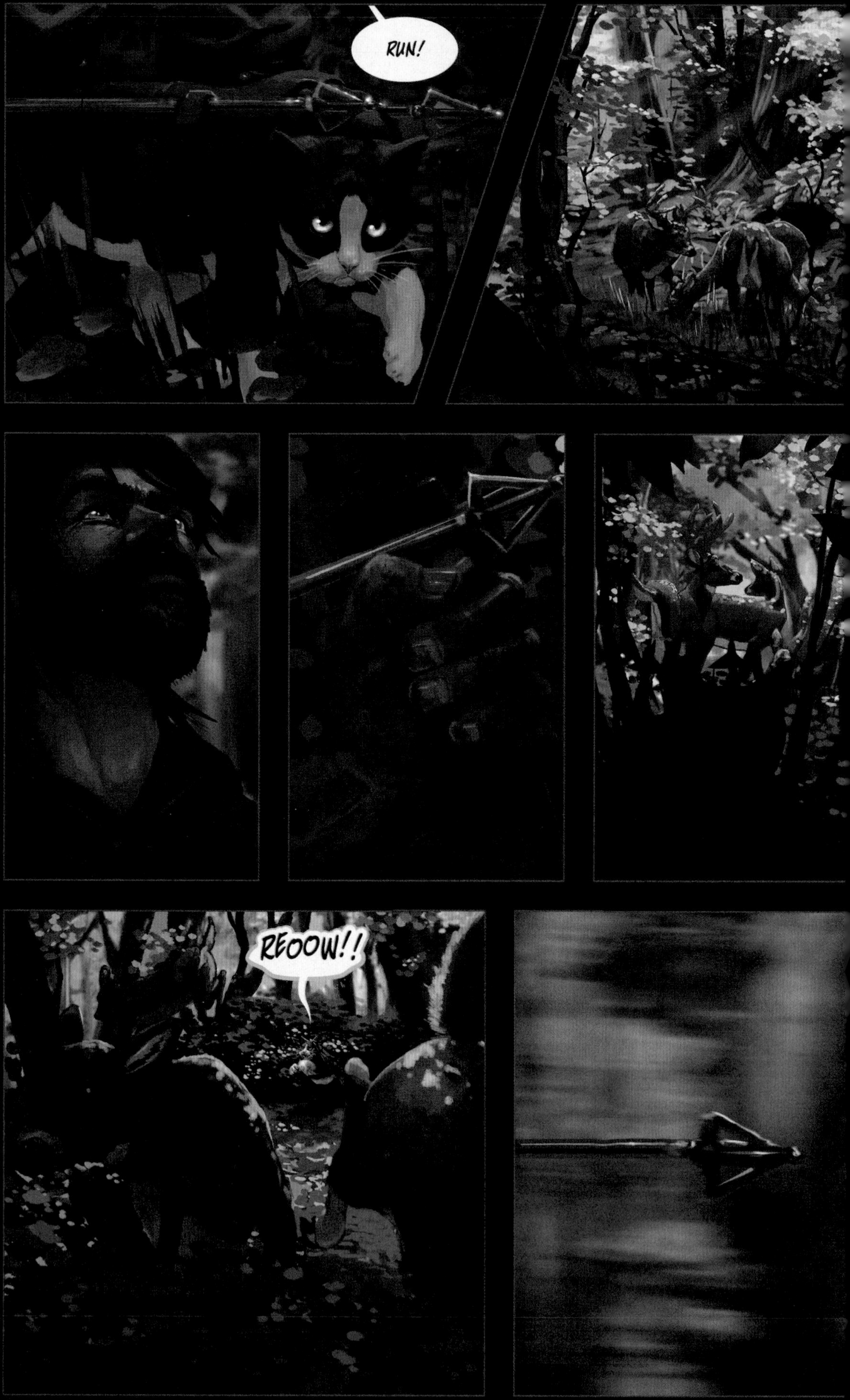
RUN!
REOOW!!

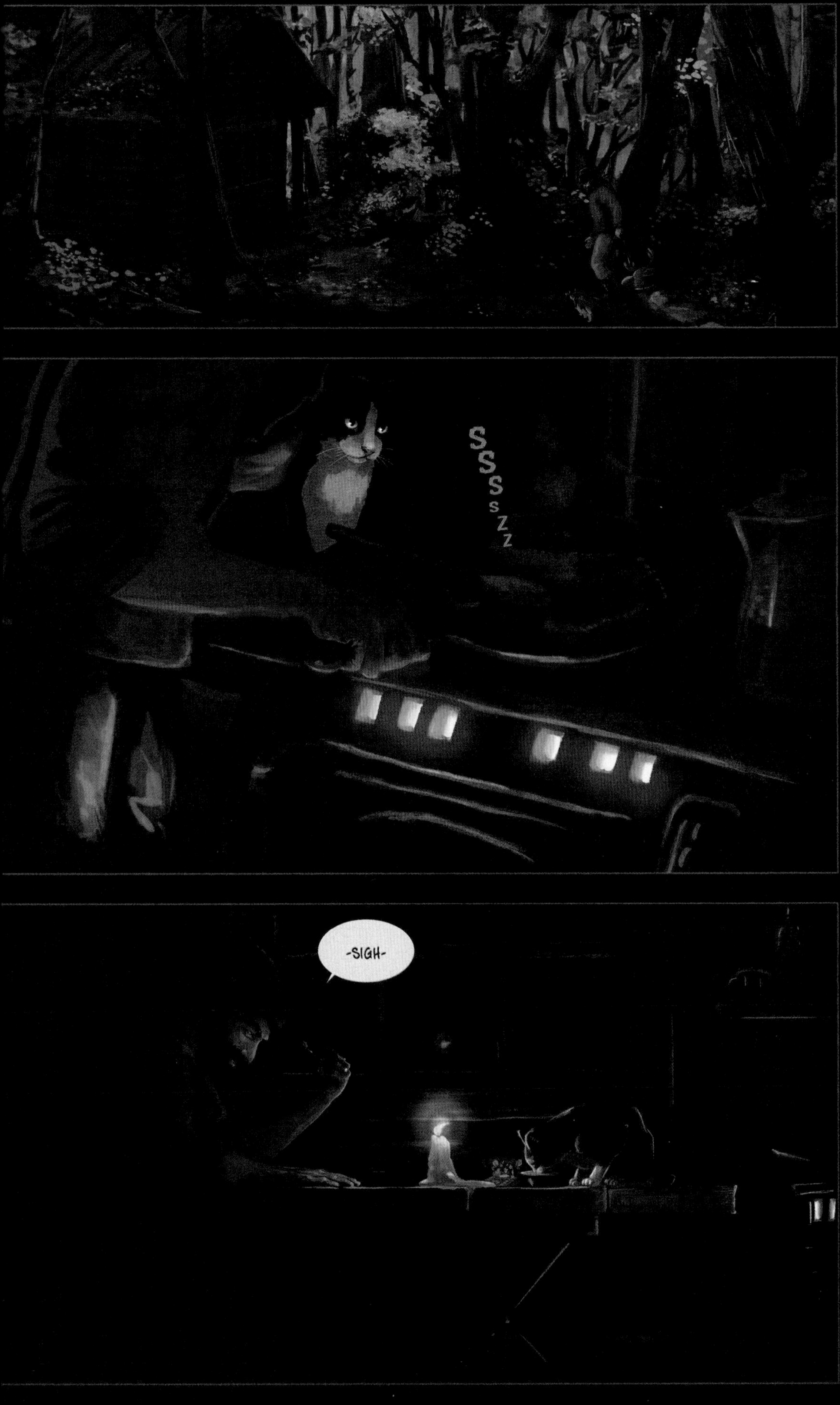
SSSsZZ
-SIGH-

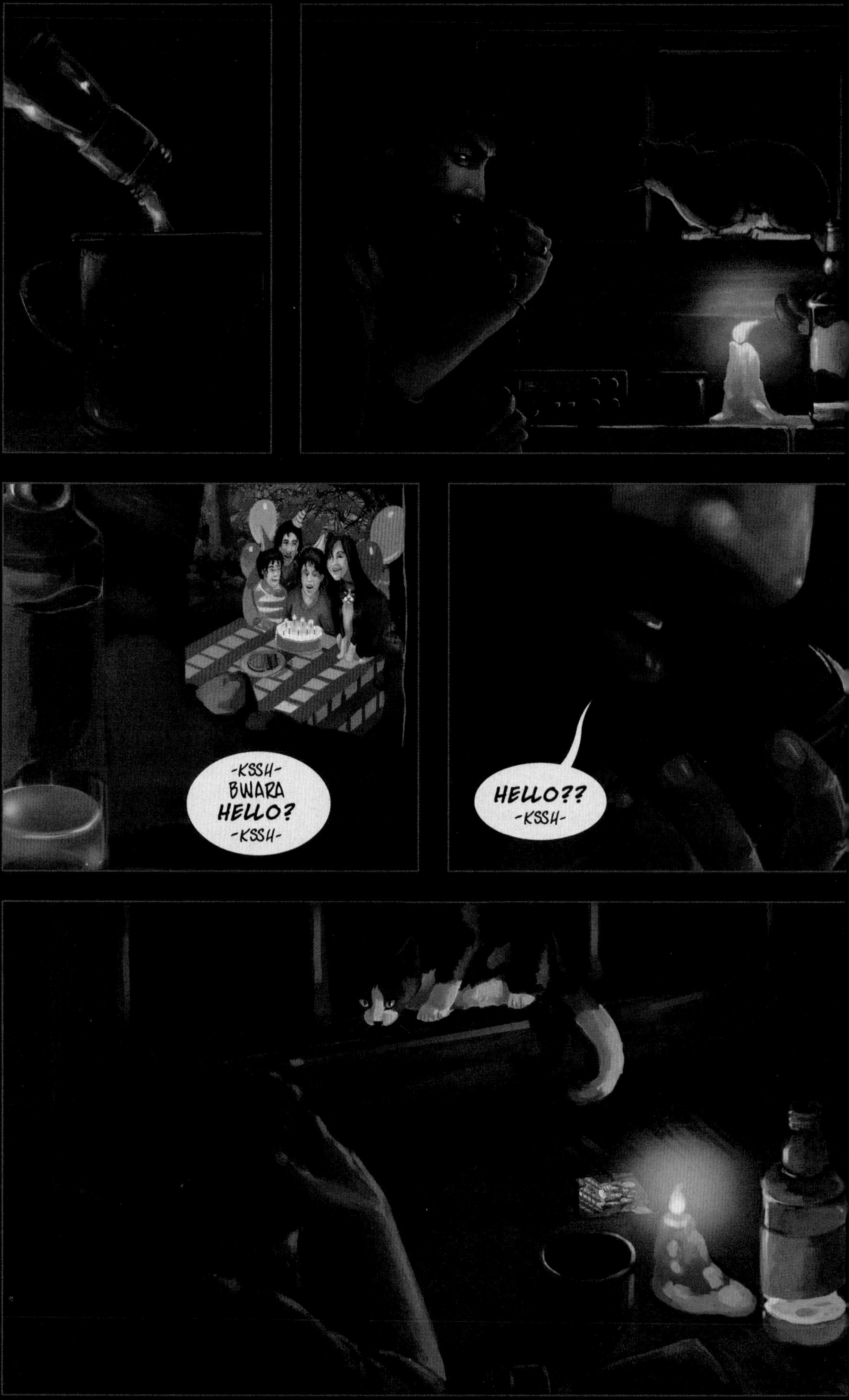
-KSSH- BWARA HELLO? -KSSH-
HELLO?? -KSSH-

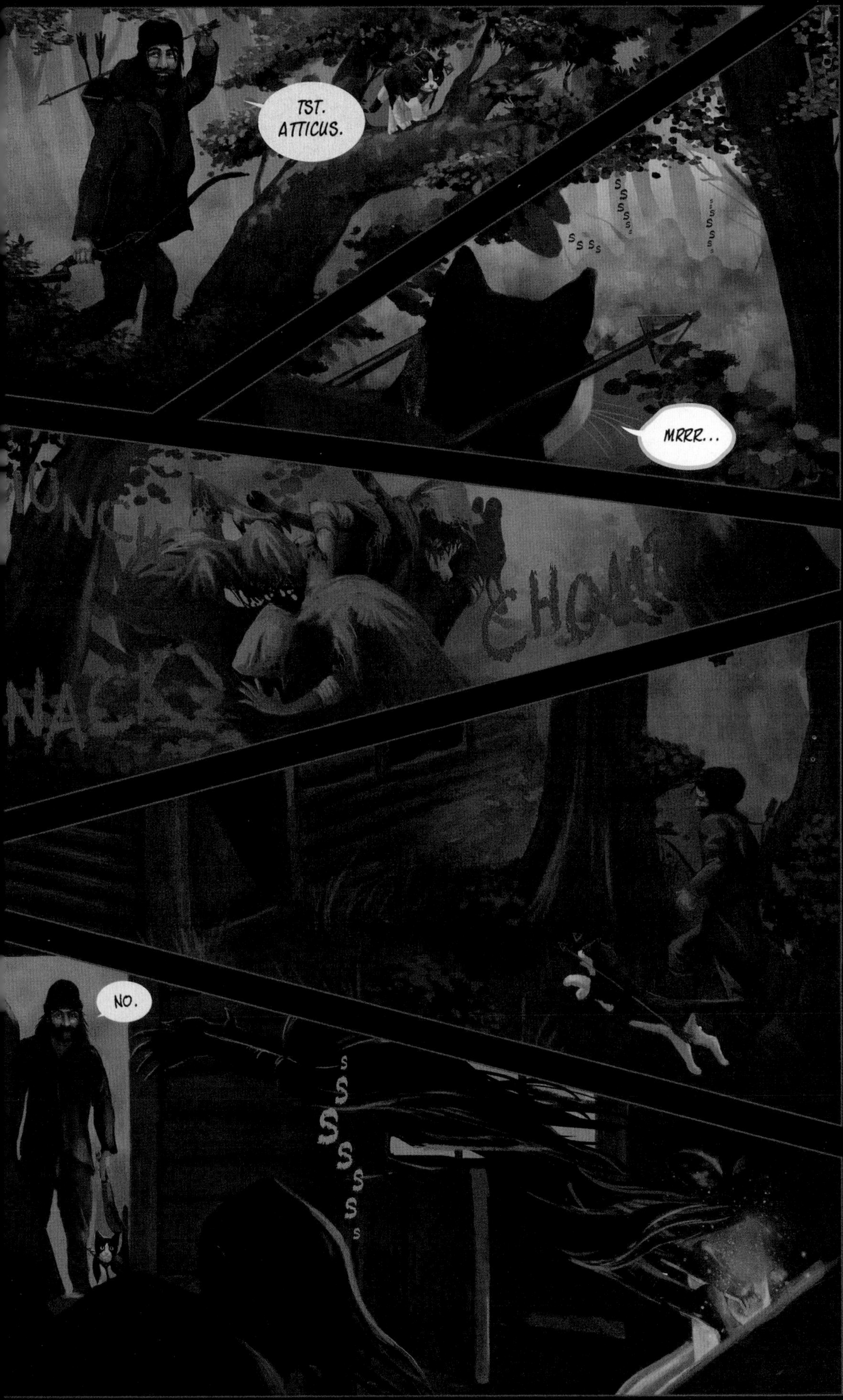
TST. ATTICUS.
MRRR...
NO.

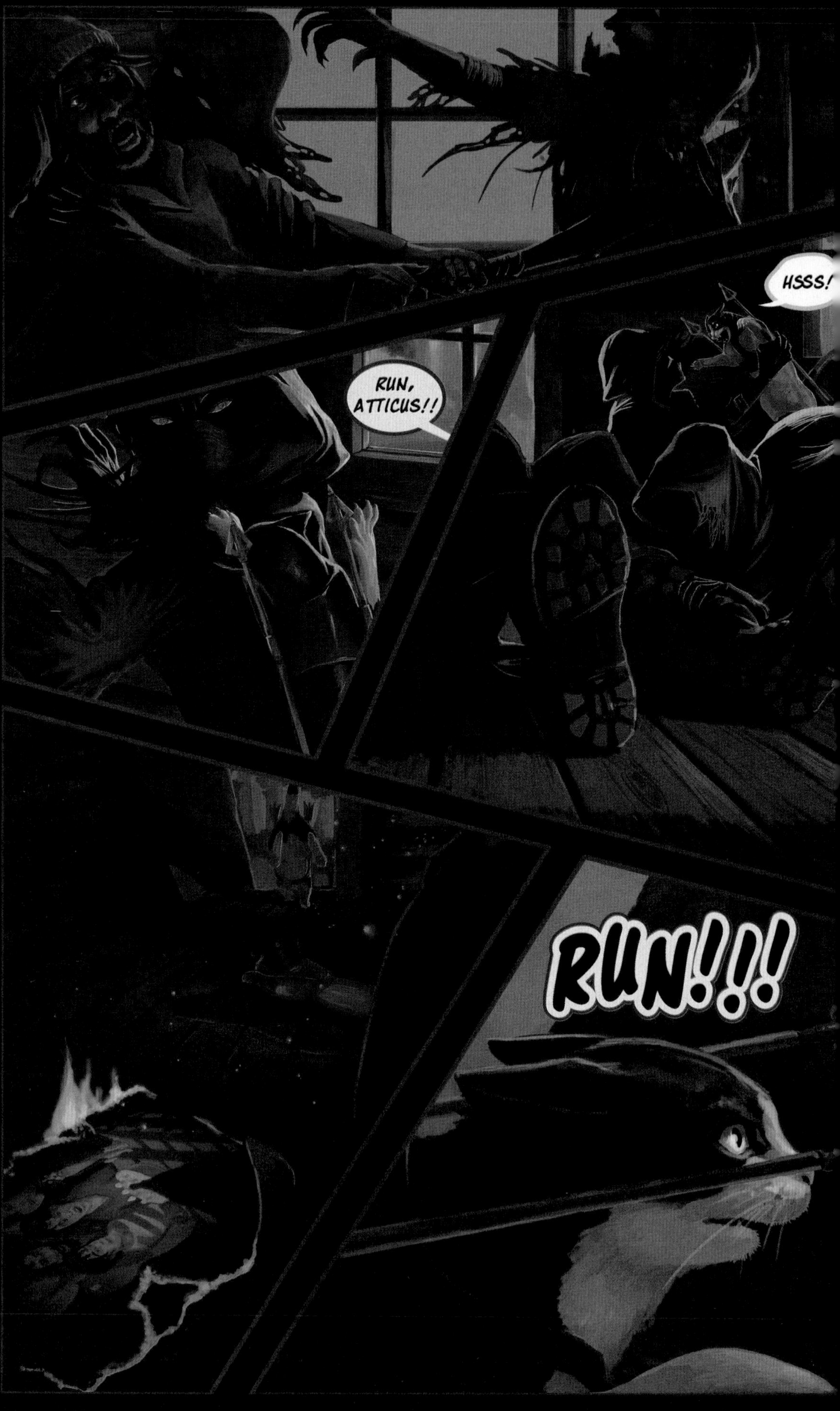
RUN, ATTICUS!!
HSSS!
RUN!!!

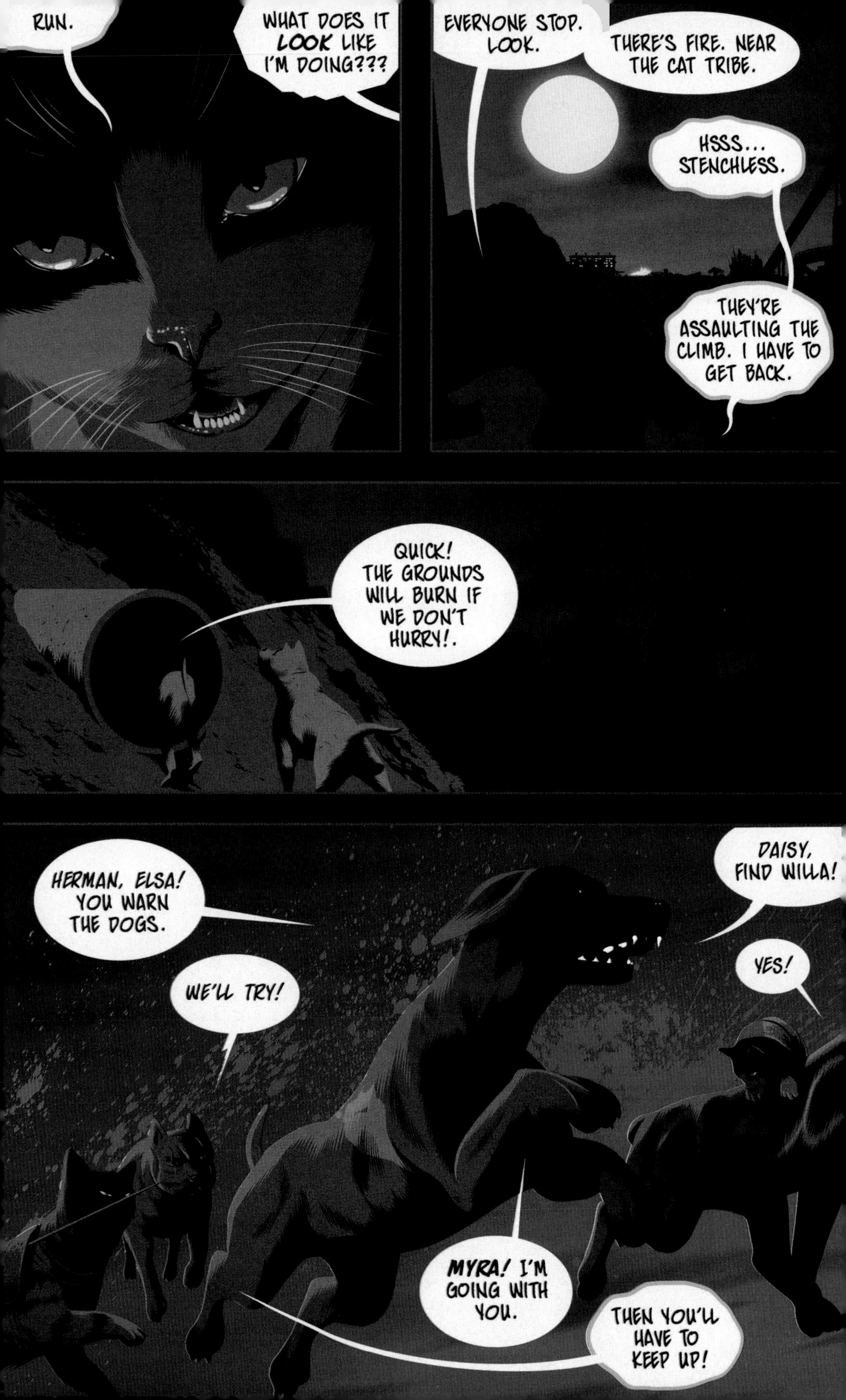
RUN.
WHAT DOES IT LOOK LIKE I'M DOING???
EVERYONE STOP. LOOK.
THERE'S FIRE. NEAR THE CAT TRIBE.
HSSS... STENCHLESS.
THEY'RE ASSAULTING THE CLIMB. I HAVE TO GET BACK.
QUICK! THE GROUNDS WILL BURN IF WE DON'T HURRY!.
HERMAN, ELSA! YOU WARN THE DOGS.
WE'LL TRY!
DAISY, FIND WILLA!
YES!
MYRA! I'M GOING WITH YOU.
THEN YOU'LL HAVE TO KEEP UP!

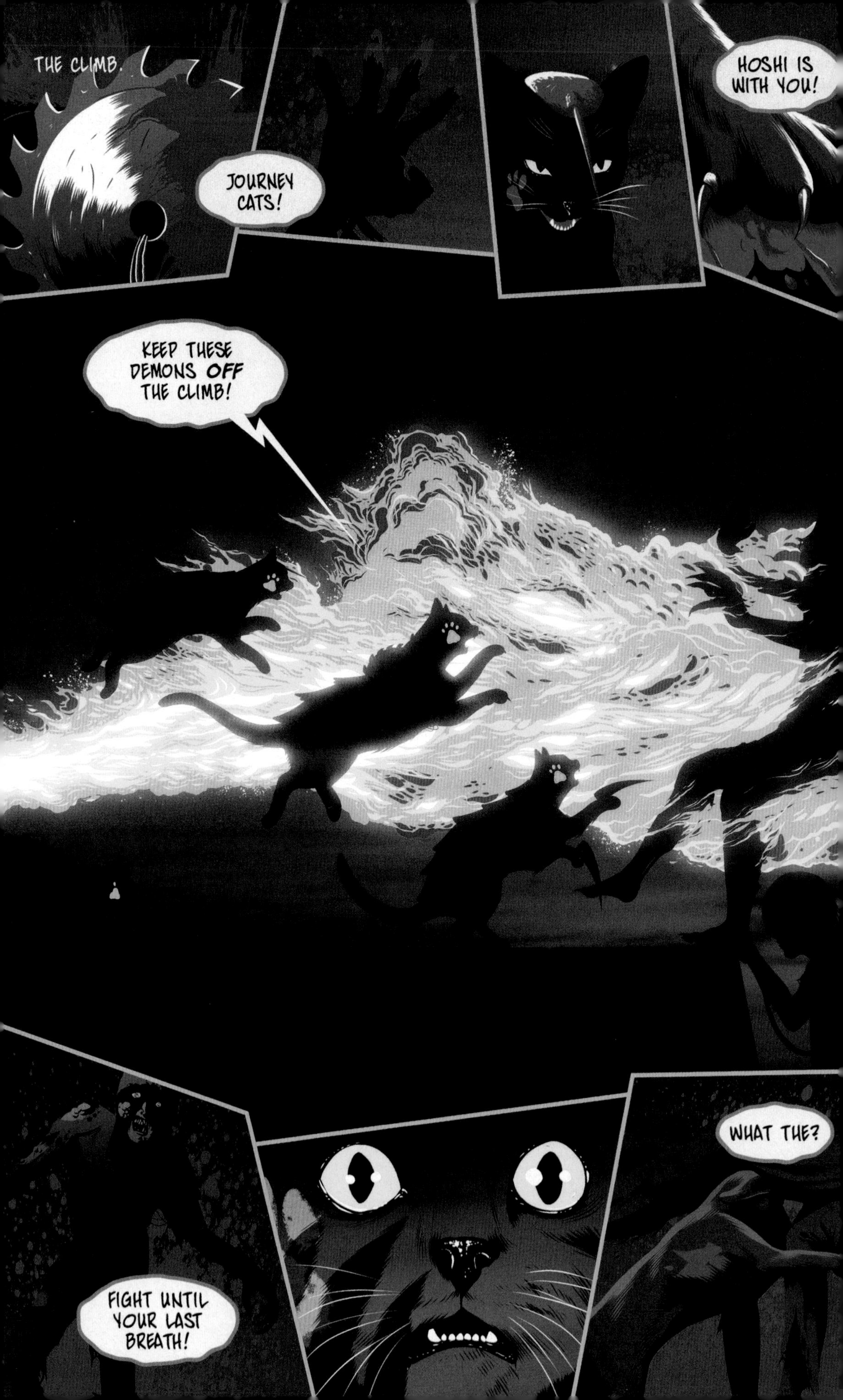
THE CLIMB.
JOURNEY CATS!
HOSHI IS WITH YOU!
KEEP THESE DEMONS OFF THE CLIMB!
FIGHT UNTIL YOUR LAST BREATH!
WHAT THE?

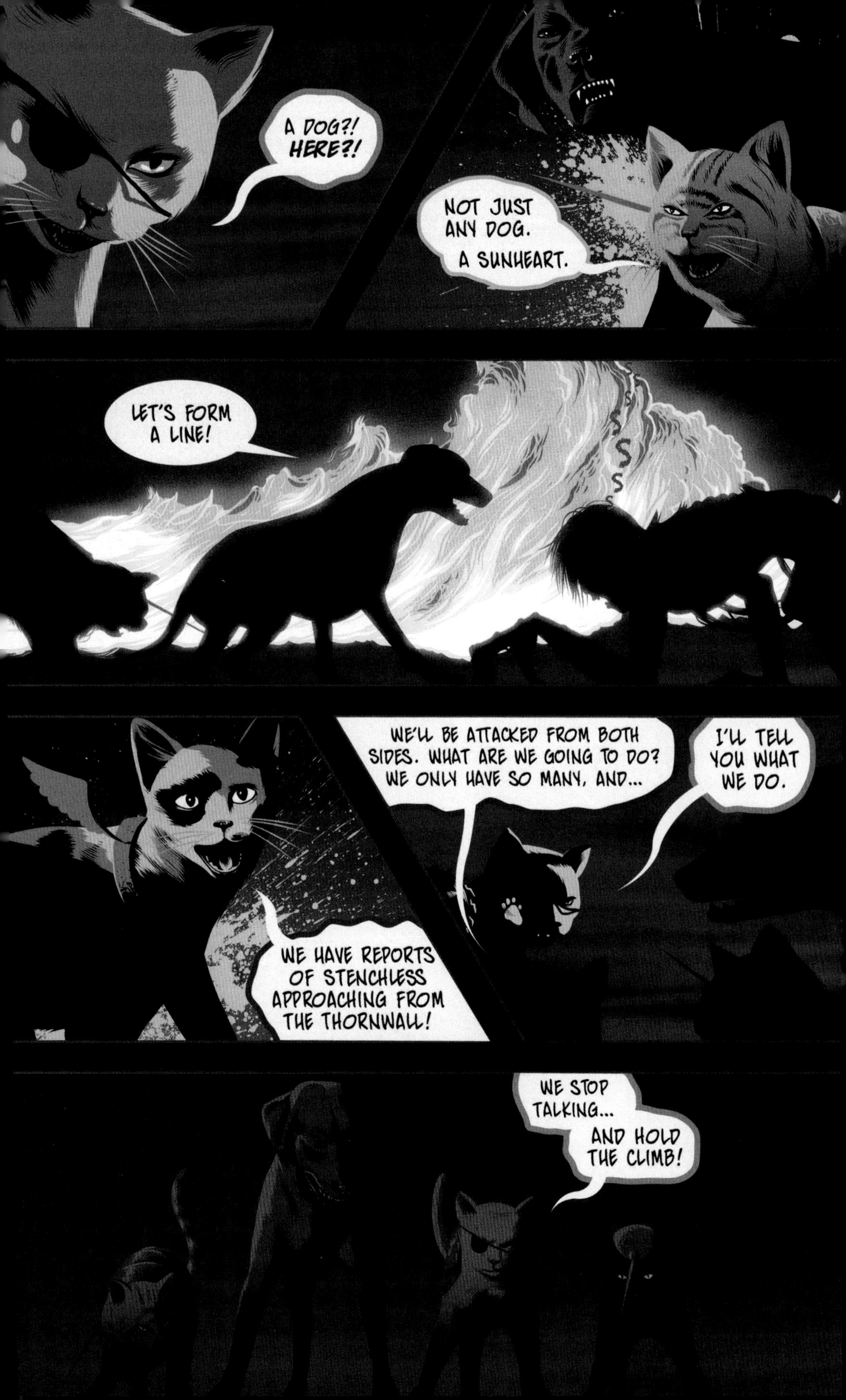
A DOG?! HERE?!
NOT JUST ANY DOG.
A SUNHEART.
LET'S FORM A LINE!
SSSS
WE HAVE REPORTS OF STENCHLESS APPROACHING FROM THE THORNWALL!
WE'LL BE ATTACKED FROM BOTH SIDES. WHAT ARE WE GOING TO DO? WE ONLY HAVE SO MANY, AND...
I'LL TELL YOU WHAT WE DO.
WE STOP TALKING...
AND HOLD THE CLIMB!

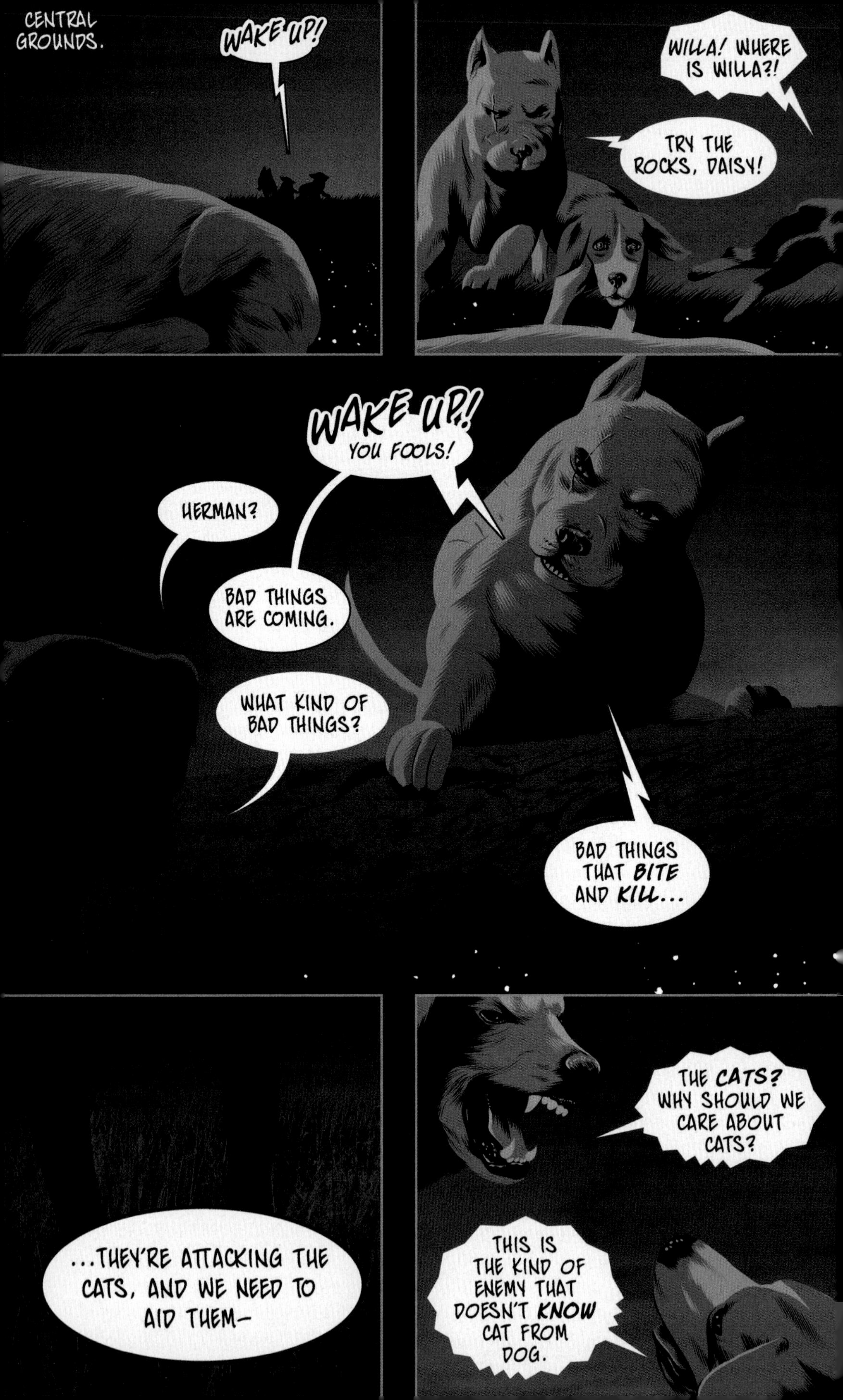
CENTRAL GROUNDS.
WAKE UP!
WILLA! WHERE IS WILLA?!
TRY THE ROCKS, DAISY!
WAKE UP! YOU FOOLS!
HERMAN?
BAD THINGS ARE COMING.
WHAT KIND OF BAD THINGS?
BAD THINGS THAT BITE AND KILL...
...THEY'RE ATTACKING THE CATS, AND WE NEED TO AID THEM–
THE CATS? WHY SHOULD WE CARE ABOUT CATS?
THIS IS THE KIND OF ENEMY THAT DOESN'T KNOW CAT FROM DOG.

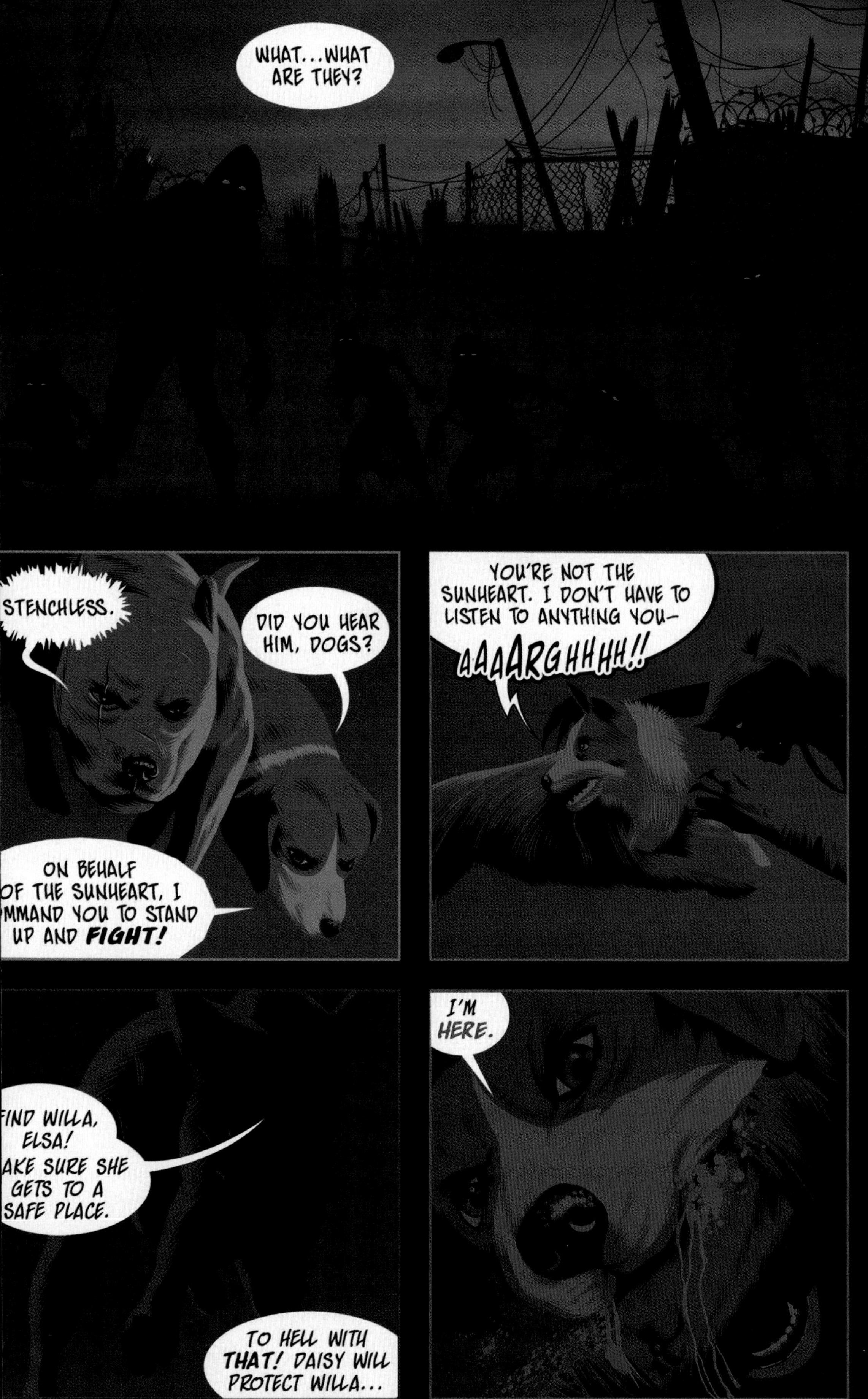
WHAT...WHAT ARE THEY?
STENCHLESS.
DID YOU HEAR HIM, DOGS?
ON BEHALF OF THE SUNHEART, I MMAND YOU TO STAND UP AND **FIGHT!**
YOU'RE NOT THE SUNHEART. I DON'T HAVE TO LISTEN TO ANYTHING YOU–
AAAARGHHHH!!
FIND WILLA, ELSA! AKE SURE SHE GETS TO A SAFE PLACE.
TO HELL WITH **THAT!** DAISY WILL PROTECT WILLA...
I'M **HERE.**

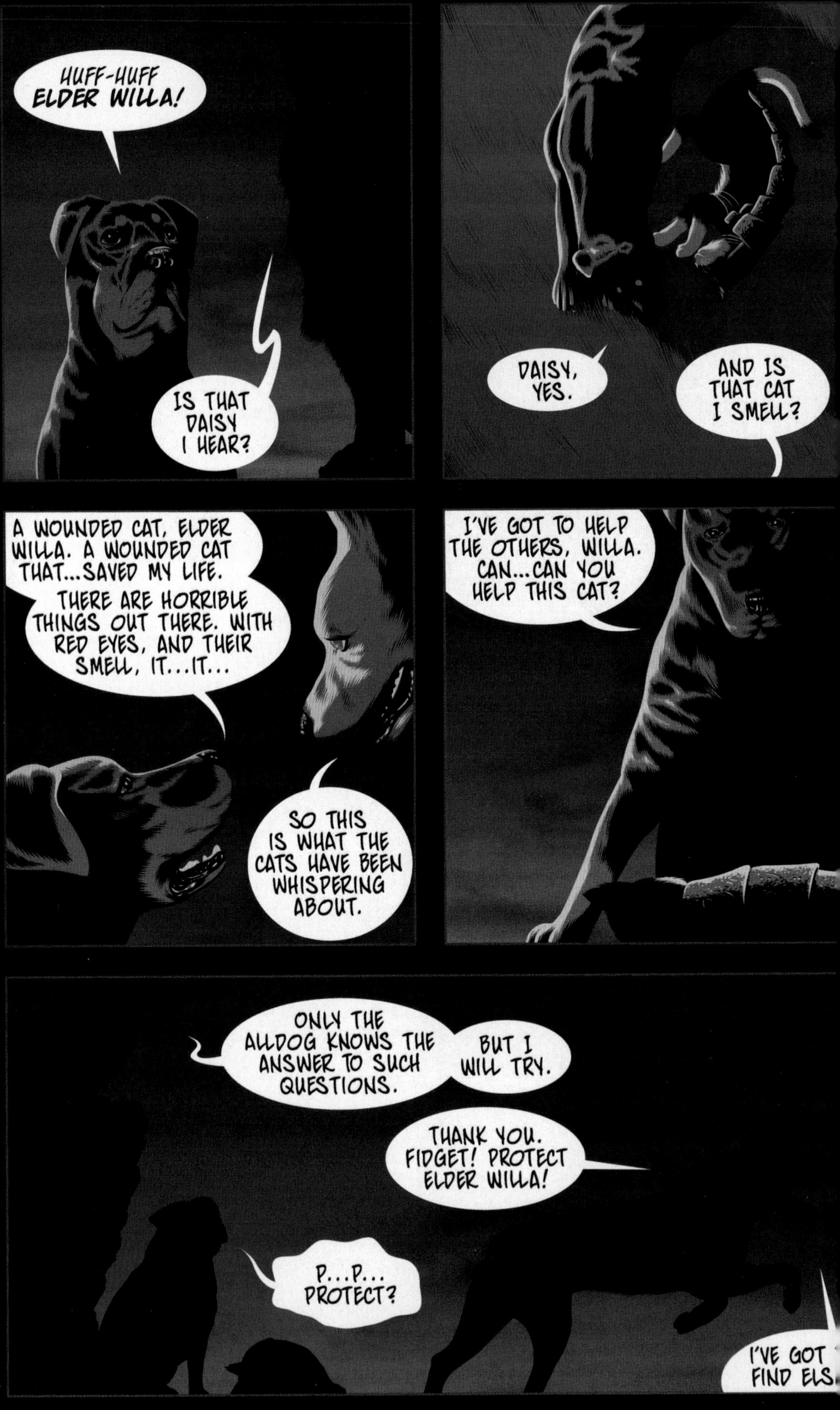
HUFF-HUFF
ELDER WILLA!
IS THAT DAISY I HEAR?
DAISY, YES.
AND IS THAT CAT I SMELL?
A WOUNDED CAT, ELDER WILLA. A WOUNDED CAT THAT...SAVED MY LIFE.
THERE ARE HORRIBLE THINGS OUT THERE. WITH RED EYES, AND THEIR SMELL, IT...IT...
SO THIS IS WHAT THE CATS HAVE BEEN WHISPERING ABOUT.
I'VE GOT TO HELP THE OTHERS, WILLA. CAN...CAN YOU HELP THIS CAT?
ONLY THE ALLDOG KNOWS THE ANSWER TO SUCH QUESTIONS.
BUT I WILL TRY.
THANK YOU. FIDGET! PROTECT ELDER WILLA!
P...P... PROTECT?
I'VE GOT
FIND ELS

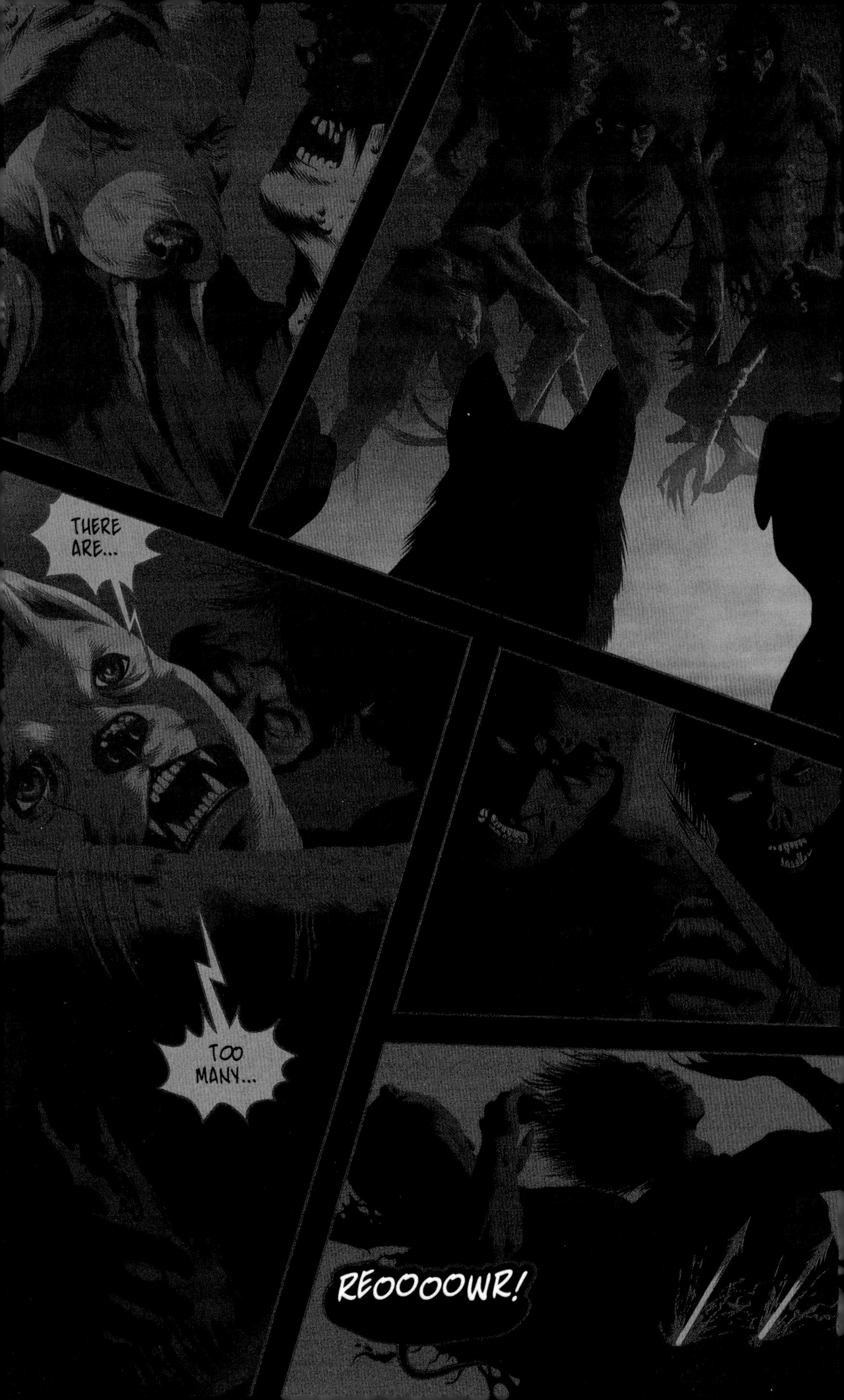
THERE ARE...
TOO MANY...
REOOOOWR!

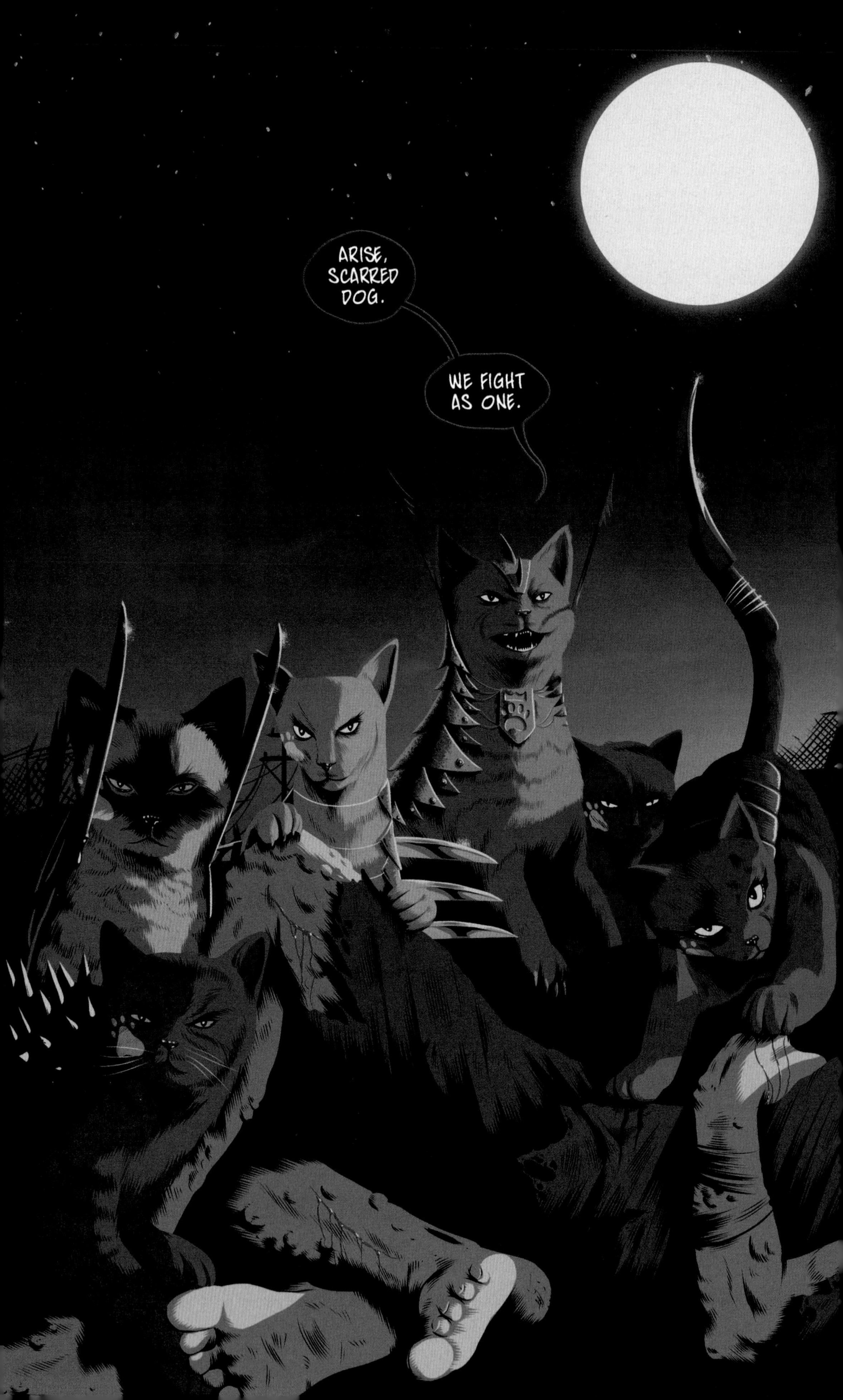
ARISE, SCARRED DOG.
WE FIGHT AS ONE.

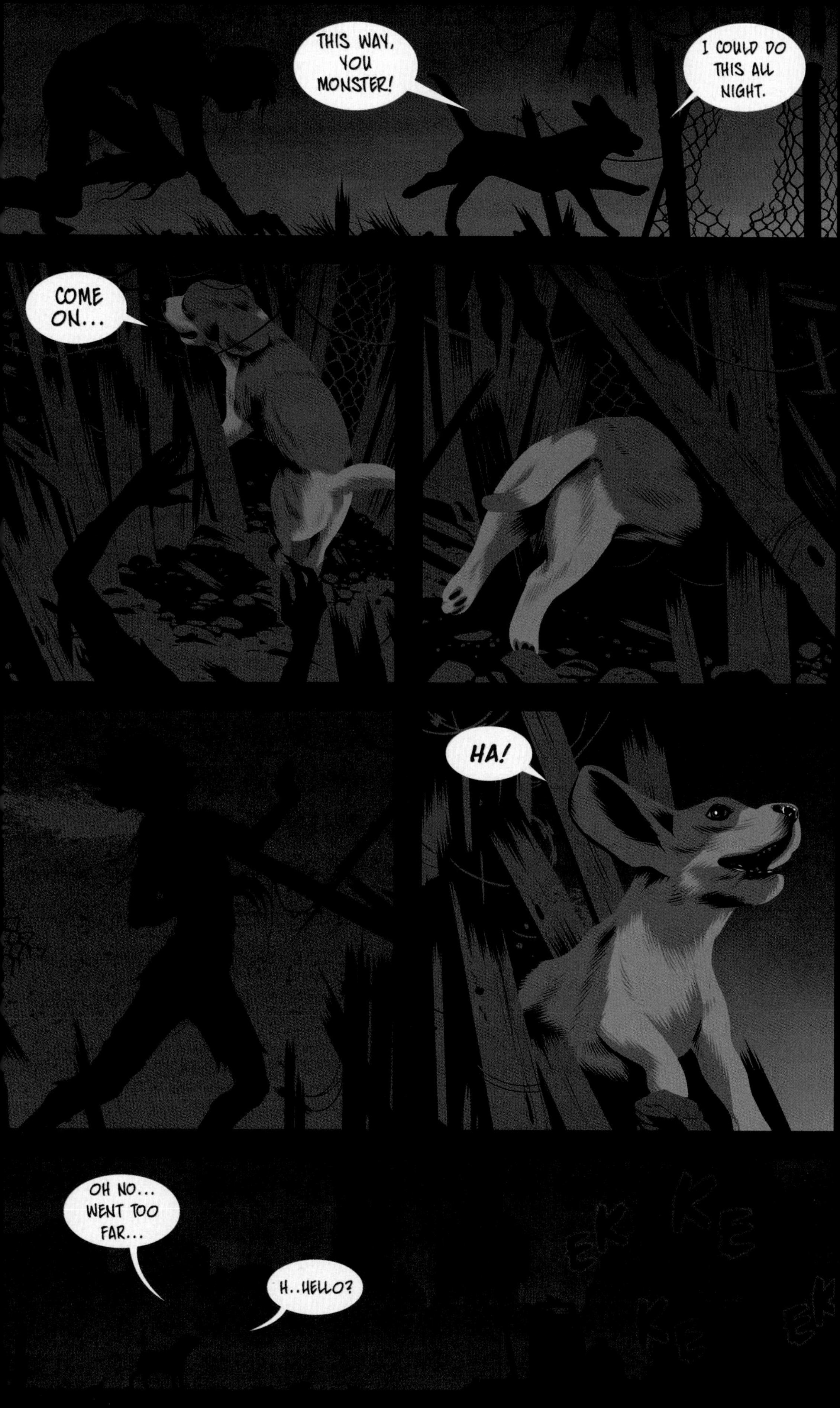
THIS WAY, YOU MONSTER!
I COULD DO THIS ALL NIGHT.
COME ON...
HA!
OH NO... WENT TOO FAR...
H..HELLO?

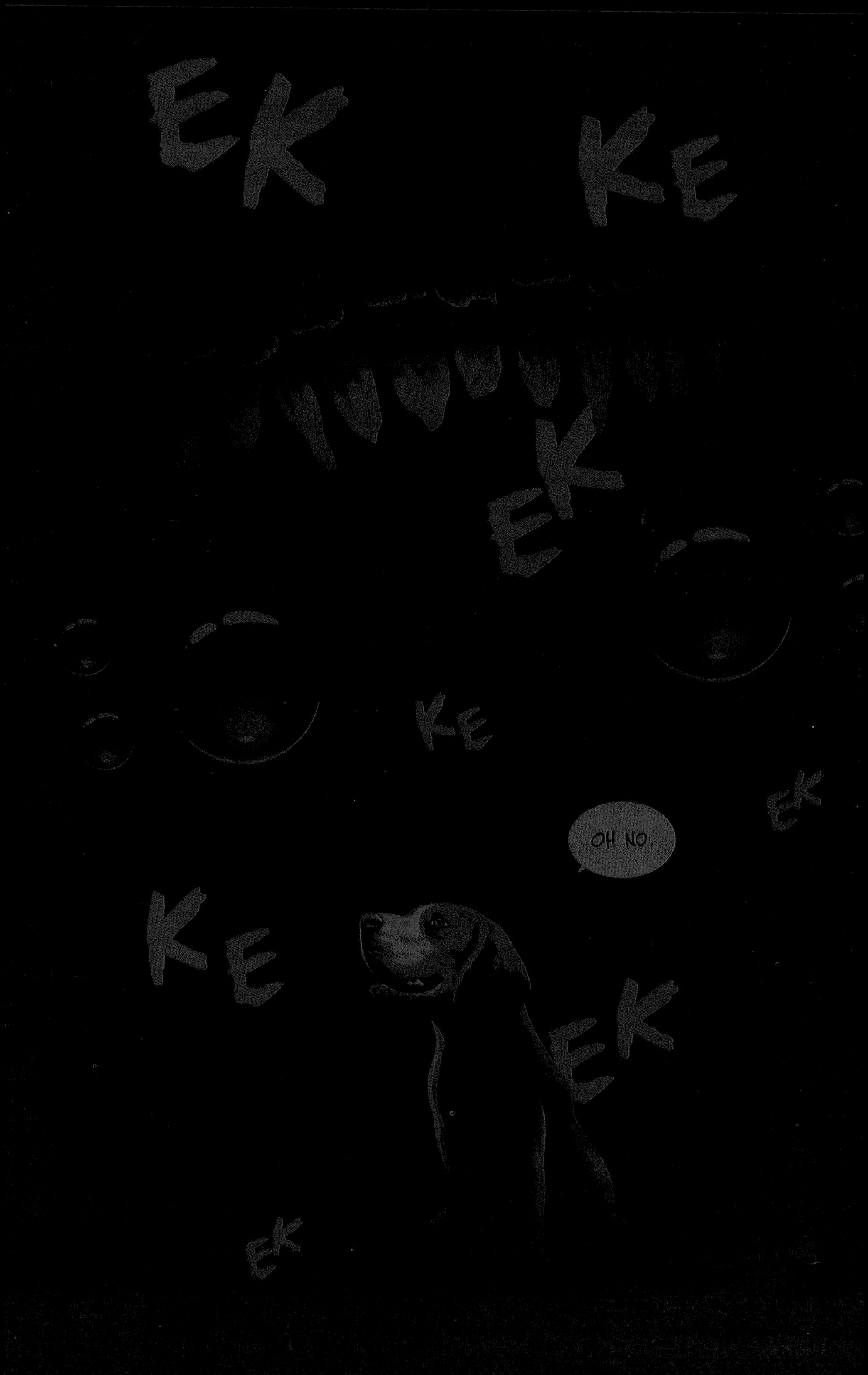
EK
KE
EK
KE
EK
OH NO.
KE
EK
EK

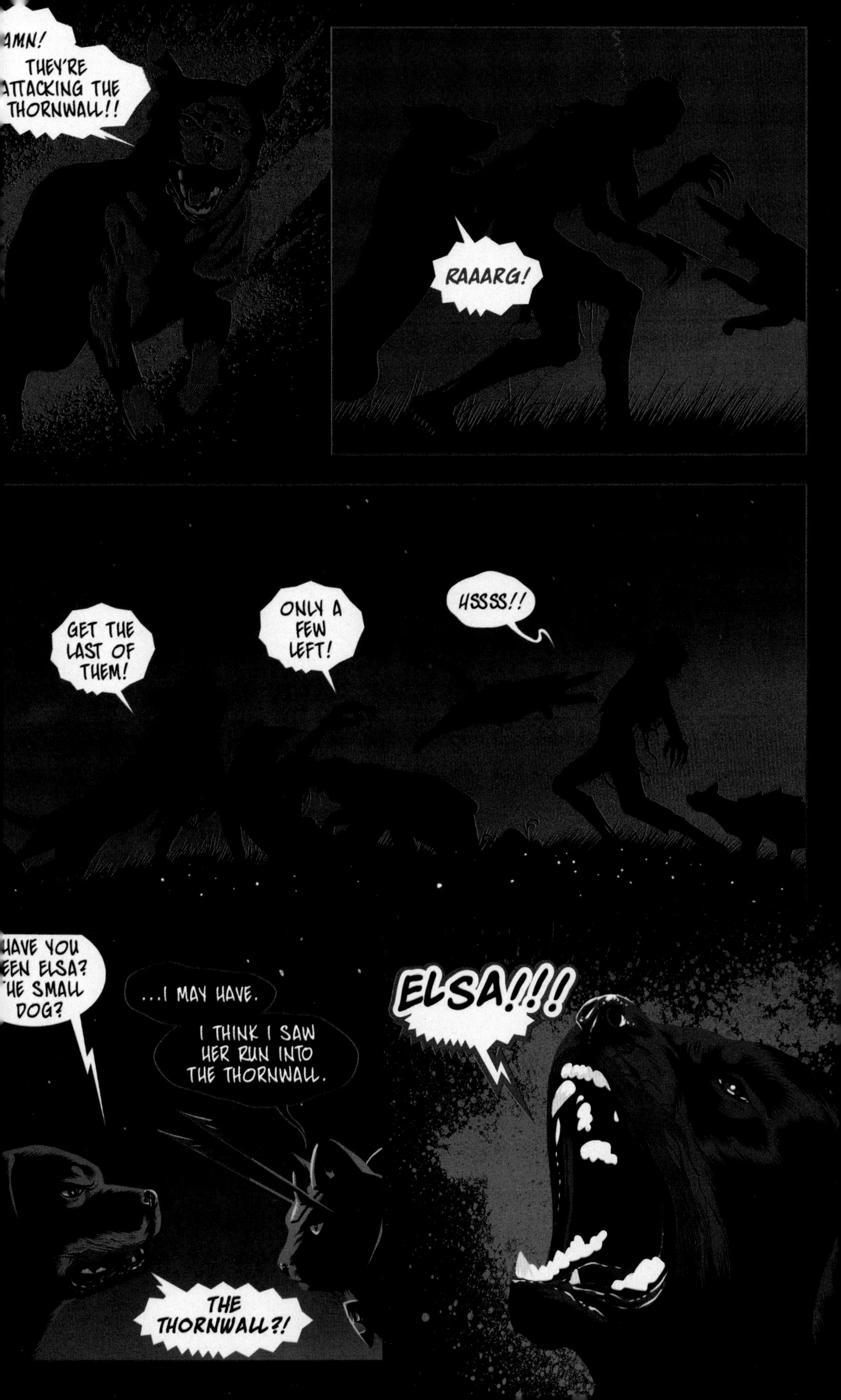
AMN! THEY'RE ATTACKING THE THORNWALL!!
RAAARG!
GET THE LAST OF THEM!
ONLY A FEW LEFT!
HSSSS!!
HAVE YOU EEN ELSA? THE SMALL DOG?
...I MAY HAVE.
I THINK I SAW HER RUN INTO THE THORNWALL.
THE THORNWALL?!
ELSA!!!

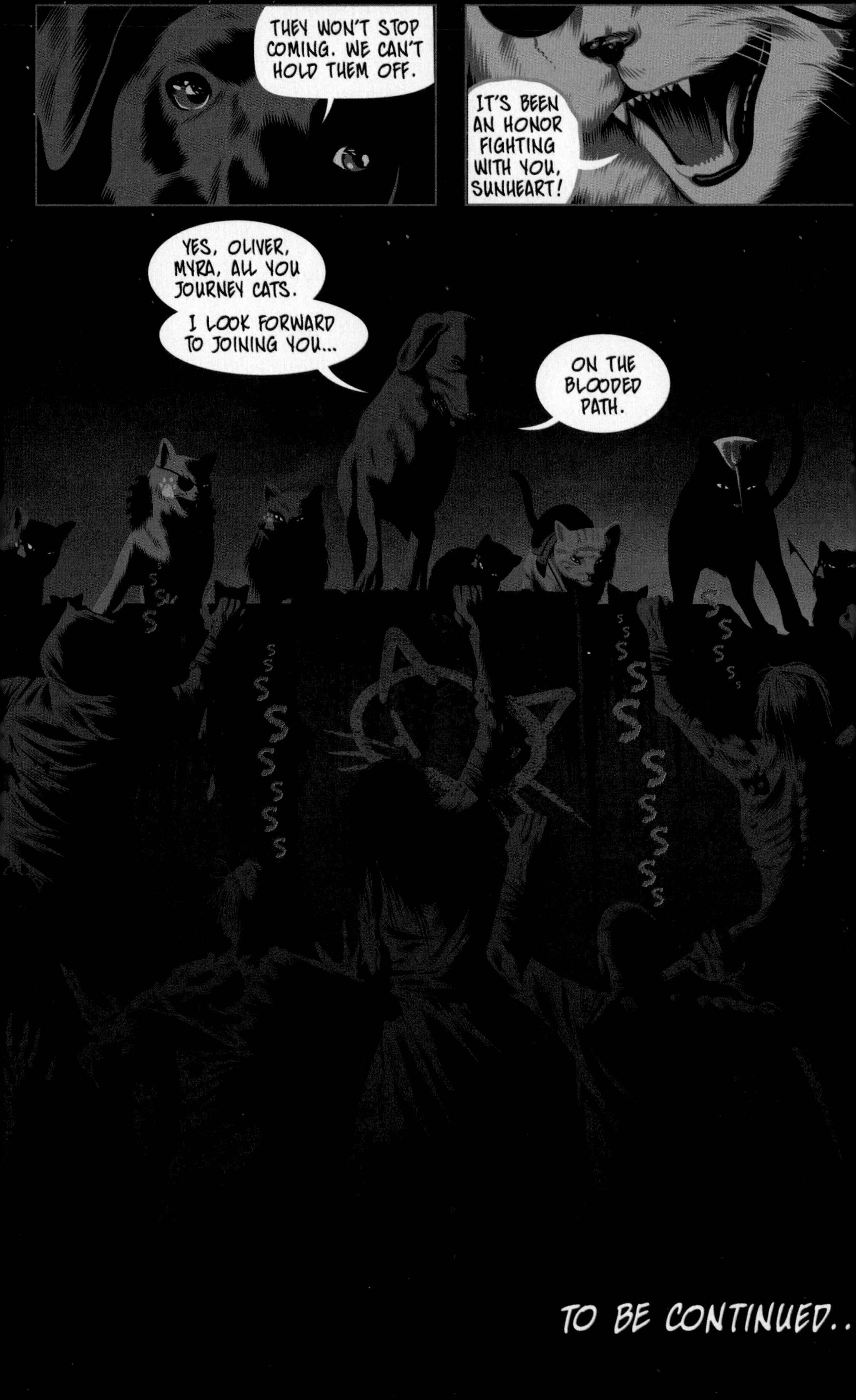
THEY WON'T STOP COMING. WE CAN'T HOLD THEM OFF.
IT'S BEEN AN HONOR FIGHTING WITH YOU, SUNHEART!
YES, OLIVER, MYRA, ALL YOU JOURNEY CATS.
I LOOK FORWARD TO JOINING YOU...
ON THE BLOODED PATH.
TO BE CONTINUED...

COVER GALLERY

ISSUE ONE THROUGH FIVE BY
CHRIS KOEHLER

ISSUE ONE VARIANT BY
TYLER BOSS

ISSUE ONE VARIANT BY
ALEX ZIRRIT

VARIANT BY
ERIN HUNTING

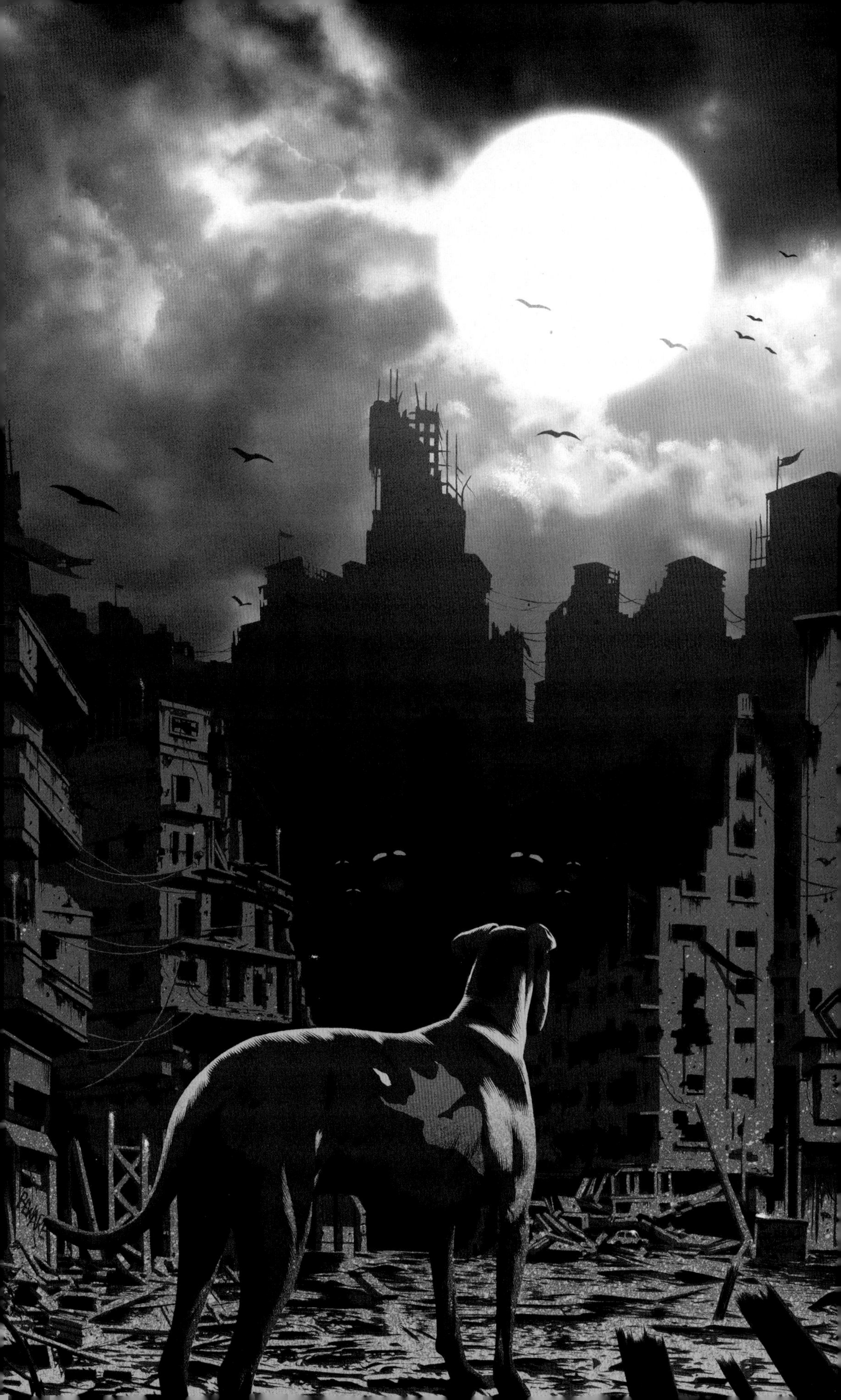

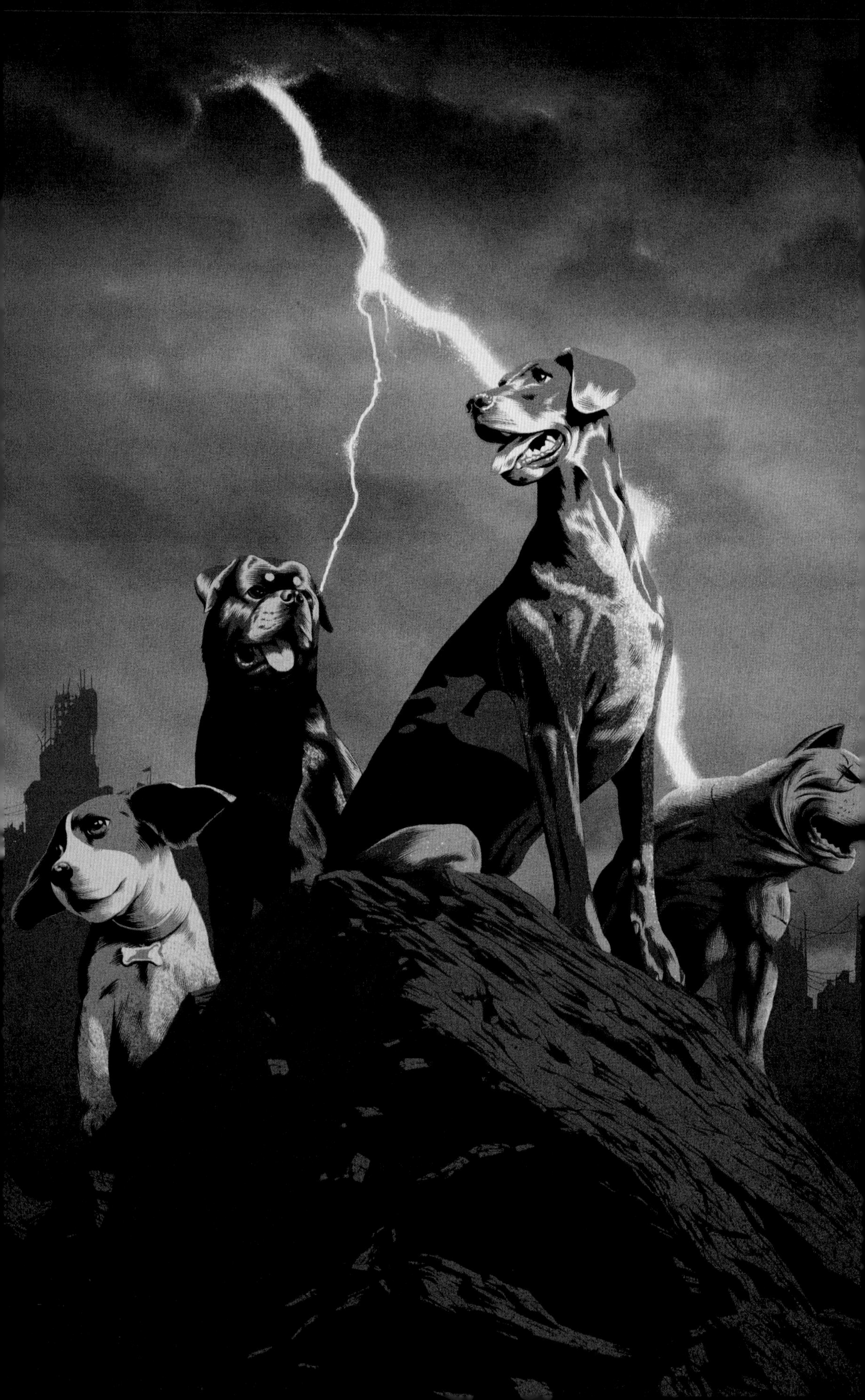

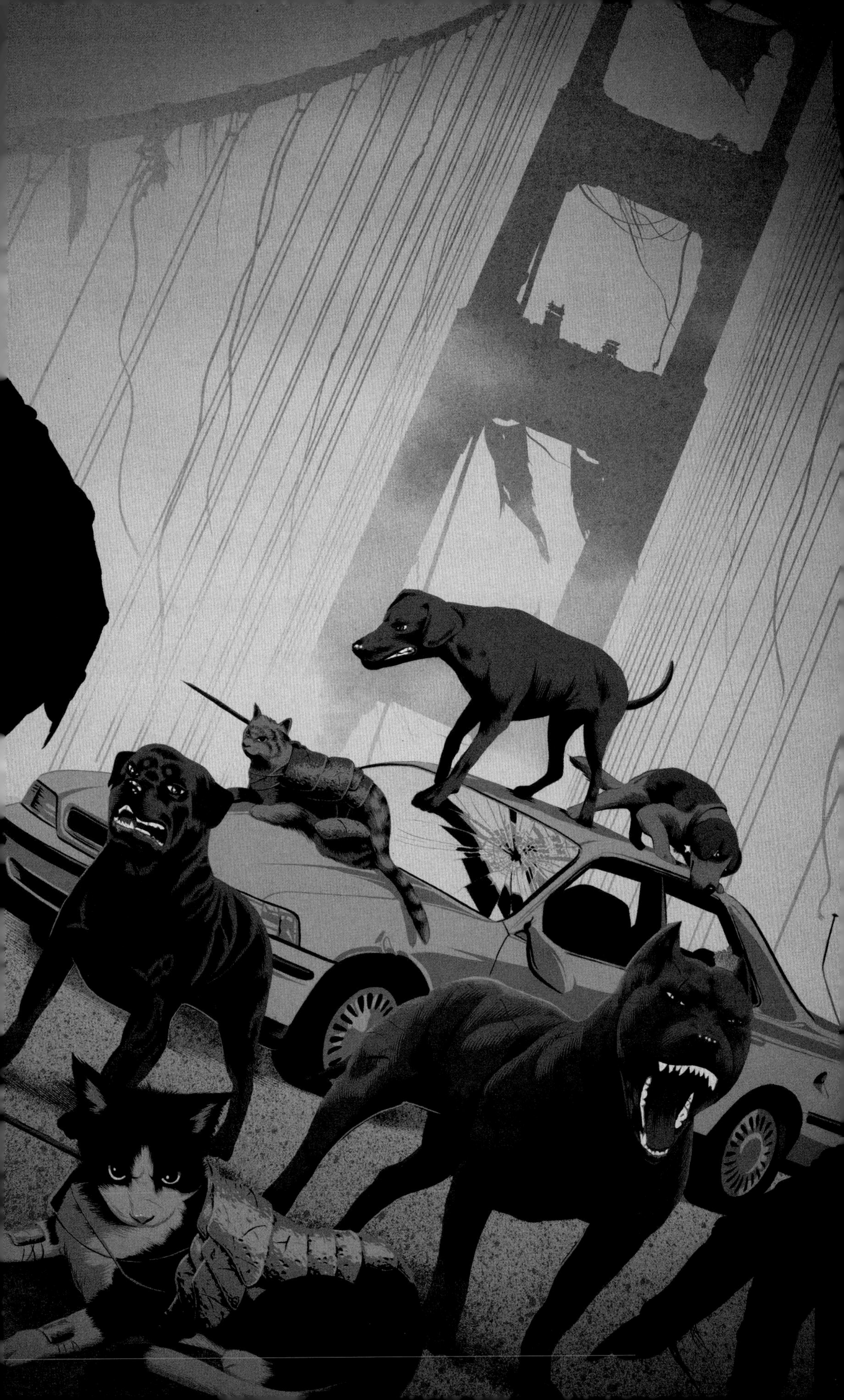

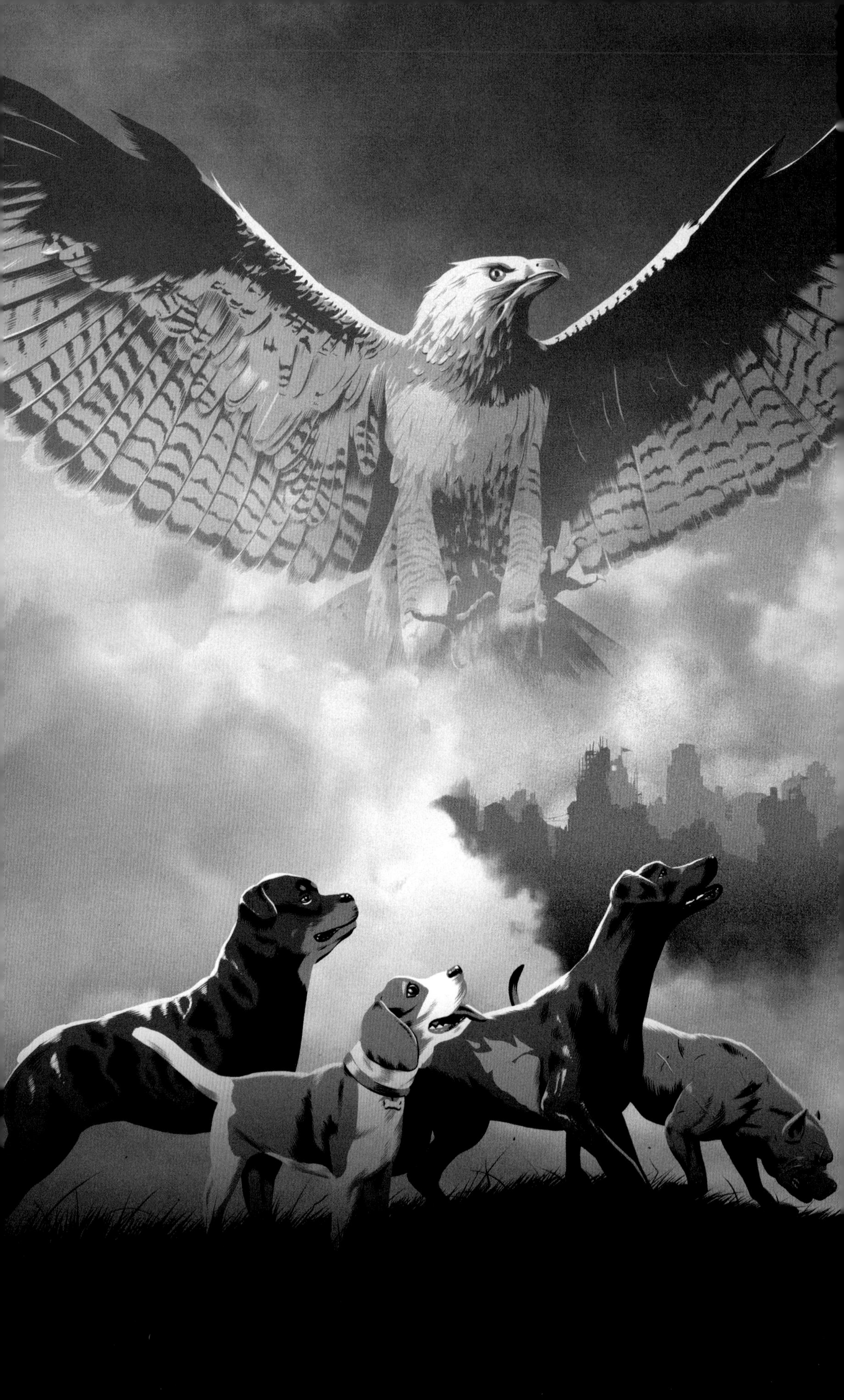

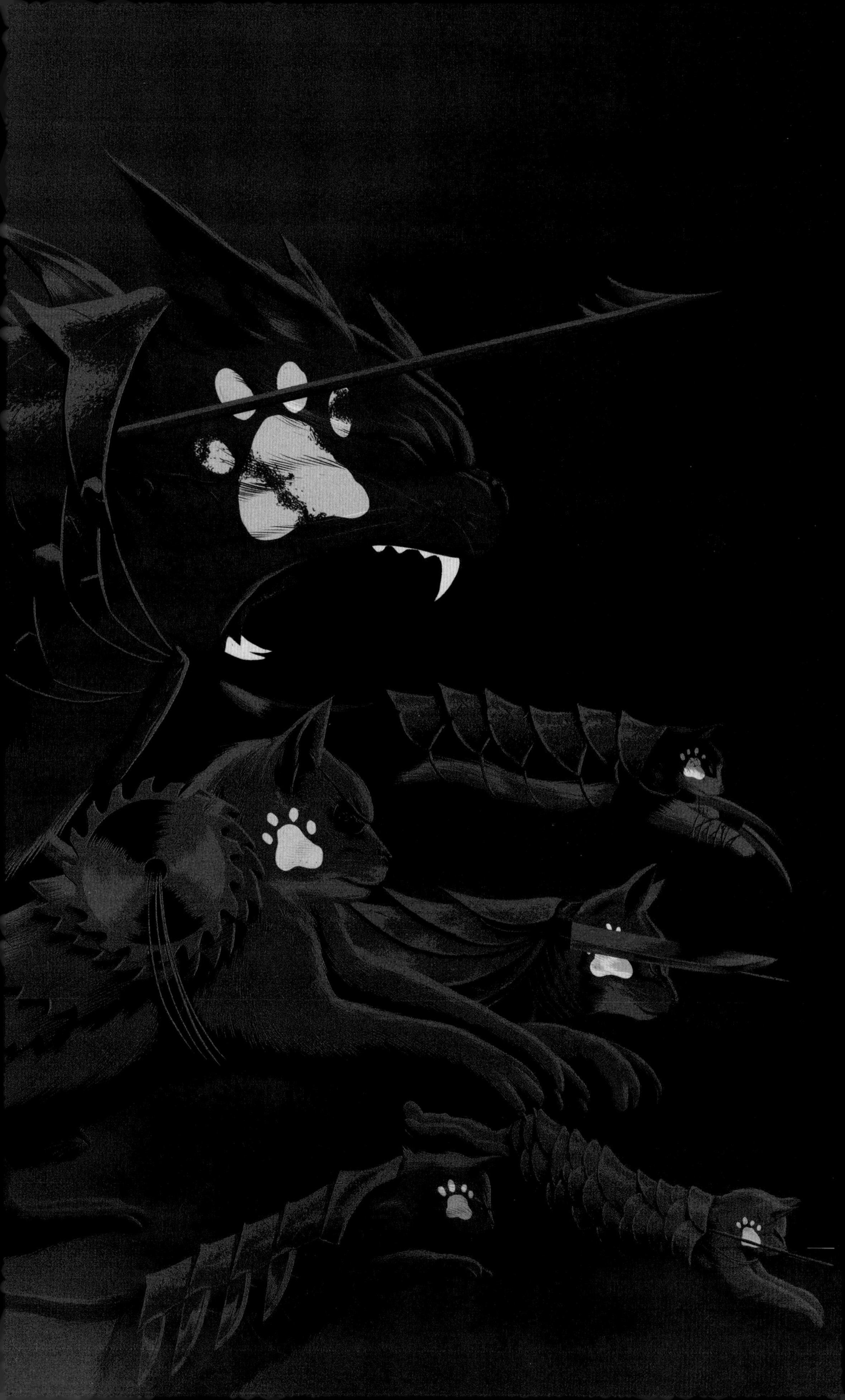

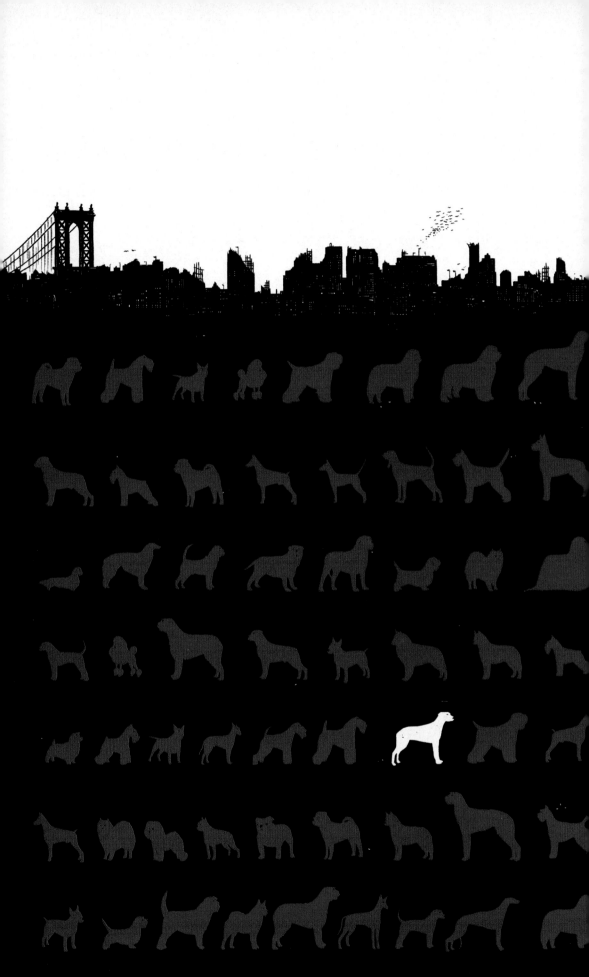

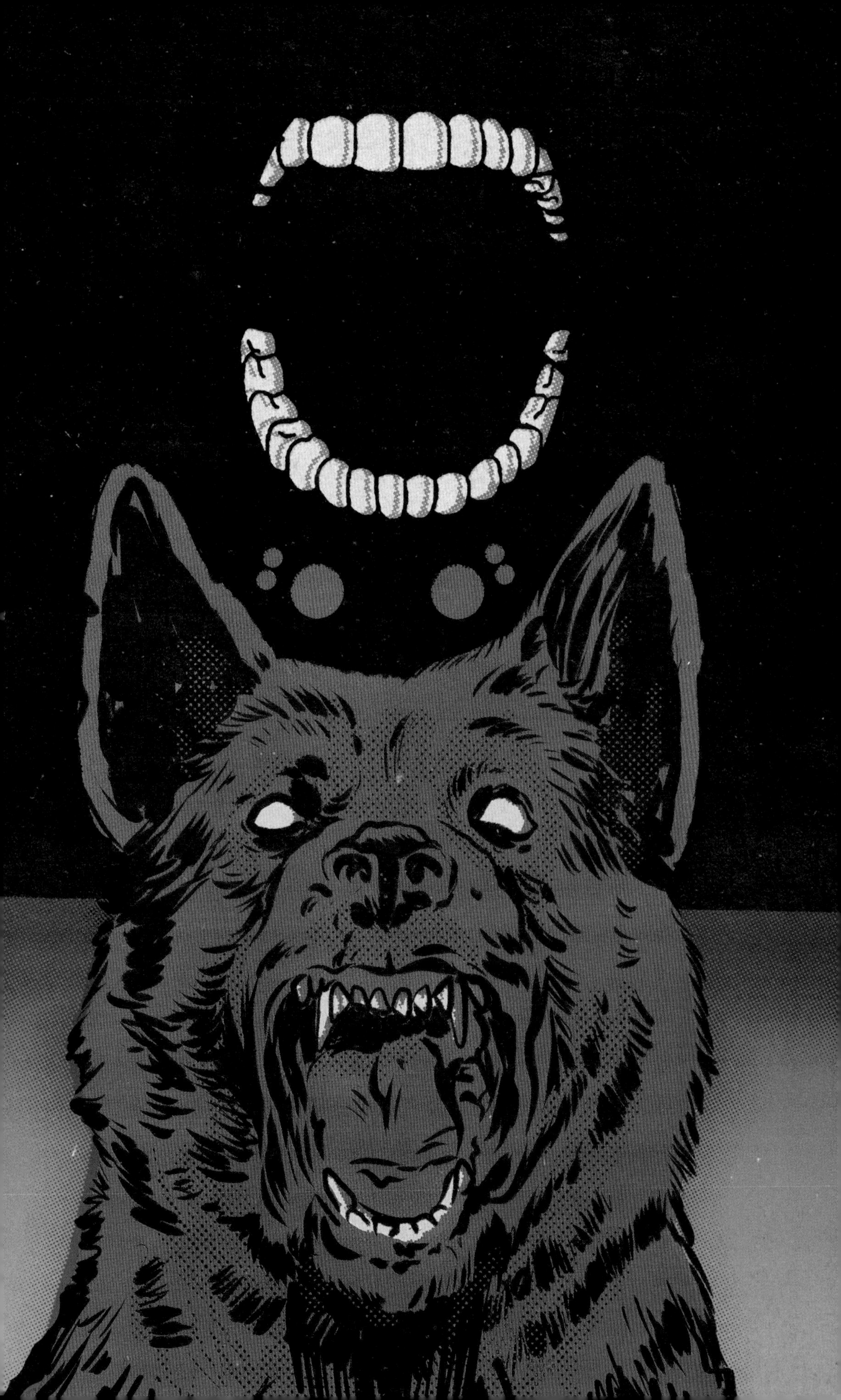

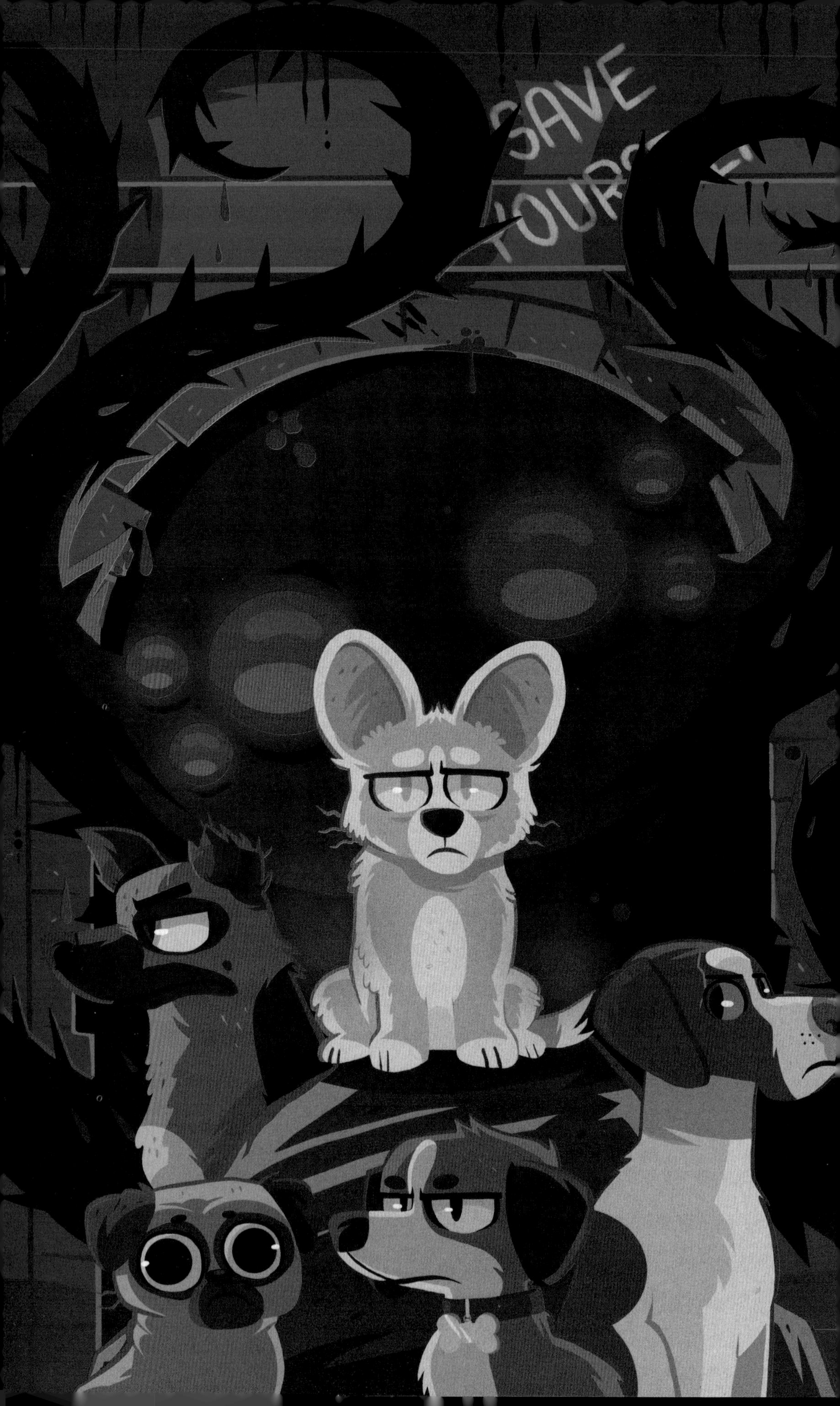
SAVE

THE LAY OF THE LAND

When we started working on *Legend*, we knew that we wanted to create a world that flowed beyond the bounds of this story alone. Our plan was to scatter seeds of mystery through every page, beyond the limited vantage of our animal heroes, hinting at a vast horizon of possibility inhabiting a planet altered beyond
reproach.

But stories are tricky, and beg for focus. While this new frontier was filled with endless stories, we also knew that ours needed to be told as if it was the most
important of them all, a tale of tails where the remaining survivors of a world doomed to destruction became harbingers of a new order.

The thing I love about Richard Adams, who wrote *Watership Down*, is that his rabbit characters, while retaining characteristics and emotions we all find familiar, are still animals. Their priorities, while somewhat dressed down, are not at all simple. Beyond enjoying patches of sunshine and the warmth of friendship, these creatures value one thing above all others: survival.

Adams was genius enough to give them a form of religion to oper- ate with, a mechanism to help them survive, an intricate mythos that plays into the psyche of smaller beings and, at the same, speaks directly to his audience: us.

This is, in part, how the story of Swyftyst the Alldog emerged.

The animals of *Legend* have an intelligence that—without giving too much away—has been sharpened since the Fault. While dogs and cats might not have mythologies of their own in real life, they do cast mighty shadows on this planet, influencing our lives in ways so magnificent that we'd be foolish to ignore them.

In the pages ahead, you will find stories of *Legend* ranging from dog mythologies to cat basement blacksmiths. Created by an array of immensely talented artists, we are pleased to present this tome of magic to you.

The world of *Legend* contains many stories, and this is just one within it. Thank you for accompanying us on this amazing journey. We look forward to bringing you the rest of what lies ahead.

-Samuel Sattin

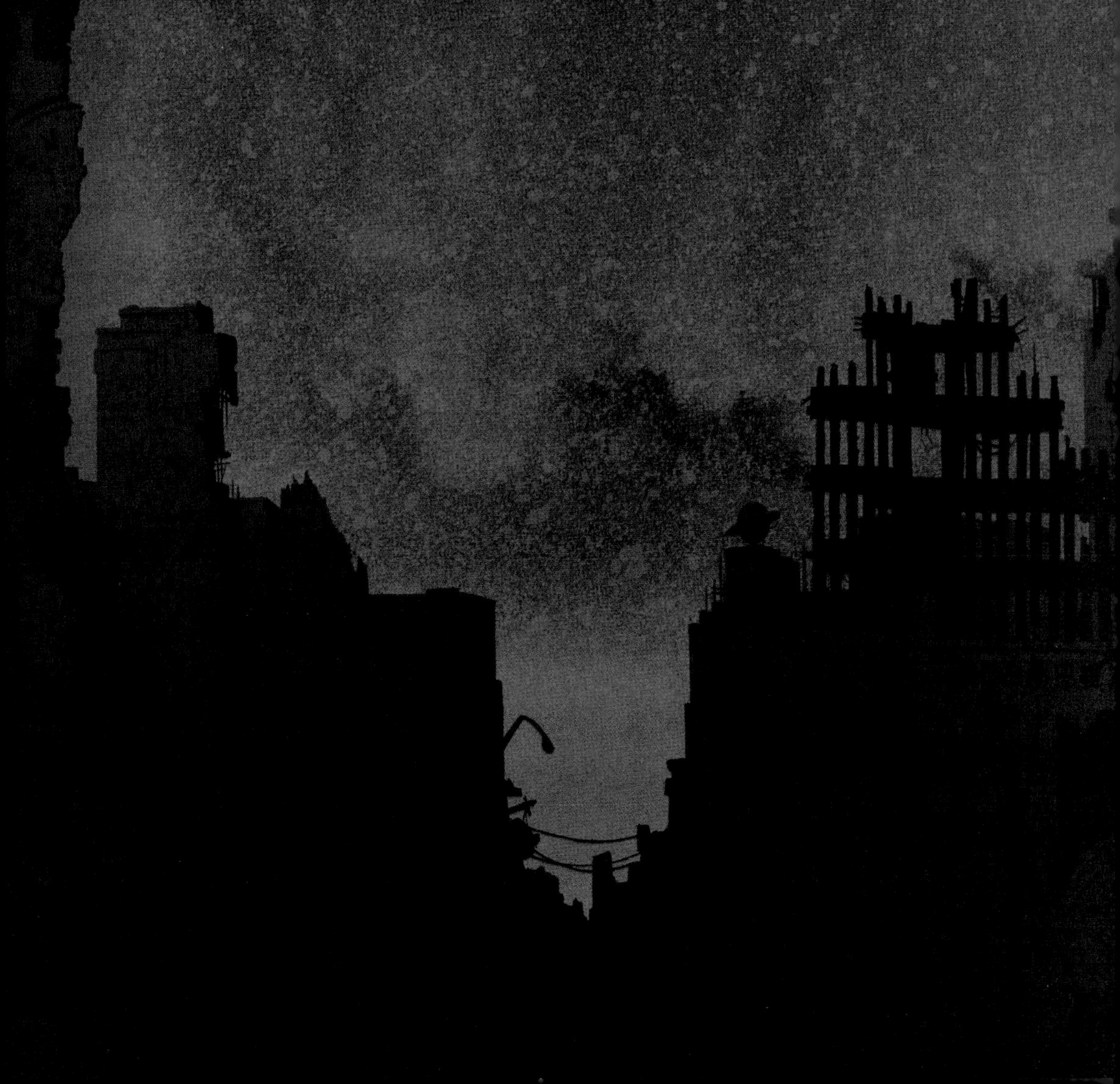

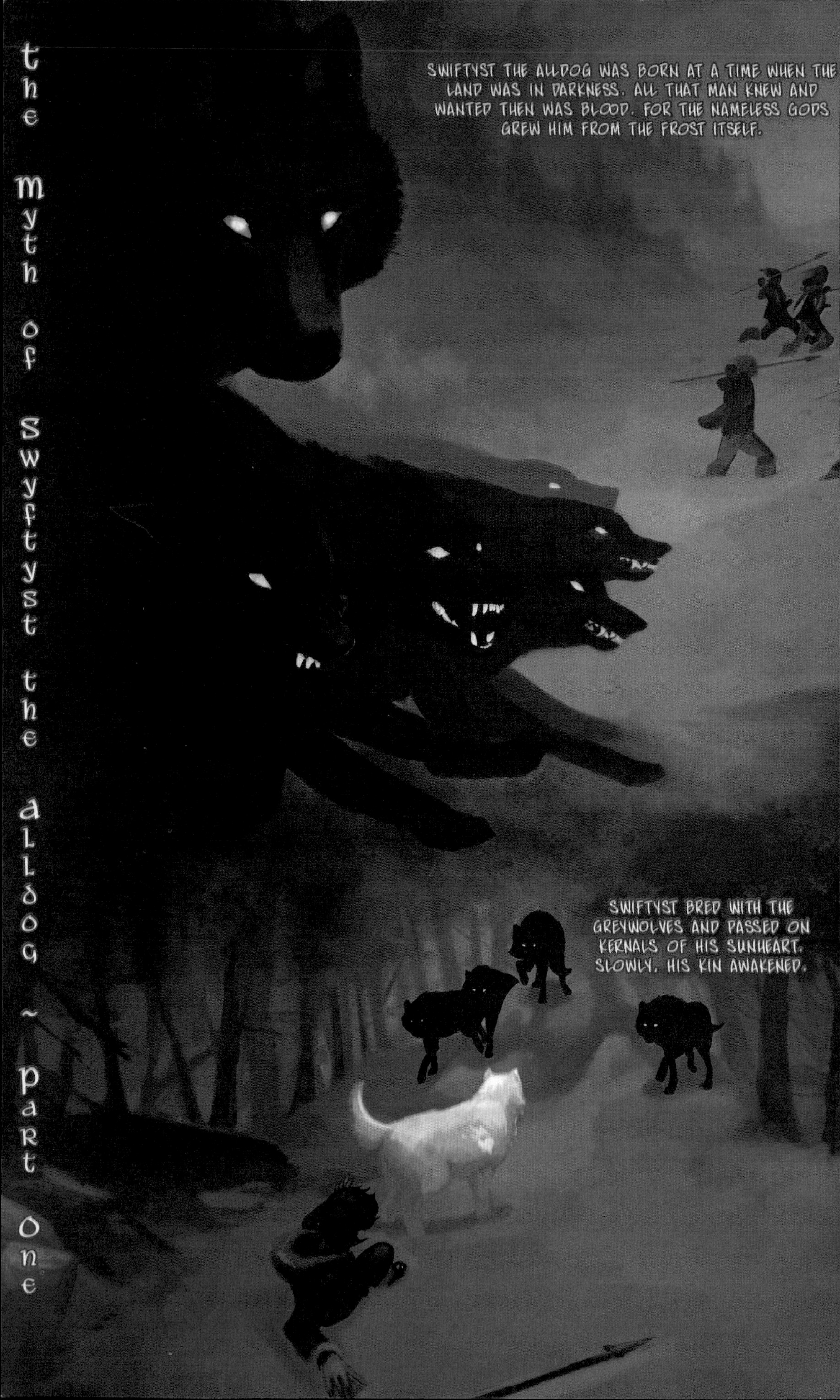
the myth of swyftyst the alldog ~ part one
SWIFTYST THE ALLDOG WAS BORN AT A TIME WHEN THE LAND WAS IN DARKNESS. ALL THAT MAN KNEW AND WANTED THEN WAS BLOOD. FOR THE NAMELESS GODS GREW HIM FROM THE FROST ITSELF.
SWIFTYST BRED WITH THE GREYWOLVES AND PASSED ON KERNALS OF HIS SUNHEART. SLOWLY, HIS KIN AWAKENED.

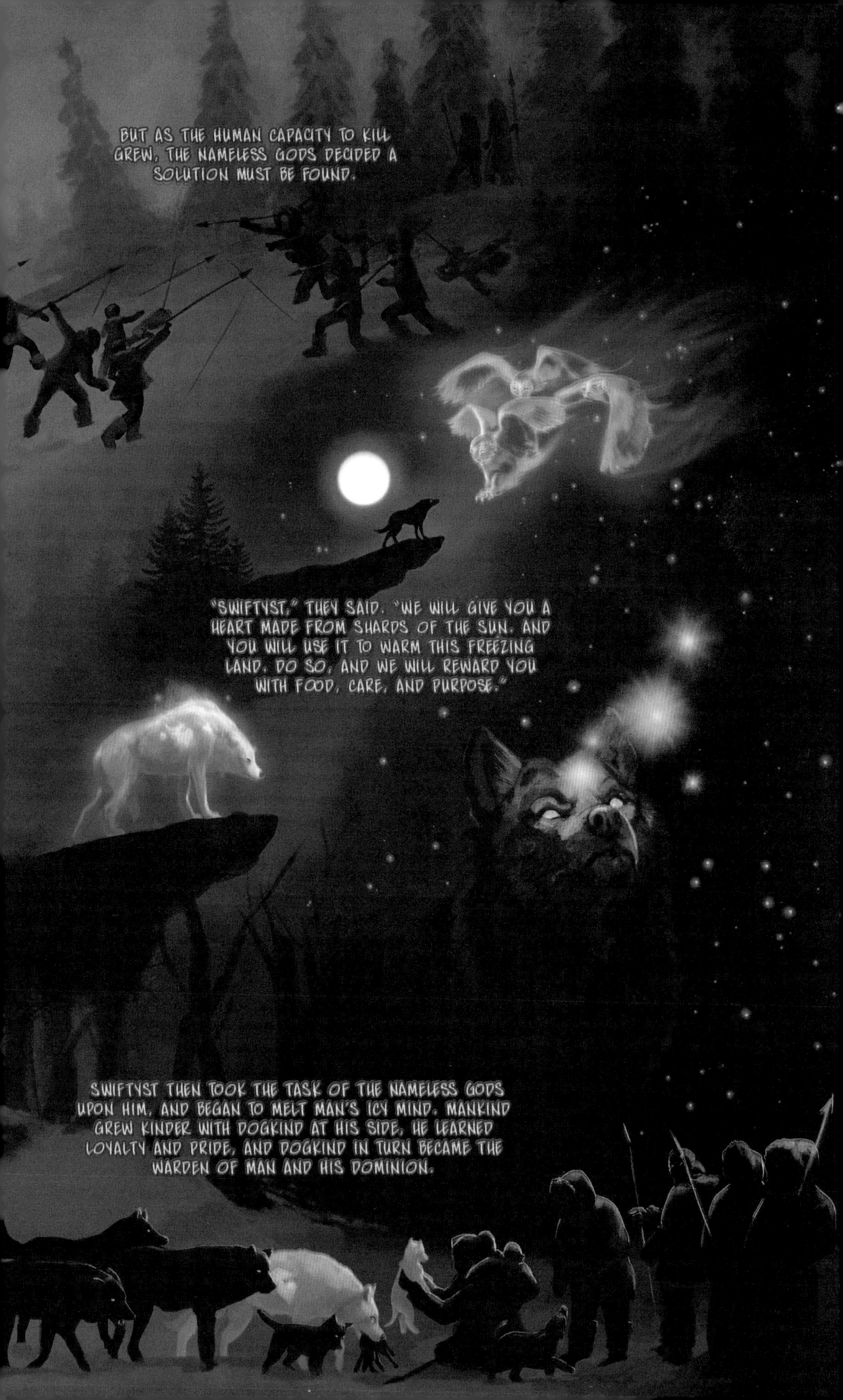
BUT AS THE HUMAN CAPACITY TO KILL GREW, THE NAMELESS GODS DECIDED A SOLUTION MUST BE FOUND.
"SWIFTYST," THEY SAID. "WE WILL GIVE YOU A HEART MADE FROM SHARDS OF THE SUN. AND YOU WILL USE IT TO WARM THIS FREEZING LAND. DO SO, AND WE WILL REWARD YOU WITH FOOD, CARE, AND PURPOSE."
SWIFTYST THEN TOOK THE TASK OF THE NAMELESS GODS UPON HIM, AND BEGAN TO MELT MAN'S ICY MIND. MANKIND GREW KINDER WITH DOGKIND AT HIS SIDE, HE LEARNED LOYALTY AND PRIDE, AND DOGKIND IN TURN BECAME THE WARDEN OF MAN AND HIS DOMINION.

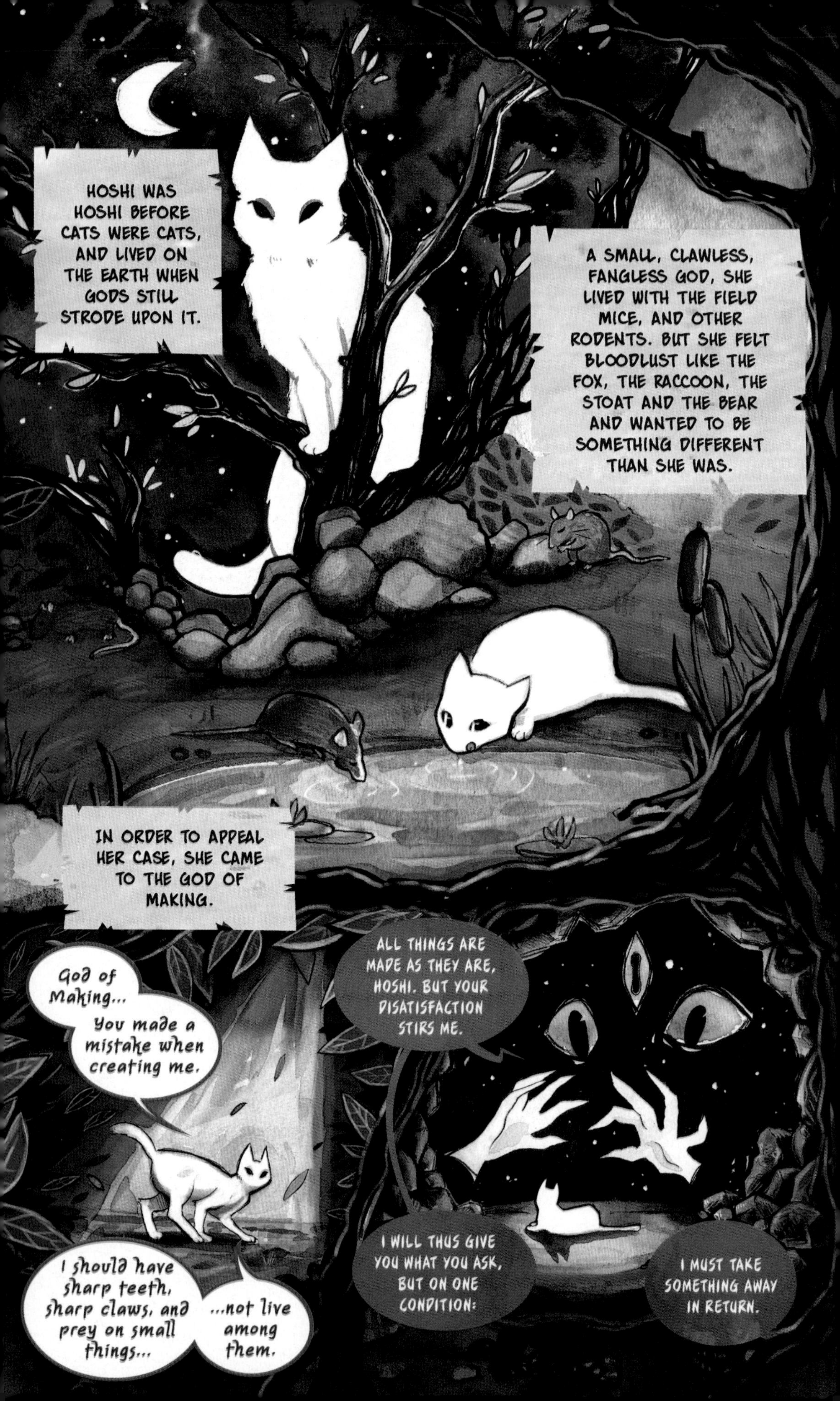
HOSHI WAS HOSHI BEFORE CATS WERE CATS, AND LIVED ON THE EARTH WHEN GODS STILL STRODE UPON IT.
A SMALL, CLAWLESS, FANGLESS GOD, SHE LIVED WITH THE FIELD MICE, AND OTHER RODENTS. BUT SHE FELT BLOODLUST LIKE THE FOX, THE RACCOON, THE STOAT AND THE BEAR AND WANTED TO BE SOMETHING DIFFERENT THAN SHE WAS.
IN ORDER TO APPEAL HER CASE, SHE CAME TO THE GOD OF MAKING.
God of Making...
You made a mistake when creating me.
I should have sharp teeth, sharp claws, and prey on small things...
...not live among them.
ALL THINGS ARE MADE AS THEY ARE, HOSHI. BUT YOUR DISATISFACTION STIRS ME.
I WILL THUS GIVE YOU WHAT YOU ASK, BUT ON ONE CONDITION:
I MUST TAKE SOMETHING AWAY IN RETURN.

God of Making...
What I care for least is fear.
would like to ve that away.
NO CREATURE CAN RELINQUISH FEAR. BUT I CAN TAKE YOUR LOYALTY...
MIND YOU, HOWEVER, THAT IF IT IS SO, THE LAND WILL ALWAYS FEEL CROWDED TO YOU, AND YOU'LL ONLY BE CONTENT IN SOLITUDE.
HOSHI AGREED, AND THE GOD OF MAKING GAVE HER CLAWS...
...AND FANGS...
...AND A LONG TAIL.
WHAT HE TOOK FROM HER IN RETURN WAS BARELY VISIBLE. FOR LOSING HER LOYALTY ALLOWED HER TO SEE IN THE DARK, SO SHE'D ALWAYS BE AWARE, AND WARY, OF OTHERS.
WHEN MAN CAME ABOUT AND THE GODS TURNED TO ANIMALS, HOSHI'S OFFSPRING WOULD OVERRAN THE EARTH. BUT WITHOUT LOYALTY, EACH WOULD TREAT ITS KIN LIKE STRANGERS.
THEY'D ALWAYS FEEL ALONE.
EVEN AMONG EACH OTHER.

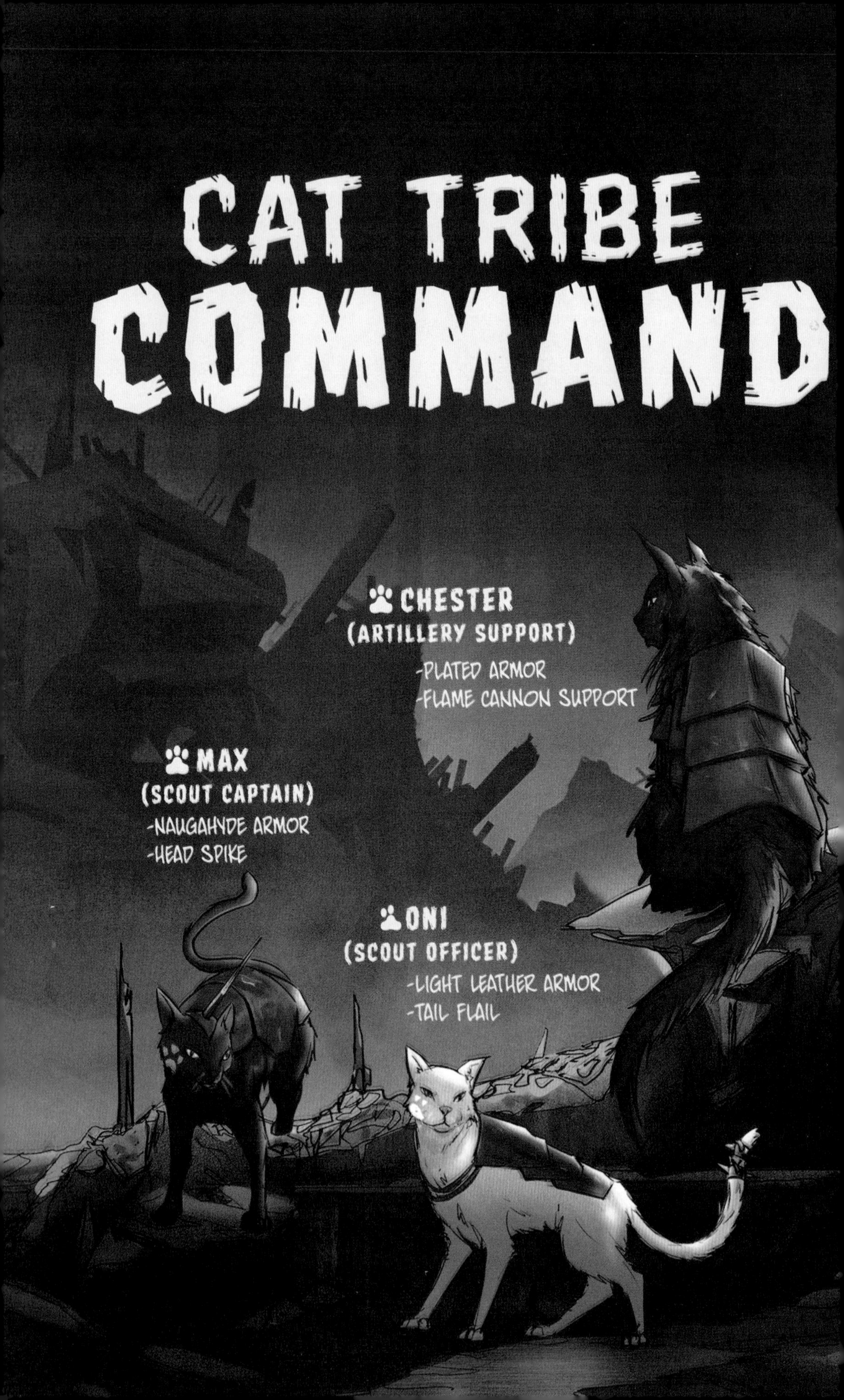
CAT TRIBE
COMMAND
CHESTER
(ARTILLERY SUPPORT)
-PLATED ARMOR
-FLAME CANNON SUPPORT
MAX
(SCOUT CAPTAIN)
-NAUGAHYDE ARMOR
-HEAD SPIKE
ONI
(SCOUT OFFICER)
-LIGHT LEATHER ARMOR
-TAIL FLAIL

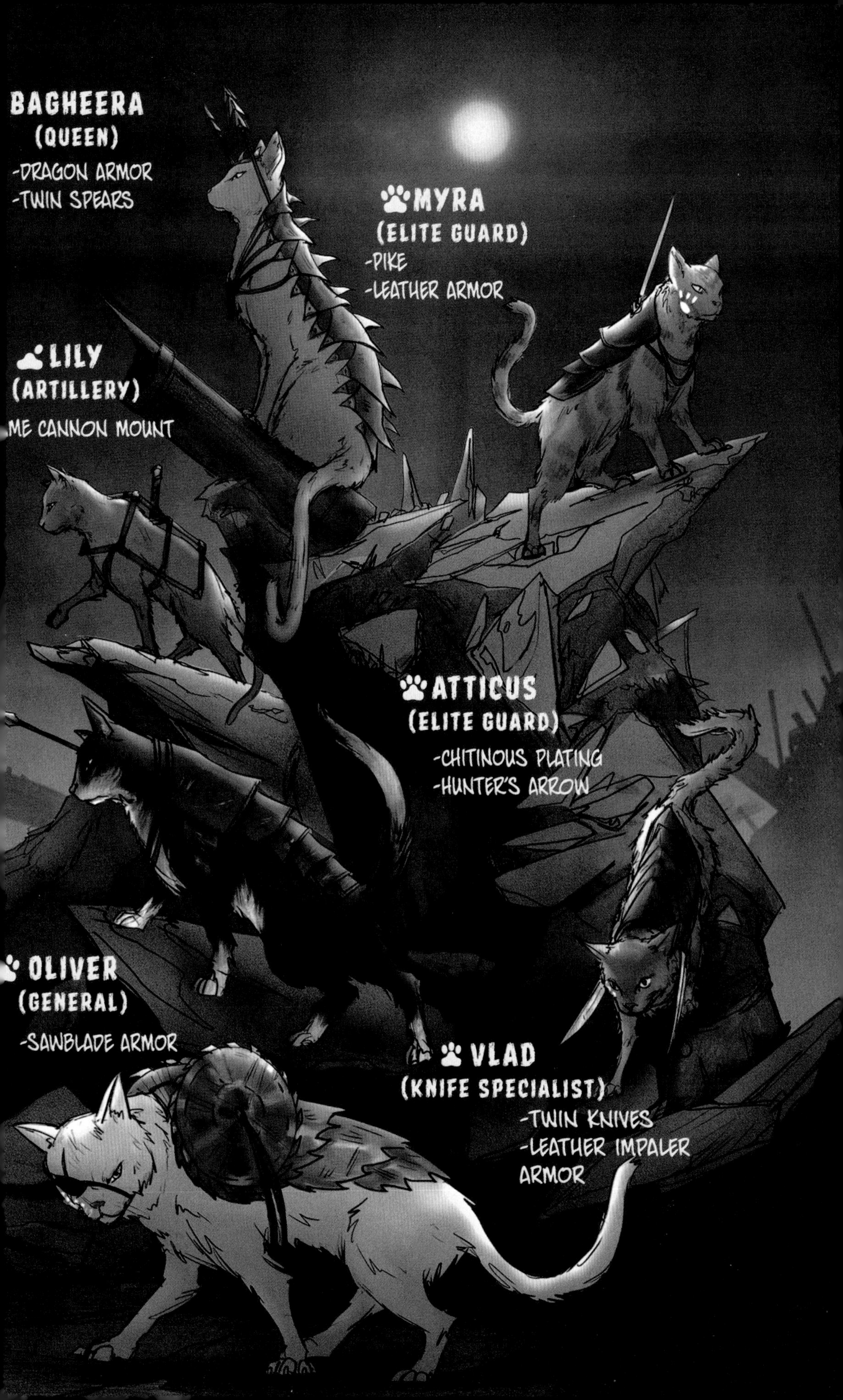
BAGHEERA
(QUEEN)
-DRAGON ARMOR
-TWIN SPEARS
MYRA
(ELITE GUARD)
-PIKE
-LEATHER ARMOR
LILY
(ARTILLERY)
ME CANNON MOUNT
ATTICUS
(ELITE GUARD)
-CHITINOUS PLATING
-HUNTER'S ARROW
OLIVER
(GENERAL)
-SAWBLADE ARMOR
VLAD
(KNIFE SPECIALIST)
-TWIN KNIVES
-LEATHER IMPALER ARMOR

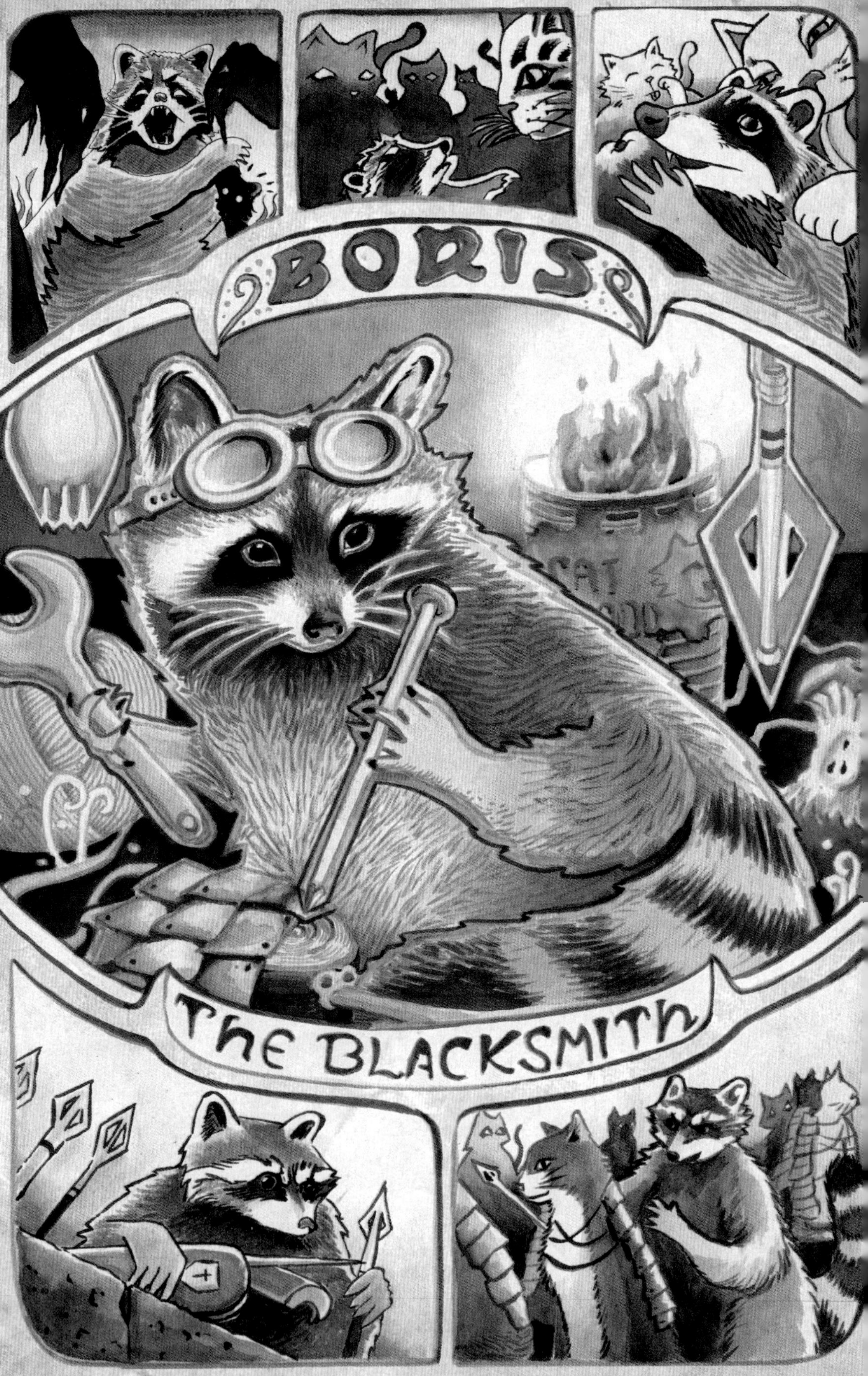
BORIS
THE BLACKSMITH

Tales of the Forge

Mother taken by red eyes when he could barely but see, cast undo death, another victim of he.

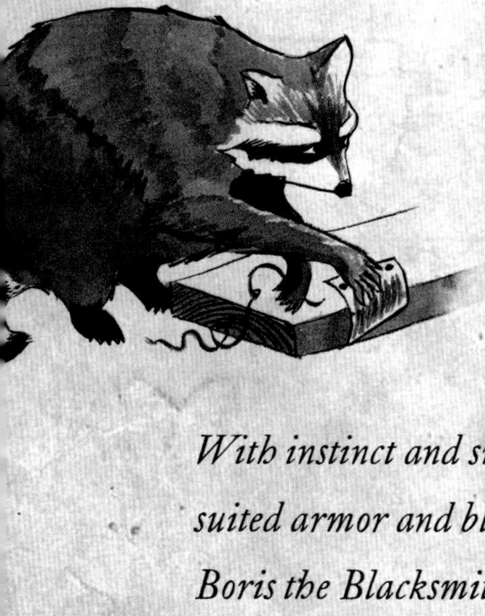

Found by cats in the Wild, they saw him as kin. A kit with good paws, and a strong take to blooming, he would make metals sing with his fire and toolings.

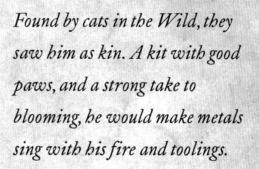

With instinct and smarts, he suited armor and blades, named Boris the Blacksmith, to remind of his ways. He now labors hard in the depths of Cat's Lair, his eyes small and black and his wits sharp as razors.

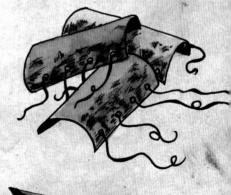

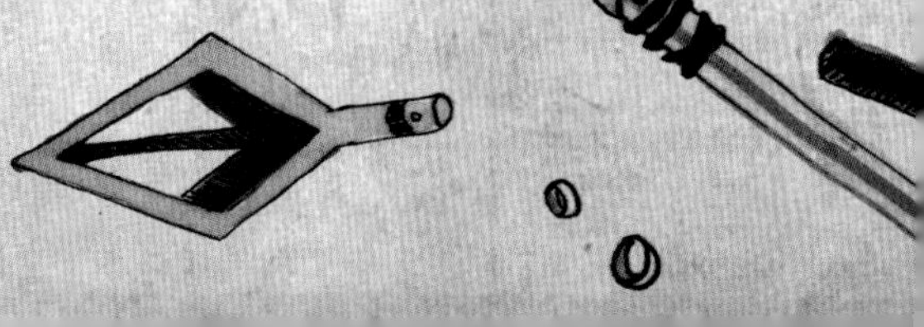

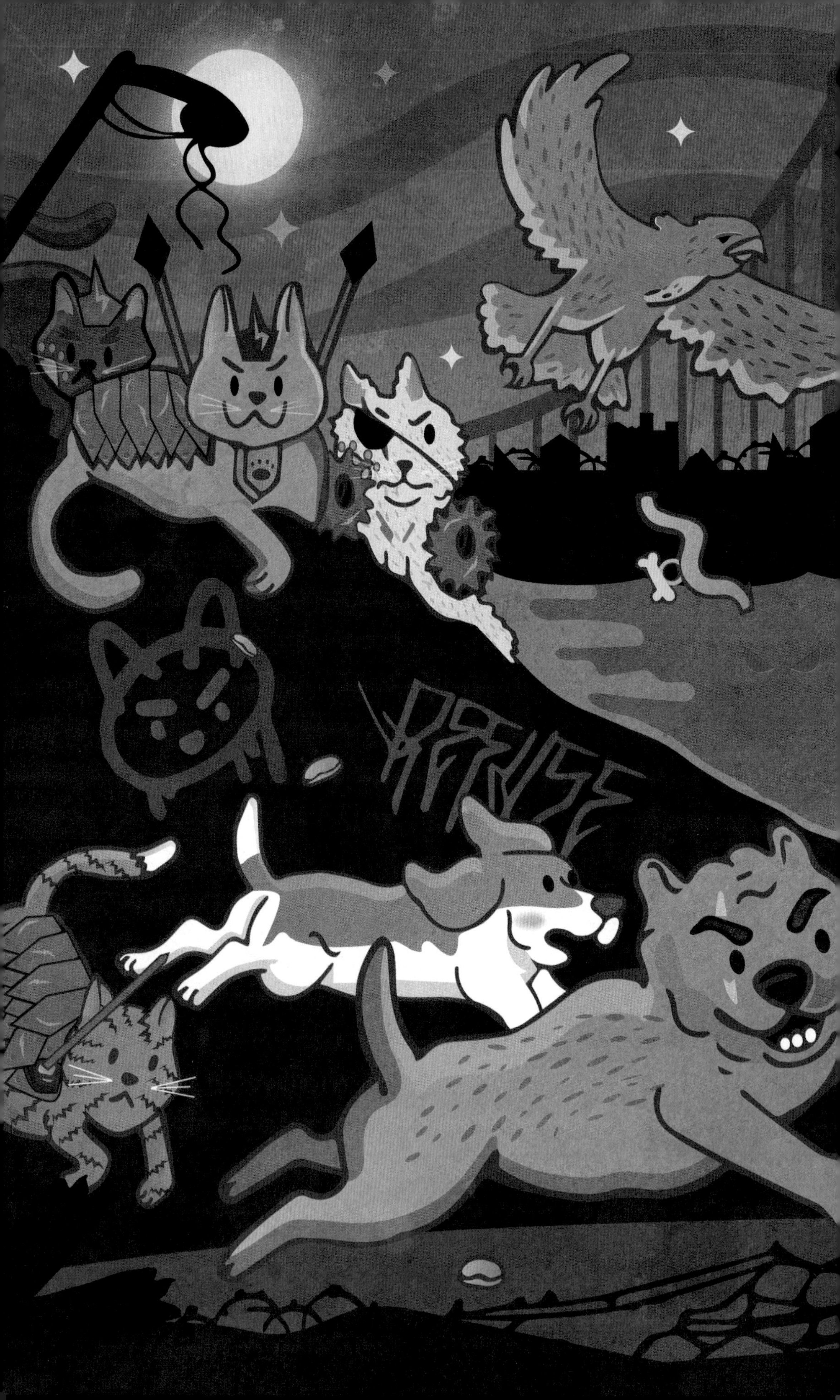

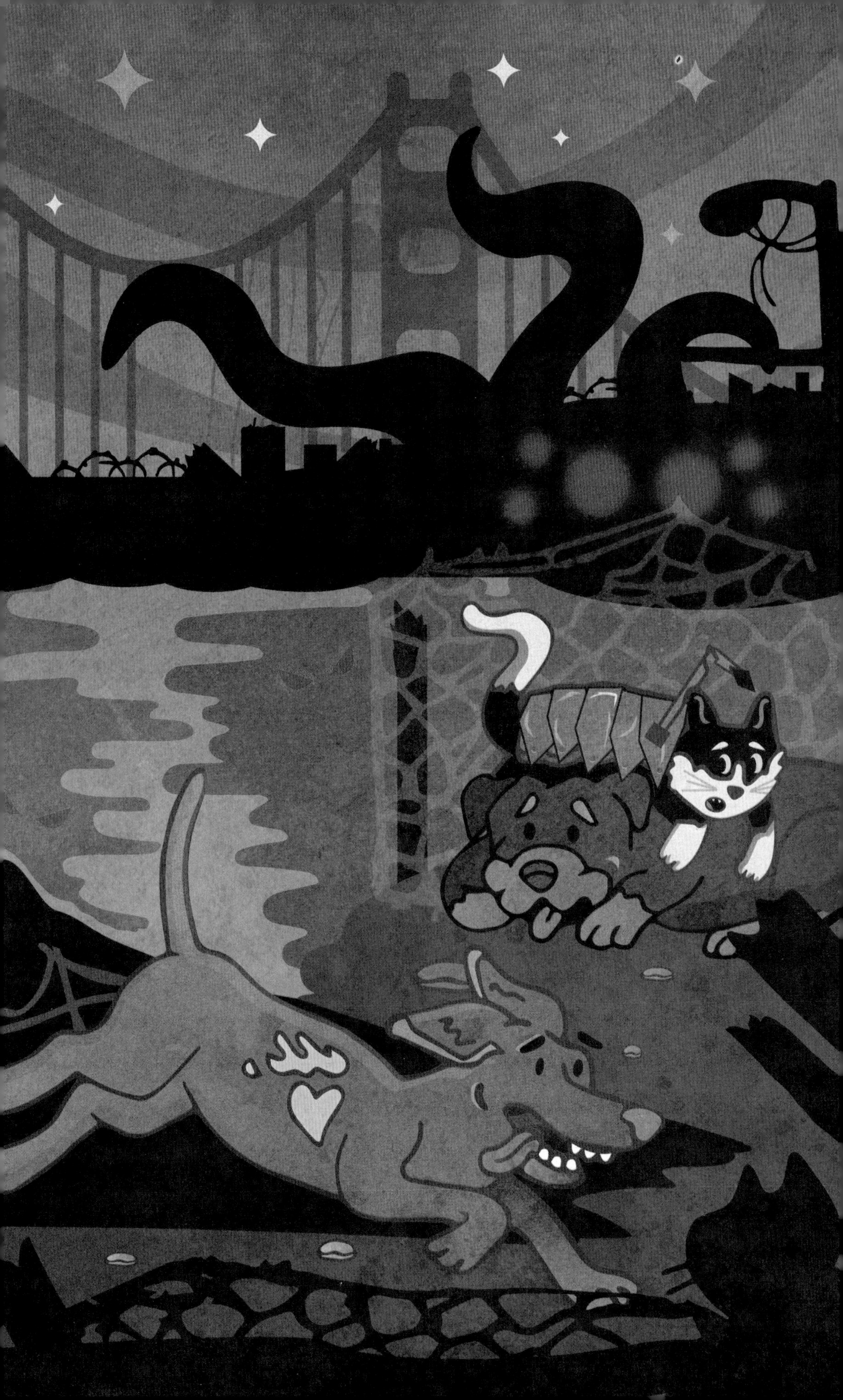

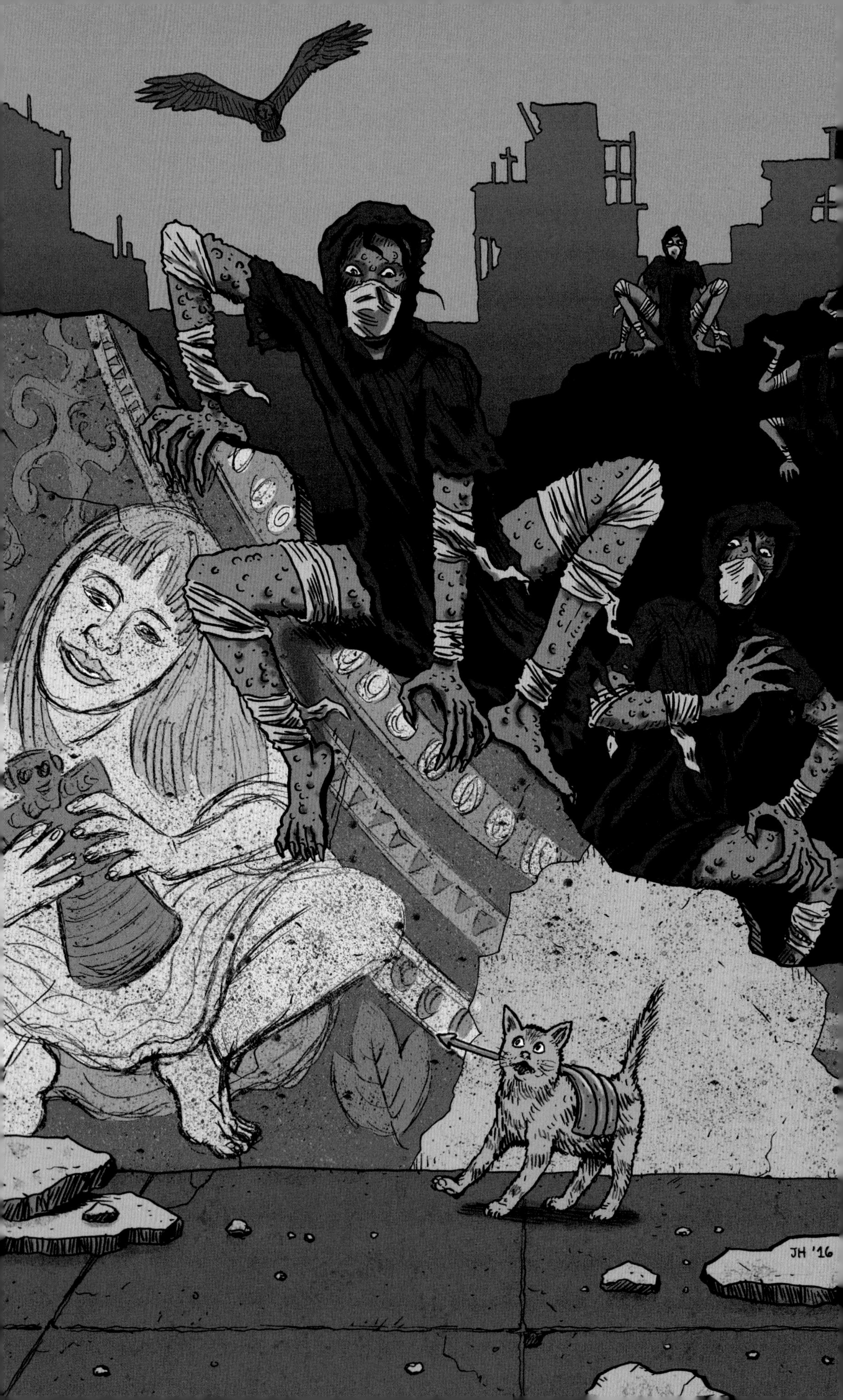
JH '16

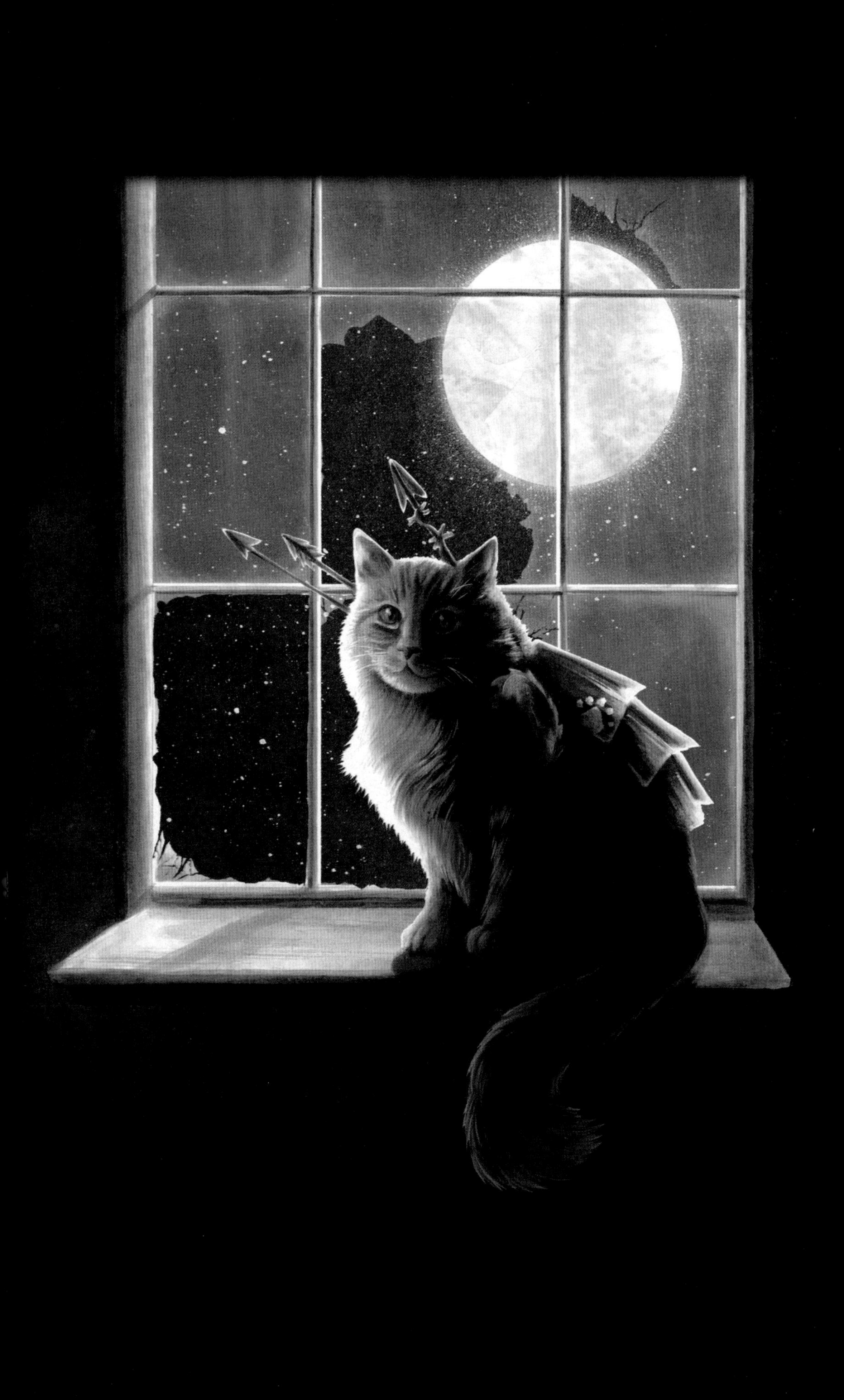

i heart

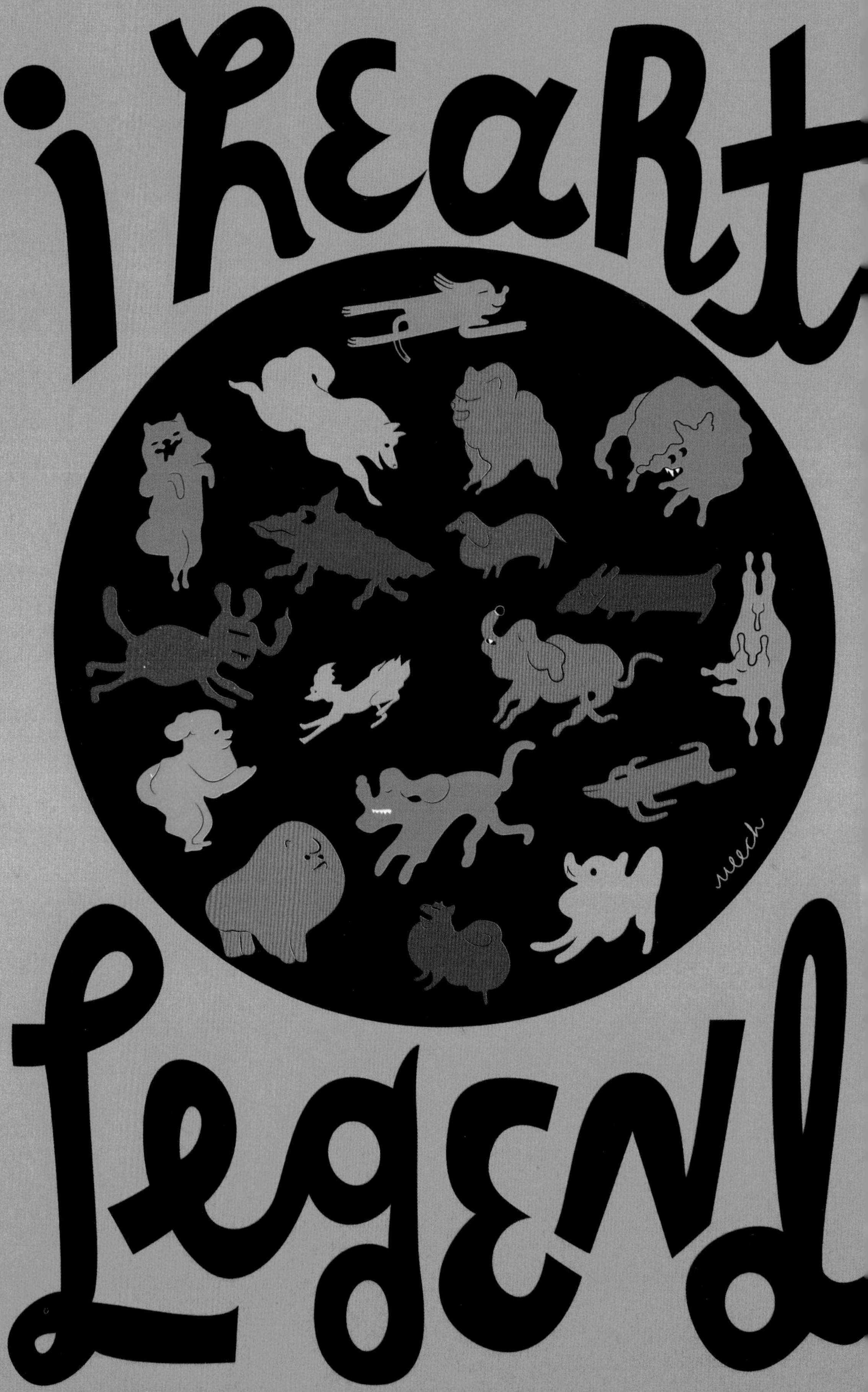
meech

legend

PROCESS

I'm not a comics' artist. The component duties involved going into *Legend* were new to me. In a lot of comics, it seems like one person pencils, another inks, another colors, and so on. Each person has a specialization, so that an efficient group of like-minded artists create pages by combining their finest qualities. This is not something I am fit to do. My pencils look like chicken scratch, my inking is done in more tones than a colorist would want to work with, and my colors... if it's not clear that I'm colorblind then you're giving me too much credit.

What I can do is make images. I am a terrible team player, but a functional lone wolf. As an illustrator, I've learned to lean into my strengths and mask my weaknesses. I work in a way that is completely unique to me and make images that I can feel a distinct ownership of, for better or worse. All this is to say: my process is as unorthodox as it is confusing. Let's take a look:

Thumbnails:
This is the ideation stage, trying out different concepts. Mostly to see if an idea translates visually at all and to try out compositions and elements.

The Final Sketch:
Once an idea is picked, I refine it into a final sketch. This resolves all details and value. There is almost nothing left to chance after this. All of the creative decisions, with the exception of color, have been resolved.

Inks:
The actual components are inked on separate sheets of paper in red and black. I use red because it is the most malleable color to manipulate in Photoshop. It flattens to a single color channel.

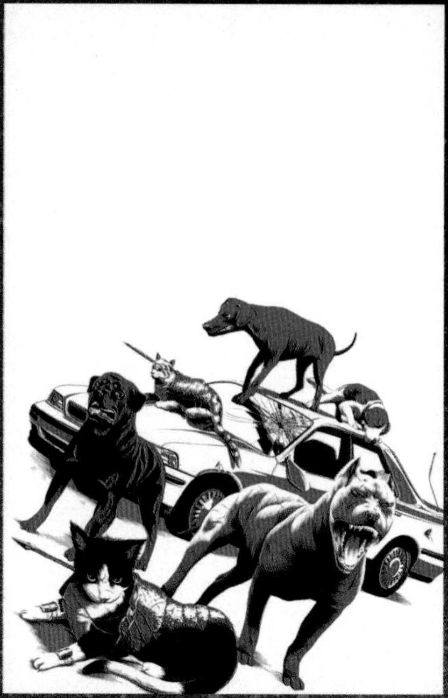

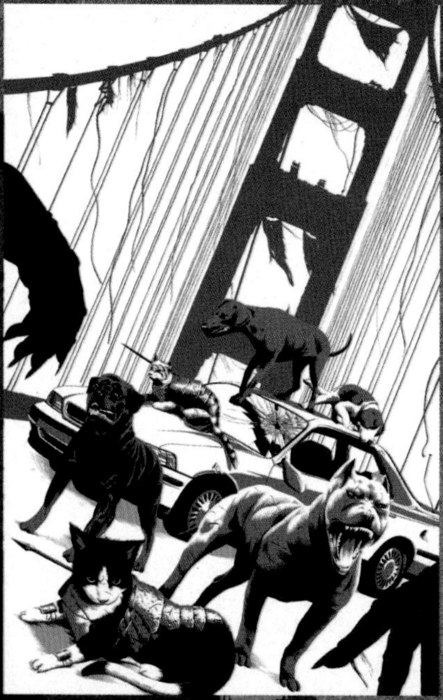

Greyscale:
I flatten the values, composite the separate drawings, and convert to greyscale. This simplifies the next steps.

Tones:
After flattening the piece to three tones (black, 50% grey, white), I add in mid-tones and different values.

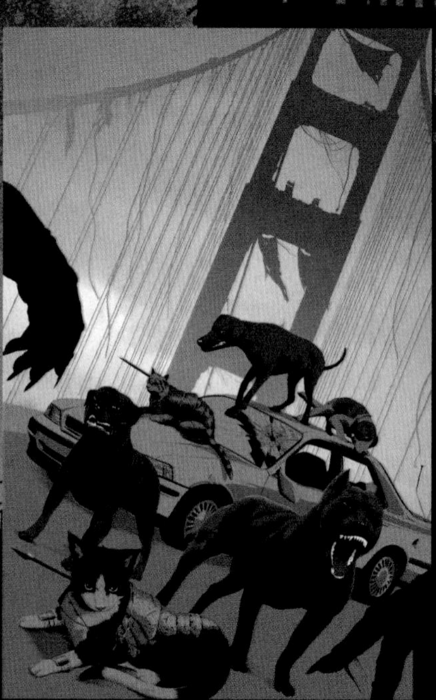

Texture:
On top of the values, I add in texture with spatter brushes and scans of my own spattering. This gives the image a more organic feel and adds some grit.

Color:
Once I have the image complete in black and white, I add in colors. For this image I wanted the light to be eerie and haunting, so I tinted it with oranges and yellows. I wanted the darks to feel unnatural, so I tinted them with purples. These colors are also complements on the color chart so they pop strongly when juxtaposed.

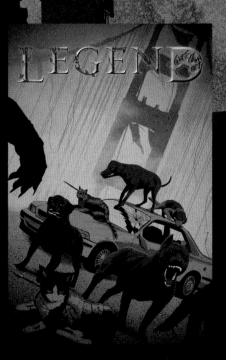

Dressing:
After the art is done, the title is added in...

...And that is how a cover is made!

-Chris Koehler

mankind has gone ~~astray~~ away. there were many before the fault took all.

mankind's hands fashioned iron and clay. but when sparks fell from the sky, his fingers turned crooked. his eyes turned red. and his former allies, the dog and the ~~cat~~ not the cat—never the cat—the horse and the sheep, were abandoned to the ruins of a new land.

we few now stand together in the land's dim ashes.

our paws are clumsy in the darkness, but the one with a heart made of ~~fire~~ sunheat keeps us warm, until the first dwellers return.

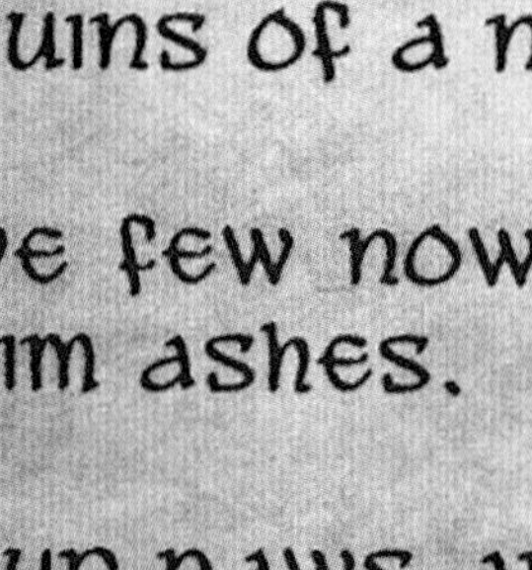

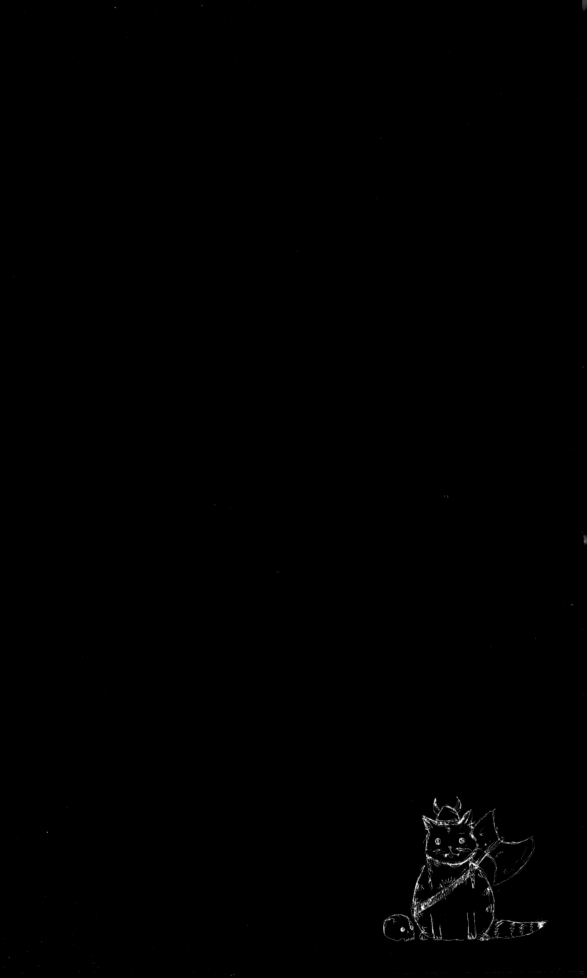